THE DEAD WALK THE EARTH
II

LUKE DUFFY

1

"Run, Chris," she urged, her voice laden with fear. "You need to run."

Behind her, she could hear the panic filled gasps of her brother. He whimpered and snorted as he ran. Tears streamed down his face and mixed with the thick strands of mucus that endlessly flowed from his nose, as he stumbled and cried his way along the dusty track behind her. They had been running for what seemed an eternity, but in reality, it had only been a few minutes and his large body was struggling to maintain the pace. His ribcage felt as if it was being slowly crushed, and no matter how hard he sucked in the air, he could barely breathe. The pain in his chest was almost too much to endure. His straining heart threatened to explode from the stress of having to pump so much oxygenated blood around such a large and unhealthy circulatory system through clogged arteries.

"I can't," he wailed pathetically, "I'm too fat."

She was well aware of that fact, and her brother's inability to look after himself had been the subject of great annoyance to her for many years. Now, with their lives depending on their capability of being able to move at rapid speeds when necessary, his lifetime of self-abuse and over indulgence was proving to be a threat to their continued survival.

Behind them, the noise of their pursuers was growing. There must have been hundreds of them by now, as their moans and cries of excitement attracted more from the surrounding area. She needed to find somewhere for them to hide, but they were miles from anywhere. The only building that they had seen in the region was an old country pub and that is where they had run into trouble.

Christopher's incessant need for food had led him to stumble clumsily into the tavern before his sister had been given the chance to have a look around. From the outside, the place had looked empty and quiet, and nothing stirred in the tranquil woods and lanes that surrounded the building. With the twitters of the birds in the trees and the lazy buzzing of the insects in the air, the immediate vicinity had seemed peaceful and he had been lulled into a false sense of security, as his insatiable appetite drove him to act prematurely.

Without waiting for Tina to come up from the riverbank after securing their boat, he charged on in through the door in the hope of finding an abundance of bar snacks. Instead, he was greeted with a wall of mottled flesh and lifeless eyes. They saw him instantly, as he stood framed in the doorway and bathed in sunlight. His plump quivering body and fear filled whimpers as he realised his mistake, were enough to work the horde into a frenzy as they came charging towards him and spilling out from the building.

Within seconds, their retreat towards the boat had been cut off and Tina was left with no choice but to drag her terrified brother along the path that led them into the woods. She had no idea where they were going, but they needed to keep moving. The dead were close on their heels, and from what she could tell, they were slowly gaining ground.

"Just keep going," she growled at him.

She stole a glance over her shoulder and saw the pain contorted face of her brother. His skin was crimson and his clothing was soaked with sweat. It was a hot day and already he was drenched with perspiration. He was clearly struggling to keep his bloated legs moving and the wretched noises coming from him were beginning to infuriate her. She paused, just long enough to allow him to stumble blindly by her. If she could not drag him, then she would try pushing him.

Hurriedly, she tucked her heavy iron crowbar into her belt. With both her hands planted between his sweaty shoulder blades, she forced him forward. His endless self-pitying sobs seemed to increase in volume and tempo as her powerful thighs drove them along the track. She was throwing everything she had into him, but he was doing very little to help himself and was even pushing back against her hands.

Tina was no stranger to testing her limits. As a Physical Training Instructor in the British Army, she could outpace and out-lift most people that she met. She loved to challenge her body and push herself beyond the threshold of normal endurance, but with death on their heels and her brother unwilling to aid her, she knew that her stamina would not hold out. On her own, she could easily outpace the lumbering corpses that were chasing them, but that would mean abandoning Christopher and at that moment, she was unwilling to do that.

"For fuck sake, Chris, you need to help me. They're getting closer."

"I can't," he wailed in a high-pitched voice. "I can't do it."

She began to hit him. At first, they were light encouraging smacks against the sodden material of his t-shirt, but as the grunts and snorts behind them grew, her gentle slaps soon turned into an assault. As she continued to push him along with the muscles in her thighs burning from the lactic acid build-up, she pounded at the heavy rolls of fat that covered the bones of his shoulders.

"You fucking *can* do it because if you don't, I'll leave you here, Chris," she snarled at him as she gasped for air. "Is that what you want? You know what they'll do to you. You've seen it happen. Do you want to die like that?"

He was crying uncontrollably but her words seemed to have had an effect upon him. With images racing through his mind of him being ditched by his sister and eaten alive by a pack of monsters, he found the energy to keep going. The tears continued to stream down his glowing plump cheeks and the snorts and gasps made him sound as though he was on the verge of death, but somehow, he managed to quicken his pace.

"That's it, Chris," she spurred from behind him as she felt his weight shift and the strain ease from her legs. "Keep going. You can do it. Just keep your legs moving and we'll be okay, Chris."

The woods all around them echoed with the moans and wails of the infected. They seemed to be converging on them from all angles, and the realisation that they may be surrounded caused a surge of panic to ripple through Tina's body. If any of them appeared on the track ahead of them, she could do nothing. There was nowhere to turn and they would be trapped. Her mind began to race. She had no idea of where they were or where they were going. All she knew was that they could not stop.

One-hundred metres further on, Christopher was back to the point of resisting her efforts to keep him moving forward. His energy was spent and it was entirely up to Tina now to keep his legs from grinding to a complete halt. His head lolled and bounced from side to side and his feet barely lifted from the ground. No matter how hard she beat at his shoulders or threatened him, he was incapable of moving under his own steam. Her brother had become an immense semi-mobile mass that needed to be pushed and shoved in order to prevent him from coming to a total standstill.

Then she saw it. Up ahead of them and through the trees, she spied a structure of some sort. It was big and dark but clearly manmade and solid. She looked back over her shoulder and saw that the infected were just thirty metres behind her.

The savagery in their movements and the noises they made while their pale lifeless eyes remained fixed upon Tina and her brother, made her blood feel like liquid nitrogen in her veins. They were not slowing and if anything, they were closing the gap. Christopher on the other hand, was losing speed by the second and it would not be long before the gnashing jaws of their pursuers caught up with them.

"Jesus, Chris," she cried out in a mixture of terror and frustration, "you need to help me. They're right behind us."

Her brother was still incapable of complying with her demands. It was all up to her now to save them both. With her lungs burning and her mind racing, she began to look for a way through the tangles of branches and roots towards the building.

"To the left. Head to the left," she ordered, but he did not change his course.

By placing extra pressure against her brother's right shoulder, she was able to steer him and change his direction slightly. She drove him towards the structure that she could see through the clumps of trees on their left. Christopher's feet left the track and began to scrape through the underbrush of the forest floor, tripping over branches and scattering the dead leaves as he trundled on. He continued to whimper and sputter pitiably and remained incapable of helping himself or his sister, but Tina refused to give up. There was a glimmer of hope now and it was enough for her to hang onto.

They began to duck and weave their way through the foliage. The thorns and thin branches lashed at their exposed flesh and whipped at their faces, but they were oblivious to the stinging pain. The grey wall of the building was soon just a few metres away, but Tina quickly realised that it was set in an area of low ground and they would have to descend an embankment and negotiate a perimeter fence before they could find a way inside. Without slowing for thought, she shoved her brother down the steep slope.

The weight of his body increased his momentum, and within a few short steps he was racing down the small hill towards the mesh fence surrounding the building. Shrieking with panic and flailing his arms as his legs ran away with him, he smashed into the corroded steel netting with a resounding clang and bounced back through the air. The fence rattled against the heavy impact, which sent vibrations running along the length of it, while Christopher was flung backwards and into the dirt. He landed in a heap, squealing loudly and sending up a small cloud of red dust into the air around him as his large body impacted with the ground.

Tina almost collided with her brother but managed to vault over him as he crashed at her feet in a saturated bundle of perspiration and urine. He lay there for a moment, crying for his mother and curling himself into a ball as his bodily functions failed him.

She reached down and grabbed him by the collar of his t-shirt. He was impossible to move and at best, she could only manage to cause his shoulders to roll with each heave, while the remainder of his enormous body stayed firmly planted in the earth.

To the left of the area where Christopher had hit, Tina saw that the fence post had buckled and the mesh had become separated from its brackets. Seeing a flicker of hope, she turned and began to kick at the quivering organic mound at her feet.

"Up. Get up," she grunted with each strike.

Her kicks were becoming more forceful and she could feel the soft tissue of her brother's ample waistline as it recoiled and rebounded with each blow.

"Get up, you fat cunt," she hollered in frustration.

Christopher cried out as his sister continued her assault. Her kicks hurt but her words and tone of voice were excruciatingly painful to him. He had never heard her speak in that way, especially towards him. She had always been caring, understanding, and protective over her brother, but now she seemed to hold nothing but hatred towards him.

"Get up, you useless bastard. They're coming and I'll leave you here for them," she growled into his face with venom-filled spittle spraying over his features. "Do you hear me? I'll fucking leave you here."

At the top of the embankment, the first of the infected appeared. Its skeletal face and bony shoulders came into view as it searched for the living. Its opaque eyes scanned its surroundings, as it stood grunting and snorting. Then it saw them. With a loud groan, it hurled itself down the hill towards them with its rake like hands reaching out before it. Its mouth gaped wide and its blackened tongue flopped from between its teeth as it let out a quivering moan of expectant lust.

There was no time left. They were cornered and Tina knew that they were about to die. Her brother was crying loudly as his self-pity and fear grew and mixed with the ear-splitting screeches of the dead who were almost upon them, as they crashed through the trees at the top of the slope.

Seeing no other alternative, Tina prepared herself to fight. Standing her ground, she pulled the crowbar from her belt and adjusted her grip on its shaft. Her heart pounded in her ears and her body began to surge with the last of her energy reserves, as floods of adrenaline poured into her bloodstream.

The first of the infected charged towards her, but just like Christopher, it was unable to slow its rapid descent. Realising that gravity was aiding her, Tina stepped to the side as the decomposing body hurtled passed and crashed into the fence. It hit the same spot where her brother had just moments before, but this time the impact was too much for the corroded metal pillars to withstand. Already weakened by Christopher's collision, the fence bowed beneath the overwhelming pressure. A loud twang rang out and the post fell with a heavy clatter, dragging a large portion of the rusted trellis with it. Brackets groaned and coils of wire thrummed as they snapped back from the tension they had been under.

The heavily decomposed body continued forward and into the space between the wall of the building and the perimeter fence. Its face hit the concrete pathway running around the structure and grinded along the hard surface, as layer after layer of putrid flesh was scraped away until the crunch of bone could clearly be heard.

Tina suddenly felt herself being tugged backwards and instinctively spun around and raised her weapon, ready to defend herself. It was her brother. For a fleeting moment, she stared back at him in shock. Somehow, he had found the energy and strength to gain his feet and take his life into his own hands.

"Come on, Tina," he was yelling as he guided her through the gap in the fence and towards a fire door set into the wall of the building.

They vaulted over the corpse that was struggling to regain its feet. It writhed on the concrete walkway and clawed at the air around it. It lifted its head and revealed the extent of the damage inflicted on its features. The face had become nothing more than a bloodied, pulped skull with strings of ground muscle and sinew hanging precariously to the smashed and pulverised bone. Its eyes were gone along with most of its teeth, but still it tried to reach after Tina and Christopher when it sensed them close by.

Christopher threw all of his weight against the door but it was locked tight. The thick steel barely acknowledged his efforts as his rounded shoulder slammed against it. Again and again, he threw his body into the impenetrable barrier, but to no avail.

"It's no use," he whined between assaults. "It won't budge."

A crowd of withered bodies and grotesque faces had appeared above them at the top of the slope. They instantly caught sight of the two people battering their bodies at the fire exit and raced down the hill towards them. Luckily, they did not have the intelligence to look for the gap that had allowed Christopher and Tina to pass through the perimeter, and instead, they launched themselves at the parts of the fence that was still very much intact. They screamed and gnashed their teeth as they gripped onto the wire netting with their bony fingers. They shook and tugged at the barrier in frustration as it kept them at bay and allowed Tina the time to decide on a new course of action.

The door was not going to open, but in a moment of clarity, her panic seemed to lift and clear her thoughts. If the door were strong enough to withstand their efforts, then maybe it would mean that the building would be secure enough for them to use as a hiding place.

"It's no use, Chris. It's not going to give," she said as she grabbed him by the arm and turned to run. "Come on, this way."

She began to follow the pathway to the right along the side of the building. The infected on the other side of the fence followed and matched their course, all the time pounding at the trellis of wire that separated them from their meal. There were more of them arriving from the surrounding land and hurling themselves down the hill to join in on the hunt. The noise coming from them was deafening and haunting, and their foul stink filled the air all around them. The reek of decaying bodies was so powerful within the narrow gap around the perimeter that Tina began to gag as she ran.

At the far end of the pathway, she turned the corner and continued to drag her brother behind her. Now that the pressure had eased slightly, he was back to being non-responsive and having to be hauled along.

Tina paused at the end of the wall and watched the area in front of the building for a moment. She could see a wide open space with a number of parked cars scattered here and there, and looking up to her left along the front of the structure, it became apparent that they had stumbled into some kind of industrial complex. On the far side of the parking area, she could see more buildings identical to the one they hid beside and on the nearest of them she could read the logos emblazoned across their fronts.

One was a household appliance warehouse and another was a stationary supply headquarters. There were others too, but she was not there to shop and paid them no further attention. They needed to find somewhere to hide and the main thing that she noticed was that there was no trace of the infected. The area was deserted.

"This way," she hissed and began to inch her way out into the open.

"I need to rest, Tina. I can't breathe."

"We'll rest when we…"

A loud crunching noise accompanied by the sound of groaning metal beyond the corner where they had just come from, indicated that the fence had collapsed. The sounds of feet trampling over the broken rails and pounding along the concrete confirmed to her that the infected were back in pursuit.

"Run, Chris, they're coming," she exclaimed and began to sprint along the front of the grey building towards what she presumed was the main entrance.

Christopher staggered along and managed to keep pace with her. Thirty metres further on, she dragged him into a doorway that led into a spacious reception area. As he fell inside and crashed against the heavy desk sitting in the centre of the room, Tina slammed the door shut and slid a number of bolts into place to secure it. She stepped back and crouched in the shadows beside the entrance, and signalled to her brother to do the same and remain out of sight.

The rampaging infected were running in all directions out in the car park as they hunted for the two living people. Some stalked between the cars, peering through the windows and pounding on the glass, while others raced across the expanse of the parking lot and towards the other buildings. Directly outside the door where Tina and Christopher had taken shelter, a large group of them crept along the wall until they reached the thick glass panes that separated them from the dark interior.

Just centimetres to her right, the dead faces of dozens of the infected pressed themselves up against the glass and stared into the gloomy reception. Tina saw the haunting shadows of the numerous heads and shoulders stretching across the carpet by her feet as they clambered at the entrance. The door juddered lightly as they pushed their putrid bodies up against it and searched for any sign of their prey, but the way in to the room remained tightly sealed from within.

Tina screwed her eyes tight and prayed that they had not been seen entering the building, and that the infected would soon lose interest and move on in their search. She remained pressed to the wall, as she listened to the nerve wrenching snarls of the monsters that were lurking just beyond the glass.

Christopher was beside her. His chest was heaving rapidly and his breath came in sharp painful gasps. She knew that if they were discovered, they would not get very far. Her brother was incapable of going any further. He was ready to collapse and his knees trembled uncontrollably. With each grunt from the crowd outside or thud against the door, he flinched involuntarily and let out a stifled yelp. He was physically and emotionally exhausted.

It was fifteen minutes before she could breathe easily again and pluck up the courage to move. She gingerly crept towards the doorframe and looked out through the thick reinforced panes. She was careful not to expose too much of herself and kept most of her body hidden in the shadows.

Out in front of the building, she could see a tribe of the infected lurching about in the bright sunlight. They were no longer running about and shrieking with excitement. Instead, they were aimlessly shuffling around and bumping into one another and the cars dispersed throughout the expanse in front of the warehouses.

They were trapped but safe for now. Tina just hoped that there were no other entrances leading into the building that their hunters could exploit. She looked at her brother who had slid to the floor. He was sitting with his back to the wall; his legs sprawled out in front of him, and his chin resting upon his chest. She quickly realised that he was asleep when she heard the grumbling snorts that emitted from his mucus-filled nostrils, and saw the drool that cascaded from his quivering lips.

She stared at him for a moment then shook her head. She knew that she had to check and secure the area, but she now realised that she would be doing it alone. Her brother was beyond help right now and was of no use to her or himself. She decided to let him sleep.

He would only be a hindrance anyway, she thought. At least he would be out of the way and she would know exactly where he was.

Remaining conscious of the bright light that shone through the glass panes of the door and illuminated a large rectangle on the floor, she carefully moved around the edges of the room and kept herself hidden within the shadows. In the centre of the reception area was a large desk with a dust covered computer, printer, and a number of files and books. It was all still neatly placed and stacked on the desktop and showed no indication that there had ever been any trouble there.

She knew that it was an exercise in futility, but she could not resist the urge to lift up the receiver from the telephone and hold it to her ear. As she expected, the line was completely dead, but from years of living with a mild form of Obsessive Compulsive Disorder, she knew that if she had not followed the impulse then it would have niggled at her until the desire had been satisfied. She could not afford to have such a trivial matter endlessly playing on her mind at that moment.

The doors leading off to the left and right towards what she presumed to be the offices, held no indication of having been forced open or barricaded shut. The place looked untouched and abandoned. She considered it as a good sign and she began to feel more comfortable in her new surroundings.

Something caught her eye as she walked around to the opposite side of the desk. It was an identification holder hanging from a hook on the wall. She reached up, removed it, and tilted it towards the bright sunlight filtering through the glass door. The photograph showed the smiling face of a young blonde haired woman, and beneath the picture, was a name stencilled in thick black lettering.

"Michelle Potts," Tina read aloud as she rubbed her thumb over the image. "Where are you now, Michelle?"

In the top right hand corner of the identification card, she was able to read the company name and it caused her eyes to widen as she realised where they had stumbled into. It was a supply depot for a large supermarket chain.

For the past four months, Tina and Christopher had been surviving hand-to-mouth and looting anything that they could find. They had been living on a small riverboat and making their way from one village to the next and treating the canals and rivers as moats, anchoring their cramped vessel away from the banks and separating themselves from the land that swarmed with the plague's victims. Almost every shop and store that they came across had either already been ransacked and was completely empty, or was teeming with the infected and impossible to get near. Pickings were always meagre. Now, stumbling upon a warehouse that supplied goods to a popular supermarket and so far seemed untouched, there was hope once again.

She needed to see for herself. With a final check on her brother and satisfied that he was completely oblivious to his surroundings, she entered through one of the doors that led off to the right of the reception.

She found herself at the head of a long narrow corridor. On her left was a solid wall and all along the right was a row of small, semi-private office cubicles that were separated by thin partition walls. The area was well lit from the sunlight that flowed in through the large windows overlooking the parking area, and filtered through the blinds of each cubicle and reflected from the brightly painted walls.

She silently made her way along to the end, pausing at the edge of each booth and listening for any sounds from within. Then she would carefully poke her head inside. Most of the offices were just empty space, but there were a couple that were furnished with desks, cabinets, and chairs. All of them remained unscathed by the panic and chaos that had engulfed most buildings and businesses. Most importantly, the windows for each office were unbroken.

She reached another door at the end of the narrow walkway. The door was thick and solid and she had to push hard in order to open it. Inside, a wall of blackness greeted her. With no windows allowing the natural light to enter, she remained at the doorway and listened into the darkness. She could smell the distinct scent of ash and as her eyes began to adjust, she could see a number of doors on either side of the passageway. In the light that managed to filter in from the windows behind her, she saw faint clouds of charred, microscopic dust rising into the air as the atmosphere in the room changed.

A fire had raged through that part of the building, and somehow it had been stopped from engulfing the entire structure. She was unsure if it had been due to the heavy fire doors or whether it had happened earlier on in the crisis before the power failed, and the sprinkler systems still worked. It did not matter but it was something she could not help but wonder about.

Eventually, she plucked up the nerve to step forward. The odour of burnt wood and melted plastic was strong in the air, and as the door slowly closed behind her, a faint draft sent up clouds of tiny cinders all around her that immediately began to obstruct her nostrils. She remained still and concentrated on controlling her breathing and listening for the minutest of sounds. Eventually, her eyes began to adjust to the gloom and she inched her way forward to begin checking the other doors.

The walls were black with soot and deformed from the heat that had ravaged the corridor. Her feet crunched against the brittle floor tiles that had cracked and shattered under the intense heat and their echoes through the darkness caused her to cringe with each step.

The first doorway revealed what she believed to be a small storeroom and after the initial fright of feeling something bristly against her fingertips, and then realising it was a broom, she moved onto the next.

Inside, she could see nothing but from the stink of the murky space she surmised that it was the staff toilets. Beyond the smell of burned wood and scorched concrete, she detected the distinct mixture of old urine and bleach, and she felt relieved at the absence of the foul stench of decaying human beings. She had experienced that particular smell all too often, and as revolting as it was to her senses, it terrified her mind more. She closed the door and continued into the dark corridor.

At the second to last doorway, she could see a sliver of light through the small gap at the bottom. Without a sound, she turned the handle and was greeted with a brilliant whiteness. After a few minutes of being unable to see and relying on her sense of smell and hearing, the brightly lit room was blinding. She squinted and shielded her eyes with one hand, and raised her crowbar in the other.

It was a cafeteria. At least it had been once. Chairs and tables that were neatly placed filled every space of the floor. All of them were blackened and misshapen from the smoke and heat that had virtually incinerated the room. The walls that had once been painted white were now streaked with the dark artwork left behind by the licking flames. Black smears reached up towards the ceiling where the foam tiles had melted and now hung from their frames like synthetic stalactites.

At the far side was a counter and hotplate, and judging by the extent of the damage to that part of the room, Tina surmised that the fire in that area had been at its most intense. In amongst the detritus, she could see what she believed were a number of bodies. They were burned beyond recognition, and had become fused to the floor in a sea of solidified ash and melted plastic. In a number of places, she noted the pale bones of hands and legs jutting out from the mess, and the longer she stared, the more she was able to see. Some of the blackened bodies were still moving. Only very slightly, but enough for Tina to see the twitching of bony fingers and writhing legs.

She watched for a moment, unsure whether to run from the room or not. Eventually, she concluded that they were no threat to her. Somehow, some of them had managed to survive the fire but their bodies were too badly damaged for them to move. She wondered if they had already been infected when they had been engulfed, or if they had reanimated after being killed in the blaze. She was curious but felt no urge to get any closer to investigate.

Set into the far wall of the canteen was a row of large windows that stretched the length of the room. They were discoloured and obscured from the smoke but a few patches remained clear enough for Tina to see that they looked out over an empty part of the car park. There was no sign of the infected around that side of the building and she hoped it denoted the area was a staff parking zone or loading bay and sealed off from the public. She would consider that side to be a potential escape route should they need it.

The final door in the hallway led out onto a platform that overlooked a spacious warehouse. The skylights high above dimly lighted it and it was hard for her to make out any details beyond the first few metres. From her higher position, she saw a few rows of stacked goods in front of her but they soon faded into blackness as they were swallowed up by shadow. She could not be sure of the extent of the place due to the low light but she was confident that given the fact that it was a supply depot for a supermarket chain and the dimensions of the exterior walls, it would be of a substantial size.

Unfortunately, it seemed that the flames had not spared the warehouse either. As in the cafeteria and the corridor behind her, the smell of fire was thick in the air. Many of the shelves closest to her had collapsed and their contents had been scattered and consumed by the searing heat. It was impossible to see any further and she could not tell whether the rest of the storage area had suffered the same fate.

She stayed by the door and listened for a while. There was no way to tell if there were any infected inside and the only realistic way of finding out would be to make her own presence known. For the moment though, she would remain unannounced.

She secured the door and made her way back to the reception area. She paused on the far side of the receptionist's desk and peered out through the entrance and over the parking area. The dead were still there but they were no longer hunting. They had gone back to their mindless meandering.

Christopher was still slumped against the wall and snoring noisily. His large stomach was rising and falling with each loud intake of air.

"Useless bastard," she grunted under her breath as she walked by him and towards the open doorway to his left.

On the other side, she discovered a flight of stairs that led up to a number of spacious offices. The Managers and their assistants had clearly enjoyed their comforts with expensive furnishings and appliances adorning each room. Every office was laid out in a manner that befitted a bank manager rather than a supermarket supply office.

In a small kitchenette at the far end of a corridor that dissected the managerial offices, Tina found a fridge loaded with rotted food. The smell made her screw her face up in disgust but the three bottles of water that she noticed sitting in the rack, were quickly snatched up before the fridge door was slammed shut.

In the cupboards, she found mouldy loafs of bread and cakes along with other unrecognisable substances that had perished through time. They were of no use to anyone, but the five tins of tuna and three sachets of dried fruit were akin to a discovery of buried treasure. She was happy with her find. They could at least stay there for the night and get some food and rest. Most importantly, there were no indications that the ravenous infected were inside the building.

They would hide there and assess the situation in the morning.

2

The world was a very different place now. Even after just four months since the plague had forced the remains of humanity to seek shelter and hide from the roaming dead, the landscape had changed considerably. Every manmade structure was already beginning to blend into the background of nature. The colours were fading and the sharp edges were starting to soften. Weeds and wild flowers sprouted from every crack and crevice and slowly began to spread their way out over the remnants of civilisation.

Sitting on the hilltop, the two of them watched the small row of stores that backed onto a sprawling housing estate. The infected were everywhere but the living men remained unnoticed. From their vantage point, they could see for a great distance in all directions and no matter which way they looked, shadowy figures stumbled through the streets or sat idle, staring at the floor.

"It's quiet, isn't it," Bull grunted.

"Yeah," Danny replied as he looked out over the jumble of rooftops. "To be honest, I find it quite pleasant."

Bull looked at him curiously for a moment and then turned his attention back to the street below them.

"Well, if you ignore the fact that there are dead people walking about everywhere you look, it's rather tranquil," Danny continued in way of explanation.

Bull nodded. He understood what Danny was saying and after a moment of reflection and comparing the old world to the new, he could see his friend's point. The world had become a much quieter place. The harsh noises of human society had disappeared and had been replaced with the soft murmur of the natural Earth. However, no matter how hard he tried, it was difficult for him to block out the reality of the situation for very long.

A sharp clang followed by a rumbling grunt that emitted from the foot of the hill dragged him back to reality. For the past couple of hours, they had been resting in the shade of a tree and out of the midday sun. It was the height of summer, a heat wave was in the process of parching the land, and as usual, the men were lying up during the hours of daylight.

At the bottom of the slope, a row of parked cars at the roadside demarcated the end of the rural and the start of the urban areas. The partially decomposed corpse of a man sat in the driver's seat of one of the vehicles and endlessly turned the wheel through its hands. It pushed and pulled at the gears and levers and it had even managed to fasten the seatbelt over its torn and bony chest.

"They're not the brightest of creatures, are they?" Bull noted.

"It's probably been sitting there for weeks," Danny pointed out. "You know how they are. They're persistent."

"Stupid more like," Bull replied. "What's Bill Gates doing?"

Danny panned to the right with his binoculars. Further along the street and sitting on a bench in front of a shop window that still displayed the latest deals on electronics and software, another of the reanimated corpses sat. In its hands, it held a laptop computer and it repeatedly tapped away at the keys as though typing up a document or writing out an email. Now and then, it would appear confused and begin examining the underside of the device as if checking to see if the notebook was connected to a power source.

"No change," Danny replied as he studied the figure. "I think he's still trying to remember his Facebook password."

Bull sniggered beside him. He rolled on to his back and let out a long sigh as he stared up at the branches that gently swayed above them. He was beginning to feel bored and wished that the night would hurry up and arrive so that they could move again.

"I don't think either of us is going to win this bet, Danny. Those things are so stupid that they'll stay there until their bodies rot from underneath them."

They had been on their patrol for almost three weeks. Their mission was to reconnoitre the harbour at Portsmouth and see whether the airfield at Farnborough was still intact. One of their secondary tasks was to check the various routes leading north towards London. Moving at night and lying up during the daytime, Bull, Danny, and Marty drifted through the desolate countryside like a band of ghosts as they moved from one place to the next and gathered the information that they needed. They avoided the living as well as the dead and on many occasions, they had found themselves in close proximity to both. Their orders were clear and they were to avoid contact at all costs.

Remaining tucked away in the shadows, they had watched as survivors scavenged and did what they could and must to stay alive. It was clear that there were still a lot of living people in the country but they were well aware that their numbers steadily declined on a daily basis. No one could hide forever and if there was one thing that they could count on, it was that eventually the infected would somehow find them.

It was never the speed or intelligence of the dead that was a concern. It was always their numbers and their tenacity. If a living person was seen or a hideout discovered, hordes of rotting corpses would converge on to the spot. Only people with strong defences and a means of escape had a chance at survival once they were detected.

While Marty took his turn to sleep, Danny and Bull had been watching the infected in the streets below. At first, they had made a childish game of naming the wandering figures after well-known celebrities and taking it in turns to identify which of the reanimated bodies the other was referring to. Once they were bored of that, a bet was made on which of the two infected, 'Bill Gates' with the computer or 'Michael Schumacher' in the car, would be the first to lose interest in what they were doing and move onto something else.

"I still can't find Simon Cowell," Danny said quietly and beginning to lose interest.

"He's long gone, mate. You couldn't miss him though. He had his trousers pulled up to his neck and a flat-top that would make Grace Jones envious."

"Christ knows how I missed that one then."

"I'd best wake up Sleeping Beauty over there," Bull declared as he sat up and began to crawl towards the tree and the snoring mound at its base.

He looked down on Marty and consciously took note of the loaded pistol that his slumbering friend clutched in his hand. In the current state of the world, awakening someone with a sudden noise or movement could easily be enough to result in a knee-jerk reaction, and Bull did not savour the idea of being shot by one of his teammates because they were in a confused state. He got down low to the ground and saddled up beside him, positioning himself in a way that afforded him the ability to restrain his friend should he need to.

"Marty," he whispered as he reached out to him and shook his shoulder.

Marty instantly woke with a start. Bull watched him for a few seconds and eyed the pistol in his hand but he did not show any indication of raising the weapon.

"It's your stag, mate," Bull continued, informing him that it was his turn to stand guard.

"What, now?"

"No, next fucking Tuesday. I just thought I'd wake you up a week early for a laugh. Get up, dick head."

"Fuck sake," Marty grunted sleepily.

Bull crawled back over to Danny while Marty slowly awoke. He turned around to check on him and watched in silence for a moment as his friend stretched and scratched at his head. Marty checked his watch and then peered up through the branches and leaves of the tree to check on the position of the sun. It was still a few more hours before nightfall and he considered rolling over and going back to sleep.

"Don't even think about it," Bull whispered across to him. "It's your turn to keep an eye out while I get some kip."

Marty rubbed at his eyes and began to crawl forward towards the others. He nestled up beside them on his stomach and peered through the grass and down the hill.

"Anything happening down there?"

"Nothing," Bull shook his head. "You sure it's worth going down there?"

"It's worth a look," Marty shrugged. "It's the last built-up area between us and the pick-up point so it would be rude not to have a rummage about. Besides, it's Danny who's mad-keen to go down there."

"I grew up not far from here," Danny said quietly when he felt Bull's questioning gaze fall upon him.

"You're not getting all sentimental on us are you, Danny?"

"Something like that," he shrugged. "Besides, that check-point down at the far end of the street may have something worth taking."

Bull looked across to his right and at the collapsed barriers. The bullet riddled military vehicles sat dark and silent with smashed windows and punctured tyres, their doors askew and their occupants long gone. There were dozens of bodies lying all around the position and it was clear that the soldiers had fought valiantly. It had done them no use and the infected had trampled the remains of the defences beneath their decaying feet while they feasted upon the overwhelmed troops.

As darkness began to fall, the three of them prepared to move. Instinctively, they silently checked that their weapons were ready and their equipment was secure with all their pouches fastened and their straps tucked away.

"Anything happens and we get split, make your way back here," Marty whispered back to them and pointed at the tree. "This will be the ERV. Wait ten minutes, if possible, then move to the pick-up."

Danny and Bull signalled their acknowledgement with their thumbs raised.

Marty stepped out to the front and began leading them down the grassy hill and towards the row of cars. The sky in the west was still a pale blue and afforded them with enough light to be able to negotiate their way down to the streets without overexposing themselves, but they knew that they would not have that luxury for much longer. The sun had long since vanished beneath the horizon and the light was fading fast. The heat of the day was rapidly wilting from the air and being replaced by a fresh breeze as darkness made its way across the night sky and changed the landscape to various dark shades of blue and grey.

Danny followed at the rear and savoured the feeling of the cool night against his flushed skin while to his left, he could just make out the jerky movements of 'Schumacher' still sitting behind the steering wheel of the car. The thing was never going to move. It was far too engrossed in what it was doing.

I just missed out on five Snickers bars because of you, Danny realised.

Down at street level they kept themselves hidden behind the row of parked vehicles and crept along towards the far end of the road. To their left, where the countryside gave way to the suburbs of the small rural town, the infected lurked. The sounds of them crashing through the darkened avenues and stumbling over debris rang out through the narrow channels within the housing estate. Their voices echoed for great distances as they moaned and cried out into the silence that surrounded them. With darkness falling, the noises of the night seemed to travel further and the three men had to be all the more careful with every step.

Every few metres they would stop while they scanned the area and listened for any sign that they had been detected. Marty was already beginning to wonder why he had felt obliged to allow Danny to indulge his nostalgically fuelled curiosity, but they were almost there now and it would be just as easy to continue, as it would be to turn back.

The three of them sat tucked away behind a vehicle and waiting as the last of the light steadily faded. The sky above them was already revealing the first of its glittering stars and as their natural night vision grew, Marty and the others were able to see more details of their surroundings. After a while, they could see clearly in both directions and as far as they could tell there were no infected in their immediate area.

They stepped out from the row of cars and began to cross over towards the darkened shops and the checkpoint to their right. Danny paused and kept an eye on the area as he covered the others. As he turned to check their rear, he almost yelled out in surprise.

All along the horizon at the top of the hill he could see human shaped silhouettes. He did not need a second glance to see that they were dozens of the infected. Where they had come from he had no idea, but they were headed towards the houses and Danny and the others were about to be trapped between the rural and urban areas, hemmed in by the dead.

He stopped and hissed to the others to grab their attention. Marty froze to the spot and turned to see what was happening and instantly recognised the threat. Bull too had seen them and the three of them took cover behind the nearest of the cars.

"Where the fuck did they come from?" Bull gasped as he peeked over the vehicle's roof and up at the hill.

Danny shook his head.

"Christ knows, mate, but in less than a minute this street is going to be full to the brim with them."

There were more of them coming from over the rise and the first of their ranks were quickly travelling down the slope and towards the row of cars. They staggered and stumbled, grunting as they advanced towards the built-up area.

"It's an entire herd of them," Bull hissed.

Marty looked back across the road and towards the buildings. They had no choice but try to stay out of sight and hope that the swarm would pass them by. He could not think of how or why they had suddenly appeared and he was sure that they had done nothing to attract their attention.

"Come on," he whispered as he raised himself into a crouch.

With the first of the infected at less than fifty metres away, they needed to move. If they stayed where they were they would be discovered for sure. Marty just hoped that their presence was not already known.

He led Bull and Danny towards the nearest of the open doors. His intention was for them to hide in the shadows and wait it out until the herd of walking dead had passed through the area and allowed them to escape back into the vast countryside.

Just metres away from them as they headed for the buildings, a number of dark figures roamed through the gloomy street. Moving slowly and deliberately the three men hoped to bypass the dead that had still not yet noticed them. The swarm of bodies from the hill were already pushing their way through the gaps between the cars and their clumsy bangs and scrapes were attracting the attention of the others that were close by.

'Bill Gates' suddenly looked up from his computer and stared in bewilderment for a moment as the dark shape of Danny crossed his path. The longing moan rising up within the corpse's throat was quickly turned to a gargle as the blade of the machete crashed down and split his skull wide open with a hollow cracking sound. As Danny pulled his blade free from the sucking mess of the man's rotting brain, he was too slow to catch the laptop before it slipped from the creature's grasp and clattered noisily to the ground.

The noise rang out like a siren. Everything in the area became still, including the three living men. The hundreds of nearby corpses slowly turned their heads and gazed in the direction of the commotion. Then their feet began to shuffle against the concrete as they converged on the disturbance. The questioning moans of the closest bodies were quickly joined by other voices as more and more of them began to follow.

"Bollocks," Bull growled as he turned and headed for the nearest of the foreboding store-fronts behind them.

It was dark but nowhere near dark enough for them to remain unseen. With the noise of the falling computer, all eyes in the area were now firmly focussed on the three soldiers. It only took the nearest of the infected to recognise that they were living people and cry out hungrily and the whole pack were alerted and moving towards them.

Within seconds, the first of them arrived and charged. Danny turned to run just as a bright flash lighted up the area around him, accompanied by a bone shuddering crack as the high velocity bullet snapped at the air. Marty was the first to fire and his round exploded by Danny's head and shattered the first of his targets. The body instantly dropped to the ground with a heavy thud as the first shot was quickly followed by another, then another.

Bull smashed and kicked his way through the debris that littered the area around the doorway of the nearest storefront. A quick scan of the interior and he was satisfied that there was no immediate threat and turned to alert the others.

"Here, rally in here."

As Danny and Marty turned and began to head for the shop doorway, Bull began firing his rifle into the closest bodies he could see through the gloom. They appeared from all around. Some ran, others lurched, and Bull carefully picked off the ones that he perceived as being the most immediate threat. His shots were accurate and his tracer rounds glowed bright red as they burst from the muzzle of his rifle and punched holes through bone and tissue.

More and more of them appeared from the murky night. They trampled the bodies with gaping wounds in their heads, pushing forward from all angles.

"They fucking definitely know we're here now," Bull called out as the howls of the infected rose to a crescendo all around them.

Marty was in and already heading for the rear of the room and hoping to find a way out through the backdoor. Danny remained at the front and helped Bull to stem the tide as more and their fire dispatched more of the infected.

"On your left, Dan, on your left."

Danny turned in time to see a body he had not noticed as it advanced along the shop's exterior wall. It was just a few metres away and approaching him from his blind side. He swivelled and fired but his aim was off. The round missed and zipped out into the night as the creature lunged towards him. Danny fired again. This time his shot was accurate. It was impossible to miss as the corpse's mouth was virtually over the barrel as the round punched a hole through its skull and spattered its decaying brains over a wide area. The body tumbled forward and crashed into the doorframe and landed in a heap at Danny's feet.

"Through here," Marty called out to them from the pitch-black interior of the building.

Bull and Danny turned and moved towards the sound of Marty's voice through the virtual blackness. They found him in the next room standing by an open doorway and waving them forward.

"Out through the back and into the next street," he whispered as they passed him. "We've broken contact so let's see if we can sneak our way out of this gang-fuck."

Bull led the way. He kept his finger running along the trigger-guard of his M-4 but he would not fire unless he really needed to. They had vanished from sight of the infected and stealth was their closest ally at that moment. It was pointless trying to shoot their way out. They did not have enough ammunition for that. They needed to find a place to hide and then hope to creep away when the streets were clear.

Behind them the infected had begun pouring into the store. The sounds of them crashing about in the darkness echoed for a great distance and attracted the attention of every corpse in the neighbourhood. In the street behind the row of shops Marty and the others hid in the shadow at the side of a house and watched as hundreds of roaming figures staggered by.

From every doorway and from behind every building they emerged. Some walked while others tore along the roads, flailing their arms and howling aggressively. Other bodies that were too badly damaged and barely able to move dragged themselves along the street to join in on the march of rotting flesh. The whole area hummed as they moaned incessantly. Swarms of buzzing insects filled the air in thick, dark, and shifting clouds that continuously swirled around the mass of wandering corpses.

"I think we should scrap the idea of having a nosey around," Bull whispered into Marty's ear as he kept one eye on the putrid river that flowed by.

The closest of the infected were just metres away from the spot where they were hiding. They trundled along, blindly following the bodies in front and headed for the next street.

Marty nodded.

All three of them sat huddled against the wall of the house and tucked in behind a large dustbin. In the street behind them, it sounded as though the dead were ripping the buildings apart with their bare hands in their search for the living. Windows shattered with ear splitting cracks and the sounds of wood splintering as doors collapsed and furniture was turned over, rang out endlessly as the crowds rampaged through the street.

They did not need to say anything but they all wondered how long it would be before the dead storm spilled into the next street and through the garden where Marty, Danny, and Bull took refuge.

"We need to move, Marty," Danny suggested when he heard the crashes and bangs coming closer from their rear.

Marty shook his head.

"There's still too many of them in the way. They'll see us."

"Fuck that, Marty. They'll see us soon enough when they…"

Danny paused and turned to look back behind them. He squinted through the gloom and saw that one of the infected had stumbled into the narrow channel they had come through just moments earlier. He stood up and took a few paces towards it as he unsheathed his long blade and calculated his approach. It was the body of a woman. He could see nothing of her features but her voice still held the feminine tones in its grunts and rasps. She saw him and reached forward with her handless stumps which were all that remained of her arms. With a well-aimed thrust, Danny drove his machete through her face and at the same time raised his boot out in front of him. As the woman's skull slid along the blade towards the hilt, Danny hit her in the chest with a forceful kick and sent her falling backwards into the darkness.

"As I was saying," he continued as he squatted back down beside the others, "they'll see us soon enough when they come crashing up our arses from the street behind us. We need to move, mate."

"Okay," Marty relented as he realised that Danny was right.

He could hear the approaching infected for himself and it was clear that eventually they would stumble upon them, en-masse. He thought for a moment as he watched the street ahead of them and began to form a plan in his head.

They could not turn back. There were far too many of them converging on the buildings there and if they attempted to hide in one of the houses, there was a good chance that they would eventually be discovered with nowhere left to run. Staying in the open was their best option at that moment. They had the darkness, along with their speed and agility to carry them through.

"Pass me your White-Phos, Bull," Marty demanded.

Bull nodded and reached into one of the pouches on his assault vest and pulled out an L-84 White-Phosphorous grenade. It was roughly the size of a fizzy drinks can and light grey in colour with the letters WP stencilled across it in yellow. While it was commonly referred to as a *'Willie-Pete'* by the American army, British soldiers had a more sinister nickname for it; a *'Warm-Person'* grenade.

On detonation, the grenade emitted a bright flash and as the phosphorous made contact with the air, it would ignite instantly and produce a voluminous cloud of white smoke. They were often used as defensive weapons, creating a smoke screen for troops to withdraw behind but they could also be used offensively too. As a trench or bunker clearing weapon there were very few devices that could accomplish the task as well as a White-Phosphorous grenade. The chemical burned at such a high temperature that it was capable of searing its way through most materials, including flesh and bone, and there was nothing that could extinguish it apart from the total removal of its fuel source, oxygen.

Marty raised himself into a semi-crouch and kept his body pressed up against the wall. Inching his way forwards he peered out into the street and looked along the length of the road in both directions. Fifty metres to their left was a junction that joined onto the street behind them. It was packed with the bodies of the dead as they streamed in from all directions and made their way towards the commotion on the outer rim of the estate.

In the street behind them it sounded as though a riot was in progress. Screams and wails mixed with the sounds of hands beating down doors and smashing their way through the building interiors.

To the right, there was still a large number of the infected making their way along the road between the rows of houses but when compared to the junction on their left, that direction was the only real choice for Marty and the others.

Marty watched for a moment and made a mental note of their numbers. There were hundreds of the staggering corpses in the street but they were spread out enough for the living men to be able to sprint through, and providing that there were not too many of them further along the road where Marty could not see, they had a chance to get away.

"Okay," Marty said as he crouched back down and informed the other two of his plan while holding the grenade up for them to see. "Once this fucker goes off, we make a run for it. Turn right onto the street and keep going until we're clear."

"That's your plan? Throw a grenade and then make like Swastikas down the fucking street?" Bull asked sceptically.

Marty blinked and then nodded. At that moment, with nothing else in the way of a real alternative, it was the best he could come up with.

"Well it's better than sitting here with our dicks in our hands," Danny countered as he watched the advancing mass of shadows that were slowly approaching them from the rear. "Let's just get on with it."

"We wouldn't be in this mess if Danny hadn't wanted to take a trip down Memory Lane," Bull grumbled to himself as he prepared himself for the coming sprint.

Marty placed his finger into the ring of the pin that held the fly-off lever of the grenade in place. He stood up, identified his point of aim, and then nodded to the others as he stepped out into the open. Before any of the infected saw him he pulled the pin free and cocked his arm back. With a powerful heave, he hurled the grenade to the far side of the street where it landed with a thud amongst the overgrown lawns of the houses facing them.

The infected closest to where it landed immediately turned and moved to investigate but before they had taken a step, the fuse ignited. A loud pop and a hiss was quickly followed by a piercing crack and a bright flash that momentarily lit up the entire street like a bolt of lightning.

Thousands of pieces of glowing phosphorous shot out in all directions at incredible speed, trailing clouds of white smoke behind them as they ploughed into the mass of reanimated corpses around the epicentre of the blast. Anything within a few metres of the explosion was instantly reduced to ash and charred remains. Further out, while a billowing pale cloud grew outwards across the street, the lighter particles of phosphorous reached the bodies that had remained unaffected by the initial detonation. They landed on flesh and cloth and instantly began to burn through their clothing and decomposing tissue. Within seconds, a number of staggering human forms were ablaze. As the soft tissue was melted away from their bones they continued to move, colliding with the others close by and spreading the fire from one to the next.

"Go," Marty hissed, "go."

The three of them jumped from cover and ran into the street. They turned to the right and began to sprint passed the infected that stood motionless all around them as they stared at the dazzling bright flames that were quickly spreading through their ranks.

A number of phosphorous particles had ignited the long, dry grass in front of the houses. The orange flames quickly burst to life and grew in size as more of the immediate surroundings caught fire. For the past two weeks the heat wave that had been slowly roasting the country and leaving everything parched made the housing estate easy prey for the flames and soon, the buildings closest to the heat were beginning to smoulder.

"Fucking hell, Marty, we only needed a distraction, not a full-on bonfire," Bull remarked as he looked back over his shoulder at the individual fires that were rapidly developing into a mighty inferno.

More of the reanimated husks of humanity spontaneously combusted as they crashed into one another and blindly staggered about, oblivious to their impending demise. While the three men thundered along the road, barging their way through dozens of frozen and mesmerised rotting statues, the area behind them became a blazing furnace. Everything that the flames came into contact with was engulfed and soon burning out of control.

Some of the infected took note of the animated men as they passed. Grasping hands thrust out in vain attempts to grab hold of the soldiers as they weaved their way through the crowd. The sluggish reactions of the dead were far too slow and Marty and the others easily avoided becoming ensnared. Figures toppled as the three men ploughed their way to safety, leaving numerous squirming bodies on the floor behind them. Against the backdrop of the bright glowing flames, the majority of the entranced cadavers failed to notice the warm flesh that was within their midst.

"Through here," Danny whispered and turned into an alleyway. He had a rough idea of where they were and found a place for them to go static.

Marty and Bull saddled up beside him in the gloom of the alley. Overhanging hedgerows that had grown out from the gardens on either side of them helped to keep them concealed as they sat watching the scene that they had created.

Out on the street, the flames roared and crackled as more of the infected were consumed. Glass shattered and roofs were already beginning to collapse in on themselves as the immense heat ravaged their wooden frames.

"So much for avoiding contact," Marty remarked.

Bull looked at him and grinned. His face was glowing brightly in the reflection from the fire. Beyond the entrance to the alley, he could see hundreds of dark figures making their way along the street and headed directly for the glowing flames. Safe from detection and tucked away in the shadows, Bull and the others sat and watched in awe for a few minutes as hundreds of diseased human shapes were reduced to nothing more than charred bones.

"Come on," Danny said as he patted Marty on the shoulder and turned to lead them off into the darkness. "This alley will lead us back into the street where we started. Hopefully, it'll be clear at this end and then it's a straight run to the PUP."

Each of them prepared themselves to move. They checked their weapons and ammunition, ensuring that they were ready to fight if necessary.

"I used up three mags in that gang-fuck," Bull grunted, shaking his head as he raised himself to his feet.

In single file they moved off. Bull brought up the rear and as they reached the far end of the alley, the roaring fire had become nothing more than an orange glow over the rooftops of the houses. The occasional pop and crunch could be heard as structures collapsed but otherwise, the night was silent again as the men made their escape through the darkness and back into the rural areas.

3

"Did you mean those things you said before?"

She turned and looked back at him. He was barely visible but she could just about see his bulk, shrouded in shadow and sitting at the far end of the sofa. She could hear his fingers scraping out the last of the tuna from the tin, quickly accompanied by the smacking of his lips.

Since they had moved up into the manager's office and barricaded the door shut, they had barely spoken a word. They had sat in silence as the light outside beyond the large windows of the spacious room slowly faded and was replaced by the oppressive blackness of night.

"You said I was fat and threatened to leave me behind. You said some really horrible things, Tina. Did you mean them?"

She thought for a while and then nodded.

"Yes, Christopher," she said softly as she realised that he could not see the movements of her head. "I meant what I said, but I didn't mean to hurt you."

There was a sudden deep intake of breath from the far end of the couch and Christopher began to reply but then she cut him short. Tina realised that she had not made herself clear in her reply and she did not want to have to listen to him during his triumphant ascent towards the emotional high ground.

"I mean," she began to correct herself. "I meant what I said about you being fat, not that I would leave you there to be eaten by those things."

Silence filled the space between them for a few minutes. At first Tina wondered if Christopher was contemplating what he was going to say next but then she heard his sniffles. He was crying again.

She was confused about her own emotions at first. Initially, she felt sorry for him as he sat with his head in his hands and his slumped shoulders quivering, but her feelings rapidly changed when she remembered the events that had occurred earlier in the day. It had not been the first time that they had been in trouble because of him, and she was confident that it would not be the last.

Her sympathy was quickly turning to anger as the minutes ticked by but now was not the time to lose her temper with her emotionally delicate brother. She held her breath and counted backwards from ten while he cried away beside her. She concentrated her thoughts and feelings on the fact that they were safe for the time being and had a place to hide. She did her best to sweep the images of gaping mouths and gnashing teeth from her mind.

"Don't cry, Chris," she said quietly in a voice that she hoped would sound caring and soothing to him.

"I can't help it," he stuttered between sobs. "You were really cruel."

"I know, but they were chasing us and they were getting closer. I had to try something and words were all I had."

"You called me names and I honestly believed you would leave me behind," he whined in a high-pitched tone. "You're my sister and you're supposed to look out for me. I've never heard you speak like that and your words really hurt me, Tina."

His voice was beginning to irritate her. Even now he did not grasp the severity of the situation they were in and the consequences of his actions. He was filled with too much self-pity to be able to see the bigger picture and he was too self-centred to understand that the world did not revolve around him. Still, she attempted to swallow her simmering rage and keep her emotions on an even keel. She did not want to hurt or upset him but on the other hand, she did not want him to sit feeling sorry for himself and playing the role of the victim. The more he wept and bleated about how much her words and actions had hurt him, the more she struggled to keep her blood from boiling over.

"Why did you say those things, Tina? You hit me and said some nasty things. I thought you were really going to leave me. I felt worthless and that you didn't care anymore."

She took in a deep breath and stared at the window in front of her. Her right index finger continually tapped against the radial artery in her wrist as she attempted to keep her cool. She concentrated on controlling her breathing and blood pressure. She had learned a few tricks over the years on how to deal with her anxiety and compulsions but at that moment, it was her burning rage that was threatening to get the better of her.

"Mum would never have said things like that to me. *She* wouldn't have threatened to leave me behind. *She* would never have…"

"Mum's fucking dead, Chris," Tina suddenly exploded as she sprang up from the couch, "and if it wasn't for me, you would be dead along with her."

She vaulted over towards his end of the settee. Her dark silhouette loomed over him menacingly as he recoiled back into the cushions under the ferocity of her outburst. Even in the near blackness he could see her clenched white teeth and imagined the sneering grimace that was etched across her face.

"For twenty-seven years she wiped your arse for you and fed you to the point where you could barely stand," Tina growled into his face as she raised an accusing finger towards him. "You have never done anything for yourself and chose to stay at home, playing fucking computer games like a retarded Japanese kid while the rest of us *real* people went out and lived our own lives. You have lived your entire life like a parasite. Then all this shit kicks off and it was up to me to pull your huge arse to safety."

"But…" he sputtered back as he attempted to defend himself.

"But fuck all, Chris. Mum died slowly and painfully while you did nothing to help her. You kept her locked in her room while you sat crying and wallowing in self-pity. It was *me* who put her out of the misery she was in. You're lucky I made it home when I did because you would still be there now, wasting away with no one to look after you. Or worse, ending up as food for mum."

She paused and pulled away from him. She sighed heavily and placed her hands on her hips as she stepped back away from the couch.

"Look at yourself. You can't and *won't* do anything for yourself. You've always been that way. You expect everyone else to take care of you and wrap you up in cotton-wool."

"But…"

"We nearly died yesterday because of you, Chris." Her tone had calmed slightly. "I had to drag and push you all the way here.

You're a grown man for fuck sake, and you weigh more than three times as much as me."

She turned away and walked towards the expansive windows and looked out across the car park and into the night.

"What if something happened to me?" She asked as she looked back towards him over her shoulder. "Would you have been able to carry me to safety? Could you have fought any of them off while you found somewhere for us to hide?"

No reply came from the dark sofa.

"Yeah, I thought as much," she continued dismissively. "It's all up to me, isn't it? I'm the one that has to keep us both safe and fed, and to come up with the plans while you sit there like a huge fucking baby."

His sobs were getting louder.

"For God's sake, Chris, shut up. Stop feeling sorry for yourself and get a grip."

"But I can't help the way I am," he pleaded in a whimpering voice. "I know I'm fat, but it's a disease. The doctor even said so."

"Fuck off, Chris. Cancer is a disease. AIDS is a fucking disease," Tina spat back at him. She raised her hand and pointed to the dark twisted shapes that hobbled around below the window. "Those poor bastards out there are a disease."

"No it's a…"

"Shut up, Chris. You're just lazy and greedy. You're the way you are because *you* made that choice. When everyone else was growing up, getting jobs, and being active, you made a conscious decision to stay at home and be a fat mummy's boy. Claiming disability benefits because it was easier than living in the real world and standing on your own two feet. Your state is self-inflicted, Chris, and you're nothing more than a fucking oxygen thief."

For a long while the room remained quiet. Christopher remained seated on the couch and wrapped in his own self-pity while Tina stood at the window, watching the infected as they staggered about in the darkness.

The moon was high and full and its glow cast out enough light over the land for her to be able to see for a good distance. It was like watching a black and white reel of film. The colours of the earth were all but gone and replaced by multiple shades of grey and black. Below the window and scattered across the parking area in every direction she looked, she saw the infected as they mindlessly wandered about, dragging their feet with their heads lolling to the side. She studied them for a while and eventually her nerves began to settle and her anger subside. She sighed heavily and turned to look back towards the sofa.

"Come here, Christopher," she called back to him in a voice that indicated he had no choice in the matter.

There was a pause but after a while he began to move. He did not want to provoke her by being stubborn and refusing to comply with her demands.

"Come and have a look, Chris." Her tone was less demanding now.

He shuffled over to her with tiny, hesitant steps and kept his hands folded protectively across his chest. His head was bowed and he stared at his feet as he approached.

"It's okay, Chris. I'm not going to lose my temper," she said as she placed her hand on his shoulder and rubbed him gently.

He nodded solemnly but kept his gaze pointed down at his feet. He was afraid to raise his head. He did not want to look out of the window and see what was outside. He knew what was out there but he did not want to acknowledge it. He wanted to stay indoors for the rest of eternity and hide from the world outside, pretending that it did not exist.

"Go on," she encouraged him, "take a look."

He slowly raised his head and reluctantly gazed out over the parking area and the warehouses. There were dozens of swaying and lumbering deformed black silhouettes that contrasted starkly against the pale concrete of the parking bays. They were everywhere and he imagined them all staring back at him, as he stood exposed in the window. He screwed his eyes shut and stepped back from the large panes of glass. He was shaking his head and mumbling something that she could not understand.

"You see, that's part of our problem," she began. "This thing has been going on for months and you *still* can't face them. I hate and fear them just as much as you do, Chris, but whether I like it or not, I have had to come to terms with having to fight them. You can't bury your head in the sand and pretend that it's not happening. You'll get your arse bitten off doing that."

"But I'm scared," he grunted.

"So am *I*, but we have to deal with it. What if something happens to me? How will you survive then? You need to be able to fight them and look after yourself, Chris."

He said nothing and remained standing behind her and staring at his feet. He wished she would leave him alone and let him go back to the couch.

Tina remained facing the window for a moment with her arms folded across her chest and her mind in deep contemplation. She made a mental note of the number of infected in the area and eyed the buildings across the other side of the car park. There was only one road leading in and out from what she could see and if the fence that surrounded the rest of the perimeter was still intact, then they could have a degree of safety and isolation from the rest of the world.

"Tomorrow, we begin clearing out the storage warehouse down stairs," she said finally as she turned to face him. "This place is pretty secure and we're safe here. All we need to worry about is food and that brings me to my next point, Chris…"

She paused and waited for him to look up at her.

"As of tomorrow morning, we begin collecting supplies and fortifying this place. At the same time, you'll start learning how to look after yourself."

4

The long stalks of grass were swaying gently in the mild night. A breeze blowing in from across the open countryside brushed against the men's faces and cooled their flushed skin. It was a full moon and visibility was good enough for them to see for a considerable distance. Marty, kneeling beside his pack, pressed the red button on the satellite phone and folded down the antenna.

"Five minutes," he whispered to the other two.

Bull and Danny were both squatting in the soft soil close by. They grunted their acknowledgement and continued to watch their arcs. The continuous rustling of the wavering stalks of unharvested wheat kept their senses turning. They honed their hearing as they stared into the blackness of the night and listened for anything that would indicate someone or *something* was approaching.

Other than the swish of the oscillating grass and the whispering gusts of the summer's night air, the land was still and quiet. Nothing moved. Gone were the sounds of traffic on the roads and people in their homes. The skies were silent and the only indigenous noises were the sounds of nature. However, it was a very different story in the towns and cities. They were packed with the infected corpses that roamed the streets and hunted the living. Their moans and wails echoed through the urban areas and anyone left alive that could do so, had long since left. The remains of the civilised world were now the possessions of the dead.

Far off to the west, the distant thump of rotor blades could be heard slowly growing in volume as they approached.

"That's them," Marty announced.

He reached into one of the pouches on his assault vest and pulled out the infrared light, known as a Fire-Fly. He held it up high so that it was facing out towards the west and switched it on. No light could be seen emitting from the device with the naked eye, but anyone wearing night vision goggles could not miss the bright pulsing signal beacon that flashed out at one second intervals.

While Danny continued to cover the area, Bull began preparing their equipment and getting ready to board the helicopter the moment it touched down. With the noise of the engines drowning out their ability to hear and the downwash hindering their view of the landscape, they would be vulnerable to attack. The sooner they were aboard, the better.

The crate was heavy and awkward to manipulate. It was over a metre long and deep and half as wide again, and weighing an estimated ninety kilograms. Bull heaved it up, grabbing it with both hands and placing it against his knee as he prepared himself to run forward with his cumbersome burden, as soon as the Chinook's tailgate was lowered.

Danny, keeping his rifle aimed into the wall of darkness that surrounded them glanced back over his shoulder and then down at the case in his friends grasp.

"For fuck sake, Bull, don't drop that thing whatever you do."

Bull stared back at him and scowled at the fact that Danny had felt obliged to remind him of the care he needed to show while handling the large heavy package. He tightened his grip on the handles at either end and growled under his breath.

"You just watch your arcs, dick head."

The CH-47 was drawing near. Already the din was enough to drown out the sound of the moving grass around them. Within seconds they would find it difficult to communicate verbally as its whirling blades hammered at the air and its motors screamed their high-pitched whine. It was then that they would need the helicopter to land as quickly as possible, leaving them exposed for as little time as necessary.

Marty, still holding the infrared light aloft pulled himself up into a crouch and readied himself to spring forward. Suddenly against the deep blue, almost black sky, an even darker silhouette emerged. The bulk of the fuselage was clearly visible as it began to slow its approach and lose altitude. The noise grew to a crescendo and the howling downwash rose into a storm as it beat at their bodies and their senses.

Within seconds, the aircraft had passed just a few metres above their heads and touched down with a bounce onto the dark earth. Its heavy wheels absorbed the landing and as the giant helicopter settled, a faint slither of light appeared at the top of the rear ramp. Moments later, the interior of the Chinook, bathed in an eerie green glow, came into view as the Loadmaster stepped forward and signalled for the men to board while he covered their withdrawal with his rifle.

Marty, Bull, and Danny wasted no time in moving. They stood together and rushed forward towards the tail end of the aircraft. Danny covered the rear while Bull who was weighed down with the heavy crate hobbled forward, puffing and panting with the strain. Getting onto the tailgate was a struggle. The big muscular Bull needed to time his approach with precision to ensure that he did not waste energy and precious seconds trying to climb aboard with clumsy footing or worse, slip and drop their delicate cargo. The thought of him taking a tumble with the crate in his hands caused a shiver to run the length of his spine.

Danny, the last to leave the ground, stepped up and onto the sloping ramp of the Chinook and nodded at the Loadmaster as he passed by. All were aboard and already the tailgate was closing and the pitch of the engines was changing.

That was when the worst happened. Unable to see the deck of the aircraft and the raising ramp causing him to constantly adjust his balance with his heavy load, Bull fell. Stubbornly gripping onto the crate, he crashed to the floor with a silent scream becoming lodged in his throat as he felt the cumbersome box slip from his grasp. He screwed his eyes shut and winced as he and his charge were sent sprawling across the interior of the helicopter.

Danny and Marty froze to the spot. They were not concerned about Bull or the injuries he may have sustained in the trip. Instead they watched in horror as the crate bounced across the hard surface of the passenger compartment. The crunching sounds of the impacts were audible even over the roaring engine as it came to a skidding halt against the long row of seats on the starboard side.

"You useless clumsy spaz," Danny howled at the top of his lungs as he leapt over the prostate Bull who was still lying on the floor with his head tucked deep into his shoulders and his eyes screwed tight.

Marty jumped across and grabbed the large heavy box and pushed his weight against it to hold it in place. He knew full well that it was not likely to move any further than it had done already but he somehow felt urged that he should secure it as best he could. He looked across at Bull and shook his head disapprovingly.

Bull opened his eyes and stared back at him, feeling ashamed but mouthing the words, *'fuck off'*.

An hour later and the helicopter was over the Isle of Wight. The three soldiers, having been on the mainland for over three weeks and tinkering on the verge of exhaustion, sat slumped in their seats with their heads lolling to the side and bouncing with the turbulence that buffeted against the aircraft. On the floor in front of them sat the bulky crate with each of the men resting their feet upon it as a way of keeping it close and secure.

"Why have you brought a coffin on board?" The Loadmaster leaned forwards and shouted across to Marty.

His voice was barely audible over the noise but Marty's senses were finely tuned and despite the fact that their mission was over, it would be a while before his brain would allow him to relax completely.

"It's none of your fucking business," Marty bellowed back at him with a grin and without bothering to open his eyes. "And it's not a coffin, it's an armoured crate."

"Looks like a coffin to me."

"Bit small for a coffin, you crap-hat," Bull barked, referring to the Loadmaster with the same insult that was reserved for *any* member of the armed forces that was not in the Parachute Regiment.

"Could be for a dwarf," the Loadmaster smiled.

"Well, unluckily for you, you'll never know, will you?"

For four months the aircrew and the team had grown to know one another very well. The team had come to rely on and trust in the abilities of Melanie and her men. The pilots were of a special breed and were never afraid to take them to wherever they needed to go, despite the dangers involved. For Marty and the others, the crew of that particular CH-47 were guardian angels, pulling them out of trouble on numerous occasions as they conducted their dangerous missions on the UK mainland.

However, despite their maverick ways and appearance, both the helicopter and the members of the team were expected to follow orders and respect the chain-of-command. Regardless of their wishes or preferences, Marty and the others were required to report directly to their headquarters on return. It was something that they always loathed.

Since their dramatic rescue at Manchester Airport by Melanie and her crew, the surviving men of the team had settled themselves into an old, partially reconstructed, barn that had been in the process of being converted into a house on the southern tip of the island. While the politicians and army commanders kept themselves in the central hub of Newport, the team considered themselves as being out of sight and out of mind. They could have chosen to live in comfort in one of the many villages and houses that had been commandeered but they valued their privacy more than the amenities of civilised life.

Still, they had not sat idle and the barn had become more than just a shelter. It was home to them. Over the months, through their outstanding ability to procure whatever they needed by whatever means, regardless of the logistics involved, they had made their own little corner for themselves within the island. They had a generator, partially running water that was gravity fed from a tank, and warm sleeping bags. The dead plague had interrupted the owners from fully installing the heating system and the kitchen, but they got by and considered themselves to be blessed to have their own place away from the daily influences of central politics and command. All three of them were looking forward to getting home but first they needed to brief the army commanders on their findings during their patrol.

As the Chinook approached the landing pad the Loadmaster hit the button to begin lowering the ramp. Bull and Danny took a handle each on the cumbersome box and stood ready to exit the aircraft. The men felt the wheels touch the pad and the fuselage rocked slightly as the machine settled into place. Marty, standing at the front and watching as the tailgate slowly lowered, suddenly turned to Danny and Bull with a sour expression on his face.

"Heads up," he shouted back to them. "I think we're in trouble, 'Kevlar Knickers' is already here, waiting for us."

Bull peered over his shoulder and saw Samantha standing beside an army Land Rover on the helicopter landing pad. She was standing with her arms folded across her chest as usual and staring back at them. Her expression was hard to read, as always, and it was difficult to work out whether or not she was there to greet them or escort them back to Newport and ensure that they reported to HQ.

"Bollocks," Bull grunted as he tightened his grip on the handle of the box. "I should've known she'd be here."

Marty knew exactly why Samantha had come to meet them. She would don the guise of being interested solely in their mission and that she wanted a summary of their report before the in-depth debrief with Gerry, the Operations Officer. However, her real motive was that she actually cared and over the previous four months, her façade of indifference had become more and more brittle.

"Why doesn't she just admit that she thinks we're fucking awesome?" Bull shouted into Marty's ear.

"Because she's a woman. She's stubborn and likes to play hard to get. Have you not figured that out yet?" Marty grinned back at him.

Outside on the concrete pad, with the sound of the Chinook's engines winding down and the hot exhaust fumes filling the air, Samantha took a couple of steps towards them. She took a mental note of each of them and silently assessed their condition. After being away from the island for so long and dragging themselves through the mainland the three of them looked dirty and unkempt. Their beards were thick with grime and the dirt and grease matted into their hair made it stand out on end from their scalp. She dreaded sitting in close proximity to them and breathing in their foul stink.

"How did you get on?" She asked while eying the crate that Bull and Danny carried between them and began loading into the back of her vehicle.

Marty shrugged.

"The usual," he replied casually as he headed for the passenger seat. "The urban areas are getting pretty congested. I wouldn't recommend buying property there just yet."

Samantha climbed in behind the wheel as Danny and Bull jumped into the rear compartment and made themselves comfortable.

"What about the airfield and the routes in?" She asked as she turned the key in the ignition and pulled the Land Rover away from the landing pad.

Marty smiled at her and watched her for a long moment. She kept her attention on the track that led them onto a narrow and twisting country lane. She could feel his eyes studying her, but she refused to meet his gaze.

"You always have to be the first one in the know, don't you, Sam?" He said finally as he reached into his pocket and pulled out a pack of cigarettes. He offered one to her but she shook her head.

"Still not smoking then? How long has it been?"

"Four months," she replied thoughtfully.

"Good for you," Marty mused. "Anyway, routes in and out; nothing special. There are a few obstacles and villages to clear along the way but in general, it shouldn't be too much of a problem to secure them. The roads will take a bit of work to clear but with the right equipment they'll be easy enough to manage. As long as there are enough troops with close air support, the corridor could stay open long enough for us to secure the objectives."

"The airfield?"

"Clean as a whistle, Sam, and the fuel tanks are full. It won't be a problem to get the place fully operational. There's a few maggot-sacks knocking about but nothing like down at the harbours. That's where I can see our main trouble coming from. Once the docks are cleared it's a straight run up to the airfield and then from there, the forward units can begin leap-frogging into London by helicopter while the support troops come up in vehicles."

"What about London itself?"

Marty shook his head.

"Not a chance. We couldn't even get near it, Sam. The roads are clogged bumper to bumper and the outlying areas are teeming with the infected. The nearest we could get to the place was about fifteen kilometres to the south-west of Hounslow. To be honest, I really don't know why we're trying to take the place back."

"The new Prime Minister is under the impression that capturing London would be a symbolic victory and would raise the moral of the people." Samantha's tone made it sound more of an automated rhetoric than a heartfelt conviction.

"A slaughter more like," Marty huffed. "Even if we managed to completely clear the city of those things, it would be a bio-hazard for the next twenty years."

Samantha nodded, still keeping her focus on the road ahead of them and snaking the vehicle through the twisting bends while doing her best to negotiate the Land Rover around the deepest potholes.

"If we had more aircraft we wouldn't need to think about the harbour," she replied, "but as it stands, it's our only way of resupply and reinforcement in the large numbers needed to keep up the momentum of the offensive. The main objective will be securing the airfield. Once the first wave has gone in every infected body for miles around will converge on the perimeter. I just hope we have enough troops and that they can get the harbour and the roads cleared to link up with the advanced units."

"Well that's up to the head-shed to work out. We've done our bit."

The vehicle suddenly jolted violently as Samantha was unable to avoid a large dip in the road. The suspension rattled and Marty was buffeted in his seat. Holding onto the dashboard he turned and looked at Bull and Danny, and then down at the crate. Bull nodded back to him reassuringly.

"You *do* know that we've kept a close eye on you, don't you?" Samantha informed Marty with an air of warning in her voice.

Marty rubbed at the inside of his forearm in the area where the bio-tracker had been implanted beneath the skin. Most of the time, he forgot that it was there but now Samantha reminded him that he was never too far away from the prying eyes of the operations staff.

"Fucking 'big-brother'," he grumbled. "Are you referring to the fact that we covered a larger area than we were tasked with?"

"Yeah. Your trackers were all over the place and quite a few questions were being asked within the Ops Room." She turned and glanced at him with a wry smile. "You been doing your own little thing again instead of sticking to the mission?"

Marty laughed.

"Hey, it's not our fault if we have to take detours. There's a lot of those things on the streets these days. Is it going to be a problem with Thompson?"

"Not at all. I just thought you should have prior warning in case they asked. Anyway, what's in the box you brought back with you?"

Marty looked over his shoulder and eyed Bull who shifted in his seat and turned his body so that his bulk was between him and Samantha, and protecting their precious crate.

"Nothing much," Marty replied, "just something we found that could be useful to us back at the barn."

Samantha knew that she was unlikely to get any more information than that from them and shrugged with disinterest.

"It can only be one of a couple of things," she reasoned aloud. "With the way that the big lump is hovering over it, it's either a box full of women's underwear or dirty magazines. Probably both, actually."

Marty smiled and shrugged his shoulders as he nodded in agreement. Samantha's logic was pretty well founded when it came to understanding Bull and his motives.

Samantha brought the vehicle to a stop at the headquarters building. Inside they passed through dozens of rooms and offices that were brimming with activity. It was clear that a high level of mission planning was in progress. Radios hissed and people spoke to one another in hushed tones as the three filth encrusted men made their way along the corridors.

"Good morning, fuck-stick," Bull bellowed out from the rear to a familiar face as he passed by an open door. "How you all enjoying yourselves here at 'slipper-city'?"

"Fuck off, Bull," came the reply. "They need *our* brains for this operation more than they need *your* brawn."

Samantha glanced back over her shoulder as they turned a corner and saw that Bull was stuffing the last pieces of a bacon sandwich into his gaping maw. She had no idea where he had procured it from and no doubt, the owner of the sandwich was probably just as confused as to where it had disappeared to. Bull never passed up an opportunity to gain nourishment, even if it was at the expense of someone else.

They passed through a doorway and approached a junction. To the left and right were corridors leading off to other parts of the complex. Immediately to their front was a set of steel grated stairs leading down into the bowls of the building and disappearing into darkness. Marty clearly heard the distinct moan of the infected rising up towards him from below. It sounded as though there were dozens of them down there.

"Experiments," Samantha whispered to him when she caught sight of the concerned look on his face. She too heard the noises but she had grown used to them by now.

"What kind of experiments, Sam?" He asked her as they took the corridor to the left and headed towards the Operations Room.

"The kind that will help us," she shrugged with indifference. "I have no idea to be honest with you. The egg-heads are playing *'Frankenstein'* down there in the basements and I have no desire to go and join in."

"You lot might be happy to have them next door to where you sleep but I'll stick to our nice cosy house on the coast if it's all the same to you," Danny murmured as he looked back towards the staircase.

Marty and the others spent three hours relaying all the information they had gathered to the Operations staff. As he finished the lengthy debriefing, Marty handed his maps and their camera's memory card across to Gerry for downloading.

While the intelligence was collated and the operations staff began pouring over the details of the reconnaissance mission, Marty, Bull, and Danny made good their escape. Bouncing across the island over the worn roads, the three men eagerly anticipated a hot meal and a chance to sleep.

"What do you think will be on the menu today?" Bull asked as his stomach began to growl up at him.

"I'm guessing either chicken or rabbit," Danny shrugged.

"It's *always* chicken or rabbit," Bull snorted back at him.

"Then why did you ask such a stupid question? Are you hoping that I'm going to tell you that it's steak or venison? The island is overrun with rabbits and chickens. So why would I guess at there being anything else to eat?"

"Fuck it," Bull grunted with a dismissive shake of his head. "I'll eat anything right now. My belly is touching my arse."

"I'll tell you one thing," Danny grinned back at him. "Sam's going to have a severe sense of humour failure when she comes out of the Ops Room and realises that we've run off with her Land Rover again."

Bull laughed. The theft of the vehicle had been an unspoken and universally agreed action between the three men, just as it had been a couple of months earlier during similar circumstances. Rather than wait for a ride they decided that they would 'borrow' Samantha's means of transport. Besides, they knew that it would give her an excuse to come and visit them later. There was method in their madness as always.

By mid-morning, they were approaching the narrow lane that led towards the bluffs on the southern side of the island and their half-built house. Once on the high ground, the refugee camp to the east was clearly visible to the men inside the Land Rover.

Thousands upon thousands of dirty white tents covered an area of two square kilometres of churned mud and human waste. A high fence topped with razor wire and a deep moat that encompassed the entire perimeter surrounded the camp. Roving patrols and regularly spaced watchtowers with armed guards maintained the integrity of the camp and kept the mass of refugees separated from the rest of the island.

Columns of wispy smoke drifted up from throughout the camp as the suffering civilians cooked whatever they could find and burned what they had to in order to keep warm during the cool summer nights. A faint murky haze of brown and green hung low in the air above the tented areas, confirming the filthy conditions that existed below and giving no illusions to the state that the remains of the Great British populous now found themselves in.

It was a pathetic sight and the three men could not help but look on at the human squalor that panned out to their left as they crested the hill and the partially completed roof of their barn came into view. Compared to the refugees, they were living in luxury and for a moment, they remained quiet in shamed contemplation.

The army and the remains of the government did what they could to supply the civilians with food, clothing, sanitation, and clean drinking water but the sheer numbers of homeless and starving people were against them. Supplies and medical care were stretched to their limits and it would not be long before the crisis reached tipping point.

"That explains why the head-shed are so keen to get the mainland back. Poor bastards," Bull muttered.

"Gerry was saying that there have been quite a few outbreaks down there over the last couple of weeks. Hundreds dead, apparently," Marty mumbled thoughtfully as he slowed the vehicle and viewed the scene.

Danny nodded.

"It's to be expected. According to the last I heard, there's almost a million people down there, all packed together like a colony of rats. If one of them dies, it doesn't matter what killed them, you can bet your arse that three more will quickly follow once they wake up and start munching their way through their friends and family."

"Well that's just put a dampener on my home-coming. I think I've lost my appetite," Bull grumbled as he leaned back into his seat and turned away from the panorama of misery.

He fell silent and thought for a moment.

"Actually, no it hasn't. Hurry up and get us home, Marty."

Releasing the handbrake, Marty complied and began slowly inching his way down the muddy track. A dark figure stepped out from behind a clump of bushes and watched them as they passed by and gave a slight nod of his head.

"Morning, Stan," Bull shouted with a beaming smile from the rear of the Land Rover as he flung the canvas flap to the side. "Did you miss us?"

"Yeah, like a boil on the end of my dick."

5

"Okay," she said quietly while standing poised by the door at the far end of the dark and unnerving passageway.

She adjusted her grip on the shaft of the crowbar. It was a good weight, heavy but strangely comforting. She had carried it with her for over four months and time and again it had proven its worth and reliability.

Looking back over her shoulder at him, she confirmed that he was still there and had not bolted for the door at the other end. She did not need to see him to know he was there, the sound of his heavy mouth breathing was evidence enough that he was standing close by her, but she felt better having confirmed it with her eyes.

"Are you ready?"

Christopher nodded and held the hammer close to his chest. He wielded it more for comfort than for defence or attack. He looked far from ready. He was completely terrified. His eyes shone wildly at her in the gloom and the beads of sweat running down his forehead sparkled in the low light.

"It's okay," she said reassuringly. "We're just going to have a look around. Stay close to me and keep an eye out behind us."

"I don't like this, Tina," he muttered, shaking his head. "Why do we have to go in there? Can't we just stay upstairs where it's safe?"

"We need to go in there and see what's left," she replied as she reached for the door leading into the warehouse. "Unless you want to starve?"

He shook his head again.

Yeah, I thought not, she heard a voice grumble from deep inside her own mind.

She opened the door and stepped out onto the raised platform. At first, Christopher failed to follow her and stayed within the relative safety of the corridor. She turned and glared back at him. He could not see her features but he could feel her eyes burning into him and since the previous day's events he was unsure of who he feared the most, the infected or his sister. He stepped out into the warehouse beside her and instantly felt the change in the atmosphere between the two rooms.

Although the light inside was barely enough for them to see beyond a few metres, he could sense the spacious room around him. The temperature was much cooler and the tiniest of sounds boomed in the expanse between the outer walls. Somewhere deep within the storage area liquid seeped out from a broken container or loose pipe. The faint echoes it made as the droplets fell into an ever-expanding puddle seemed magnified in the crushing silence and near blackness.

Christopher was beginning to feel the icy tendrils of panic slowly creeping upwards along his legs and into his gut. His flesh was covered with goose bumps and the hairs of his neck and forearms stood out from his skin. His breathing was coming in short gasps and his heart was beating rapidly and thumping in his ears as he fought to keep control on his fear.

Tina reached out and touched his forearm to get his attention. As her fingers made contact with his bare flesh, he flinched and almost let out a scream.

"Chris, it's okay," she whispered soothingly. "Stay calm and stay close to me. We're okay. We just need to make sure there's no one here. It'll soon be over."

She could not see his face but she was sure that his lips were trembling. She kept her hand on his forearm for a while longer to comfort him and she could feel him shaking in her grasp. She wondered how long it would be or how far they would need to travel from the safety of the doorway before he lost control of his bladder again or worse, his bowels.

That reminds me, we need toilet paper, she thought fleetingly.

She turned to her right and began to descend a set of concrete steps that brought her to the same level as the warehouse floor. Christopher did as he was told and remained close behind her. He was actually too close for her comfort but she did not bother to say anything. If it made him feel better then she would let him stay virtually on her shoulder. The fact that she had managed to get him to follow her at all was a victory in itself.

Slowly but surely their eyes began to adjust to the lack of light. It was still extremely dark but they were now able to make out shapes and changes in depth and distances as they quietly made their way along the first row of incinerated and collapsed shelves.

A minefield of burnt and destroyed stock lay strewn all over the cold floor of the supply room and they needed to be careful of where they placed their feet. They had heard nothing that indicated there were any infected within the warehouse but that did not mean that the place was free of danger.

Tina had learned over the months to rely on all her senses and not to trust any of them on their own. Until she could see, hear, smell, and feel that the place was clear she would assume that the infected were there, waiting for them in the darkness.

They reached the end of the first fallen aisle and entered into the main walkway that split the warehouse in two. From what she could tell, they were in a wide channel that ran the length of the building and dissected the storage area with smaller aisles branching off to the left and right at ninety degree angles. In her mind's eye, she imagined forklift trucks moving up and down the central passage as they collected pallets of stock from the rows of steel shelving. Behind her, she saw an area of wall that looked much lighter than the rest of the interior and she made the assumption that it was the large loading bay doors where the trucks would wait to be loaded by the forklifts. A thin shard of light that managed to penetrate through the bottom confirmed her assumption.

Their intention was to clear the building systematically, beginning at one end and making their way along the rows. She stepped back to check along the aisle to her right and Christopher followed closely. His eyes never left her dark silhouette and wherever she went, no matter if it was a single step to the side, he stayed in extremely close proximity.

Starting at the bay doors, they slowly made their way down the centre of the storage area. The racks of burnt and crumbling goods towered high up towards the ceiling and the light crunches of charred debris beneath their feet seemed to echo on for an eternity. The oppressive darkness and eerie silence were playing havoc with their nerves and they needed to stop regularly to allow their senses to clear.

The faint ping of the drips continued to resonate from somewhere deep within the dark warehouse. They resounded at five second intervals and Tina found herself relying on their frequency as a way of preventing her from losing her nerve. It was something for her to cling on to and so far, it seemed to be working.

Each aisle gaped out at them like a terrifying cave holding an untold number of horrors that lurked within their dark recesses. It was virtually impossible to see into them and Tina needed to rely on each of her senses to judge if they were clear. She watched intently as they passed by and scrutinised the wall of blackness that greeted them from between each of the high stacks of shelving.

She paused and cocked her head. She was sure that she had heard something other than the light crunch of their footsteps and the steady drip. Before she was able to identify the sound, her brother ploughed into the back of her. He had not noticed that she had stopped and as they collided, the scream of terror that he had been holding back for the previous fifteen minutes erupted from his mouth.

Tina froze as the cry shattered the silence and thundered around within the confines of the spacious room. Her blood solidified within her veins as she corrected her stance to prevent herself from falling over after her brother's colossal weight had knocked her off balance. She remained immobilised for a moment, rooted to the spot with every muscle tensed and all her nerve endings virtually protruding from her flesh. She listened intently as she held the crowbar aloft, ready to swing at anything that came towards her from out of the sinister curtain of blackness enveloping them.

As the echoes of Christopher's squeal subsided, the smothering silence returned. She straightened herself and turned to face him. His dark bulky shape loomed over her, but despite his immense size, he appeared to her like a little child. Her rage was at the point of bubbling over and her hands shook as she fought hard against the urge to hit him.

She was about to say something to him but then stopped as she detected something moving close by. She sensed it more than anything else. She reached out and grabbed her brother by the collar, and with a forceful heave, she pulled him towards her. As he tumbled forwards, she stepped to the right to avoid colliding with him again and released her grip on him. With the momentum of her sudden and powerful yank, Christopher staggered by her and slammed into a shelf, unable to slow himself.

He turned in time to see the faint shape of his sister as she leapt forward with her bar raised and slammed it down onto a dark form at her feet, close to the spot where he had been standing just seconds earlier. The iron crowbar smashed against something solid that cracked loudly. The force of her blow propelled the heavy shaft through the object and into the hard concrete of the floor with a resounding clang.

Christopher looked on in shocked silence as once again his sister saved him from one of the infected. He watched as Tina raised the weapon high in to the air and slammed it down against her victim again and again, pummelling her prey and growling under her breath with rage and fear. Each time the hefty crowbar impacted against the hard surface beneath the body the high-pitched chime of the metal rang out around the warehouse, sounding like a hammer being beaten against a blacksmith's anvil.

Finally, when there was nothing left of the head but tattered chunks of flesh and shattered bone, she stopped and took a shaky step back. She wiped her face on the back of her sleeve and urgently checked her immediate surroundings for any further danger. She was breathing heavily and trembling with the rush of adrenaline but the terror that she now felt was much stronger. The mixture of fear for the unknown, the darkness, and the noise she had created made her mind race with impending dread as she expected more of the infected to come racing towards her.

Christopher looked on in shock and awe. To him she was like something from one of the thousands of computer games he had played, or one of the movies he had watched. She moved with a grace and swiftness that he could only fantasize about. She was terrifying and fearless. She was unflinching in her resolve and ruthless in her attack. Christopher suddenly felt inferior, even pathetic, compared to his sister. She was more of a man than he was and he knew it all too well. Her damning words from the previous day echoed around inside his head. Once again, she had saved him from the monsters that were out to get him. She had looked out for him and seen what he had missed and reacted when he could not. He felt ashamed and worthless and began to wonder why his sister even bothered with him.

Before he could slump into another self-pitying abyss, Tina huffed loudly and blew out a sigh of relief. It had been over ten seconds since her attack had ended and there was stillness once again all around them.

"Well at least we know one thing," she gasped as she rested her hands on her knees and concentrated on settling her heart rate back to normal. "That must've been the only one in here. Otherwise, they would've made an appearance by now. What do you reckon?"

Christopher grunted as he looked around at the dark corridors that led off between the shelving units. While Tina had saved them from attack and then remained on guard for a while afterwards, he had stood inactive. It had not even occurred to him to help her or at the very least, protect them from further, unseen dangers.

"I suppose so."

She could sense his dejection in the tone of his voice.

"Don't worry about it, Chris. You made a mistake but it's all okay now. It's not your fault that you didn't see it. It's as black as a witch's tit in here."

She did not believe her own words and beneath the façade of understanding and casual forgiveness, she was still fuming over his clumsiness and inability to steady his resolve. The crawling, legless infected had come from the left, the side that *he* was supposed to have been watching. His lack of concentration and courage could have resulted in one of them being bitten. Worse still, there could have been many more of them in the warehouse, lurking in the shadows.

"It nearly got me," he whimpered.

Tina shot him a look. She took a deep breath and began her silent countdown again as she maintained her faltering grip on her temper.

Yeah, that's right, Chris. It nearly got you. Don't worry about me, she thought but stopped herself from speaking the words out loud.

"Yeah well, it didn't get *us* and at least we know the area is safe," she reasoned, hoping that he would pick up on her highlighting the fact that there were actually two of them at risk. "Let's carry on our search and see if there's anything good left in this place."

They continued forward. Tina remained alert, watching every shadow and listening intently while Christopher trailed along beside her, absentmindedly swinging his hammer like a child's book satchel as he walked home from school.

"Chris," she hissed across to him, "keep your fucking eyes peeled."

"I thought you said we're okay and there were no more of them?" He replied innocently and far too loudly for her liking.

Again, she could feel her feathers being ruffled. They *hoped* the area was clear of infected and the evidence pointed to that fact but it had not yet been confirmed. Her brother's complacency was another issue that she would need to confront in the near future. She made a mental note of it and added it to her growing list.

The light crunch of their footsteps as they walked over the charred debris at their feet continued to herald their presence. With each noise they made, Tina cringed and dreaded the thought of something taking note. Mixed with the sound of their heavy breathing and light footfalls, the steady drip continued to echo across the warehouse. It had become louder now and Tina knew they were reaching its source.

Something had changed in their surroundings. At first, she could not put her finger on what the change was. She hesitated and stood her ground while squinting in an effort to see into the gloom. She sniffed the air. It was still the same. The unmistakable smell of fire and melted plastic remained heavy in the atmosphere, but there was something else now. Something she could not quite place. It was a taste more than a scent, almost metallic.

She looked across at the dark shape of her brother. He was standing upright and looking more bored than alert. He glanced back at her questioningly. Despite her having to remind him constantly, he still could not grasp the idea of remaining watchful. His sister had proven their need for vigilance on many occasions and by now he should have learned that if *she* was standing still and searching their surroundings with her eyes and ears, he too should do the same. Instead, he relied on her to carry that burden.

Tina looked beyond him and then turned her attention to the shelves on her immediate right. In the low light, she was able to make out bright labels. A multitude of shapes and faint colours began to materialise within the stacks on either side of them. Gone were the black shapeless lumps of burned stock. She realised that at that point the fire had somehow been stopped. She took a quick glance to her rear and estimated that roughly one-third of the warehouse had been reduced to a smouldering ruin, but the remainder appeared to be untouched.

Cases, cartons, bottles, and all manner of objects and containers unfolded before her eyes. She could see crates of tinned goods and stacks of boxes reaching high up towards the ceiling, and they all appeared to have been spared the ravages of the fire that had consumed the stock behind them. She smiled to herself in the darkness and let out an involuntary huff of triumph while she stared up at the high reaching stacks of food and supplies. Christopher had not noticed the change and looked across at her in confusion.

"What is it?" He whispered.

"Food," she answered, simply.

Christopher's eyes grew wide at the pronunciation of that particular word, but before he could step across to her and begin rummaging through the stacks of goods, she held out a hand and stopped him in his tracks.

"We still need to check the rest first, Chris."

He paused and glared down at her. She was standing in the way of his feast and he could feel the hairs on his neck begin to prickle. His stomach constantly growled and he felt light headed from hunger but here she was, standing before him and telling him that he could not have that which he coveted so much.

She could see by the way he was standing that he was beginning to feel angered. She kept her hand raised in front of her and just centimetres away from his chest. He remained where he was, as though there was an invisible force emitting from her palm that prevented him from moving any further.

"But…" he began in a pleading voice.

"Chris, listen to me," she reasoned, "we will check the rest of the warehouse all the way down to the end and then we can take whatever we need. Just be patient. We need to make sure we're safe before we begin grabbing stuff off the shelves."

He did not like her tone of voice. To him she sounded patronising, speaking to him like he was a child and telling him that he could not have anything to eat just yet. As far as he was concerned, the place was already safe. If there were any more of the infected they would have come when they heard his yelp.

"Okay?" She asked him as she tried desperately to make him understand.

Finally, he nodded and grunted his reluctant agreement. She could see that he still was not happy. Reaching out behind her, she grabbed something from one of the shelves and handed it to him. He looked down into his hand and recognised the cereal bar. With no other option at that moment, he gladly accepted the food, savouring the thought of having his fill once they had finished looking around. He hurriedly tore the wrapper away and virtually inhaled the cereal bar as he obliviously followed after his sister.

They quietly passed row upon row of fully stocked shelves and carefully checked the aisles in between. The sound of the drip was getting louder and the strange scent that Tina could almost taste at the back of her throat was becoming stronger.

She stopped before the last unit. In the gloom, she could see a large open space with what she believed was a small office to the left. It was hard to be sure but in the dim light, she was able to see a door and a window that would have probably been the staff area. At that moment however, she was not concerned with the left side. Whatever was making the dripping noise was off to the right and beyond the final stack.

She clicked her fingers and indicated that her brother should move closer to her. With her back against the steel frame of a rack, she readied herself. Clutching her crowbar tightly in her hands she took a deep breath and turned the corner.

Instantly the smell hit her. It struck her in the face like a hard slap and she recoiled from the sharp tang of festering blood. A dark shifting cloud of angry flies swarmed up in front of her and took flight through the aisles. The air came alive with their loud buzzing and it was almost impossible to hear anything other than the sound of the surging insects. Her foot slipped in something and she stumbled and crashed into Christopher as he rounded the corner from behind her. He too gasped at the overpowering stench but he managed to keep his balance and even stopped his sister from falling in the swathe of the dark sticky substance that seemed to carpet the floor over a vast area.

"Fuck me," Tina gagged as she held her hand up to her mouth and nose.

The noise of the flies faded as they continued their flight towards the far end of the warehouse and relative silence settled upon the scene again. Tina and Christopher remained still for a moment as they watched the mess on the floor slowly begin to form as their eyes took in more detail from the gloom. Distinct shapes began to stand out from the darkness and they soon realised that they were looking upon a pile of mutilated human corpses. They had been torn to pieces, gnawed beyond recognition, and mixed together into a mound of bloodied flesh and bone.

Tina's foot knocked against something metallic. It shifted when she came into contact with it and began to roll away from her. She could not be sure of what it was but she *had* to reach down for it. Something in her subconscious told her that it was safe to do so and that it would be of use to her. She crouched and felt for the object. Her fingers made contact with a cool cylindrical shape and she instinctively knew what she had found. Rising back to her feet, she fumbled for the switch.

A bright light suddenly bathed the area in front of them in a luminous brilliance. The beam flitted about as it reflected from the shelves and Tina adjusted her hold on the tacky blood soaked aluminium handle.

She pointed the light down at the floor. In the glowing beam, they looked on as the carnage was revealed. Twisted limbs that had been eaten down to the bone lay tangled within the human wreckage and pointing outwards at various angles. Ribcages that had been torn open and emptied sat amongst the organic debris with their spines still holding them together. Skulls and leg bones, having been ripped from their owners' bodies, sat festering around the pile while the bloated and discoloured innards and putrefying soft tissue filled the spaces between and swamped the cold floor beneath.

"Fuck me," Tina gasped again.

It was impossible for her to tell how many bodies there were. None had remained intact and all were chewed and torn beyond any recognisable form. She panned the light to the left and right and took in the scale of the massacre. Subconsciously she counted the heads that she could see and concluded that there were at least fifteen people in front of her.

Christopher stood beside her and followed the light with his eyes. He too struggled to take in the scene. He was still battling with his gag reflex and with every second that ticked by, he could feel his composure slipping from his grasp.

"What do you think happened here?" Tina asked rhetorically. She knew that her brother had no answers but the question needed to be voiced.

Close by, she could still hear the distinct sound of the dripping liquid. It echoed in her ears like the slow steady beat of a drum. She moved her light around the area and paused when she caught a glimpse of something at shoulder height on the shelving stack in front of them. The beam of her torch shone onto a white plastic container and made it almost opaque as the particles of light filtered through and illuminated the interior. Inside she could see a dark shape and from the bottom, a steady flow of dark fluid seeped from a small crack in the plastic. The blood spread out across the steel shelf and dripped from the edge and into an expanding puddle on the floor. Morbid curiosity was getting the better of her and before she could control herself, she stepped forward and reached up for the container. Her fingers folded over the lip and she tested its weight with a gentle tug. It was heavy and she would need to grip it more firmly to stop it from slipping from her fingers. She raised the pale tub, lowered it to the ground, and shone her light down into it.

A set of cold dead eyes stared back up at her. They were flat and pale but there was no mistaking that they could see her. They remained fixed on her, unblinking and showing nothing in the way of humanity. They were monstrous and terrifying, and made all the more so by the fact that they were attached to a severed head that disobeyed all the natural laws that Tina had ever come to understand.

She was shocked, revolted, and horrified at what she saw but she could not take her eyes away from it. Beneath the tangle of black matted hair was the emaciated face of a woman. Her skin was a deep green with brown and blue traces that created a marbled effect. Her soft tissue looked as though it had shrunk and was stretched over her skull, making her cheekbones protrude and her eye sockets appear like deep chasms. Her lips had shrivelled away revealing her yellowed teeth and her nose was nothing more than a thin and lifeless sliver of withered flesh. The jaw continued to flex as the lifeless eyes intently watched Tina.

Christopher stepped over and peered into the bucket. Still holding his nose and struggling against the stench of the mass of corpses around him, he finally lost control. With his large body suddenly throwing itself into convulsions, vomit spurted out over his hand and gushed from between his fingers.

Tina felt the splash of the warm bile as speckles hit her across her face. She turned the light towards him and if it had not been for the horror of the situation, she would have laughed. Caught in the beam of light and frozen to the spot, Christopher stood staring back at her with bulging bloodshot eyes. Orange tinged gloopy liquid sprayed out from behind his hands in all directions as the pressure thrown up from his churning stomach forced its contents to push through his attempts at damming the flow. It was akin to trying to stop a sudden fast flowing leak by placing his hand over a burst high-pressure hose.

She stepped back away from him and out of range from the spraying vomit. She kept one eye on the ground and where she placed her feet. The thought of slipping in the intestines of a human being and tumbling into the festering remains made a shiver run down through her spine and ricochet back up into her brain.

Christopher slowly recovered behind her while she stepped further out into the open space and began to pan the light in a three-hundred and sixty degree arc. Forklift trucks, handcarts, large rolls of plastic sheeting, and many more warehouse objects were sitting within the spacious area, but there was no sign of any movement. That was her main concern at that moment. For all she knew there could have been survivors hiding in the darkness, or worse, more infected slowly crawling their way towards the two newcomers.

"Looks clear," she whispered loudly over to her brother and turned to check on him.

He was wiping his face on the material of his t-shirt, leaving dark smears of filth that would leave him smelling far from agreeable. He rubbed at his eyes with his screwed fists and wiped away the tears that had begun to cascade along his plump cheeks when his stomach had given up all it could and only dry retching had remained.

"You okay?"

He nodded and closed his eyes as he took in a deep breath. He was far from okay. He began to heave violently again. The noise of his gag reflex forcing him to sputter and groan loudly echoed through the rafters of the warehouse ceiling. It went on for a long time and Tina began to worry that her brother was going to have a heart attack. His face was a burning red and the veins in his neck and forehead protruded angrily from beneath his skin. His eyes were streaming again and thick viscous trails of drool hung from his slack mouth as his guts continued to twist and spasm.

"Come on," she coaxed as she placed an arm around him and guided him to the left of the storage area and towards what she believed to be the floor manager's office. "Get away from the stink and you may feel a little better, Chris. Here, sit down for fuck sake and sort yourself out before you keel over."

He allowed himself to be guided downwards by her. With his back against the wall and his ample rear on the cool floor, he sat with his head spinning and his knees shaking.

Tina looked down at him and shook her head while he gasped up at her with his eyes rolling backwards into his skull. Once again, he had proven himself to be of absolutely no use to her.

Right now, he was nothing more than a burden. If they were attacked she would face having to make the decision between dying as she tried to help him and leaving him to be a feast for the infected.

In her hypothetical thinking, she liked to believe that she would stand her ground and refuse to abandon him, but she knew all too well how human instincts worked. Over the months, she had witnessed families and friends take flight and desert their nearest and dearest as their own self-preservation had gotten the better of them. She had even seen people deliberately feed loved ones to the infected so that they themselves could get away.

I'll burn that bridge once I've crossed it and live or die with whatever decision I come to, she thought to herself as she watched her brother sitting slumped against the wall.

She still needed to check the office and on further inspection, she realised that there was another room beside it. The light in her hand reflected off something shiny and metallic. It was large and she knew what it was before she had taken another step towards it. It was the cold storage room. Inside would be where the meat, fish, and vegetables were stored to keep them fresh. At the rear of it would be the freezer. The door was closed and appeared to be secure. However, the office entrance was not sealed and she could see there was a gap between the door and the frame of about ten centimetres. She would check that room first.

She did not need to check on her brother. She was well aware that she would be doing it alone and no help would be coming from him. She could not even rely on him to keep an eye out for her while she went inside. He sat there grunting and sputtering, and breathing heavily through his mouth. Each intake of air was a wheezing gasp.

She paused at the door and looked back across the open space of the warehouse. All was quiet and still apart from her brother's panting. She glanced down at him. She knew he could not hear her but she had to voice her thoughts.

"Jesus, Christopher, I hope to God I find a treadmill in this place because you'll be spending a fucking lot of time on it."

In the office, she found nothing. Desks, filing cabinets, and the usual stationary equipment that could be found in any administration area was all that was inside. With a sigh of relief she stepped back out into the cool spacious air of the warehouse.

Next, she turned her attention to the cold storage door. She hesitated for a moment and took in a deep breath. The crowbar was held aloft and to her rear and was ready to be brought forward with all the power she could muster. With her left hand, whilst keeping a precarious grip on the torch, she fumbled with the handle. It needed to be pulled towards her and she would have to use all the skill and dexterity that she could in order to keep hold of the light and manipulate the locking mechanism at the same time.

With a heavy clunk, the lock slipped from its housing and the door came open. It was thick and heavy and needed to be heaved away from the frame. As the black rectangle of the dark interior grew before her, Tina jumped back and angled the torch so that the light illuminated the inside of the room.

A gust of icy air moaned out towards her. She could detect the scent of cold meat within the breeze as it mixed with the warmer atmosphere inside the main storage area. Inside, from within the blackness and set into the far wall, a red light was blinking away and another open doorway appeared from within the murky interior. The room still had power.

"Hello?" She hissed in through the doorframe.

The inside of the cold storage was not the only thing that was chilled. Her blood was becoming frozen from the terror she could feel creeping through her system. She could leave the door locked and barricaded but there could be things of use to them in there and if there *were* any infected inside, they needed to be dealt with. She did not like the idea of any of them being inside the building with them, no matter how difficult she made it for them to break free and get to her.

There was nothing but utter silence greeting her from within the darkness. Tentatively, she crept forward and over the threshold. Her breathing was shallow and silent. Each breath quickly misted before her eyes as she exhaled and concentrated all her efforts on making no sound, but her heart was beating like a brass band in her ears. Her feet crunched against the frost that had seeped out from the open door of the freezer and everywhere she looked, the ice crystals that coated every surface sparkled back at her like a blanket of stars in a clear night sky.

The further in she went, the colder it became. Shelves loaded with frozen vegetables and fruit flanked her on either side as she made her way along the central aisle. They were devoid of their usual colours and had become a mixture of white and cold blue as the frost had coated them along with everything it touched.

She was soon standing before the doorway that led into the freezer compartment. Its dark opening gaped back at her forebodingly, almost daring her to step inside. She shuddered. It was not the cold that made her muscles and nerve endings twitch. It was the almost impenetrable blackness of the next room that gave absolutely no hint of what lay beyond.

Again, Tina steeled herself and drew on every bit of her resolve to continue forward. She took in a deep breath and stepped towards the open wintry chasm. Her light flickered across more of the same that she had seen in the space behind her. A thick blanket of whiteness coating every surface. More shelves revealed more frosted goods but there was something further along filling the centre of the aisle. At first, it looked as though some of the large slabs of meat had fallen from the stacks on either side but in the back of her mind, she knew that they were not sides of frozen beef.

"Oh my God," she gasped involuntarily.

What she was seeing were dozens of people. They were all sitting huddled together on the floor of the freezer compartment and perpetually frozen in time. The frost clung to their cold flesh and formed icy stalactites that hung from their features. Their skin was a multitude of greys, blues, and deep purples and some of them still remained with their eyes open and staring out at their surroundings. There were men, women, and children of all ages among the petrified heaps. They had sheltered there, hoping to get away from their attackers and had slowly frozen to death.

Tina was unable to move. She stood in the doorway staring at the unfortunate families who had tried to save themselves but had inadvertently sealed themselves into an icy tomb. She guided the beam of her light over the faces of the dead. Their flesh glittered and the open eyes seemed to stare back at her accusingly as her torchlight caused them to sparkle.

It was the bodies of the children that horrified her the most. Some of them could not have been much older than two or three, and they would not have understood why they were slowly freezing to death. She could almost hear their quivering, echoing voices and cries as they beseeched their parents to provide them with warmth and comfort. Their faces, frozen with the innocence of youth, looked almost peaceful in their deaths. They did not look as though they had died in pain but Tina knew that the latter stages of hypothermia were usually accompanied with a feeling of euphoria and sleepiness. It was the uncontrollable shivering and excruciating pain of the cold, creeping along their limbs and over their bodies in the earlier stages that would have been the hardest to suffer. She could only imagine how it must have been for the parents to watch their children slowly die around them when they realised that they had locked themselves inside the freezer with no way out.

Most of the adults were virtually naked, having removed their clothing and wrapped them around the children. It had done them no good and had more than likely only prolonged the suffering of the young.

A shadow flickered across from behind her, accompanied by a low rumbling groan. She spun and raised her heavy bar as a stifled yelp forced its way up from her throat. She released the tension, brought the curved end of the crowbar forward, and aimed for the head of the lumbering figure behind her.

Christopher stood staring at her in fright. He could not speak or even raise his hands to protect himself. Instead, he winced and waited for the inevitable impact of the heavy metal against his skull. It did not arrive.

Before it was too late, Tina realised that it was her brother and averted a catastrophe by throwing herself off balance and slamming her body into the doorframe.

"You dick," she gasped. "I nearly killed you, Chris."

"Yeah, I'm glad you didn't, sis," he quipped with one eye open as he watched Tina correct herself and regain her balance.

Tina showed him what she had found and for a while, they both remained at the doorway, unable to take their eyes away from the scene. Both remained silent and lost in their own thoughts as they took in the tragic spectacle.

"Poor buggers," Christopher sighed thoughtfully as he imagined the suffering that had taken place within the room.

"Yeah," Tina nodded as she turned and made to walk away.

"What do you think happened?"

"It's obvious, don't you think?" She shrugged as she pushed passed him. "They froze to death in here."

"Yeah, but how?" He replied as he turned after her. "I mean, why would they all go and lock themselves in here?"

"Desperation," she grumbled over her shoulder. "Maybe they had absolutely no choice and preferred dying in here instead of out there with the others? Who knows what happened and why it happened."

"Yeah, but why lock themselves in?"

Something had been troubling her and Christopher's final question reminded her of what had been on her mind when she first entered into the cold storage room. She paused and slowly turned around. She caught sight of the blinking red light again and realised what it was. Subconsciously she had wondered to herself why they had not shut down the power to the freezer but when she examined the control box, she realised that it had not been through their lack of trying. The shutdown switch was set behind a thick glass panel and it was obvious to her from the damage to the surrounding casing that they had repeatedly attempted to open it and turn it off. For whatever reason, they had been unable to access it and the freezing air had continued to be filtered in through the vents. To add to their misfortune the interior door handle had failed them and left them trapped inside with no way out and no way of turning off the power.

"They had no chance," Tina sighed as she stepped back out from the cold storage room and into the warmth of the warehouse.

Christopher followed her closely. He did not like being separated from her and he especially did not like being in the freezer while she was outside.

"Do you think the place is safe now?"

She nodded.

"Yeah, I think it probably is," she replied solemnly.

"What about all those people that are in the fridge? Do you think they'll come back to life, Tina?"

"They're frozen solid, Chris. I don't think we have much to worry about from them at this moment in time."

Christopher stayed standing behind her for a while. He could tell that what she had seen in the freezer had deeply affected her but his sister's upset did not distract him from the painful rumbling that emitted from his empty stomach. He silently agreed to himself that he would give her a few moments to herself before they began rummaging through the food stocks. He owed her that much at least.

As Tina turned and walked towards the wall of the office, her torch light reflected from something close by to where Christopher was standing. While his sister pulled out a chair and sat herself down with a heavy sigh, he stepped closer to investigate what the dull black glint had been that he had seen in the light for just a fraction of a second. He checked over his shoulder and could barely see her. She was too far away to be able to see what he was doing and he crouched down, blindly feeling for the object over the dusty concrete floor. Then his hand brushed against it.

It was cold and heavy and made from metal. He folded his hand around the hard plastic grip and raised it up close to his eyes for inspection. He kept his body turned away from Tina so that she could not see the treasure he had found. Affectionately, he ran his fingers over the smooth steel and along the length of the top-slide. He could feel the tiny grooves of the lettering stencilled along the side of it and although he could not identify the exact make of it in the darkness, he had played enough video games and watched enough movies to be able to make an educated guess that it was a nine millimetre calibre.

He felt for the bottom of the pistol grip and the magazine that was still securely inside the housing. He did not want to release it and check if there were any rounds inside. The noise would alert Tina to his find. Instead, he tucked it into the waistband of his jeans and ensured that his t-shirt covered any sign of it. He would examine the weapon in private later and away from prying eyes.

"Should we get some food?" He suggested merrily as he turned back to his sister and hungrily rubbed at his bloated abdomen.

6

Back at the barn, Danny and Bull hefted their cargo out from the rear of the Land Rover and carried it towards the house. Stan was standing, watching them and as usual, he gave off no indication of whether he was happy to see them or not. The large red scars, sustained during the battle at Manchester airport, running down the side of his face and neck made him appear more ferocious than ever.

"How did you get on?" He asked.

"No dramas," Marty replied as he climbed out from the driver's door, clutching a cigarette between his teeth. "I think they have everything they need now and I get the impression that the counter offensive is going to begin pretty soon."

"You think so?"

Marty slung his rifle and pack over his shoulder, and shrugged violently to encourage the heavy equipment to sit comfortably on his aching muscles. Stan turned and they walked side by side back towards the front of the house.

"Well, yeah," Marty grunted as they entered in through the wide doorway and placed his kit down beside it. "There's a lot of prep going on down there at HQ and all the brass are running about like headless chickens."

"Yeah, I've had a warning order from Gerry," Stan replied while his attention was focussed on the crate that was being placed in the centre of the floor. "He says that it could begin within the next couple of weeks but since most of our forces never made it back from the Middle East and Korea, they have decided on narrowing the spearhead instead of the Blitzkrieg style offensive they were hoping for. They're concentrating their efforts on just a handful of cities to begin with now and then, moving on to further ops once the initial objectives are complete and secure. What have you brought back?"

Bull looked across at Marty then grinned back at their commander. He snapped the locking clasps up and with the toe of his boot, he kicked off the lid to the armoured box and revealed its interior.

Inside Stan saw the four car batteries, fuse boxes, transformer, and a mass of cables and other electronics and testing equipment that he had ordered them to bring back. There was another crate within the box and Stan blinked with disbelief when he read the yellow stencilling and saw the warning labels. He took a cautious step back and looked at Marty.

"What the fuck are you doing with a bunch of S-Mines?"

"We found them," Marty replied casually.

"We thought they would come in handy when the fight for the mainland starts," Danny added as he looked down into the box with an admiring eye.

Stan rubbed at the irritating fresh skin around the scars on his cheek and continued to stare down into the box. He had seen the carnage caused by those mines throughout Africa and Bosnia. They were effective and completely indiscriminate.

Commonly known as a 'Bouncing Betty', the S-Mine was an anti-personnel mine that when triggered, would spring up from the ground and detonate at waist level. Throwing out hundreds of high-velocity ball bearings, they were designed to maim rather than kill. As a result, soldiers that would otherwise be continuing the battle would instead find themselves trying to help their wounded comrades. Designed by the Germans in the Second World War, they had since ceased to be used by western armies but variants of them still existed in the east and other parts of the world.

"It's okay, Stan," Danny assured him as he reached in and removed the box of deadly explosives. "We've checked them and they're safe. I'll keep them stored out of the way where they can't do any harm."

"Whatever you say," Stan shook his head and watched as Danny carefully walked away with the mines. Then he saw the bottles of whisky and vodka and just as Samantha had guessed, a pile of adult magazines.

Realising that Stan was saying nothing, Bull felt obliged to justify their other items. He stepped closer to the box and began pulling out various items.

"Well we had to bring something back for the rest of the kids, Stan. You couldn't be the only one getting presents. That wouldn't be fair, and besides," he grinned, "pickings are pretty slim around here in the way of female company. Danny won't wear the lingerie we got him so what else are we supposed to do?"

"Fuck off, Bull," Danny called from the next room.

"Hey, Danny, it's not our fault you have an arse like a ten year old boy, is it?"

Stan knew that it was pointless to protest over the alcohol and now that the stuff was splayed out in front of him, the idea of having a few glasses of whisky in the evening were becoming more appealing. He shook his head and leaned in to retrieve the batteries with his good arm. Since the explosion at the airport that had killed Brian, the nerve and tissue damage to his right arm had rendered it almost useless and he had come to rely more upon his left.

Bull was watching him intently as he manipulated the heavy batteries.

"You right or left handed, Stan?" He asked innocently and with a frown of contemplation creasing the skin on his forehead.

"Right handed," Stan replied. "Well I used to be before it was shredded and turned into Swiss Cheese. Why?"

Bull shrugged indifferently as he picked up one of the adult magazines. It had been a Christmas edition from the previous year and displayed an extremely attractive blonde woman dressed in a provocative and seductive version of a Sanata Clause outfit on the front cover. He began to flick through the pages, pausing briefly when a particular picture caught his eye.

"Just wondering how you manage to wank is all."

There was a sharp audible intake of breath from around the room but Bull was not deterred. He barely noticed that everyone had become frozen statues, waiting to see what was going to happen next. He trundled on with his vocalised thoughts in spite of the glares from his commander. As usual, the big man did not have his filter in place and his thoughts were pouring from his lips with no consideration to where his words could lead, or the damage they could cause.

"I've tried it with my left but it just ends up doing its own thing. I don't have as much control, the elbow goes in different directions, and I lose rhythm. Before I know it, I'm pretty much just battering away at my plonker and almost ripping it from its foundations. Actually it's a bit like…"

"Bull," Stan said calmly and stopped him in mid ramble, "shut up."

Bull paused and looked around the room at the faces of the others. Even Emily who had entered from one of the adjacent rooms, smiling and about to welcome the men back from their long and dangerous mission was staring back at him with her mouth hanging open and a look of disgust and horror etched into her features.

"Oh, right," Bull said with embarrassment as he realised that he had allowed his mouth to slip into autopilot again. "Sorry."

"Bobby," Stan shouted into the next room as he shook his head in bewilderment at Bull, "get Richie over here and have these hooked up to the generator. Get him to work his magic on all this as soon as possible."

Bobby appeared at the doorway, and after a short reunion and exchange of insults with Bull and the others, he left through the front door to carry out Stan's orders. He still walked with a slight limp and was careful of every step. The cracked vertebrate he had suffered along with the broken ribs after jumping from the control tower were healed but he was still not back to full fitness and he had spent the better part of two months in a hospital bed and undergoing a number of operations and treatments for his injuries.

For months, the men had been having to scrounge and save on fuel. It was one of the many things that the island was short of. The barn had been in the process of being converted into a house and there was still a lot of building materials lying about. They had discovered that the owner had been intending to have the power partially supplied from solar panels and that the battery system had already been installed. Danny had come up with the great idea of hooking up their generator directly to the house power cells and fuse box, and almost blew himself up, along with the barn, in the process. The batteries had been overloaded and were now useless since then they had decided to use the fuel consuming generator thriftily and leave mauling with the electronics to the experts.

Then Bobby had met Richard, a Civil Engineer who agreed to take care of their problem but since the army were reluctant to part with the necessary equipment that he needed, they would need to find the parts elsewhere. The units who had arrived before them had already rifled the island and much of the equipment had been claimed. That did not deter the men from thieving what they needed when they had the chance but most encampments soon began posting guards specifically to watch out for people breaking in to steel from them. Instead, Stan's team had to turn to the mainland in order to get what they needed.

Now, with battery power and the generator and solar panels keeping them charged, Richard would be able to install a basic water heating system from the equipment that had been abandoned there. The huge oven, which had a habit of consuming the diesel from the generator's fuel tank almost as quickly as they could put it in, could also now be used from time to time. With each scavenging expedition things were looking better, and despite the gaping holes in the roof and walls that were covered by canvas sheeting and sandbags, they were comfortable.

Taff, his arms laden with chopped wood, entered into the house through the large bay doors that led out to the rear and overlooked the English Channel. Young William was in tow and as equally burdened and concentrating on keeping the logs from slipping.

"Ah, Billy the Kid," Bull roared when he saw the boy. "How the devil are you? Have you been keeping up with your pistol training?"

William placed the wood down onto the pile by the chimney breast, smiled up at the large man, and indicated the pistol he had strapped to his waist. Stan had insisted that everyone, including Emily and her son, should train regularly with the weapons they had. Emily had been reluctant but William had been more than willing to learn. Bull looked down at the holster attached to the boy's belt, saw the dull glint of the weapon, and instantly turned to Stan with a look of concern in his eyes.

"Oh, it's not loaded," William assured him, pulling the slender Browning High-Power from its holster and turning it so that Bull could see into the hollow magazine housing. "Stan said I should keep it with me so that I get used to carrying it and practicing with it."

Bull smiled down at him and patted him on the head with his huge hand that almost covered the whole of the child's cranium.

"Good drills, mate. Make sure you always keep it within arm's reach. We'll make a proper soldier of you yet, Billy."

"Not if I can help it," Emily called across from the doorway with a smile. "He'll be staying here, on the island, with me, until the mainland is safe again."

"Sounds like the lady of the house has spoken, Billy," Bull said down to him with mock disappointment. "You'd better listen to what she says, mate."

William looked up and then quickly turned away in annoyance. It was clear that he and his mother had already argued extensively over the matter and for the time being, Emily had the final say. Since their rescue from Manchester, Emily and William had kept themselves close to the men of the team and became a part of the group with their own roles and responsibilities. There were no objections from any of them over the unspoken arrangement and with the only other option, being to live in the refugee camp, the mother and son had been adopted by Stan and his soldiers and kept under their protection.

Taff was slowly rising from a squatting position after dropping the heap of wood onto the pile by the fireplace. He grunted and winced with each movement as he straightened his legs and back, grimacing with each painful movement. Bull watched him and could not help but find it amusing as he witnessed his friend's suffering.

"So how's the little princess?" Bull taunted.

Taff turned and glared at him for a moment and could already feel the blood within his veins beginning to heat up. The moment he heard them arrive, he knew that there would be a degree of abuse headed his way. It was how they were. It was never meant to offend or upset and it was just their way of conveying their affection for one another. Still, there were always times when the ridiculing would go too far or the person on the receiving end was just not in the mood.

"I'd like to see you jump about like a gymnast after a broken ankle, dislocated knee, and a cracked pelvis. Other than that I'm fine. Now wind your neck in."

"You poor little lamb," Bull continued with a sneer as he sat himself down onto the large couch in front of the chimney breast. "Do you need a cuddle? While you cripples are busy mincing about here, we able-bodied sorts are getting things done and risking our lives on the mainland. I really don't know how you sleep at night, Taff. Now if you don't mind, make us a brew and run me a bath. There's a good boy."

As Stan and Marty began emptying the box, Bull made the mistake of allowing his attention to become focussed elsewhere and away from tormenting Taff for a few seconds. That was all the time that the Welshman needed.

A heavy thud from the area in front of the fire prompted Stan to turn around. Taff was standing by the couch and Bull's limp body was slowly sliding downwards, slipping from the cushions and onto the floor. With lightning speed, as Bull was busy watching Stan and Marty, Taff had stepped in and sucker-punched the huge man in the left side of his jaw. Instantly, Bull's consciousness had been snatched away from him.

Emily, still standing in the doorway as she watched and listened in amusement to the men and their banter had not seen Taff move. She must have blinked at the moment he launched his lightning attack but she had clearly heard the thud and the fact that Bull had suddenly disappeared from sight and his voice could no longer be heard was enough to tell her that he had somehow been incapacitated.

"Dear God, Taff," Emily huffed as she realised what had happened and made her way across to the sofa. "Not again."

"I told him to shut up," Taff grunted in a tone reminiscent of a child who was being told off for fighting with one of his siblings.

Kneeling down beside the unconscious Bull and after scooping her fingers into his cavernous mouth to ensure that he was not going to swallow his tongue, she turned to look up at Taff. Her face conveyed the level of her annoyance.

"I know you told him to shut up but it's always *me* who ends up having to deal with him. You know what he's like. He's not much different from a kid at times." She paused and looked about at the rest of them. "In fact, none of you are. You're all a bunch of overgrown bloody five year olds."

"Well, I'll keep doing it until he learns to back off when I tell him to." Taff leaned over her and peered down at his friend. "Is he okay?"

"Of course he's okay," Emily replied with a sigh. "It's *you* that won't be okay when he wakes up, Taff. I'm not playing 'mother' for you all and getting in the way of your silly squabbling when he comes to."

Stan and Marty looked on in amusement from the other side of the room while they continued to inspect the contents of the box. Neither of them were electricians but the item numbers on the equipment matched the list that Richard had given them.

"You'd better make yourself scarce before he wakes up, mate," Marty advised Taff as he handed a bottle of whisky across to their team commander.

Below average in height but powerfully built, Taff knew that in a fair fight he would not be able to take on the mighty Bull in a slugging match. None of them could. Instead, he always resorted to using his wits and speed and on a number of occasions, Bull had made the mistake of dropping his guard and leaving himself wide open to attack.

"Aye, good idea," Taff agreed as he stared down at his drooling friend on the floor. "I'm due for my daily walk anyway. I have to keep working on getting my ankle strong again. You coming, Billy?"

Bobby returned a couple of hours later with Richard and set to work on improving their power issues. With his wiry grey hair that stood out in strands from his scalp and leathery skin, Richard looked nothing like one expected from a man who had once sat on the London City Council. He was short and lean, to the point where he looked malnourished, and the burning cigarette that always seemed to dangle between his nicotine stained lips and discoloured stubble made him appear like a man who had been living on the streets for most of his life.

"All right, Bull?" Richard grinned as he walked through the door revealing the four discoloured teeth he had remaining within his mouth.

Bull was still brooding over the incident with Taff but Stan had managed to calm him down from his rage and convinced him that he was overreacting.

"I'm good, Richie. How about you?" Bull replied from the table where he continued to strip and clean his weapons. "Taff hit me again. Sucker-punched me when I wasn't looking, the wanker."

Richard shrugged.

"Well what else is he going to do, arm wrestle you? You're lucky he didn't go with the gun option, mate."

By nightfall, the house had become a little more civilised. Bull was happy to bury the hatchet over a few drinks and the oven and hot water boiler were fully functional. Each of them took it in turns to have hot showers and finally began to feel human again while they sat down to a hefty meal of mostly locally caught meat. Taff was an expert tracker and trapping animals in snares was something that had come as part of his skill. Knowing what to look for and how to read the ground helped when setting his snares and had kept them all reasonably well fed compared to the rest of the island's inhabitants.

Marty gave Stan a full report on the reconnaissance mission that he and the others had conducted over the previous three weeks and what they had seen.

"Sounds like it will be a hard job getting into the city from the west then," Stan concluded. "Aviation fuel is one of their main concerns at the moment, but if they decide to try a heli insertion, we'll have those things all over us before we even get close."

"You sound pretty sure that we'll be going in ahead of everyone else on this one, Stan," Bull said as he reassembled his pistol after giving it a thorough cleaning.

"What else would we be doing? Taking it easy here on the island?"

"Aye, I suppose so," Bull shrugged.

Marty nodded and poured himself another glass of whisky.

"Getting us in there is their problem. We can let them figure that out. Plus, with the shortage of aircraft I get a sneaky feeling that they won't risk losing one while dropping us in. As you said, fuel is also an issue. Obviously we'll have the final say on it but as

THE DEAD WALK THE EARTH II

long as they don't try dropping us in by parachute then I'm happy enough to consider their ideas."

"That might explain the meeting I'm having with Gerry in the morning," Stan pondered as he rubbed at the bristles on his chin.

"What meeting?"

"Just a rough head's up on the outline of the coming ops. More of an in-depth warning order really and he's bringing an old friend of mine who I didn't even know was on the island. Anyway, what about the other stuff?"

Marty nodded as he swallowed a mouthful of the golden fiery liquid and twisted the map around on the table so that he could get a better orientation. Stan was referring to the secondary task that he had given them in secret and was not a part of the orders from the Operations Officer or the army commanders.

"Here's where we left the first cache," he said as he pointed to an area on the mainland that was north of the island and directly south of Swindon. "There's weapons, ammunition, food and water, and cold weather gear too. We piled it all into the back of two SUVs and both are fully fuelled with battery chargers inside in case it's a while before we use them. The cache is off the beaten track too, so we shouldn't have any trouble with unwanted attention while approaching it."

"Upavon," Stan read the name of the closest town aloud. "That's about what, seventy kilometres?"

"Roughly that, yeah," Marty nodded and then tapped another point on the map with the sharpened point of his pencil.

"I have the exact grid for you and a cache report," Danny cut in. "It's close to an old Cold-War bunker and away from the built-up area. The other cache is here, about a hundred kilometres further north towards Birmingham."

"You covered quite a distance on your visit to the mainland, didn't you? Did you see any survivors? What about infected?"

"Plenty of both," Marty confirmed. "The infected are sticking mainly to the urban areas but there are still a lot of them scattered through the sticks. Survivor wise; we watched a few units of soldiers carrying out raids and so on. Not sure whether they were from any of the FOBs or acting independently though. We passed quite a few families who were still barricaded inside their homes too."

"Anything that's likely to give us problems?"

Marty shook his head with confidence.

"Nah, I doubt it. People on the mainland are too busy just trying to survive. Besides, I'm one hundred percent sure that we weren't seen by anyone. We only moved at night and laid up during daylight hours."

Remembering the incident of the fire that engulfed the better part of a town, Danny glanced across at Marty. The look was only fleeting but Stan saw it and wondered what exactly they were holding back from him. He decided not to push the subject and reasoned that if there were something that was operationally critical, they would tell him. Other than that, he did not want to know what they got up to on the mainland so long as it did not get in the way of them doing their jobs or affected their continued survival.

"Good work," Stan nodded.

With the caches that Marty and the others had left in the south of the country he was satisfied that they were not placing all their eggs into the same basket as the remains of their government and military forces. If the worst came to the worst, they knew that everything they needed could be located in the same spot. Their only problem would be getting there, and in one piece.

Later, as they sat eating and drinking, Samantha arrived. She did her best to appear annoyed over the theft of her Land Rover but her face betrayed her amusement at the men's complete disregard for the rules when it came to taking care of themselves. Within minutes of her appearance she made an excuse to leave and as per their routine, Bobby left shortly afterwards with his own excuses.

"Those two kids must think we're stupid," Richard remarked as he topped up his glass. "Hey, Stan, what's the latest on that Marcus guy and his blokes?"

Richard was referring to the transmissions they had been listening to on the High-Frequency radio over the previous couple of months. Each night they had tuned in to catch up on the latest developments concerning a group of men who were fighting their way back across Europe after battling their way out of Baghdad and crossing over from Turkey and the Middle East.

"We haven't heard anything from them for a few days," Stan replied. "The last message they sent was that they were approaching the French coast and that there was strong evidence of a rogue militia in the area."

"Yeah," Taff added as he sat back in his chair and looking more than a little inebriated. "They were up against tanks and all sorts, apparently."

"Jesus," Richard whistled through his well-spaced teeth, "they fought their way out from one shit hole to the next, all the way from Baghdad, only to run into a bunch of Frogs with chips on their shoulders?"

"French Fries, you mean? They had French Fries on their shoulders," Taff quipped as he sat swaying in his seat.

"Good one, Taff." Richard sniggered.

The joke was sharp but Richard really did hope that Marcus and his men had somehow come through. For weeks, Stan and the others had all been listening intently to their progress as they dragged themselves across Europe. There had been many transmissions over the months from various sources across the world, but the saga of Marcus and his men had drawn them in. It was something they could relate to and not completely dissimilar to predicaments they had found themselves in.

Bull had compared it to a soap-opera. With very little in the way of entertainment, the team of mercenaries from Iraq and their adventures had it all. Drama, action, excitement, and tension. It even had the love interest and intimacy between Marcus and his wife, Jennifer.

"Do you think they made it?" Marty asked with interest.

"I doubt it," Stan shrugged as he emptied his glass.

"That's shit," Bull grumbled, "I was rooting for those boys."

The next morning, while Taff attempted to scrub the permanent marker-pen drawing of a penis from his forehead that Bull had settled upon as payback for the sucker-punch, Stan headed off to meet with Gerry.

7

"There, that should do it," Tina said with satisfaction as she stepped back away from the door and rubbed her hands together.

"Do you think it'll be strong enough?" Christopher asked with scepticism as he eyed the barricade that they had both spent the better part of a day building.

For hours they had both toiled, hefting large heavy desks from the offices and dragging them into the foyer where they stacked them at the main entrance to the building. With each piece of furniture that they piled up against the door, less light filtered in from outside. The reception area was steadily becoming darker.

Tina had conducted the construction of their defences like a military operation. Each time they brought in a desk or cabinet she would insist that they place it down and wait while she crept forward through the maze of obstacles and took a look through the glass. She was terrified of any of the infected that were scattered about the car park noticing them as they worked. She knew well from experience that it did not take much to attract their attention and if one of them saw her there would soon be an immense crowd of the things beating away at the door.

She nodded confidently while she stood back, placing her hands on her hips and admiring their handiwork.

"I don't see why not, Chris. As long as we're careful not to make too much noise and we remain conscious of any light we use during the night, they won't know we're in here. Hopefully, if the worst came to the worst, the barricade will hold them off long enough for us to come up with a plan if things went tits up."

He nodded to her. He was confident in her judgement. Since she had arrived home in the early days of the infection's spread, she had never been proven wrong in her decisions. He was more than happy for her to take the lead and sit back while she did all the thinking for both of them.

For a number of days they had spent their time making their new home safe. After clearing the warehouse, Tina had gone about the grisly task of dealing with the frozen corpses in the cold storage room. She had dragged their stiffened carcasses out through the door beside the loading bay and out into the open air.

She discovered there that she had been correct in her assumptions and the area on that side of the building was a sealed off parking lot for staff vehicles and delivery trucks. There were a number of cars dotted about the area, but she doubted that any of them were capable of starting and did not want to risk attempting to turn the engines over. At that moment, the area was clear of the infected and she wanted it to stay that way.

The entrance gate was still open but it was at an odd angle from the main parking area in front of the buildings and obscured by a row of tall bushes running along the fence line. Tina considered closing the gate but decided against it. Leaving it open would provide them with an alternate means of escape and they would be extremely unfortunate for the infected to wander into the area due to its location and lack of accessibility. At the very worst, one or two meandering bodies could stumble into the staff parking area from time to time but she could easily deal with that.

Out in the private car park they also uncovered the source of the power that had kept the cold storage units working. Solar panels were connected to a large bank of batteries that had originally been charged from the main-grid. When the power had failed, the batteries kicked in and the unusually good English summer had provided enough solar power to keep them topped up. It made sense. Stock being ruined and costing the company money due to a power cut would have been unacceptable in the old world.

Tina set about taking care of the icy cadavers. One by one, she crawled over the unfortunate people with a long screwdriver in her hand and delivered the final death to each of them. She still could not bear to look at the children and driving the long shaft of the screwdriver through their tiny heads had been heart breaking for her.

With minimal help from her brother, she loaded the bodies onto one of the handcarts and made five separate trips to and from the loading bay before all the dead were gone from the freezer. She piled them at the far side of the staff parking area and did her best to afford them a degree of dignity under the circumstances. The bags of lime that she found in the DIY section of the shelving units were cut open and poured over the remains to help with decomposition and to keep the smell down to a minimum.

Collecting the half-eaten skeletal corpses in the main part of the warehouse had been the toughest test of their resolve. For that particular task, she insisted that Christopher helped her and no excuse would be listened to. Using shovels and plastic sheeting, they scraped the gruesome remains from the floor and scooped them into large plastic waste bins before dragging them out to add to the growing funeral mound.

To complete the mass grave, she covered the heap of defrosting bodies with a large canvas sheet she had found on the back of one of the forklift trucks. She bowed her head in respect for a moment then walked away and never looked back.

The cafeteria was of no use to them. It was destroyed beyond repair and all the furniture and utensils were too badly damaged from the heat and smoke. Rather than sift through the charred ashes of the canteen, both Tina and Christopher unanimously agreed that they would settle for sealing the room off completely. They closed the door and used the strongest adhesive they could find to seal it shut. The place was a tomb and neither of them had any desire to open it up again.

With all the various entrances around the building checked and secured they began rummaging through the warehouse and collecting anything they could use. It had been a storage depot for a big supermarket chain, supplying all the outlets in the region with stock. To that end, they were able to find virtually everything they needed. Food, water, clothing, it was all there in abundance.

There was also an entire section dedicated to tools and gardening supplies. It was there that Tina swapped her crowbar for an extremely attractive hatchet. She fell in love with it the moment she picked it up. Grabbing a builder's work belt down from the rack, she made herself a crude but extremely effective harness to carry her new weaponry. She kept her crowbar as a backup, tucked into the straps of her harness. Its length was useful for keeping the infected beyond arms' reach and she had, to a degree, become sentimentally attached to it through months of reliability. The long shafted screwdriver that she had used to deal with the frozen corpses completed her arsenal.

In another aisle, they found camping equipment and wasted no time in grabbing what they needed. Each of them had a pack filled with a sleeping bag, gas stove, spare clothing, and food and water. Tina, much to her brother's annoyance, made a point of taking an inventory of what they had in their gear. She wanted to ensure that they had everything they needed should they find themselves in a situation where they had to grab their packs and run. With everything they could ask for right at their fingertips, she reasoned that it would be foolish not to make sure that they planned for all eventualities.

On the upper floor they made themselves comfortable. They stocked the place with piles of food and water. They used gas camping stoves for cooking and once they had covered the windows with thick blackout curtains taken from the homecare aisle, they were able make use of the battery powered lanterns they had snatched from the warehouse. Compared to how they had survived for the previous four months, they were now living in splendour and with a degree of safety that neither of them had experienced since before the outbreak.

"We did okay, didn't we," Christopher remarked as he scooped up another spoonful of hot spam and baked beans.

Tina nodded vigorously, unable to speak due to her bulging cheeks. She reached over, picked up the bottle of beer from beside her, and washed the food down her throat with the cool liquid. She wiped her mouth and stifled a burp.

"Yup," she replied, smacking her lips with glee and reaching for another helping of their gourmet meal. "We did pretty fucking okay, Chris."

Both of them sat in silence for a moment and savoured the luck that had befallen them. They were lying on the floor on top of their thick sleeping bags. They had tried the couches in the offices but after having to rough it for so long neither of them could get comfortable on the soft springy cushions. Instead, they both opted for a compromise and compared to what they had grown used to, their new home was akin to a five-star hotel.

"Do you think we'll be safe here?"

"I don't see why not," Tina replied thoughtfully. "As long as we're careful and don't attract any attention to ourselves, we should be fine."

She paused for a moment and let out a sigh that made Christopher believe that there was something else on her mind.

"What is it?" He asked with concern.

"The boredom," she replied simply.

"What boredom?"

"The boredom that will eventually set in once we've been here a while. Think about it. What will we do with ourselves, Chris? Just sit here and eat, and slowly grow old? That's not for me I'm afraid. Within a week I'll be climbing the walls in here."

He huffed and shook his head in dismay. Her point of view was completely alien to him. They did not want for anything or need to go anywhere. They had it all there and he could not understand how she could ever want to step out into the open air again. Staying safe and away from the infected from then until the end of time would be easy for him.

"Don't be daft, sis. Why would we get bored? We can just sit here and wait it out. This thing can't last forever."

Tina leaned back. Having had her fill, she now wanted to stretch out and allow the sugars and carbohydrates to carry her away on a lazily flowing river of bliss as her body transferred much of her energy into digestion. She was craving for a cigarette. She always did after a meal, but before the world had ended, she had given them up and saw no reason to reverse her decision and begin smoking again.

"You know this how, Chris?" She asked as she stared up at the ceiling. "How do you know it won't last forever?"

He shrugged as he continued to eat.

"It just can't, can it? I mean, those things out there will eventually die, won't they? They can't just keep walking about for all eternity."

"I don't know. Maybe they'll never die? Maybe they will continue walking about forever and keep searching for the living? I haven't a clue. No one has ever seen or dreamed of anything like this before. The scientists couldn't work it out so I'm fucked if I can."

"But you've got a degree, haven't you?"

She looked over at him and then turned away with a slight shake of her head. She wanted to laugh but it would upset him and she did not want to hear his bleating at that particular moment. Especially while she was attempting to digest a large meal.

"Yes, in Business Management, not virology or any of the sciences. Having a degree in one thing doesn't make you an expert in another, Chris."

"Oh, right," he murmured with embarrassment. He looked back up at her with a puzzled expression. "So why did you join the army? You could've made lots of money working in an office somewhere and telling everyone what to do."

"I didn't join for the money. No one joins the army for the shitty money they pay. I did the degree and when I hit twenty I realised that I was fooling no one, especially myself. I'm not cut out to be in an office. There are other careers I could've chosen I suppose but I really wanted to see what life in the army was like."

"What was it like then?"

He had always been curious about the life of a soldier and on many occasions, he had fantasized about one day having the ability and drive to become one. He read the books, watched the movies, and played the games, but he had never taken the step towards changing his life for the better.

"It was great," she nodded as she stared into thin air and seemed to focus on something from her past. "Nine years of travelling the world, going on operations, and doing things that the average person could only dream about. I had money in my pocket, a roof over my head, and needed to worry about nothing. I was fit, healthy, and had everything I needed. Then there was the social life. Jesus, we had some great times. I had the best bunch of friends on the planet, Chris. A tight-knit group of lunatics that wanted nothing more than to enjoy themselves and live life to the full." She paused for a moment then smiled mischievously. "Plus, I had as much cock as I could handle."

After her last statement, she looked across at him with a glint in her eye. His face was glowing red with embarrassment and she was sure that she could see the steam rising from his flushed skin. She burst into laughter.

"Seriously though, I loved it. I never regretted my decision to join up."

Christopher felt extremely awkward. He had no idea on how to continue the conversation. After the announcement his sister had made with regards to her *other* activities, he instantly got a vision of her having sex. The thought revolted him and made him squirm internally. He wanted to shake it from his mind but it stubbornly and vividly clung to the forefront of his imagination and refused to be dislodged.

"Did you ever kill anyone?" He blurted finally.

She rolled her eyes. That same question was the one that all soldiers dreaded from naïve and tactless civilians.

"Not all soldiers end up killing people, Chris. In fact, ninety percent of them never fire their weapons in anger. The infantry do all that stuff. I would've loved to have been in an infantry regiment but the army don't allow chicks to serve in frontline units. I was Royal Logistics, so to answer your question, no; I never got to kill anyone."

She fell silent for a moment.

"Not until all this shit started that is," she said with a heavy tone of sorrow.

Christopher made to ask another question but she quickly cut in and changed the subject before he could probe into her secrets.

"Anyway, you should finish eating then try to get some sleep because you have a busy day tomorrow."

He looked up with surprise and intrigue.

"Really? Busy doing what?"

She let out a laugh and rolled over to face him.

"You really didn't think we were just going to sit here and get fat, did you?" She paused and watched his reaction. The expression on his face was quickly turning from confusion to dread. "As of tomorrow, we start your training."

"What training?"

"Your end of the world training," she smiled. "For months I have been saving your arse and pulling you from one disaster to the next but from now on, you're going to learn how to look after yourself, *and* me if you have to. There's two of us in this mess and we'll begin by pounding you into some kind of shape that resembles a twenty-seven year old man instead of a useless blob. No matter how long it takes, Chris, you *will* learn to survive in this world. I can't keep wiping your arse for you."

"You really do make me feel like shit at times, Tina," he said quietly as he stared down into his lap.

Her eyes narrowed as she watched him in the glow of the lamp. She could see that he was about to tumble into the same deep, self-defeating hole that he was so fond of and always used as an excuse to do nothing with his life.

"Oh really? Has all this come as a shock to you? When you look in the mirror, who do you see? Gerard-fucking-Butler dressed as a Spartan?" She huffed as she turned on to her back again and folded her hands across her chest. "You seriously need to grow up. You're fat, unfit, and incapable of holding your own in a fight against anything living *or* dead. That's the truth of it, Christopher, and you'd better face up to it. I'm not going to mince my words and smear it in honey for you to avoid stepping on your sensitivities. You've been wrapped up in cotton-wool your whole life and it's time for that to change."

She adjusted her position on the floor and closed her eyes for a moment. Growing up, she had never been the sort to hold off on speaking her mind but as she matured and joined the professional world where anything she said could have consequences, she had learned to control her tongue to a degree. Now was not the time for her to tiptoe with her words and her brother needed the truth spelling out for him.

"As of tomorrow, we begin rectifying all that. You're on a diet from now on and we'll be doing plenty of physical training, brother. You'll be sick of the sight of those stairs once you've been up and down them a few thousand times."

Christopher remained silent and staring down at his feet. He snorted back the tears and mucus that was threatening to flow from his eyes and nose.

"Go to sleep, Chris. It's late."

He stood up and walked across to the far side of the office and towards the bathroom. He paused at the door and looked back at the red and blue mound of his sister who was now wrapped up within her sleeping bag.

Why is she so cruel to me? He wondered as his vision blurred with tears. *I can't help being fat. She knows it's not my fault. It's a disease.*

Christopher seated himself down on top of the toilet inside the branch manager's personal bathroom. It was a spacious room with a shower cubicle fitted into the far wall and a large sink facing the lavatory. The floor and walls were made from marble, or a material that was made to resemble marble, and the fittings and fixtures looked grand enough to have been taken from an expensive hotel room.

However, none of its grandeur was of any use to either of them. Water no longer flowed from the taps or the showerhead and the toilet could not be flushed. The light inside the room was provided by one of the camping lamps they had looted from the warehouse and the shower cubicle now had a portable shower-bag hanging from the ceiling. Water was not to be wasted but Tina had insisted that they do their best to keep a good level of hygiene whenever possible. She had lectured him on how important it was to keep clean in the field.

'*A debilitating infection, caused through lack of personal administration, is a self-inflicted wound,*' was how she had described it to him.

In place of a functioning toilet, they had installed a large bucket with a seat attached to the top of it. It was half filled with sand and a dozen bottles of bleach sat beside it for disinfecting after use. Christopher stared at the makeshift latrine for a moment and then looked up at the wall above it. Tina had written the house rules in big black letters over the tiles. They included things such as the washing of hands, the use of the bleach, and the consideration of others. The final commandment was double the thickness and size of the other letters and below it, connected to a self-adhesive hook, dangled a small plastic spade like the sort used by children at the beach.

'*YOU POOP, YOU SCOOP!*'

All the rules and regulations that his sister was piling upon him were beginning to wear him down. She decided when they would eat, when they would sleep, and how they went to the bathroom. She had even gone to the length of checking him over to make sure he had been washing himself. He wondered how much longer it would be before she began stripping him down and scrubbing him herself.

Now she was telling him that he could not eat what he wanted anymore. That really affected him because it had been, and still was, his only real joy in life. Computer games and movies had been a welcome distraction from reality but he had always had to drag himself away from them at some point. Food, however, was his only true friend. It had comforted him throughout his twenty-seven years and it was always there for him. Now, his sister was trying to snatch it away from him.

He began to weep. He was miserable and wanted the world to leave him alone. He missed his mother and he missed his bedroom at her house. There he was treated well and he wanted for nothing. He was allowed to sit playing his games all day and into the early hours of the morning. He never needed to worry about anything because his mother did it all for him. She washed his clothes for him and brought him his food. She was a great cook and she even prompted him when she thought he needed a shower. He did not have to think for himself or deal with the day-to-day hardships that the rest of the human race had to contend with.

Rivers were now pouring down his cheeks and cascading from his voluminous jowls. Even his t-shirt was beginning to become soaked through. His shoulders shook with each quivering sob as he fought hard to remain quiet so that Tina did not hear him and launch a fresh assault on his already delicate mind.

I hate her.

Deep down, he always had. When they were young, he had felt inferior and threatened by his sister. By the time he was eight years old he was grossly overweight and incapable of being anywhere near as active as she was. From his bedroom window, he used to watch her playing football with the boys from the estate or racing up and down the street on skateboards and bikes. She was accepted as one of them whereas he had been shunned. They had called him names and chased him into his house when he had tried to befriend them, but they had readily welcomed his sister into their ranks.

She was pretty but never bothered with the things that most girls were in to. She was not interested in dolls and make-up, and always preferred jeans filled with holes and stains as averse to frilly dresses and pretty shoes.

She was popular with everyone that she met. She was witty and outspoken and regardless of what she said or did, Tina always seemed to come out on top of things and could do no wrong in the eyes of the people around her.

While he sat in his room, lonely and rejected, she would disappear for hours on end climbing trees, building camps, and generally being one of the boys. It was always made worse with the fact that their father clearly favoured her more than him. She was a 'chip off the old block' as far as their father had been concerned. Tina was an adventurer like him and they did a lot together when she was growing up.

Christopher had barely notice when their father died. He was only thirteen at the time and felt nothing of the kind of grief that befell his sister when he passed. While Tina struggled to come to terms with the loss, Christopher was smothered all the more by his mother and that suited him just fine as he revelled in her loving warmth.

Growing up, he had never had a girlfriend either. He was shy and had no idea how to talk to them. There were many that he had fancied in school and such, but he had never plucked up the courage to approach them. The fact that he was always being told that he smelled bad by the girls as they looked at him with expressions of revulsion never helped his confidence or self-esteem. He slowly withdrew into his room and became a recluse. He found contentment in food, movies, and computer games. However, he had an abundance of virtual friends all over the world who he communicated with via the internet gaming forums and settled for that as his lot in life.

All that suddenly changed though when the dead began to walk. His mother contracted the flue and died a few days after the first government announcements about the spread of the plague. After seeing the effects of the virus on the news and the World Wide Web, he locked her in her room, unable to do the terrible thing that the world beyond his front door advised him to do and ensure that she did not come back.

Tina had arrived a few days later, her clothes tattered and soaked with blood. It was *she* who killed their mother. It was *she* who dragged him out from the safety of their home and into the dangerous world. It was *she* who forced him to scrounge for food and shelter, and it was *she* who forced him to run everywhere.

Now she was telling him that he had to train every day, even though they were safe and did not need to worry about what was happening outside. He hated running. He hated any kind of physical exercise and she was going to force him to endure pain and suffering while she shouted at him to keep going and treated him like a diseased dog. She was going to make him starve and suffer from the pains of hunger.

Fucking bitch.

He wiped away the tears that had ceased to flow as his anger grew and his bitterness swelled within him. In their place came a rage he had never felt before. His temper flared and his skin became hot to the touch as he thought about how much he loathed his sister. His teeth began to grind as he simmered with anger.

"I'll show you," he whispered as he reached behind him and pulled the pistol from the back of his jeans. "Yeah, I'll show you who's tough, *sis*."

He looked down at the dull black metal of the weapon as he held it in his hand. He stroked it lovingly with an affection that most people would reserve for a pet. It was a Glock-19. He had seen them in movies and had read about them on Wikipedia when researching the net for the weapons he was using during his online gaming. Out of the fifteen rounds that the magazine was capable of holding, he had six left. The pistol did not have a safety-catch so he had decided against keeping a round in the chamber for fear of it going off while tucked into the waistband of his trousers.

He hefted it in his palm as he admired its sleek shape and cold steel black finish. Standing up from the toilet, he stared back at his reflection in the mirror above the sink. For a fleeting moment, he saw *Gerard-fucking-Butler* and he smiled broadly, as he raised the pistol into the aim.

"You think you're better than me, don't you, Tina?" He huffed. "You think I can't look after myself, don't you? Well, I'll show you. You'll regret the things you said and I will show you how wrong you are about me, Tina."

Holding the gun in one hand, then with two, he tried out a number of different stances and pulled various faces as he fantasised about being the strong tough man he had always wanted to be. Next, his eyes glazed slightly and with a half-cocked smile, he adopted the stance of an extremely casual and nonchalant character from a movie he had once seen as the hero coolly took on a band of bad guys that vastly outnumbered him. With assured death hanging over him, he lazily raised the Glock in his hand with a less than steady aim and pointed it towards the sink.

"You talking to me?" He asked as he began a conversation with the man staring back at him in the mirror.

"Well who the hell else are you talking to?"

He raised his free hand and pointed to his own chest.

"You talking to me?"

He paused for a moment and shook his head with a menacing glint in his eyes, the half-smile still creasing his lips.

"Well, I'm the only one here. So who the fuck do you think *you're* talking to?"

Christopher turned himself side on to the mirror and folded his hands across his chest with a cocky and dismissive shake of the head.

"Oh yeah? Yeah, okay," he said as a final statement before pulling his pistol out from beneath the rolls of fat that encased his upper arms and pointing it at his reflection. The movement was clumsy and slow and resembled nothing of the speed that the hero of the movie had been able to manipulate the weapon with.

"Yeah, fuck you, Tina," he snarled and made a noise similar to that which a child would make when trying to imitate the sound of a gunshot.

He rubbed his sweaty palms over his face and then grinned at himself in the mirror as he tucked the pistol back into his jeans and headed for the door.

"You're wrong about me, Tina," he whispered before opening the door. "I'll show you that you're wrong."

8

The sound of the alarms blasted out over the entire island. Shattering the morning air, their rising and falling wails sent panic coursing along the nerves and through the minds of everyone who heard their mechanical and endless shrieks.

Stan and his men gathered on the crest of the hill close to their home and looked down into the valley below. They were armed and ready to face whatever threat came their way. A habit grown from years of soldiering, their weapons and ammunition were never more than an arm's reach away from them. They travelled with them, sat with them, and they even ate and slept with their rifles close by.

Although they were at a distance of nearly three kilometres, they could clearly hear the terrified screams of men, women, and children as they tore through the dense clusters of tents and makeshift corrugated iron shelters within the fenced areas of the refugee camp. They ran in all directions in fear and confusion as the outbreak spread like wild fire and up on the high ground, it was impossible to identify the healthy from the infected. It was complete chaos. Soon, the sounds of gunfire drowned out the horrified cries of the refugees and the blasts from the sirens. While the shots echoed out across the landscape, the team watched on as dozens of civilians died.

"Take William inside," Stan ordered to Taff without taking his attention away from the scene in the low ground. "Get the place locked down and secure until we're sure that none of them have broken out beyond the barricades."

"Will do, Stan," Taff replied gruffly. He turned to the young boy and began leading him back towards the barn. "Come on, Billy, let's get you and your mum safe. You don't need to be seeing this sort of thing."

"What do we do?" Marty asked as he scanned the length of the camp with the scope attached to the top of his M-4 rifle.

"Nothing," Stan replied indifferently. "It's up to the camp guards to sort out. We'll just stay put and keep an eye on our own perimeter."

When they first arrived on the island and selected the barn as their base, their first action had been to make the area secure. While Stan, Bobby, and Taff lay recovering in the field hospital the others had set about building defensive positions that utilised the lay of the land. Obstacles and barbed wire entanglements were placed in key locations, denying access from the various routes in and channelling anyone who approached the house into a killing zone. It was virtually impossible for a person to sneak up on the position without someone having them in their sights. Any blind spots or dead ground was laced with trip-wires attached to a rudimentary early warning system of cans and bottles that would clash together and alert the team to someone approaching. It was simple but extremely effective.

Danny and Bobby remained on the hilltop observing the outbreak and guarding the area around their home. For a long while they did not speak. They just looked on in silence as the anarchy spread amongst the refugees.

"You see much?" Bobby asked as he reached across to Danny and took his turn with the binoculars.

"Not really, no," Danny replied quietly and still watching the sprawling refugee camp. "I can see the militia at the fence line and in the towers, but not much else. Everyone seems to have disappeared over to the other side."

Bobby scanned along the length of mesh fencing and barbed wire. At first, there was nothing of note, then something caught his eye. To the left he saw what he took to be a gaggle of infected but he soon realised that they were in fact living people who were running from the outbreak. After a moment of scrutiny, he guessed them to be a family group, trapped and attempting to find a way through the fence. He watched as they managed to make a hole big enough to squeeze themselves through but they were soon struggling to fight their way out from the multiple rolls of razor wire that encircled the entire compound. They became ensnared within the steel coils and the more they thrashed and struggled, the more entwined they became. Their fear was evident in their desperate actions and it was easy to make out the people shouting to one another for help as they wriggled and squirmed and all the while became more enmeshed by the sharp barbs of the wire.

Bobby presumed them to be a mother and father with a teenage boy and girl, along with another child who could not have been older than five or six. As the gunfire continued to reverberate up to them on the hilltop, he saw a vehicle approaching along the fence line from the north and come to a halt in front of the area where the family were trapped. He tightened his grip on the binoculars and adjusted the focus.

The truck, a large civilian flatbed, blocked his view of what was happening but he could clearly identify the small band of militia guards as they climbed down from the cabin. They disappeared from sight around the far side of the vehicle and a few moments later, they emerged again and climbed back inside the truck before driving away. Once that the flatbed was gone, Bobby could see the limp and bloodied family lying in the mud beneath the heavy coils of wire. None of them were moving. The guards could have helped the defenceless people but instead they had executed all of them with single shots to their heads to ensure they did not return. He felt his blood run cold and his anger rise within him.

"Bastards," he snarled.

He panned the binoculars to the right and watched as the militia vehicle headed further along the fence to join up with the rest of their group and continue the battle to regain control of the outbreak. They jumped down from their truck and moved towards the fence where they began firing indiscriminately into the camp and at anything they saw moving within the enclosure. Their rounds boomed across the open ground and with each report, Bobby blinked involuntarily.

Danny glanced at him nervously and then back towards the city of tents that continued to echo with the sound of gunfire and screams.

"Some of those civilian militia are worse than concentration camp guards," he murmured after having witnessed the events for himself and seeing the disgusted and rage fuelled expression on

Bobby's face. "You never know though, those people may have been bitten and infected."

"Fucking bastards," Bobby repeated, shaking his head and flexing the muscles in his jaw as he ground his teeth.

He knew in his bones that the family had not been infected and were just trying to escape from the virus. He looked back at the flatbed and watched it as it began to move again and finally came to a stop outside a small brick building that was used as their main guardroom. He counted the men and eyed the approaches along the track on the outer perimeter of the fence line. He grunted and nodded to himself as he made his mental notes. There were four of them stationed in that particular building. There may have been one more, possibly a regular professional soldier to act as their commander, but Bobby could not be one-hundred percent sure from that range.

When the 'all clear' was given and the clearance teams had confirmed that none of the infected had escaped from the camp, life returned to normal on the Isle of Wight. The doctors and soldiers moved into the refugee enclosure and cleared the dead for collection and incineration details. They checked on any wounds sustained during the battle and although it was never openly acknowledged, everyone knew what happened to the people who were taken away for 'treatment' of suspected bites. They were never seen again.

Bobby wondered how many men, women, and children had been dealt with in this way through wrongful diagnosis. The doctors and soldiers took no chances and to a degree, he could not blame them, but there was always the time and facilities available to afford a more thorough examination. Death and reanimation from a bite was never instantaneous.

Bobby's mind drifted back to Danny's statement about the militia being no different from the guards of a concentration camp. They rounded the civilians up like cattle and arbitrarily set aside anyone they did not like the look of.

"Bastards," he snorted again.

"It's done now, Bobby. There's nothing we can do and besides, it's none of our business what goes on down there. We have our own shit to worry about."

Bobby said nothing but continued to watch the militia guards through his binoculars for a considerable length of time. He memorised every detail of them that he was able to see from that distance and watched how they contentedly returned to their posts in the guardroom once the emergency was declared as being over. He grunted and nodded to himself.

"You okay, Bobby?"

"Fine and fucking dandy, mate," he replied with a nod and a grimace that conveyed his disgust.

That afternoon the six remaining members of the team were called into headquarters to be given a set of preliminary orders on what their upcoming tasks would be during the counter offensive and from there, the team would build their own execution and concept of operations on the way they would conduct their mission. They all knew full well that in one way or another they would be leading the spearhead for the entire campaign but their exact role could only be speculated.

"You know we'll be in the thick of the shit when it kicks off," Taff grunted sourly as he sat down beside Stan and began sipping at his coffee.

Stan blew out a long sigh in agreement. They were *always* in the thick of it so Taff's predictions were not exactly enlightening to him.

"You hoping for a cushy number, Taff?"

Before the Welshman could answer, the door opened and a long lean figure sauntered into the room. They recognised the man instantly even though his face was cast in shadow beyond the area that was illuminated by the bright spotlights set into the ceiling.

"Good afternoon, gentlemen," General Thompson greeted them in his deep gruff voice as he strode across the briefing room.

His long legs covered the distance in a fraction of the number of steps that it would have taken a man of average height. He looked up at Stan and along the line of his men seated in a row and waiting for the briefing to begin.

"Are you and your boys up to this, Stan?" The General asked with a wry smile. "I know we managed to break a few of you recently."

There was nothing malicious in his words and he had already expressed his deepest and sincerest sympathies for the losses the team had sustained. He knew each of them personally and had the utmost respect for each and every one of them. It was a friendly taunt that Stan was not going to allow himself to be sucked into. General Thompson was a tough man but he was well aware that the team were tougher still and there was very little that could pose a serious obstacle to them.

"Just a few cuts and bruises, sir," Stan replied flatly. "Far from broken."

Thompson placed his hands on his hips and nodded to the men with approval. He was proud of the team and relied heavily on their skill and capabilities.

"Good to hear it. I'm well aware of the hardships you have faced and the losses you incurred, but I wouldn't send you back out there if I didn't *need* to, Stan."

Thompson nodded to a figure standing close to the door and the lights were dimmed. On the wall behind him, a large map of the United Kingdom was illuminated and a number of symbols of various shapes and colours, denoting troops and assets, were overlaid onto it from a projector stationed above their heads. For the next two hours, they were informed of the general plan to reclaim the United Kingdom.

London was the main objective for Group-South, which included the forces stationed on the Isle of Wight, Guernsey, and Jersey. Liverpool was to be taken by Group-West operating from the Isle of Man and Glasgow was to be cleared and secured by Group-North who were occupying the islands off the west coast of Scotland, namely Jura and Islay. Both cities in the north had deep-water ports and could be used as jumping off points for further operations once they were cleared and secured.

There were other units already on the mainland within the numerous fortresses' that had been built at the beginning of the outbreak. These strongholds would act as Forward Operating Bases for support, intelligence gathering, and further offensives once the primary objectives had been secured. Although many of the hastily erected outposts had been overwhelmed during the rapid spread of the plague, there were still enough of them dotted around the country to allow the creation of a network of safe enclaves to facilitate forward command and control, as well as resupply and reinforcement.

Stan and his men watched with interest as the 'Prince of Darkness' pointed to the various cities and then the supporting FOBs. In theory, the operation was pretty straightforward. Although there were multiple objectives and large numbers of troops to support, the primary goals were feasible.

The General then moved onto the next heading in the orders' process and began describing the situation of enemy and friendly forces.

There was very little to tell in the way of the enemy. The cities were swarming with the dead and in London alone, their numbers were estimated to be upwards of three-million. Biologically nothing had changed in the make-up of the infected or the virus itself. They were still easily despatched in small groups but it was their numbers and instinctive inability to retreat that posed the biggest threat to the offensive. The scale of the opposing forces caused a few members of the team to raise an eyebrow or two.

"We mustn't allow their numbers to be a deciding factor in this operation. Their size counts for nothing. They're dumb and very predictable. We need to take advantage of their weaknesses and utilise bottle-necks and choke-points when selecting our battle ground," Thompson stated before moving onto the next heading.

The situation with friendly forces was a different matter. Since the military were ordered to withdraw from Korea and the Middle East, very few of them had made it back to home waters. They had arrived in small groups or as stragglers, bloodied and battered after suffering heavy casualties in the counter attacks that had been launched against them by Iranian and North Korean forces during their extraction. It was estimated that less than a fifth of the British military had survived.

Three aircraft carriers and all of the nuclear submarines had been destroyed. The Royal Air Force, having lost huge numbers while supporting the retreat, were down to a glimmer of their former glory and spread very thinly on the ground, and many of the ground forces had either been killed in battle or consumed by the dead before making it to the extraction points from their respective operational theatres.

Rumours were rife that the Russians had been involved in the sinking of a number of Royal Navy ships and troop transports during their journey home, but these suspicions were never confirmed. Large numbers of aircraft that were carrying much needed men and material had strangely disappeared from the radar screens, never to be seen again. Threats had been swapped between the eastern and western governments over the suspected attacks but they were soon forgotten as the catastrophe grew in scale. Soon they had a much larger threat on their hands and what mattered was that every soldier, sailor, and airman was needed for the coming fight and every serviceable piece of equipment, vehicle, and craft was thrown against the enemy.

The military was short on manpower and resources. As a result, a number of high ranking officers and politicians were leading the charge on recommending the use of nuclear weapons. Colonel Gibson, the commander of Group-North, had been voicing this opinion from very early on in the planning stage of the campaign. Slowly but surely, he had rallied support from other commanders and a degree of infighting had erupted within MJOC, Mainland Joint Operations Command, controlling the various elements of the army, navy, and air force.

At that moment, the control of Britain's nuclear arsenal still rested in the hands of the government and commanders stationed on the Isle of Wight. A limited amount of tactical missiles were in the possession of Group-North but these were smaller weapons that were dropped from aircraft and Gibson did not have the quantities needed to have any real impact on enemy numbers. It was the heavy yield missiles, still sitting in their silos on the mainland, which Gibson was wanting to launch but luckily, he did not have the access codes or knowledge of their locations.

Opinion was split and the new Prime Minister, with the backing of his senior military advisors, recommended that the offensive begin at the soonest opportunity once the preparations were completed. It was widely believed that any further delay to the invasion would cause the delicate cooperation of the disagreeing factions to fragment and the operation to fail.

To add to the deteriorating political situation there was also the humanitarian factor. Thousands were dying within the refugee camps. Disease, hunger, and the outbreaks of the plague were taking their toll on the civilian population. Already on minimal rations that were barely enough to sustain them, the refugees were once again being told that their food supply would be cut by a further fifty percent in order to provide for the large numbers of troops being used in the coming battle. Riots were common and murder had become a regular part of day to day life within the camps.

"The sooner we can get the civilians back into the towns and the cities, the better," General Thompson declared. "That is our main objective here. Taking back the capital will be symbolic to the refugees and will prove to them that we are not beaten. Our population is dying a slow and inhumane death on these islands while the infected own the mainland. If we delay any longer then there won't be anyone left to resettle."

Everyone was in agreement. Only that morning Bobby and Danny had witnessed first-hand how desperate the situation was within the camps.

After Thompson had finished briefing them on the strategic goals, the team were left to begin their own tactical planning. The General had informed them that they would be inserted into the city of London and that their job was to mark targets of densely packed infected for the bombing runs being conducted by the RAF. The air-strikes were intended to decimate the enemy numbers and ease the pressure on the ground troops as they began sweeping through and securing the urban areas.

"You won't be alone on this one, Stan," Thompson informed them. "We have some of the boys from Hereford who will be inserting into other parts of the city along with the Pathfinder Platoon from Sixteen Air Assault Brigade."

"How do we get large numbers of the infected into the same place?" Stan asked, hoping that the general was not expecting the team to use themselves as bait.

"Gerry will give you a heads up on that one, Stan. He'll go through the Concept of Operations and the Service and Support elements," Thompson replied and nodded towards the Operations

Officer who was standing to one side. "Good luck gentlemen and if there's anything you need, just let us know."

General Thompson left the room and handed over to Gerry. There was someone else with him and as they stepped forward from the shadows, Stan recognised the man, even without the grime covering his face or the terror in his eyes.

"I believe you have already met," Gerry said to the team as he gestured towards Dr. Joseph Warren.

The doctor nodded to the men and smiled briefly.

"I never got the chance to properly thank you all," Doctor Warren said with a hint of shame and regret in his voice. "I'm afraid that for the moment you will just have to content yourselves with my humble words until this is all over and I can find a more fitting way to convey my appreciation to you. I truly am grateful for all that you did for me in Africa and I am sorry for the loss of your friend. I have been told that Nick was a great man and I regret that I will never be able to express my gratitude for the sacrifice he made."

The team said nothing but nodded their acceptance and appreciation of the doctor's words. Nick's loss was still felt amongst the men, as was Brian's, but they did not dwell on their deaths. They could not afford to.

Doctor Warren stepped back and allowed Gerry to continue until he was needed again. Later in the briefing he would be called forward to answer questions but for now, he would remain in the shadows.

Before Group-South could begin their assault on London, the Portsmouth Ferry Terminal needed to be cleared and secured in order to bring in troops, equipment, and vehicles. This would open up a line of resupply between the Isle of Wight and the mainland. Eventually, the civilians would travel along this protected corridor when they began the reoccupation of the land in the south.

While the beachhead was being created, the few remaining transport helicopters that the military had left would be sent in to drop troops into the airfield at Farnborough. Their job was to secure the area and hold it while the ground forces pushed up from the harbour in the south. With the airfield in friendly hands, the helicopters would then be able to refuel and provide support for the men on the ground.

Ammunition stocks were not an issue but aviation fuel was. Ferrying troops into London all the way from the island, one load at a time, would not be viable and the advance would quickly lose its momentum as the helicopters' tanks ran dry. So it was imperative that the airfield was taken and secured.

Instead of a single direct overhead assault on the capital, the bulk of the ground forces would be going in by vehicle via the harbour at Portsmouth initially and then thrusting northwards from the coast with the air force giving limited close air support in the form of bombing and strafing missions.

At the same time, once the assets and troops at the airfield were consolidated and strong enough in numbers they would begin the advance on London. With the Chinooks refuelled, the forward elements would be flown in to make the initial break-in while the remainder followed on in vehicles. Making their break-in from the outskirts in the south-west of the city, the ground forces would push forward, block by block, until the southern side of the River Thames was secured. All the while, the Royal Air Force would be overhead and clearing their path.

The CH-47s would run resupply and reinforcement missions into the parts of the front that were struggling to force their way through or looked as though they would be overwhelmed and forced to retreat. The plan was not dissimilar to conventional operations from the past. The principles were still very much based along the lines of the 'assault, supress, reserve' doctrine, using assets from land, sea and air.

"So what you're saying is, that we're re-enacting 'A Bridge Too Far' but the Germans have been replaced with dead people?" Bull asked.

"The concept is not dissimilar," Gerry replied with reflection.

Stan leaned back and shook his head.

"Seems like a lot to do with just twenty-thousand troops, Gerry. Holding the harbour and airfield, and keeping the supply corridor open is going to take up most of our manpower. Then there's the casualties and reinforcements issue. How can you do all that with just a handful of soldiers?"

Gerry looked back at him. He had been waiting for the question but still felt uncomfortable giving the answer.

"Civilian militia," he replied. "We have around fifty-thousand of them supporting us as auxiliary troops."

Stan said nothing. He understood that every able-bodied person needed to join the fight but he did not like the idea of the success of the offensive hinging on the performance and ability of untrained refugees.

"They're quite keen, I assure you," Gerry continued, unconvincingly.

"They're quite keen?" Bull replied with sarcasm. "Oh, thank fuck for that. Now that you put it that way, Gerry, I feel loads better about the whole thing,"

"They will only be used to protect the supply lines and to plug any gaps that form at the front. We have armed them and training has been going on for quite some time now. They're not exactly elite troops but we're not up against a conventional enemy either."

With the general concept of operations covered by Gerry, Stan and his men were advised on their own task.

London would be split into 'assault lanes' and it was their job to guide in the RAF on their bombing missions along the separate corridors. Along with Stan and his men, teams from the SAS and Pathfinders would be operating in their own individual assault lanes and calling in the air assets on separate targets while giving up to date situation reports to the command element of MJOC.

Their mission was to form the infected into dense clusters and mark them with lasers for the pilots to identify. In this way, huge numbers would be dispatched with minimal ordinance and casualties. In theory, and providing that all went according to plan, the ground troops would be conducting a simple mopping-up exercise.

"You will be inserted a few days before the attack begins. That's seven days from now and should give you ample time to get things ready. Weapons, ammunition, equipment, and anything you need will be supplied as best as possible. Just let me know once you've come up with a plan and I will see to it that you get the full support of operations staff and the Quarter Master."

Stan nodded over to Taff. As the second in command of the team it was his responsibility to oversee the administration and ensure that all their equipment was up to the task.

"Knock up a list and get it over to those blanket stackers once you're happy, Taff. We have plenty of ammo but the more the merrier on this one."

"No worries. I suggest taking those S-Mines along on this one, Stan."

"Yeah," Stan replied as he remembered the cache that Marty and the others had found on the mainland. "Any doubts with them though, ditch them in the sea. I don't fancy one of us being fragged through faulty kit."

"Uh, I have a question," Bull spoke as Gerry finished rounding off their mission. "Two questions actually."

"Go on," Gerry nodded. He believed he knew full well what the questions were going to be but he could never be sure, when it came to dealing with Bull.

Bull looked around at the others to make sure that he was not jumping the gun and that his timing to ask was right. They all looked back at him expectantly. Like Gerry, they could not be sure of what was about to come from his mouth.

"How do we get there? Going on foot will take forever and if the head-shed can't spare the helicopters and fuel, what you got in mind? Secondly, as Stan has already asked, how do we get those things to form large groups?"

Gerry stepped back and nodded over his shoulder.

Doctor Warren stepped forward. He was carrying a large cylinder made of mesh steel. It did not look too dissimilar to a waste-paper basket but it was clearly more robust. Inside, it was reinforced with a cross-section of metal bars and in the centre was a silver box and what appeared to be a set of speakers attached.

"Music," the Doctor said plainly. "You plant these in the desired location then trigger them remotely from a safe distance. We know that the infected are attracted to sound so this should work quite well."

The team stared back at him for a moment and shifted their gaze to the bulky object he stood holding in his hands.

"Did all those years of learning and the PhD you have hanging from your wall help you to come up with that, Doc?" Danny asked.

"You hadn't thought of it, had you, Danny?" Bobby nodded with a smile of appreciation to the Doctor. "Simple, but effective."

"Well, while some of us are still trying to work out what is causing all this and searching for a cure, the rest of us have dedicated our time to more practical purposes. All the tests we have carried out have revealed nothing, from a scientific sense that is, about this virus and how to stop it. So understanding what makes them tick and using their disadvantages against them is our greatest weapon now, I believe."

"Okay," Bull continued, satisfied that one of his questions had been answered. "How do we get there then?"

Stan looked at Gerry and then across to Bull.

"We're getting a ride from an old friend of mine."

9

The reception area echoed with the thumps of his heavy footfalls as they pounded against the stairs. His breathing came in short strained gasps and resounded loudly inside the open space of the foyer. Each step was physical and mental agony and his pace had reduced to little more than a lumbering stagger as he slowly moved up towards her. His legs trembled uncontrollably and his body quivered as he struggled to prevent himself from vomiting, all the time forcing his tortured thighs to continue their agonising ascent. Sweat poured from him and dripped on to the floor. Pools of perspiration, drool, and snot swathed the rubber-coated steps that were set into the steel staircase. He grunted and wheezed his way upwards. His heart pounded and his lungs felt as though they were pathetically incapable of sucking in the precious oxygen that he so desperately needed. The blurred vision and his spinning head added to his misery but *she* would never let up on him until he had finished.

"That's it, Chris," she encouraged from the landing above him as she stared at the stopwatch in her hand. "Only a few more steps to go and then you can rest."

For the entire week, she had hounded him relentlessly. From the moment that the sun rose until it set on the opposite horizon, she pushed him to the point of collapse and beyond. He was exhausted and each night as Tina slept soundly he lay awake for hours, wincing with aching bones and muscles and crying quietly as he lay enveloped inside his sleeping bag. He had never experienced pain and suffering like it. At the end of each day when darkness shrouded them and he was left with his thoughts he silently wished that he would not wake up the next morning.

But as the sun made its appearance again and the night gave way to the brightness of day, she would wake him and assault him with her sadistic regime. He was suffering from severe anxiety and faced each new day with a feeling of cold dread in the pit of his stomach. Pain and exhaustion were all that was waiting for him. There was no joy, not even a simple comfort. He would suffer until the sun set and then it would begin all over again when the morning came. He had grown to hate the sounds of the morning birds. They were the harbingers of aching bones, burning muscles, and misery.

In his eyes, Tina's training programme was brutal to say the least. For breakfast, he was allowed nothing more than a few dried crackers and a tin of sardines, followed by a litre of water to wash it down. That was one of the hardest parts for him; water. She made him drink litre after litre throughout the whole day and it never failed to make him sick. He would have done anything for a Coke, even a diet one.

From there she would drag him to the warehouse and starting at the loading bay doors, force him to run from one end of the building to the next, over and over again. All the time she would be howling at him to move faster and to keep going until he was at the point where he could no longer hold on to the meagre meal he had been given and was forced to throw it up, all over the concrete floor.

He would have to keep going like that for thirty minutes at a time and without rest. Her words of encouragement did nothing for him and the fact that Tina did everything alongside her brother was of no comfort. He failed to understand that she was helping him or that the tough love she was showing him would be for his own benefit in the long run. He saw it as torture and her way of taking out her frustrations.

After recovering from his morning run, she would allow him to rest physically but the mental training continued. While he lay recovering, sweating profusely, she would begin asking him questions with hypothetical scenarios built in and he was supposed to answer with tactical thinking. She would draw diagrams and maps on a whiteboard and begin grilling him on what he would do in certain situations. In his state of physical exhaustion, he was rarely capable of forming any kind of clear thought in his clouded mind. Instead, he would just sit there staring back at her, feeling numb throughout his entire body.

After yet another miniscule lunch, she would then go on to instruct him on how to defend himself against the infected. She demonstrated how to use their weapons and how to move and take advantage of the slow and uncoordinated attacks of their enemies, even when greatly outnumbered. Again, he struggled to handle himself in any way that could be of benefit. He was almost as clumsy and uncoordinated as the corpses that lumbered about in the car park outside.

"We always keep one foot on the ground," she explained to him in the hope of making him understand the principle of mutual support. "If one of us is dealing with something, the other is watching their back. Whether we're fighting the infected or changing a light bulb, we *have* to look out for one another."

"Why would we need to change a light bulb?" He had asked in confusion.

"It was a figure of speech, Chris. The point I'm trying to make is that we don't let our guard down or become complacent. One of us is always covering the other and we stay prepared and ready to fight, or run."

He stared back at her with blank heavy eyes and a throbbing head.

Still, Tina persisted. She was determined to mould him into something of use. His cries and whimpers fell upon her unsympathetic ears and his pleadings for respite were ignored as she continued to bark orders at him.

At the top of the stairs, Tina looked down at his sweating hulk as he struggled to lift his feet up onto the final step before reaching the landing. He was bent almost double with his face pointing down towards the steps. From her vantage point, she could only see his wide trembling shoulders and well-rounded back quivering beneath the sodden blue t-shirt that clung to his huge frame. She smiled fleetingly. It was pride that swelled within her. She checked the stopwatch and stepped back as Christopher reached the landing and collapsed into a heap on the cold linoleum floor. He turned onto his back, coughing and sputtering with thick globs of frothy saliva and glistening mucus smeared across his face and down the front of his t-shirt. His skin was bright crimson and even in the semi-light of the corridor that dissected the upstairs offices, she could see the steam rising from his hot skin.

"Well done, brother," she said with respect as she bent down and patted him encouragingly on his shoulder.

She immediately regretted touching him and stood back up, wiping her sweat soaked palms on the front of her trousers.

"You did it in ten minutes and thirty-five seconds, Chris. That's twenty seconds faster than yesterday."

Christopher was incapable of responding to her words. His eyes were screwed tight and his tongue flopped from the side of his mouth like an overheated dog. He coughed and retched in reply and rolled over onto his side as he continued to gasp for breath. He cared nothing for her enthusiasm. Timings, repetitions, distances, all of it held no meaning for him and he loathed each of them just as much as the next. He was just glad that it was over and that he could rest... for now.

"Go on, Chris," Tina said softly. "Go and get yourself cleaned up. I'll crack on with my session then we can get something to eat before we do our perimeter checks."

"Why are you doing this to me?" Christopher groaned hoarsely. He was still lying on his side with his eyes shut, unable to move from the spot.

Tina had already begun to make her way down the stairs where she would then begin her own training. She had made a point from the very beginning of never asking her brother to do something that she was not willing to do herself.

"We're doing this so that we are ready to fight or run if need be," she replied with a hint of frustration. She had explained it to him repeatedly over the previous week. "You know that and one day, you'll thank me for it."

Christopher slowly peeled his pain-racked body up from the floor. He made it to the point where he was on his hands and knees and quickly realised that he would not be able to raise himself any further than that. Slowly, with shaking arms and legs that threatened to collapse from underneath him at any moment, he crawled towards the manager's office where he had every intention of crumpling back to the floor again.

"We don't need to run... or fight, you fucking cunt," he grumbled under his breath as his sister began hammering away at the thirty-five steps behind him.

He still could not understand why she would ever want to leave the building. They were safe and away from the infected.

They had everything they needed and there was no need to set foot out into the open for a long time to come.

Still puffing and panting, Christopher crawled through the door and into the plush office. The beating sounds of his sister's feet against the hard stairs faded into the distance as he dragged himself over towards his billowing soft sleeping bag that lay sprawled across the floor at the foot of the smallest leather couch. It called to him seductively, wanting to wrap him up in its comforting embrace.

He paused for a moment and looked to his left and at the door of the storeroom that was set into the wall beside the huge television screen facing the manager's desk. Just beyond the wooden barrier lay an Aladdin's cave of food and delicacies. Tina had moved it all in there at the beginning of the week, locked the door, and kept the key in her possession at all times. She had even gone to the lengths of securing the door to the warehouse so that he could not sneak in there when she was asleep and gorge himself on sugar and carbohydrates. All the vending machines within the building had been broken open and emptied of all but water. There were no safe havens for him or his eating disorder and he was so hungry that the pain in his stomach was unbearable.

He stared at the storeroom longingly, imagining the stacks of tinned food and boxes of biscuits and chocolate. It was all so near, yet so far away.

"Fucking bitch," he whimpered.

He was about to allow his aching elbows to buckle and his body to collapse but something stopped him from doing so. A noise out from beyond the huge panes of glass that overlooked the parking area grabbed his curiosity. It was the sound of struggling grunting voices. They were aggressive and savage and Christopher had no doubt in his mind that they were the voices of the living dead. His fear rose inside him and as his body crawled towards the window, sucking on the last of his energy reserves, his mind screamed at him not to look. He was still terrified at the sight of the dead, even from beyond the protection of the upper floors of the building, but now he felt compelled to see what was going on.

Maybe Tina is right? Maybe I am getting stronger… and braver? He thought and smiled proudly.

Only a week ago, he would never have dreamed of approaching the window on his own accord. It was always down to his sister to force him into facing his fears. At one time, even the sounds of a brass band playing in the car park would not have encouraged him to venture across towards the glass but here he was, brushing his trepidation to the side and forcing himself to confront the dead, albeit from the safety of the top floor of their fortress.

He pulled the thick blackout curtain to one side slightly and peered out into the bright sunlit car park. There they were. Roughly thirty of them scattered over a wide area and wandering aimlessly. They were revolting figures, all twisted and grotesque. Their flesh torn and their bodies distended with the gases of decay, they stubbornly refused to follow the laws of nature and remain dead.

Christopher shuddered as he watched their dark menacing forms drifting between the vehicles and swaying with each step. Their arms hung limply and their heads lolled from side to side with blank vacant eyes staring at the ground beneath them. Each had its own eco-system of insects swirling around them that feasted upon their rotting flesh and the grubs that squirmed beneath the surface of their putrefying tissue. Now and then, a bird would dive out of the sky and swoop in to feed on the bloated tiny creatures that buzzed around the corpses.

A sudden clatter, quickly followed by hostile snarls and groans, erupted from the right of the car park. Christopher snapped his head around and saw two of the infected tussling with one another. They clawed at one another's faces and snapped their jaws angrily, tearing chunks of flesh from each other's bones as they grappled, but neither of them paid any notice to the gaping wounds that they inflicted or received. They were fighting over something and on closer inspection Christopher saw that they were having a macabre tug-of-war over what appeared to be the remains of an animal, possibly a cat or a small dog, but he could not be sure from that distance and angle.

He looked on for a while as both corpses continued to beat at one another. Finally, the larger of the two, a creature that had once been a well-built male, was able to wrestle the remains from the grasp of its smaller opponent. Turning away to protect his meal, the dead man stuffed his face into the carcass and began chewing vigorously, smearing his pallid features with dark red blood and tufts of fur.

The smaller reanimated body continued trying to retrieve the unfortunate animal and attacked the feeding ghoul from behind. The large man twisted and turned, keeping his back to his challenger whilst continuing his feast. Finally, he had had enough of the interruptions and turned on his adversary. With a single thrust, he grabbed the other's face in his massive hand and drove it backwards towards one of the cars, all the while keeping a tight grip on the animal in his free hand. The smaller body was caught off balance, and with its attacker's hand pushed hard against its face, it flew backwards and slammed into the doorframe of the parked saloon. Its head snapped backwards and thumped hard into the roof of the vehicle with an echoing hollow clang, but the big corpse did not leave it there. To ensure himself of no further disturbances while he ate, he continued to pound the smaller creature's head against the steel frame of the door. Eventually the body became limp and slid to the floor with a large opening in its skull. Its fetid brains oozed out from the cracked bone and ran down over the corpse's face and dead staring eyes.

Satisfied, the dead man turned and stumbled away to a secluded area at the side of the car park where he could finish his feast in peace.

Christopher, far from scared, had watched them with fascination as they fought over the remnants of the poor animal. He stood witness to their unflinching savagery and ravenous hunger as they battled for the scraps of meat. He eyed the other infected bodies that continued to stumble about, unaware of him watching them from the safety of his hideout. They were slow and benign, completely unthreatening in their movements, but fearsome in their appearance. It would not take much to rile them up though. He would not even have to step outside to gain their attention and work them into a frenzy. Just his appearance at the window would be enough to turn them from shambling husks to tearing and snapping monsters.

He turned his head to the left and attempted to see along the front of the building and towards the gate that led into the loading area and staff car park. From that angle, it was impossible to see the entrance but he knew that it was there at the end of the fence and that it was still wide open. A thought flitted into his mind and immediately, he shook his head forcefully and shivered.

Tina was working hard on the stairs. Her stopwatch indicated that she too was about to shave off a number of seconds from her training session of the previous day. She had just two more repetitions to go. Breathing hard and soaked in sweat, she was feeling good. She smiled at the thought of how she had grown to love, even crave, the pain of hard exercise. She relished the dull ache in her thighs as they were flooded with lactic acid and she had become accustomed to the feeling of her chest tightening as her lungs battled to take in oxygen. So many times, she had tried to convey this to her brother; that he would one day grow to yearn for the discomfort. That it would make him feel alive and filled with euphoria, but he could never seem to accept or understand.

She reached the bottom step and turned to begin her last ascent. As she placed her foot on the first rung, a large shadow drifted over the stairwell. She looked up to see Christopher standing at the top and staring down at her.

"Hey," she began, "you're recovering faster already. You would still be breathing through your arse at this point last week. See, I told you."

Christopher said nothing but continued to watch her as she sprinted up the final flight and came to a panting stop in front of him. She clicked the stopwatch and checked the time.

"Thirty-five fucking seconds faster," she whooped with a wide grin.

He nodded and looked down at the timer in her hands and smiled fleetingly at her. He was still sweating and beads of moisture continued to drip from his hairline and over his flushed face but she was right, he was recovering much quicker now. Apart from his legs that were still shaking slightly and the slowly receding burn in his chest, he felt fine.

She stood with her hands on her hips and breathing deeply in an effort to slow her heart rate and speed up her recovery. Shifting her weight from one leg to the other, Tina shook her feet alternately in order to keep the blood flowing and preventing her limbs from cramping up.

"So," she blew out a long breath, "that's us done for the day, Chris. Good effort and tomorrow we will do some…"

"I think we should close the gate," he cut in flatly.

Tina hesitated, unsure of what he meant but then realised that he was referring to the side gate leading into the loading bay from the main parking area in front of the building. They had left it open as a possible escape route. Through the gate and along the front of the adjacent warehouses, they could make their way up to the access road leading into the industrial complex and away to safety if the situation called for it.

"Why?" She asked in confusion. It was not just the fact that Christopher believed the gate should be closed but also the cold blank expression on his face. "We don't need to. It's out of the way and it's our escape route."

She turned and headed for the offices.

"I saw some of those things over in that area, Tina," he informed her. "I think it's only a matter of time before they wander in there and if they do, we'll be trapped in here. We can't go out through the front door and the back fire escape is on a blind wall with no windows. We won't know what's out there and could walk into a hundred of them."

Tina stopped in her tracks and spun around to face him. She thought for a moment and recapped herself on what he had just told her. He had a point. Even with the gate closed they still had breathing space to consider climbing the fence as an escape. He was also right about the front and rear doors. If the side gate was left open indefinitely, there was always a chance that a horde of them could eventually stumble into the staff car park and cut them off.

Could this really be you talking? She wondered as she studied his bemused face carefully. She struggled to understand where his sudden logical and strategic thinking had come from.

"Hey, what can I say?" He beamed at her and shrugged. He could almost hear her thoughts beyond the shocked expression in her eyes. "I'm learning."

"That you are, Chris, and you're right, I think we should close the gate."

10

"What the hell is that?" Bobby gasped with his mouth hanging open.

The six of them were standing close to the massive floating dock. It had been moved into position on the south side of the island early on during the evacuation of the mainland. With The Solent, the strip of water that separated the island from the mainland, being so heavy with traffic at the outbreak, the military had built a Mulberry Harbour beneath the bluffs close to the village of Niton Undercliff to the south of Newport. The few remaining war ships of the British Navy remained in the area, protecting the Channel and out of harm's way from the south coast of England.

The dock stretched out from the beach and on to the sea for about two-hundred metres then formed into a number of manmade mini harbours over deep water. The Channel in that area was far too shallow to allow the larger ships to approach the coast and any supplies being brought ashore or loaded onto the vessels would have needed to be flown over or carried on smaller boats. With the harbour in place, the heavy ships could remain in deep water and their cargo and passengers could be transferred along the joining sections of the Mulberry Harbour stretching out from the shoreline. The design had changed very little since it was first used in 1944 during the D-Day landings in Normandy and was a testament to the engineering of the time.

The Channel was mostly empty. Far off to the east sat the aircraft carrier, HMS Illustrious, with a small number of destroyers and frigates scattered around her. The harbour itself was deserted of ships. All except for the last birth on the far right of the floating structure. Tucked up close to the dock wall sat a grey shape that was roughly eighty metres long. Compared to most navy vessels, it sat low in the water and from a distance it would have been easy for it to go unnoticed.

"It's a submarine, Bobby. What do you think it is?" Taff replied as he puffed away on his cigarette, the blustery Channel Sea air whipping the smoke away as he exhaled. "For the past week we've known we were going to be inserted by sub, so what did you expect to see, the Titanic?"

"Yeah, I was expecting to see a sub, Taff, but that doesn't look like any submarine I've ever seen."

None of them had seen a vessel like it. When they were told that they would be inserting by submarine up along the River Thames, they had all expected to see one of the big black nuclear versions with its smooth sleek hull and tall conning tower reaching high above the water. Instead, they were looking at a long grey monster that appeared like something from a history book.

"Me too," Bull nodded. "They usually look like giant black dicks."

"It's a German Type Twenty-One from World War Two," Danny said from the rear as he continued to eye the ship. "It's a U-boat."

"A U-boat?" Bull snorted. "Fuck off, Danny. I've seen that movie, 'Das Boot', and that looks nothing like a U-boat. I suppose you'll be telling us we'll be exchanging our M-4s and Minimis for muskets next?"

"Honestly, it's a U-boat. It was one of the later models, built by the Germans towards the end of the war. All the submarines of the world's navies that followed on afterwards were based on its design. It was the first true submarine. Up until that point, all its predecessors were classed as surface ships with the ability to submerge."

"Head's up, everyone," Bull announced in a raised voice and a smirk creasing the corners of his mouth. "Sounds like we have a nerd in our midst. You're not a re-enactor as well are you, Danny?"

"Danny's right," Stan said as he became bored of listening to their squabbling. "The Captain is an old friend of mine and I expect you all to watch your manners around him. He's very protective of his boat and crew, so be careful what you say."

"How did he end up driving a U-boat?" Taff asked in confusion.

"He used to be a nuclear sub commander in the late eighties but he had a falling out with his bosses that resulted in one of them losing a few teeth. Rather than kick him out of the navy, they busted him down to riding diesels and this is what they gave him."

A dark figure appeared out from the top of the conning tower. He paused for a moment when he saw the team standing at the far end of the dock then waved with long sweeping gestures. Stan raised his hand in return and the man began to climb down the ladder rungs fitted into the boat's superstructure.

"Just remember what I said," Stan reminded them as he watched the man making his way towards them. "Watch your Ps and Qs and that includes you, Bull. Otherwise, Taff won't be the only one you have to worry about putting you on your arse."

Taff grinned broadly and his shoulders juddered with a silent laugh. Bull shot him a look that instantly wiped the smile from his face.

As the boat's commander drew nearer, they were able to see him more clearly. He was tall and lean and walked with a charisma that seemed to spread out around him over a wide area. The man definitely had an aura about him. He did not strut or swagger but his gate was that of a man of extreme confidence in his own skill and abilities. He seemed to know where he was going and how to get there and already, even from a distance of fifty metres, the team could see that he was a man of presence.

He wore a dark sheepskin jacket with a white woollen collar over a pair of grey trousers, and the thumps of his heavy black boots could be heard as he pounded across the planks of the Mulberry Harbour. His footfalls made him sound twice as heavy as he looked. On top of his head, he sported the distinctive white Captain's hat. It was discoloured from years of wear and tear and crumpled down around the rim around the sides, sitting at a skewed angle to the rest of his face.

"Jesus," Bull grunted, "he even looks like he belongs on a U-boat."

Stan turned to them and nodded.

"Wait till he tells you his name then," he said.

Stan stepped forward as the Captain approached and they shook hands heartily and smacked each other on the shoulder. Stan actually managed to smile and the rest of the team wondered just how far back and how deeply their friendship reached.

"How the hell are you still alive, Stan?" The man asked with a broad grin. "I thought you would've been finished off a long time ago."

"I'm still ticking, I'm happy to say," Stan replied. "For how much longer, none of us know, but I'm here today."

"Good to hear it, old friend."

They turned and walked a couple of paces back towards Stan's men. For a short while the submarine Captain stood in silence, watching the five soldiers intently with his piercing pale grey eyes. His face was narrow and long with a nose that seemed to stretch far out from the rest of his features and the visor of his cap, giving him the appearance of an ever vigilant hawk. His cheeks and chin were covered with a thick growth of almost black hair but the grey moustache and silver streaks around the corners of his mouth contrasted greatly with the rest of his beard.

Finally, the Captain smiled. His eyes flashed with a genuine gladness to see them. His white teeth shone brightly from behind his beard and he stepped forward with his hand outstretched towards the first man in line.

"Great to meet you," he began in a gruff voice that had been created from years of cigar smoking. "I'm Captain Werner."

Bull was not sure if he was being lined up for a practical joke and as he took the man's hand in his own he looked across to Stan for confirmation that the navy officer in front of him really did have a German name. His face was etched with doubt and confusion and for a moment, he was unable to speak until he had clarification.

Stan nodded back at him.

"I'm Bull, pleased to meet you too, mate. Uh, sir, I mean, Captain."

Werner laughed and shook his head. He moved along the line and introduced himself to each of the team. When the preliminaries were out of the way he turned and raised his open palm towards his vessel.

"Well, what do you think? She's beautiful, isn't she?"

The affection he held for his submarine was unmistakable in his voice. The rest of the men could also see in his eyes how he looked on at his boat and they saw a love that could only have come from years of familiarity and dependability.

"Grab your gear and come have a look," Werner continued as he led the way along the floating dock.

The rest of the men fell into line behind him, carrying their weapons and packs over their shoulders as they headed for the submarine. Without anyone saying a word or asking for it, Captain Werner launched himself into a verbal tour and history of the boat.

"It's a Type Twenty-One Unterseeboot, built by the Germans at the Blohm and Voss dockyards in Hamburg in late nineteen-forty-four. Her original designation during the war was U-3514 and according to the official records, she was scuttled as part of Operation Deadlight in February of forty-six."

He turned and flashed the men a mischievous smile.

"But she wasn't sunk. The Royal Navy kept hold of her in secret. At first, she was used as an operational boat to help offset the ever-growing armada of submarines and surface ships that the Russians were developing during the late forties and early fifties. Eventually, as we caught up with and surpassed the technologies involved in building the Twenty-One, she pretty much became redundant but the navy held onto her as a spy-boat and eventually, she became a research vessel."

Werner stopped short of the gangplank that was resting against the hull and leading up on to the foredeck. He turned to Stan and his men, folding his arms across his chest and staring back at them with an intense expression.

"Here she is," he said in a low voice that was filled with pride.

He turned and made his way up the gangplank. As he reached the top, his footsteps rang out with a metallic resonance as averse to the dull thuds of the wooden planks on the Mulberry Harbour. He stopped by the conning tower and affectionately brushed his hand over the grey painted steel of the outer hull.

"These things could've turned the war completely on its head if they had been set loose on the Atlantic convoys," Werner said as he continued his tour into history. "They were faster submerged than they were on the surface, outpacing most of the hunters of the day. It could dive twice as deep as the other models of U-boat and had a hydraulic, automated torpedo loading system. In the earlier kind, it took ten minutes to reload just one tube. This thing could fire all her torpedoes and reload all six tubes within twelve minutes."

He paused for a moment and looked up at the conning tower. He pushed his cap back from his weather-beaten brow and stood with his hands on his hips as he gazed up towards the bridge.

"Unfortunately for the Germans, they came too late in the war and in too few numbers. Lucky for the Allies I suppose." He turned to the men assembled at the bottom of the gangway and waved them up towards him. "Come on up, I'll show you around and introduce you to my boys."

As Stan and the others began the precarious journey up the narrow walkway, Captain Werner began scaling the ladder leading up towards the bridge. He continued to talk as he made his ascent.

"You know, the MoD thought that sending me to command this boat would really piss me off, but nothing could've been further from the truth. After sailing on nuclear attack boats for all those years, commanding a diesel of this sort is a dream. There are less things to worry about and its simplicity compared to the nuclear types makes you really appreciate them all the more. I could never really get a feel for the modern ones after being with this old tub for so long."

One by one, the men began to climb down through the conning tower hatch and into the heart of the submarine. At the bottom of the ladder, they stepped onto the steel grated floor of the Control Room and found themselves in an open space roughly five metres wide by eight metres long. The room was filled with pipes, gauges, handles and levers, and a mind-spinning array of wheels and dials with workstations and machinery squeezed into every possible space. Everywhere they looked, they could see wires and cables running through conduits over the ceiling and along the walls, linking into circuit boxes and a countless number of instruments.

Although the boat looked clean and well maintained, there was a distinct smell of mould and diesel inside the cramped pressure hull and despite the ventilation, there was condensation forming on the curved ceiling above them. A faint but continuous drip could be heard echoing throughout the interior. Small patches of rust had formed around some of the hatches and seals and a number of pipes had a steady rivulet of slow trickling water leaking from them along the walls and down into the bilge below.

Werner was standing close to the periscope housing beside another man who was much shorter than he was and slightly built. The man watched them, as they stood huddled around the ladder in the cramped confines of the boat and staring about them in bewilderment.

"This is my Chief Engineer," Werner said as he placed his hand on the shoulder of the man beside him. "He's the heart and soul of the boat."

Stan and the team nodded to him and one by one, they leaned forward and shook hands as they introduced themselves. Each of them came away with a palm covered in grease and oil and they began vigorously rubbing their grime-smeared hands against their trousers and shirts. The Chief Engineer appeared as an extremely serious man and he eyed the team with suspicion. He clearly did not like having non-submariners on his boat and his body language made no attempt to disguise that fact. Eventually he shrugged with a single nod of his head as if to accept the arrangement.

"She's had a few modifications over the years," the Chief began. "New batteries and radar and such things like that but all in all, she's still the same boat we swiped from the Germans at the end of the war."

"Thank fuck for that," Bull whispered sarcastically to Marty standing beside him. *"For a moment there I was beginning to worry that we were sitting in a rusty old tube that was more than twice my age."*

"This is the Control Room," the Chief continued. "Forward, you have the Sound Room with the Captain's quarters and beyond that you have the Officers' living area. At the very front, in the bow compartment, is the Torpedo Room. Aft of the Control Room is the galley and crew quarters. Next is the Diesel compartment and beyond that is the Electric Motor Room with the Stern quarters behind that. That is where you will be spending most of your time during the voyage, gentlemen."

Compared to its wartime compliment, the boat only had a skeleton crew. Originally, the vessel would have been crammed with more than fifty men and piles of equipment and provisions to last them for over six weeks at sea, leaving virtually no room for personal items. With just a handful of men on board, they were able to live much more comfortably, compared to their predecessors.

However, all that was soon to change. Over the next three hours, as Stan and his men settled themselves into the Stern quarters and stored their weapons and equipment, other troops began to arrive and squeezed themselves into the ever-increasing cramped confines of the boat's interior. As the teams from the SAS and Pathfinder Platoon filled every available space inside, the boats atmosphere quickly began to change. Before long, it had become stiflingly hot and the air had turned stale, reeking with a mixture of diesel fuel and body odours.

"Well this is going to be a lovely trip," Bobby grunted as he nodded to a fearsome looking man with a shaved head who was trying to make himself comfortable while pressed up against the rear bulkhead.

"Living the fucking dream," the man mumbled back to him with no expression in his face. He turned away and pushed his shoulder against the pack he was leaning against then closed his eyes in an attempt to get some sleep.

Bull was busy trying to make a bed for himself. The bunks were far too small for his bulky frame and he had to settle with tucking himself into the area between the propeller shaft and a number of other pipes and ducts. He huffed and grunted as he twisted himself into a position that was something that resembled comfortable.

"Hey, what do you think of the whole murder mystery thing then?" He asked as he stretched his legs out and reached for his flask of tea.

Danny rolled over on his bunk and peered over from the book he was reading. It was impossible for him to sit up due to the tiny space between his head and the bunk above him so he settled for propping himself up in a half-lying position.

"What murder mystery thing?"

"On the island," Bull replied as he continued to carefully pour the steaming brown liquid into his cup. "Four men were murdered sometime during the last week. All shot in the head and dumped on a deserted stretch of beach."

"Nope, not heard anything about it," Danny admitted shaking his head. "Who were they? Anyone we know?"

Bull shrugged as he sniffed at the contents in his Thermos mug. He took a sip and winced, then smacked his lips with satisfaction before handing it up to Danny.

"No idea, but apparently, they were guards down at the refugee camp. Obviously they must've pissed someone off in a big way and they were given the good news. Can't say I blame them for it though. I've heard those guards are a right bunch of sadistic bastards and get a real kick out of making the refugees suffer."

Danny suddenly remembered the events that he and Bobby had witnessed the week before during the outbreak at the camp. He turned and looked over to Bobby and raised a questioning eyebrow. Bobby looked back at him but his features gave nothing away. He shrugged indifferently and went back to reading a fishing magazine. Danny knew that Bobby was responsible and his only problem with it was that his friend had not seen fit to involve him. After watching the guards firing indiscriminately into the fleeing crowds and then executing a family who needed their help, he had hated them just as much as Bobby clearly did.

Bull was oblivious to the silent exchange between the other two and went on rambling about the event and then suddenly changing the subject to food as his mind flitted from one thing to the next, as it usually did.

Up on the bridge, Taff and Marty stood smoking vigorously as they took in as much nicotine as they could before the mission began. They knew that it would be a while before they would next have the chance and wanted to stock up while they were still in port.

Stan stood beside Captain Werner as the final preparations were completed and the bow and stern lines holding the submarine to the floating dock were cast off and the vessel was cleared for sea.

"Engage electric motors. Back one-third, Chief. Come left full rudder," the Captain called into the voice pipe.

From inside the conning tower a low hum started up as the motors began to drive the submarine back out of its birth and towards the Channel. A number of commands were called down into the Control Room as Werner carefully manoeuvred the boat away from the harbour. When they were a few hundred metres away from the dock, the Captain called for an 'all-stop' on the electric engines. He turned to Stan and smiled.

"I love the sea, Stan. I'm never really happy unless I'm amongst the waves, regardless of the weather. Actually that's probably why I've gone through two messy divorces in my time. My real wife is the ocean."

Stan nodded. He could understand where Werner was coming from. He too had been a professional soldier his entire life and women had always come much further down in his list of priorities. He had never been married and now he could never imagine there being any change to that fact.

With the bow of the U-boat facing eastwards, the men on the bridge stood looking out over the English Channel for a while. The only noise they could hear was the sound of the waves slapping lazily against the hull, joined by the occasional screech of a seagull. The wind was down to little more than a breeze and the sun was slowly setting in the western sky. Its rays bounced off the surface of the darkening sea, causing it to glitter with orange and red sparkles of light. It was peaceful and almost hypnotic as the submarine gently rocked in the swell of the current and the cool wind brushed against their faces.

"Okay, let's go to work," Werner finally said, breaking the silence. He leaned forward and placed his mouth close to the voice pipe. "Right full rudder. Come to heading one-five-zero degrees. Both main diesels ahead full, Chief."

From the hatch below, the sound of the order being repeated in the Control Room could be heard as the sailors set about getting the boat underway. A rumble began to grow from within the U-boat and a gentle vibration travelled through the hull as the diesels were fired up. The engines growled noisily and within seconds, the bow of the boat had begun to cut its way through the murky green waves and steadily began to gather pace. Before long, it was impossible to have a conversation at normal speaking volume up on the bridge. With the engines hammering at full speed and the wind blowing into their faces, the men up top had to shout to one another in order to be heard.

"Once we get some depth below our keel we'll go under and run on the batteries," the Captain hollered to Stan as he held onto the handrail fixed to the interior lip of the conning tower. "That way we save on fuel and it will give you and your boys something to write home about."

Within an hour, the boat was locked down tight and gently slipping beneath the surface. The diesel engines were disengaged and the electric motors kicked in and powered the U-boat down into the depths.

"Take her down to thirty metres, Chief," the Captain ordered in the Control Room as he stepped down from the ladder.

As the conning tower disappeared beneath the waves, the hum of the electric motors began to resonate through to the stern section of the submarine. Bull had been busy chomping away on a large piece of dried beef from his rations but as the Captain announced the dive over the intercom speakers, he stopped in mid chew. His cheeks were puffed out from being overstuffed and his eyes grew wide as he automatically gazed up at the ceiling of the pressure hull as though he was able to see through it and witness the sea as it flowed over the upper deck.

In the Control Room, Stan watched as the crew expertly handled the boat and automatically worked the controls. Men moved about pulling levers and turning wheels, allowing water to rush into the diving tanks and then closing them off once the ship had begun her descent. The Chief stood back beside the Captain and observed, keeping his eyes on the men sitting at the diving controls and controlling the bubbles in the glass tubes that indicated the angle of the diving planes.

Within thirty seconds, they were completely submerged. Stan observed the needle on the depth gauge and watched as its point gently passed the fifteen metre mark and continued towards its desired depth.

"Bow planes on zero, stern planes on zero," the Chief said as he leaned forward and tapped the shoulders of the two men sitting at the helm and then turned to face Werner. "Boat level at thirty metres, Captain."

Captain Werner nodded and thoughtfully rubbed his hand over the long bristles that covered the lower part of his face.

"Very good, Chief. Shut all main vents and check all valves and seals."

He turned to Stan and smiled.

"And there we go, Stan. We should be able to manage a nice gentle ten to thirteen knots, depending on the current, and still have plenty of battery charge left over. You and your boys may as well settle in and get some sleep."

In the stern compartment, no one was yet considering sleep. Bull was still transfixed with the ceiling and many other sets of eyes had joined him. Deep resounding groans and creeks echoed within the hull as though some huge hand was trying to squeeze the life out of them. With each crunch and wine, Bull flinched.

"What the fuck is that? Have we run into something?"

Danny was the only one that appeared unaffected by the noises. He remained in his bunk and reading his book.

"Water pressure against the hull," he said casually. "Even at just thirty metres the pressure is four times as much as it is on the surface. It's just the sound of the boat's ribs protesting as they're being pushed inwards."

"Pushed inwards? Is that supposed to make me feel better?" Bull grunted without taking his eyes away from the ceiling.

"It'll settle after a few minutes. This sub could go to two-hundred and fifty metres if it needed. The movement of the ribs is barely detectable at this depth."

"Well I'm detecting it plenty enough, Danny," Marty mumbled. "I wish to fuck they'd decided to parachute us in now."

11

Tina and Christopher were both standing ready. Or at least as ready as they could be before leaving the safety of their hideout and facing the walking corpses that wanted nothing better than to feast on their warm flesh.

Standing beside the hatch set into the left hand side of the huge bay doors, Tina began checking her equipment. They wore thick jackets made from nylon and denim with a number of layers beneath to prevent the teeth of the infected piercing through to their skin. In the reception area, lying in the drawers of the desk, they had found stacks of magazines and newspapers. Now, over their forearms and lower legs they had secured copies of Vogue and Cosmopolitan with duct tape to act as greaves and vambraces. They completed their rudimentary armour with thick work gloves and steel toecap boots.

Tina was wearing her utility belt with her various weapons attached. In her hand, she held her trusty crowbar with her hatchet safely tucked through one of her belt loops for easy retrieval. She looked at her brother. He was pale and sweating heavily but he gave her a decisive nod that indicated he was ready and willing. Again, she paused and watched him for a moment. She could still not understand where his sudden bravery and eagerness had come from.

Was it just the fact that he was terrified of being trapped?

"Okay," she nodded as she began taking deep breaths in readiness. "Remember the drill, Chris? We head straight for the gate. I close it and you cover me. Stay close and if any of them appear before the opening is sealed, you twat them. Got it?"

"Got it," he nodded back to her with assuredness. He lifted the heavy steel pipe he had brought with him and gently patted it against his left palm.

"One, Two…" Tina began to count.

Christopher screwed his eyes shut for a moment and sucked in a lung full of air through his whistling nostrils. He was terrified, but despite his trembling hands and thumping heartbeat, he heard his own voice rattling around within his head.

Don't fuck this up. Don't fuck this up…

Tina pulled the door open and stepped out onto the loading bay ramp. She moved to the side in order to allow her brother to climb through the narrow opening without crashing into her. The loading area was empty of the infected and she wanted to keep it that way. One of them taking a sudden fall could alert the wandering corpses to their presence before they were able to close the gate.

In the far corner, nestled against the edge of the adjacent building and the fence line, she could see the pile of bodies that were covered with the canvas sheet. Clouds of flies buzzed around the heap and even from a range of fifty metres she could smell the sickly sweet tang of the decomposing cadavers. To the right of the loading bay were a number of parked cars slowly rusting away, caked in dust, and overlooked by the large windows of the cafeteria. On their left sat an abandoned heavy goods truck, its windows shattered and its doors lying open. There was no sign of the infected having stumbled in through the gate.

"I thought you said you'd seen some of them down at this end?" Tina muttered back at her brother without taking her eyes off the gate. She had expected to at least see a few of them lumbering around within the space.

"Maybe they left?"

"Come on," Tina whispered and began to move out into the open and away from the protection of the building.

She took the direct route, heading straight across the open space and towards the gate area in the far right hand corner. As she stepped out from the stretching shadow of the tall building and into the fading sunlight, she felt the difference in the temperature within the multitude of layers that she wore.

Christopher was close behind her, as instructed. His eyes darted continuously from side to side but he kept his face pointed in the direction of Tina's back. He was determined not to make a mess of this one. More than anything, he wanted to prove to himself that he was capable of overcoming his fears and doing what was necessary.

They were close to the bushes running along the inside of the fence line to their right, separating them from the main parking area in front of the warehouses. The foliage was thick and in full bloom, but now and then, when the light wind managed to catch them in its gusts, the branches would part fleetingly, long enough to allow them a momentary glimpse out on to the car park from between the fluttering leaves. The infected were still a distance away and it appeared that none of them had detected the presence of the two living people. Their shuffling footsteps and low groans could still be heard though. With nothing else to blot out their sounds, the haunting voices were easily audible across the expanse of the parking lot.

Tina, moving in a low crouch, suddenly stopped and Christopher immediately followed suit. His eyes remained locked on his sister's back, and at her sudden halt, the dread he had been fighting so hard to control began to bubble within his stomach.

"What is it?" He whispered, unsure whether or not he wanted to hear her reply.

She said nothing and kept her attention focussed upon the gate that was just ten metres away from them.

"Tina…"

She turned to him and raised a finger to her lips. Her eyes burned into his and conveyed the urgency of the situation that he was still oblivious to. She held his gaze for a moment, ensuring that he understood that he was to remain still and silent. Then, tentatively, she pointed to the fence beside them.

He turned and followed the line of her finger. At first, he was unable to understand what it was that he was supposed to be seeing. He stared blankly at the wire mesh and blinked. Finally, he realised what she was trying to tell him. The line of bushes had suddenly stopped and the last stretch of the fence line was empty and exposed. The moment they took another step they would be visible to any of the lifeless eyes in the car park that happened to look in their direction. He nodded his understanding and took a small step backwards.

However, Tina was still pointing at the fence and staring wildly at him. He nodded again, thinking that maybe she had not seen his acknowledgement the first time, and went as far as raising his thump to ensure she understood.

She shook her head. Her thickly gloved finger continued to jut out to her side while the remainder of her body, still squatting low to the ground, was frozen to the spot. Christopher realised that there must be more to see than the absence of greenery along the perimeter. He gingerly leaned forward and peered out from behind the last of the bushes. His sister was directly below him now as he towered over her and balanced himself precariously on one leg as he strained to see.

Tina cringed. His colossal body was hanging over her like an unstable protrusion of rock jutting out from a cliff face and she was swallowed up in his shadow, unable to make any sudden movements and get out of his way. She *had* to stay where she was and had no choice but to place her faith in Christopher's ability to stay upright for once. She prayed that his balance did not falter. If he fell, he would land on top of her and as she was in a squatting position, she imagined herself sustaining all sorts of damage to her back, hips, and lower limbs beneath his crushing weight.

He finally saw what she wanted him to see. His eyes bulged and his mouth instantly lost all its moisture, leaving his tongue dry and feeling as though it was caked in sand, as his body seemed to shrivel with terror. Forcing his weight back onto his planted leg, Christopher brought his raised foot, which had been thrust out behind him and acting as a counterweight, to the ground and placed it firmly beside the other. He stared down at Tina and began to inch his way backwards.

She shook her head slightly and raised her finger to her lips once more.

Just a metre away from them, perched right up against the fence, sat one of the infected. Luckily, it was facing away from them with its back leaning against the steel mesh but Tina could tell that it was far from inactive. Its head twitched as it sat watching the movement of the other bodies in the car park and the birds fluttering about overhead. It gargled and sputtered lightly, as though holding a conversation with itself and commenting on the goings on in the area around it. It was impossible to tell how long the thing had been there for but it must have been for quite some time. Its decaying tissue appeared to have become fused with the intertwining strands of the wire fence. Globs of decomposing skin and muscle seeped through the mesh and a large pool of sticky dark fluid had leaked out from its rectum and formed itself into a black viscous puddle that spread out around the creature.

Its backbone and ribs were devoid of flesh and its white scapulars were laid bare, branching out from the spinal column like a small set of wings. The head, with just a few strands of wispy white, sun-bleached hair clinging stubbornly to the leathery cranium, bobbed continuously, accompanied by low rumbling grunts.

Tina stared at her brother and signalled him to remain where he was. He had been steadily creeping further away from her with terror-filled eyes and quivering shoulders. He was back to his normal self, Tina noted. Gone was the glimmer of hope that she had held for him in becoming an asset to their duo. She glared at him and pushed her hand out a little further in an attempt to reinforce her need for him to stop.

Finally, he halted and watched her. He did not want to be there. The safe and secure warehouse was just a short walk away and he could feel it beckoning him. He wanted to turn and run and allow the building to envelop him in its protective walls but his sister demanded that he stay out in the open, surrounded by the walking dead and risking his life.

Tina crept back beyond the safety of the bushes. She moved along in a crouch, almost hopping from one foot to the other until she was out of sight. She raised herself back to her full height and approached her brother. Again, she raised her fingers to her lips but the expression in her face had softened and seemed more understanding of his fear.

"It's okay," she whispered as she pulled herself close to him and raised her mouth towards his ear. "It doesn't know we're here. We can still do this, Chris. We just need to be very careful and make sure we don't make a sound."

Christopher pulled away from her and began shaking his head. He started to say something but Tina pushed her fingers up against his mouth.

"Chris, we *have* to do this. It was your idea to close the gate and a good one too," she continued encouragingly and attempting to appeal to his own sense of pride. "We can't leave it open now.

If we do it right, it'll be over in just a few seconds and we will be back in the warehouse before you know it."

He looked at her blankly and then up at the gate. It was just a few metres away and it would not take long at all. He glanced at the area of the bushes where he knew the body of the infected sat, just out of sight. It would all be over before the corpse managed to climb to its feet and he would be gone from the area long before it reached the gate. He gulped hard and nodded, closing his eyes and fighting desperately to swallow his fear and force himself into positive action.

Tina smiled and lightly brushed her hand against the thick material that covered his bulky shoulders. He looked down at her glove as she began to turn her head and body away from him. It was the first sign of physical affection she had shown him in months.

Shaking himself internally, Christopher began to creep along behind his sister. As he passed the end of the row of bushes, he glanced nervously to his right and saw the corpse still sitting with its back to them, completely unaware of their presence. He focussed his attention back on the shoulders of Tina and remained within arm's reach of her.

Don't fuck this up, he heard the nagging voice in his head say again.

At the gate, Tina paused and quickly surveyed the area for anything she had missed. Then she turned and glanced back at the sitting infected body just a few metres to her right. She had a clear view of its profile now. Its face looked flat with very little protruding in the way of its features. Its nose had rotted away to nothing more than a hollow stub and its eyes were sunken deep into its skull. She wondered to herself how good its vision was but she quickly shook the thought from her mind. It did not matter and they would know the answer to that particular question soon enough when they slammed the gate shut.

She took a quick glance over her shoulder to check on Christopher. He was close, very close. Stretching her arm out in front of her she began to reach for the rolling gate, but something made her stop dead in her tracks. Something was wrong. They remained unseen but there was definitely a serious threat.

Subconsciously she had seen and recognised it but it was taking a while for her brain to register what it was.

The danger was behind her.

Tina slowly turned her body, keeping her feet planted against the tarmac so that she did not create any noise with a careless foot movement. Christopher's bulk came into view and his face appeared as she slowly panned around to her right. His eyes were blazing at her and his lips were curled back into a snarl. Then she recognised the barrel of the gun that was being pointed directly at her face.

Where the fuck did that come from? She gasped internally.

Christopher's hands were shaking but the muzzle remained firmly pointing into the area between her eyes. He had taken a step backwards, careful not to get too close to her and allow his sister the opportunity to snatch the weapon from his trembling hand.

Tina recognised the hatred and anger in her brother's face. The insanity in his eyes raged like a bush fire and his sweat soaked, pallid skin added to the appearance of a man that was on the verge of madness. A knot suddenly formed in the pit of her stomach and the blood in her veins seemed instantly to freeze, sending a shiver through her entire body and causing her cranium to tingle and the hair of her neck stand out.

At that moment, it did not matter where the pistol had come from or the reasons why her own brother now stood poised to put a 9mm round through her face. The glare in his eyes and the vile expression etched into his features told her everything she needed to know at that moment. He was going to shoot her.

"Christopher," she began in a hushed and calming tone, "listen to me. Whatever it is I've done wrong, please don't do this. We can talk this through, Chris. Whatever the problem is, we can fix it. I'm your sister and I want to help you."

His fingers tightened their grip on the Glock and his face became more twisted and unrecognisable as he stared back at her in hateful silence.

"Please, Chris," she pleaded, "you don't have to do this. If you want, I will just leave and I will never come back."

He remained impassive to her reasoning. His face held its snarling grimace and his aim did not falter.

She suddenly realised that any attempt at negotiation or compromise was futile. Her brother was clearly committed to putting an end to her life. Her shoulders sagged and her body threatened to collapse from beneath her. Her death was just moments away. She felt nauseous and dizzy and her skin flushed with a dread filled sweat. It felt as though her bowels were contorting and writhing and her bladder suddenly felt particularly full as a surge of adrenaline flowed into her bloodstream. Her survival instincts were preparing her for 'flight or fight' mode but there was nothing she could do. Christopher was too far away for her to make a grab for the pistol and too close for her to turn and run. She was completely at his mercy and the expression in his face told her everything she needed to know about his intentions.

He was going to kill her. She had no doubt in her mind.

Suddenly, with a speed that she had never seen from her brother, he barged forward and threw out his foot. It happened so fast that she was unable to move in time and the kick caught her squarely in the stomach. The wind was instantly knocked from her and she was sent flying backwards through the air. Her left shoulder struck the edge of the roll gate with a loud clang and she felt a shooting pain rip through her upper arm and into her neck as the joint dislocated from its socket. The loud rattle of the fence and the high-pitched ringing sound of her crowbar falling to the floor immediately caught the attention of the infected that were scattered about the car park.

The corpse sitting against the fence line just a few metres away from the gate opening also turned its gaze in their direction. Struggling to pull itself free from the steel mesh, the body writhed and kicked as it saw the warm radiant flesh of Tina as she sailed through the air and crashed into the hard asphalt with a yelp of pain and fear. The pitiful cries of the walking dead began to echo as they converged, their voices joining in a mournful wail.

Tina rolled onto her side, unable to breathe and almost blinded by the pain in her shoulder. Her right glove had come away from her hand in the violence of the kick and she became distantly aware of the grated skin across her palm caused during her rough landing. She attempted to push herself up and regain her feet but her legs were refusing to cooperate. They slipped from under her and she fell back against the floor. Again, she attempted to stand as she began imploring her brother.

"Please, Chris, don't leave me like this. Help me."

Taking a second to glance at her surroundings, Tina quickly saw the corpses making their way over to the corner of the parking area where she lay helpless. She was crying with pain, fear, and the hopelessness of her situation. She looked back at her brother.

The terror and desperation in her eyes were plain to see but he was beyond caring now. He had committed himself to his actions and he was determined to see them through. Her cries and pleas did not register in his hate filled mind as he reached out for the gate and began pulling it towards him, he raised the pistol in his free hand and pointed it at Tina.

"No, Chris, no," she screamed as he squeezed the trigger.

The first shot boomed out across the expanse of the car park as the round smashed into the asphalt beside her, peppering her with sharp chips of tarmac and particles of disintegrated rock from beneath the surface.

Tina screamed and rolled to the side, hoping to get out of the way of the next shot. Again, the gun roared and the bullet snapped through the air beside Tina's head. She twisted and turned away from it and slithered across the ground in an attempt to escape. He had missed with his first two rounds but she was sure that his next would be accurate.

"Please," she was screaming as she crawled away from him and towards the nearest of the parked cars that were no more than twenty metres away.

Tears were streaming down her face from agony and terror. She suddenly felt alone and utterly vulnerable as she lay at the mercy of her murderous brother. She had been taken by complete surprise, and even now, as bullets smashed into the ground around her and the moans of the dead rang out from all directions, confusion and shock was taking their toll.

The decomposing body at the fence had managed to pull itself free, leaving large portions of its decayed flesh still clinging to the wire and forcing the swarms of flies to choose between the static remains smeared over the fence or the moving corpse. It climbed to its feet on rickety legs and began to lurch towards the writhing form of Tina as she scrambled away from the gate.

With blurred vision, ringing ears, and searing pain, Tina continued to crawl. Some of her nails had been torn away from her fingers as she desperately clawed at the ground and dragged herself along. Another two rounds cracked loudly beside her in quick succession and showered her with debris as the impacts sent up small fountains of stone and dust.

"Stop, Chris. Please stop," she croaked desperately between sobs.

Her voice had weakened substantially. She was now just waiting for the shot that would end her life but she could not sit idle. Her instincts forced her at least to attempt to survive. However, she had only managed to crawl a few metres and the protection of the nearest car was still a long way off.

"Please, stop..."

The gun blasted again and this time it felt like someone had suddenly hit her with a hammer in the lower right limb. She felt the muscle tear and her calf spasm as the bullet ripped through her trousers and punched a hole through her leg. Then she screamed as the true pain hit. Her blood-curdling howl reverberated over a vast distance, reaching far beyond the industrial estate as the agony of her shredded flesh assaulted her brain like an electric shock. Her head spun and her vision danced as an instant nausea loomed over her threatened to cause her to black out.

Reaching down and clamping her hand over the wound, she could feel the warm blood soaking through the material of her trousers and pouring out over the shredded magazine that was still wrapped around her damaged limb. The pain was excruciating but somehow, she managed to remain conscious and still moving away from the gate, kicking and clawing at the tarmac with her remaining good arm and leg.

Behind her, she heard the heaving clang as the gate was pulled shut and the clunk of the bolts as they were slid into place. She stole a quick glance over her shoulder and saw the huge shape of Christopher standing beyond the railings, still holding the pistol in his hands and staring out at her as she slowly pulled herself along the ground. She also saw the corpse from the fence line staggering towards her. It was still a few metres away but already its arms were outstretched in anticipation. Its mouth hung open and black bile seeped from its shrivelled lips. It grunted and gargled, stumbling after her and grasping at the air with its long bony fingers as it closed in on her wrecked body.

Tina gritted her teeth and renewed her efforts to escape. Her fingers were torn and bloodied from scraping along the rough surface of the car park but she was numb to the pain. Her shoulder, though wrenched from its socket and being dragged limply at her side, had become a distant burning sensation and even the hole in her leg had faded into a dull ache as the terror of being eaten alive filled and overwhelmed her senses.

The creature closed in as Tina attempted to climb to her feet. She pushed herself upwards and roared as a torrent of pain shot up from the bleeding wound in her calf. She almost collapsed back to the floor but the excited wail and snapping teeth of the corpse as it lunged towards her drove her forward. It missed her by just a few centimetres and careened off to the side before turning to pursue her again.

Tina stumbled on, her damaged shoulder rendering her left arm useless and her wounded leg slowly her dramatically. She had no idea where she was trying to get to or what she would do when she got there. All she could think of was getting away from her brother before he fired again, and the infected monster that was now close on her heels.

She made it to the first of the cars and reached out, placing her hands on the hood to stabilise herself and pushing her weakened body around to the other side. There was more of the infected coming. They were closing in fast, much faster than the pathetic hobble that she could manage. She needed to hide somewhere, anywhere, but there was nowhere that she could escape to.

She stumbled and fell, crashing to the floor and hitting her head against the solid surface of the parking area. Her shoulder slammed hard against the tarmac and the pop of the socket as the bone slipped back into place echoed loudly in her ears. Stars erupted across her vision and her head swam as her senses were knocked off kilter. She rolled to the side and groaned with pain and confusion. She tried to stand but fell again. It was impossible for her to get her body to obey her mind. It was like trying to swim in oil. Her movements were slow and clumsy, uncoordinated and feeble.

She rolled onto her back and looked up in time to see the rotted corpse from the fence reaching down towards her with its mouth agape. Its knee landed on her upper thighs and she was pinned to the ground beneath its weight. She pushed against it with both arms, ignoring the searing pain in her shoulder as her hands sunk into the cold mushy grey flesh of its chest and her fingers slipped through the bones of its ribcage.

The infected man did not acknowledge the damage caused to its body. Its entire focus was on sinking its teeth into the warm tissue and muscle of the writhing woman beneath it.

Tina desperately struggled to push the creature away from her but its grotesque face continued to descend towards her own. Its putrid stench filled her nostrils and its gurgling groans assaulted her ears, threatening to drive her into a dark pit of madness as she screamed and roared with fear and frustration. She thrust hard against it, and brought her left arm, the shoulder burning and aching immensely, down towards her belt in a desperate attempt to reach one of her weapons. She did not care which one, anything would do. Her fingers clutched and grasped as she frantically felt for something that could be brought up to help her, but there was nothing there.

Her ear splitting screams of terror and agony shattered the silence of the countryside for miles around the complex.

Christopher stood in the darkened warehouse, his back pressed up against the locked hatch set into the loading bay doors. He panted and gasped for air. His hands shook uncontrollably and his knees trembled. The sickness he felt rising up in his stomach threatened to burst through its floodgates at any moment. He was crying and shaking his head, blubbering away to himself incoherently, unsure if he had done the right thing in killing his sister.

Her horror-filled shrieks still echoed through his mind, freezing his blood and torturing his darkening soul.

"Shut up," he screamed into the darkness, "shut up."

He smacked himself on the side of his head, forgetting that he still had the Glock pistol clutched tightly in his hand. The sharp pain as the magazine housing crashed against his skull sent spasms of irritating throbs through his brain.

"Cunt," he snarled through gritted teeth, "fucking cunt."

He turned and staggered towards the door leading out from the warehouse and into the administration offices. He was mumbling and wailing to himself as he made his way through the doorway, cursing himself in one breath and then justifying his actions in the next.

"How could you?" He called out in disgust as he made his way through the incinerated corridor on unsteady legs.

"How could you do that to her? You killed your own sister, you piece of shit."

He slammed himself against the wall and then threw himself against the door at the far end, as though trying to punish himself or knock the feelings of remorse from his mind. He burst out from the darkened passageway and into the long sunlit room of office cubicles. Saliva foamed at the corners of his mouth as his bloodshot eyes focussed on the doorway at the far end. He launched himself forwards, his massive legs rippling as the layers of fat were jolted from the impacts of his heavy feet against the floor.

"She was a bitch," he snarled as he ran. "I *hate* her and she deserved it. I warned her. I told her not to push me."

The fact that he had never spoken a word of warning to her or made any sort of threat, other than to his own reflection in the mirror as he wrapped himself up in a world of fantasy, did not register with him.

He raced through the offices and out into the reception area. He ploughed on, charged his colossal body up the dreaded thirty-five steps of anguish, and headed for the manager's office. He could no longer hear his sister's screams but he wanted to see the feeding frenzy that was no doubt taking place in the car park by now.

Barging through the door, he covered the distance to the large windows in just a few strides and hurriedly swept back the thick curtains and flooded the room with dazzling sunlight. He squinted in its brightness and raised his hands to shield his eyes while they adjusted to the sudden change.

Out in the car park he could see a large number of corpses appearing from the peripherals of the industrial estate and around the edges of the various buildings. Some walked and others ran but they all headed in the same direction. The commotion had no doubt attracted many of them from the surrounding areas but Christopher did not care about that. The parking area could hold thousands of bodies for all he cared. He was safe inside the supply depot and was confident that the barricades would hold out. He had no intention of stepping outside again now.

"It's okay," he whispered to himself reassuringly as he took in the amount of moving corpses that were steadily filling the industrial complex. "You're safe. They can't get in here. You're safe now."

He looked across to the area where he had last seen Tina. She had gone down behind a blue saloon that was parked in front of the warehouse situated at the end of the staff parking area and running at a ninety-degree angle to the one he and his sister had been sharing, roughly seventy metres away. He squinted and craned his neck in an attempt to see, pressing himself up close to the large panels of glass and paying no consideration to whether or not the infected below could see him.

A number of other cars blocked his view of what was happening on the ground but the dozens of bobbing heads around the vehicles and adjacent building's entrance confirmed that the feast had indeed begun. More infected arrived and joined in and soon it became a seething mass as they tore into his sister.

Christopher imagined her lifeless body being ripped to shreds, her limbs pulled from their sockets, her abdomen being tore open, and her intestines devoured. He hoped that she had been alive long enough to suffer the slabs of flesh being savagely gnawed from her. He particularly savoured the image of her eyes being gouged out and her tongue wrenched from her mouth while she lay screaming in pain.

Christopher grinned ruefully.

"Fuck you, *sis*," he sneered.

12

Samantha was pacing. Her nails were becoming shorter by the minute and she had gone through over a dozen hair-clips over the last six hours as she nervously twisted and pulled at them with her fingers. The atmosphere within the Operations Room was becoming tense. Samantha herself was causing the vast majority of the tension as she hounded every person around her for updates and ensured that they had checked and double-checked every detail of their duties.

"For Christ's sake, Sam, will you relax?" Gerry hissed across to her, as he remained seated behind a desk with his feet up on the table top. "You're like a bloody dog with a bone. They've just got underway and you're driving everyone around here nuts."

Samantha stopped and checked herself. He was right. The mission was in its early stages and already she was on edge. She needed to calm down.

"If you're like this on phase-one, Sam, what will you be like when the attack on the harbour begins? You'll be no use to any of us and I need you at your best, not a quivering wreck because of self-induced pressure."

"Yeah," she nodded, "you're right, Gerry."

She looked around at the rest of the operations staff. Some of them were watching her expectantly. They appeared like caged animals with skittish movements and wary eyes. From the moment, that the signal had been received from Captain Werner that they were en-route to the drop off, she had been hovering over them to provide her with information. She had even lost her temper with a young corporal from the Royal Corp of Signals when he stood up from his workstation to get a drink from the fridge. If she continued in that way, they could snap under the strain.

"They're submerged now, Sam. So we won't hear anything from them until they surface again and if all goes to plan, that won't be for another sixteen hours or so. In the meantime, I suggest you go and get some sleep or do whatever it is you like to do to relax around here."

"Like what, Gerry?" She asked with a hint of aggression.

"I don't know, Sam. Go and paint a frigging watercolour landscape or something. I really don't care, as long as you're not hanging about here like a fart in an airtight room and putting people on edge."

Gerry was conveying it as a suggestion but she knew he meant it as an order. He did not want her burning herself out in the early stages of the operation. She paused for a moment and held his gaze. She felt like running over and hitting him. Finally, she nodded, brushing her stubbornness to one side and heading for the door.

Outside in the corridor, Samantha ran into Melanie coming in the opposite direction and making a beeline for her. Since their ordeal in the bunker complex below the city of London and Melanie's dramatic rescue of the team stranded in Manchester, Samantha and the young pilot had become close.

"I was just coming to find you," the helicopter pilot said as she approached. "I was wondering if you wanted to join me for a coffee."

"You mean Gerry got in touch with you and told you to come and get me out of the way for a while?"

"Uh, yeah, something like that," Melanie smiled sheepishly.

There and then, Samantha made a conscious decision that as soon as she came across any person holding a cigarette, she would snatch it from them and begin puffing away again. She had fought against her cravings throughout the crisis and had beaten her addiction each time, but now she was ready to give in to it.

I'm running out of hair-clips, so I need to do something, she thought.

"How's it going in there?" Melanie asked.

Samantha shrugged. There was nothing really to tell and at that moment, she really did not want to speak about it. Gerry had been right. She was getting herself all bent out of shape for no reason and it was best if she took a step back from the operation until it really began. Stan and his men knew what they were doing and they would not need her input until they were in their over-watch positions.

They began to walk away from the command room. At the junction in the corridor, they made to turn right but something brought them to an abrupt stop. A long drawn out howl filled the air around them. It was a distant sound but clearly coming from somewhere within the building. It clawed at their ears and nerves and sent shivers running through their spines. The gut wrenching wail was suddenly cut off. It did not fade out but finished swiftly, as though someone had put an end to the lament.

"What the fuck was that?" Melanie gasped with dread.

To their left was the set of steel stairs that led down into the basements where the scientists carried out their experiments. To most people, the area was off limits but Samantha was one of the senior operations staff and had clearance. She leaned over the railing and peered down into the darkness deep below them. She could see faint traces of light that seeped through the doors leading into the laboratories but there was no sign of any disturbance. She moved down onto the first of the steps and turned to Melanie.

Melanie hesitated but then began to follow her. She was used to running in the opposite direction whenever she heard that unmistakable sound, but now she was deliberately heading towards it. Her guts tightened and a light sweat began to seep from her pores as she followed after Samantha, gently placing her hand over the butt of her pistol.

The further they descended the cooler the air became. Even if they were blindfolded and had no idea where they were, they would automatically come to the assumption that they were below ground. The staircase had that hollow, dank subterranean feel about it and the slightest noise echoed hollowly.

As they reached the bottom, a guard stepped forward out of the gloom and almost caused both Samantha and Melanie to jump out of their skins. They expected a soldier to be there but his sudden appearance still surprised them. He recognised the Captain and gave a questioning nod to the woman standing beside her.

"It's okay, she's with me," Samantha said with authority.

The soldier was not about to argue. He knew the reputation of Captain Tyler and being an obstacle in her path was far more trouble than it was worth. He nodded and handed them a pair of surgical masks then allowed them to pass through the door and into the brightly lit corridor of the underground labs. Originally, the place had been a large wine cellar and storage rooms. When the military had occupied the island, the basements had been retrofitted to suit the needs of the scientists conducting their research and experiments. They insisted on a cool environment and rather than waste fuel to power air-conditioning units, the naturally chilled environment below ground was chosen.

They walked passed a number of offices and small laboratories where people stood scrutinising data on clipboards and computer screens, or sat staring through microscopes. At the far end of the corridor, they came to a large open space that was separated from the labs by a thick sheet of opaque plastic hanging from the top of the doorway. They pushed through the split in the centre and into an area that was roughly half the size of a tennis court with bare brick vaulted walls and ceilings. A strong smell of damp, decomposition, and disinfectant lingered in the air and plucked at their nostrils.

Along each side of the room, they saw numerous operating tables and hospital gurneys with monitoring equipment and instruments beside them. Bright surgical lights that were connected to retractable brackets reached down from the ceiling above and shone onto the tables, casting the area directly below them in a brilliant white glow. On each bed, Samantha and Melanie could see a body. A number of men and women, dressed in protective surgical clothing, stood around each of the individual workstations, talking amongst themselves while one of them conducted the procedures.

Beneath each of the operating tables, the floor was awash with blood and gore and in the far corner of the room, Samantha saw what she believed to be a pile of bodies that had been unceremoniously dumped there, awaiting disposal.

At one of the gurneys, a number of doctors were watching as a surgeon cut out each of the internal organs of a specimen, one by one. Samantha could not hear what they were saying but as the man held up the discoloured and shrivelled heart of a reanimated woman, the rest of them nodded vigorously. Next, he reached into the exposed ribcage and began to pull out the rotting liver, kidneys, and bloated stomach. All the while, the corpse beneath them violently thrashed and pulled at the restraints that held it in place. Its head swivelled continuously and its jaws snapped at the living people around it from beneath the thick leather gag that had been strapped over its mouth.

The doctors paid very little attention to the infected body that was struggling to break free and tear into them. They continued to be engrossed in the work they were conducting. They were clearly used to handling reanimated corpses and had become numb to the horror of the situation or the plight of the human beings they worked on. They had an almost blasé and casual demeanour about them as they poked, prodded, and sliced through the flesh and organs of the dangerous creatures lying at their mercy. The shock and revulsion that the scientists had no doubt felt at the beginning of the outbreak, even the terror at the sight of the infected, had been replaced with inquisitiveness and a detached and completely emotionless approach to their patients.

"Good God," Melanie exclaimed, as she raised her hand to cover her mouth and nose from the overpowering smell of rotting blood. The foul odour found its way into her senses despite the mask she was wearing. "It looks like Frankenstein's laboratory down here. What the hell are they doing?"

"You tell me," a voice suddenly said from close behind them.

Samantha gasped and spun around with fright. She was ready to strike out at anything she saw, despite the fact that the owner of the voice was clearly alive. A tall slender man with wispy light brown hair stood staring back at her. He did not flinch or step back from her sudden turn but merely stood his ground with an indifferent expression upon his face. He was not wearing the same protective clothing that the other scientists had covered themselves in. Instead, he opted for his lab coat and did not even bother to wear a mask.

"Sorry, I didn't mean to startle you," Doctor Warren said with a brief smile as he stepped closer and took a sip from the cup he was holding. "But to answer your question, Lieutenant Frakes, I have no idea what they're doing down here. For the last three months I have been telling them that we should stop with anatomical and biological experiments and concentrate on more important, *practical* matters, but no one will listen. I'm just the crazy guy who failed to find a cure before it all got out of hand."

"So what *are* they doing, Joseph?" Samantha asked as she nodded over to a rubber-clad surgeon who was holding a severed head aloft and showing his assembled audience how the creature's senses were still functioning.

"Supposedly, they're looking for answers," he sighed. "Personally though, I think they're just curious and behaving like kids with a magnifying glass over an ants' nest. They're learning nothing that we don't already know and wasting time and resources if you ask me. They're pretty much reinventing the wheel down here.

"Very early on in the epidemic we learned that the process of decomposition slows dramatically after a while and despite our best efforts, we were unable to understand why. Some doctors are still searching for an answer to that riddle even though it's utterly superfluous now."

He took another sip and nodded to the gurney holding a woman's corpse as the doctors continued to strip out her internal organs.

"Over there, they're still trying to work out why the reanimated cadavers attack and feed on the living. They have no need for nourishment but still, they do it. Personally, I gave up trying to work that one out a long time ago. Some are still studying the virus itself and trying to understand it and where it came from. Others are studying the brains of the victims in the hope of finding answers.

"As for me, I just look for easier ways to kill them now, and in large numbers without causing casualties to our own side. Not exactly deep scientific stuff of course, but *someone* needs to keep their head out of the clouds. We've tried all kinds of methods. Chemical weapons were our most recent attempt but they proved to be completely ineffective. More hazardous to our own people than the infected. Some believe that radiation might have a more positive outcome but I have my doubts. At the moment, fire and massive trauma to the brain are still the leaders in dealing with the plague."

The three of them fell silent for a short while and stood staring at the macabre experiments that were being carried out on close to a dozen individual bodies. Grunts and muffled wails continued to fill the air all around them, interrupted only by the high-pitched whirling sounds of surgical drills and the grating of bone saws.

"Looks like you're not running short on specimens, Doctor," Melanie noted and indicated the pile of corpses in the far corner. "Where you getting them from?"

For the first time, Doctor Warren suddenly looked uncomfortable and his gaze dropped to his feet. He shuffled nervously as he considered his answer but Samantha interjected before he was able to speak.

"The camps," Samantha said flatly, as she eyed the pile of rotting human corpses at the other end of the room. "You're getting them from the refugee camps, aren't you?"

He nodded.

"Are they all dead when you bring them in, or are you taking the living as well?" Melanie asked as she turned to him and scrutinized the expression in his eyes.

"All our specimens are infected, Lieutenant, but yes, some of them are still alive when they're collected," he replied with a heavy hint of regret and shame. "Some of us are still trying to find ways of reversing the infection and live specimens are the only way they can carry out their tests."

"Jesus," Melanie gasped, shaking her head as she stared at the grotesque experiments being conducted around her and the doctors who were enthusiastically carrying them out. "It makes you wonder if there's anything worth saving."

"What about that one over there?" Samantha asked as she pointed to a bed with the still corpse of a man lying on top of it.

"Died twenty minutes ago," Warren replied. "He was brought in two days ago with the flue and kept under observation. He was actually a soldier and not one of the civilians. I assure you that he was treated humanely and his comfort was a priority. We have accommodation units down here where we house the living and keep them under quarantine. When he passed, they immediately brought him here and the clock was started."

As if on cue, a door to their left opened and a figure appeared carrying a pile of food trays, empty water bottles, and used plastic cups and cutlery. Before the door closed again, Samantha was able to catch sight of a pair of soldiers guarding the entrance to a long corridor with a number of doors leading off into separate rooms on either side. She made the assumption that they were the accommodation units for the living that Doctor Warren had just mentioned.

"The clock?" Melanie asked.

"Yes, the clock. To see how long it takes him to revive. Some of the doctors believe that the time between death and reanimation is slowing down."

"And *is* it slowing down?"

"It's hard to tell, Sam. Each and every case has always been different. Some have revived within minutes and others have taken as long as eight hours. I guess we'll find out when he wakes up," Doctor Warren shrugged.

Samantha had seen enough. The atmosphere in the underground laboratory was nauseating and she could feel her skin becoming cold and clammy. She wanted to get out of there and into the fresh air above ground. She understood that studying the virus and its effects was important, but she could not bear to look at the doctors who treated living people as nothing more than just livestock while they anxiously waited to begin ripping them up.

Five minutes later Samantha and Melanie burst through the doors of the main building and out into the pitch black of night. The air was cold on their lungs as they breathed in deeply and savoured its effects. It was the best Samantha had ever tasted as far as she was concerned, and she was more than happy to pollute it with the carbon monoxide from the cigarette she placed between her lips and proceeded to light.

"Christ, I needed that," she gasped as she felt the influences of the nicotine rush to her head. Her vision spun for a moment and she felt lightheaded due to her body not being used to the influx of the drug through her bloodstream.

They sat for a moment in silence and lost in their own thoughts. They had seen more than their fair share of horror since the plague began but watching the scientists as they clearly enjoyed their work was sickening. To the men and women in the basement, the world had become nothing but a huge playground where they could indulge their macabre theories and conduct unrestrained experiments with the government's backing.

"Do you think they'll ever find out what's causing this?" Melanie asked with a sigh as she stared up at the stars.

Samantha took another drag from the cigarette and stared down at her feet.

"I don't think it matters whether they do or don't, Mel. Whatever this thing is though, I don't think the human race is *supposed* to understand it." She paused for a moment and blew out a long cloud of smoke. "Or *survive* it."

To their left and at the far end of the building they could see an area lit with spotlights and vehicle headlamps. They saw a number of figures moving within the beams, and recognised the silhouettes of soldiers and heard the anxious voices of frightened civilians. Melanie and Samantha moved to investigate and found themselves standing on top of a wall and peering down into a walkway that led into the basement from the rear of the building. Soldiers stood flanking a number of trucks as doctors, wearing protective equipment, unloaded men, women, and children, then bustled them in through the doors that led into the accommodation beside the laboratory.

The eyes of the civilians shone wildly in the reflections from the lights and their frightened, questioning voices betrayed their uncertainty. Children clung to their mothers and the men argued with the guards and the doctors, demanding answers and the opportunity to speak with whoever was in charge.

The doctors assured them that they were being taken to a facility for treatment and good care would be provided for them. They were trying hard to sound soothing but their voices came across as more mechanical and automated with very little in the way of understanding or sympathy for the terrified refugees.

A man to the rear of the group decided that he was going to stand his ground and refused to go any further until he had spoken to the senior doctor. Before he could complete his demands, a soldier stepped forward and struck him across the side of his face with the butt of his pistol. The man yelped and dropped to the ground with a gash suddenly appearing around his eye and blood pouring down over his face. Two other soldiers stepped forward and hauled him to his feet. They grabbed him under each arm, dragged him along the walkway, and in through the doors ahead of the group while his feet trailed behind him and scuffed against the cold, hard concrete.

Samantha caught sight of Doctor Warren standing to the side of the vehicles as he watched the wretched procession. He glanced back at her and shook his head slightly. She could see that he was just as disgusted with the situation as she was and his dishevelled appearance and exhausted expression was evidence enough that the circumstances were beginning to wear him down.

"Looks like there's been another outbreak at the camp," Melanie said as she watched the civilians disappear through the doors.

Samantha said nothing but nodded as she stared at the unfortunate group.

A mother and child who had been at the very rear of the line were the last to enter into the basement. They walked holding one another's hand and with their heads bowed in silence as though accepting of their fate. They passed the two guards at the entrance and before the doors swung shut, the little girl turned and stared back up at Melanie.

The child's eyes, still sparkling with life behind the fever that burned beneath her flesh, almost glowed in the darkness. They held a sadness that penetrated deep into the soul of Melanie as they held each other's gaze for that fleeting moment. For the short while it took the door to close behind her, the little girl spoke a thousand words and asked a million questions. Her eyes held no accusations or blame but Melanie felt guilt and regret stabbing at her heavy heart.

The entrance was sealed and a sob suddenly sprang from Melanie as she was overcome. The child's unflinching eyes remained imprinted upon her memory long after the doors had closed on them.

13

All was virtually silent inside the pressure hull of the U-boat. Many of the men were still asleep and all that could be heard was the low electrical whine of the motors, the occasional drip, and the dull clunk of the deck plates as the crew on duty moved about within the cramped and dank interior. They had been travelling submerged for almost a full day and the humidity within the boat had risen substantially. The air was stale and the lack of space was beginning to make some of the soldiers feel claustrophobic and short tempered. Those that were not used to life on a submarine could not wait to get out into the fresh air and feel dry land beneath their feet again.

Up on the surface, the sun had already set and fifteen minutes earlier the Captain had ordered them to switch to red light to help their natural night vision adjust in anticipation of continuing their journey above the waves. As the boat entered into the Thames estuary, Werner ordered them up to periscope depth so that he could take a look around and check their bearings. A few minutes later, after confirming their exact position, he turned to his chief engineer and gave the order to surface.

The Chief blew the ballast tanks and ordered an upward angle on the diving planes. With a loud hissing noise and a series of gurgles as the compressed air was pumped into the tanks, the men on board could feel the boat begin to rise. In the dim glow of the red light, the crew moved about and attended their stations with an expertise that came natural to them due to years of practice. They barely had to look where they placed their hands. They knew exactly what each valve and wheel did, and they were able to carry out their duties in pitch darkness if the situation occurred when they needed to.

"Tower is clear, Captain," the Chief announced a minute later.

The Captain nodded and instructed the Chief to equalise the air pressure inside the hull and began to climb the ladder leading up into the cramped conning tower. As the atmosphere inside the boat changed, Werner threw open the hatch and pulled himself up onto the bridge to have a look around. The watch crew, along with

Stan and the other team commanders followed him up into the cool night air.

The wind had picked up considerably while they had been submerged and the clouds had grown heavy overhead in the dark sky. A few cold droplets of rain splashed against the faces of the men on the bridge and they knew that it would not be long before the heavens fully opened up on them.

"Visibility is shit," Captain Werner grumbled to Stan who was standing beside him in the conning tower. "But we have radar and at least the wind and rain will allow us to use our diesels without being heard for miles around."

Stan nodded as he continued to scan the blackness all around him. It was hard to distinguish where the sky finished and the water began. It was virtually impossible to see anything beyond the bow of the boat, and he wondered just how many untethered vessels there were adrift within the river and across their intended path. Crashing into a rogue ship would not be his idea of a good start to the mission.

"All stop on the electric motors, Chief. Start-up both main engines and ahead standard. Come to bearing two-six-five degrees."

The diesel engines sputtered to life and began to chug rhythmically from within the hull while the exhaust spewed out the noxious fumes into the cool night. The boat picked up speed and made a slight alteration to its course. Ahead of them, they could see the bright white glow of the bow wave against the rolling black sea as the submarine reached a cruising speed of thirteen knots. Behind them, an almost luminescent wake stretched out into the darkness as the starboard and port screws churned the water to a bubbling froth.

Minutes later and the Type-XXI was cutting its way through the swell towards the River Thames and the heart of London. Before long, they had made their break-in on the main river and as the channel began to narrow, they saw the first of the ships that were sitting at the river's edges. Their huge shapes loomed out from the wall of gloom surrounding the boat. They were dark and silent with no signs of movement and the black silhouettes of the city's buildings behind them were just as devoid of life.

"This place is nothing but a graveyard," Captain Werner mumbled thoughtfully as he stared out at the dark landscape.

Stan grunted and nodded beside him. He could feel the chill in the air against the bare flesh of his neck but the cool temperature was not what made him shiver. As soon as he and his men stepped foot off the boat, they would be virtually on their own and cut off. No help was immediately to hand and he had serious reservations about whether or not they would all make it back.

With each passing minute, they ventured deeper into the infested capital. Even on the submarine and in relative safety, the mood was tense and fear burned brightly in the eyes of many of the crew. They were in the heart of their nation but it was a heart that was no longer beating. The city was as dead as its new occupants were, and the crew of the boat were deliberately sailing right into it.

More and more ghost ships emerged on either side of the river. Some were small fishing craft and others were huge cargo transports and tankers. All were silent. The abandoned vessels sat slowly rusting away at their births, still tethered to the dock walls by their mooring lines and rocking gently against the tide.

"Right full rudder, Chief, right full rudder. Make it quick," Werner suddenly called into the voice pipe in alarm.

Stan snapped his attention back to the front of the boat and saw the stern of a river ferry just metres in front of the bow of the submarine. It had appeared out of nowhere and they were almost on top of it before they knew it was there.

Down in the Control Room the Chief acted quickly. The Captain had not explained why he needed the sudden turn to starboard but the urgency in his voice relayed the importance of a fast reaction to his commands. They avoided a collision with just centimetres to spare as the rudder was thrown over into a tight turn.

Werner continued to curse under his breath as he watched the towering ship pass by on the port side. Visibility was worse than he had expected and their outdated radar was clearly struggling to cope due to the volume of ships that were still in the river.

"Slow to one-third, Chief," he ordered then turned to Stan with a shrug and a wry smile creasing the corners of his mouth.

"Slowly does it I'm afraid. It would be embarrassing if we sunk ourselves."

At a reduced speed, they continued westward along the Thames. By now, the anticipated rain had begun to pour and it was not long before the men exposed on the bridge were saturated through to their skins. It beat down upon them in thick sheets and reduced visibility to less than one-hundred metres as the watch crew tried desperately to see through the squalls that lashed against their faces and the outer hull of their boat. Werner ordered a further reduction in speed and they continued to crawl along the river.

"Well, I think it's safe to say that the summer has come to an end," the Captain commented as he turned his face up towards the rain.

An hour later and they were approaching the Thames Barrier. The rain and wind had begun to ease off and visibility had increased slightly, allowing the sodden men on the bridge the ability once again to see their surroundings. Carefully, they squeezed through the narrow gaps between the gates and were soon approaching the prominent curve of the river that passed by the Isle of Dogs. To their left, a giant white structure emerged from the darkness. The buildings close by were dwarfed in comparison to its sheer size. It reached high above anything in the vicinity and spanned a wide area close to the river's edge.

"Fucking *Millennium Dome*," Captain Werner grunted with disdain as he eyed the colossal structure. He spat over the side of the conning tower and glared at the arena with loathing. "A complete waste of money that turned out to be."

Stan looked back at him and studied his expression for a moment as they passed by the dome that was situated on the northern tip of the Greenwich Peninsula. The man clearly despised the building and the motives for its construction, but Stan was not going to get into a political debate over the reasons why at that moment.

"Stand-by on the first drop off," Werner called down through the hatch in a loud whisper. "We'll be at the pier in about five minutes. All stop on the main engines, Chief. Switch to electric motors."

The diesels suddenly cut out and once again, the air around them became silent as the batteries took over the responsibility of propulsion in order for them to remain undetected. The wind was down to a blustery breeze and visibility was improving steadily.

In the city surrounding them, the ghostly wails of the dead drifted out from the streets and buildings and floated across the choppy waters of the Thames River towards the men in the boat. They sounded tortured and lost in an eternity of agony and misery. Their woeful cries protesting against their existence as they continued to walk the earth while their bodies decayed from around their bones. Then there was the reek of rot. It hung in the air like a heavy cloud. All the bodies that packed the streets between the buildings had been decomposing during the particularly hot summer and their foul stench was seeping out across the waters of the Thames like a creeping fog.

The men on the bridge staring out into the darkness swapped nervous glances. They watched the first soldiers as they gathered on the foredeck and prepared to go ashore. The crew in the tower observed them with a muted respect and a deepening sympathy. Everyone knew that not all of the men aboard the boat would return from their tasks. The soldiers themselves understood the high risk and were extra aware of the fact that some of them would never leave the city.

There were to be six drop off points along the river. At each stop, a team would disembark and move off towards their task locations and set up their positions. The first men to step onto the soil of London would be a team from the Pathfinders. As Werner brought the vessel in close to the pier, he stopped the engines and allowed the momentum of the slowly turning screws to bring them in at a drift.

The first men that were gathered on deck prepared themselves in silence. Their heavy equipment was secured on their bodies and their weapons were held at the ready. In the conning tower and on the aft deck, dozens of weapons were trained on the pier and its surroundings as the submarine slowly drew up alongside it in silence.

Every eye was focussed on the dock and the multitude of shadows and dark recesses that could hold the spying eyes of the dead. There was no sign of movement on the shore and when the boat came to a shuddering stop as the hull came into contact with the huge rubber tyres along the dock wall, the four sailors in charge of handling the gangplank went to work and secured the aluminium walkway against the pier.

The first team quickly moved off and spread out around the pier head, taking up fire positions as they waited for a few minutes. A short while later and Captain Werner saw the flash of green light from the team commander that indicated the area was clear and they were about to move off towards their patrol lane. One by one, the men disappeared into the darkness of the harbour and headed inland.

"Good luck, boys," Werner whispered then mumbled down into the voice pipe for the Chief to manoeuvre them away from the dock wall.

Stan and his men were the second to last team to be dropped off. All had gone well with virtually no incidents during the landings, except for when one of the SAS troopers had misplaced his footing and slipped from the deck and into the river. His splashes and cries of panic as his equipment attempted to drag him under rang out into the surrounding area and soon began to attract the attention of hundreds of infected.

They appeared in droves and came out from behind every shadow and every building. They lumbered towards the dock and their moans of excitement and aggressive snarls grew louder as the mass advanced. As the boat pulled away and the sailors hoisted the half-drowned soldier back on board, dozens of ravenous walking corpses surged towards the water's edge. They tumbled into the river and were sucked under by the currents as they blindly reached out for the U-boat. The landing was aborted and a secondary drop off was chosen a few hundred metres further along the river.

"Okay, Stan, this is you, old friend," Captain Werner said quietly as they approached Tower Bridge.

Stan looked out at the iconic structure and saw nothing of the internationally recognisable bridge that it had once been. During the outbreak, the government had ordered the quarantine of the entire southern half of the city and most of the crossings had been blown. The only one to escape the carnage of high explosives was the Dartford Bridge, situated further to the east. All that was now left intact of Tower Bridge were the suspension spans on either side of the river. In the centre sat the smashed ruins of the two towers still sitting on top of the piers and the twisted fragments of the bascules that had once formed the centre. Its black shape stood out against the charcoal coloured clouds that swept by overhead. Its broken and warped remains looked like the carcass of some colossal monster that had fallen there and rotted away to its bones.

Down on the foredeck, Taff and the remainder of the team waited patiently for the boat to slowly manoeuvre into position. Stan turned to Werner and nodded. He thrust out his arm and took the Captain's hand in his own.

"I'll see you back at the island when it's all over. Good luck, Stan," Werner said as he locked eyes with his old friend and forced a smile.

"You too, and thanks for the lift," Stan replied, simply.

Down on the deck, Stan positioned himself at the head of the team and waited for the gangplank to be brought into position. He would lead the way, as was his habit. *A good commander always leads from the front*, he was always fond of saying. He turned and looked at the faces of his men lined up behind him. He could see the tenseness in their eyes and he would have been lying if he said he did not feel apprehensive himself. They were about to walk into a city holding an estimated three to four-million reanimated corpses so it was understandable to feel a degree of trepidation. However, he refused to show it. His men were extremely experienced and tough but the sight of fear etched into their commander's face would undermine the resolve of any man.

They all looked back at him and nodded that they were ready. No words needed to be spoken and despite the radios that they carried, they would work entirely on hand signals and well-practised drills. They all knew their jobs and what needed to be done, and from there on in, they would be relying on the ability of the men beside them knowing exactly what was expected from them.

Stan leaned forward and shrugged against his heavy pack. The straps had already begun to cut into his shoulders and the weight was pressing down on his pelvis and spine. He carried his weapons and ammunition in his assault vest and along with the pistol on his hip, he held a Heckler & Koch MP-5 in his hands. It was a much smaller and lighter weapon than the M-4s and Minimi Light Machineguns that the others were carrying. It was a 9mm sub-machinegun and much easier to handle with the reduced mobility and dexterity in his damaged right arm. He could fire the MP-5 one handed if he needed to and at close quarters or in confined spaces, with its high rate of fire and easy handling, it was the ideal weapon.

All of them were carrying a large amount of equipment. Along with their personal ammunition of twenty magazines each, pistols, and three high-explosive grenades, they were carrying spare rounds for the two Minimis carried by Danny and Bull. Every man had an extra two-hundred rounds of belted ammunition tucked into his vest for the gunners. In their packs they had the 'music-bins' that had been supplied by Doctor Warren and his team of scientists. S-Mines, enough water and rations to last them up to a week, medical kit, and a range of other items to suit the individual jobs of each man were crammed into every available space. There had been very little room amongst their equipment for comforts and sleeping bags had been exchanged for lightweight quilted army blankets that scrunched down to a size that was no larger than a grapefruit.

The deck crew silently placed out the gangplank and stepped back. Stan moved forward. He looked up towards the conning tower and saw the faint outline of the watch crew. He recognised the head and shoulders of Werner and gave a nod before he turned and headed up the narrow bridge towards the dock.

One by one, the six men stepped on to the solid ground of the city of London. Suddenly they felt exposed and vulnerable as they took up defensive positions amongst the debris and equipment that littered the dockside. They snapped on their night vision goggles and waited for a few minutes as they watched the shadows and adjusted to their new settings.

The ground was still wet from the rain that had now ceased. Drips continued to fall from the tin roofs of the sheds that lined the small harbour and sent up a cacophony of high-pitched rings as they splashed into the puddles that covered the ground below. The wind blew litter and loose materials around but there were no sounds indicating that the infected were in the area or signs that they were coming.

Stan turned and raised his small green light and flashed his signal to the men standing on the U-boat's bridge. A few moments later, after quickly checking his GPS and then consulting his compass to confirm their position and intended direction of travel, he stood and began to patrol towards the gates leading out from the dock. Beyond was the dead city.

For a while, as the team patrolled through the streets close to the riverside, they saw no hint of the infected. The area seemed deserted but the signs of the plague were everywhere around them. Cars jammed the roads and every door and window that they passed by was smashed inwards. Barricades all around the city had failed to hold back the grotesque hordes of reanimated corpses. No matter how well constructed, all of them had collapsed eventually. When London had finally been abandoned, it was estimated that more than sixty percent of its population had been killed or added to the ranks of the walking dead. Much of the remainder of the survivors died as they fled and according to the scientists, many had gravitated back towards the urban areas out of instinct when they reanimated.

Stan stopped at a junction and checked his navigation again. The rest of the team went static around him and took cover in the shadows. Ahead of them was a long street that was headed in the direction of their intended LUP, Lying Up Position. A tall apartment building attached to a factory complex had been chosen by Stan to be their base of operations. From the high rooftop, they would be able to see clearly the three large junctions where they intended to place the sound devices and attract the swarms of dead. They were large open spaced intersections that would allow large numbers of the infected to congregate, making it easy for the air force to despatch while the over-watch position remained far enough away to keep the men out of the danger zone.

The other teams had picked similar locations within their AoRs, Areas of Responsibility, and providing that the plan worked, vast numbers of the dead could be destroyed before the ground troops began their break-in from the south. As the ground troops pushed forward through the city, the Special Forces teams would leave their over-watch positions and link up and join in on the advance as they swept through the streets.

Stan peered down along the dark grey street. He could see nothing but the lines of the buildings and the deep shadows that were cast around them. Even through the NVGs, it was difficult to penetrate the dense blackness that was surrounding them. There was no movement but he could not be sure if it was safe or not. For all he knew, there could be a million sets of eyes staring back at him and lying in wait for the men to stumble into an ambush of rotting flesh and snapping teeth.

He wondered if he had made the right decision to stay above ground for the insertion. Two of the other teams had opted to travel through the sewers and underground train tunnels but Stan had felt that they would be more or less trapped if they were detected and staying above the streets was also easier for navigation and communications back to the command centre if the situation dictated.

The street looked desolate. Nothing moved except for the light pieces debris that drifted on the wind and the bloated rats that scurried through the gutters. Stan looked across to Bobby and Marty and nodded, signalling them to lead off. The team followed closely behind in two columns, one on either side of the road, hugging the shadows and the static vehicles at the curb's edge.

Somewhere in the next street a tin can rolled along on the breeze and rattled loudly as it bounced its way over the tarmac. Somewhere else up ahead of them, a heavy object crashed to the floor and echoed out over the rooftops of the surrounding buildings. As the noise dissipated, the lingering moan of a dead woman drifted out along the street.

Marty raised his hand and the men instantly stopped and dropped to one knee. They waited patiently, scanning their arcs with their weapons at the ready while Marty and Bobby inched forward towards a junction just ahead of them.

There they stopped and watched the streets to their left and right. Through the green glow of their NVGs, they could see a number of distant dark figures wandering aimlessly through the stalled traffic and making their way towards them, but it did not appear as though the team had been detected. The dead were clearly just staggering in whatever direction their bodies faced, with no particular destination. They lurched and waddled, and looked almost comical in their sluggish and ungainly movements, but the sight of their silhouettes stalled any amusement in their observers. Some were bloated to the point of near bursting as the gases continued to expand within their rotting stomachs, and others, having been consumed to near skeletal, appeared demonic. All infected were terrifying to behold. Even the fresh ones were devoid of anything human and their pale lifeless eyes and their horrific poignant moans, tested the steel of the toughest and most experienced men and women.

Bobby looked back to the others and signalled for them to move up and begin crossing the open junction and into the next street. In the old days, during conventional operations, they would have covered the gap as quickly as possible to avoid being shot in the open by snipers. Now, they were facing a very different enemy from the men they had fought against over the years. They kept their pace slow and deliberate. The dead were attracted to sound and sudden movement, and in the darkness of night, it would be difficult for them to distinguish distant shapes moving at an unhurried pace.

Once they were clear of the intersection, the six men continued ahead. Bobby and Marty moved back up to the front and took on the role as lead scouts for the team. They checked the vehicles as they passed, the open doorways of the buildings, and the gaping dark windows. Their heads swivelled continuously and their weapons pointed in the same direction that their eyes moved. The silencers they had attached would keep the noise of their fire down to a minimum. However, in a closed and confined area such as the streets between the buildings, the sharp crack of muffled shots and the inevitable snap of their speeding rounds would quickly attract a large number of corpses that would overwhelm them, despite their attempts at stealth. Using their weapons would be a last resort. Instead, they relied on their ability to remain undetected and seeing the dead before they were a threat.

A short while later and the team abruptly halted again. Up ahead of them, the street was blocked. It was not stalled traffic, collapsed buildings, or debris that prevented them from going any further. It was the dead.

A wall of darkness stretched from one side of the road to the other, cramming the street as the infected stood shoulder to shoulder in a mass of rotting flesh. Stan and his men waited for a minute and observed the crowd. They were not moving and seemed to be just standing still and completely inactive. An incessant murmur hummed out from within the horde like the sound of a million uttered words that were impossible to understand.

Marty and Bobby began to inch their way back towards Stan as the remainder continued to observe the multitude of static corpses in front of them.

"Fuck me, this place stinks," Marty whispered as he crouched down beside Stan and took cover behind an overturned police car.

They were nestled in what had once been a hastily constructed defensive line. Police and army vehicles were parked across the street in an attempt to block the road. At some point during the early days of the spread, they had attempted to halt the advance of the infected into the central part of the city. Soldiers and police officers had stood side-by-side, firing into the hordes that charged towards their barricades.

It had been a futile attempt. Amongst the piles of brass cases that littered the ground, sat the stripped bones of the fallen defenders. Dozens of dismembered skeletons lay strewn over a wide area and hundreds more littered the road on the enemy side of the barrier. As valiantly as the men and women had fought, they had done nothing to slow the dead. They had been overwhelmed and consumed by the plague as the ravenous creatures had swept on through and into the city centre.

Stan was staring at his GPS but due to the buildings around him, the signal was taking its time finding a link with the satellites in orbit high above them. He looked up, eyed the dark windows and doors on either side of the street, and then looked back the way they had come, considering their options. He did not cherish the idea of heading back and trying to find another way around, but moving through the dark buildings that lined the street was just as unappealing.

"Which way, Stan?" Bobby asked as he took a tentative peek over the vehicle towards the dark throng at the end of the road.

Stan did not reply immediately but finally, he nodded towards the front of a department store to the right of their position.

"We'll cut through there and see if we can skirt around them. We're a kilometre short of our LUP."

Marty and Bobby exchanged a nervous glance but they trusted Stan's judgement and they both preferred that to going back in the direction they had already travelled. They silently approached the doors and peered into the eerie darkness.

The six men moved in through the gaping smashed doorway and began to push forward through the wreckage of the store. Inside, through their night vision goggles, they saw a landscape of various shades of green and black as they scanned the ground floor for any movement. Displays and counters were upturned all over the place, and mannequins littered the floor, having been torn to shreds by the infected in their confusion while they ripped their way through in search of the living.

The team moved slowly and fanned out into an extended line as they advanced through the interior. They could smell death lingering in the air but could see no infected inside. Evidence of their presence was in abundance but nothing moved or lurched towards them from within the blackness. They did their best to remain completely silent but it was inevitable that the occasional crunch of glass would ring out from beneath their feet. Each time, they all froze to the spot and scanned their weapons in all directions as they expected to see dark figures racing for them.

They passed by the escalators leading to the upper floors and continued towards the rear of the department store. Above their heads, they could hear the occasional dull thud and thump as something moved about in the darkness. It could have been the infected or it may have been survivors, but they were not there to investigate.

Marty led them through a door and they emerged into the storage area of the shop. Racks and boxes filled nearly every space in the cramped room and for a while, they remained still as they scrutinised their surroundings. One behind the other, they headed for the rear doors that they hoped would lead them into the alleyway of an adjacent building.

Bobby raised his rifle and pointed it at the exit while Marty counted backwards from three and then pushed the bar of the fire escape, allowing the heavy door to swing open. Immediately, Bobby stepped back and began to squeeze his trigger up to the point just before firing.

A figure stood framed in the doorway and silhouetted in the pale light that filtered in from outside. Its body was emaciated with the white bones of its ragged shoulders shining brightly in contrast to its dark and withered skin. Its scrawny neck appeared far too delicate to support the weight of its head and hanging around its knees, the fetid remains of its intestines spewed out from the gaping cavern of its abdomen. Its long wiry hair stood out in strands from its scalp and it cocked its head continuously as it emitted questioning grunts and groans. It was completely blind. Its eyes were gone, along with much of the soft tissue of its face. In their place were colonies of maggots that squirmed through the remains of the flesh and slowly ate away at the muscle and sinew that was left behind. The creature could see nothing but it was obvious that it could detect movement and sound close by as it stood, trying to zero in on the source.

Marty reached out and slammed the stock of his rifle into the side of the figure's head. The dull crack echoed in the narrow passage behind the store and was quickly followed by the sound of the body hitting the ground as it collapsed under the heavy blow.

Marty stepped forward, slammed his heel down into the side of its head, and felt the skull collapse beneath his boot. The infected let out a low grunt then remained still as the men filed out from the building and into the anticipated alleyway.

It took some time before they had managed to circumnavigate the large build-up of infected in the area. Sneaking through shattered buildings, along narrow backstreets, and over the numerous corpses that littered the pavements, the team slowly advanced. They stopped regularly, taking cover in the shadows or behind the debris of civilisation as groups of meandering corpses staggered by, completely unaware of the living men that were

THE DEAD WALK THE EARTH II

close by and watching them through the green glow of their night vision.

By the time they were approaching their destination the sky above had begun its slow transition from night to day. Thick banks of cloud still raced across from one horizon to the next but the slowly rising sun was beginning to penetrate through the blackness of the night and illuminate the earth below. Stan and his men soon had no need to wear their NVGs. They could see clearly enough the city around them and the remains of the thousands of bodies that filled the streets.

After four months of abandonment by the living, the buildings were already showing signs of decay. The pavements were beginning to become overgrown with weeds and the smaller animals and insects had not hesitated to take up residence in every available space. Nearly every window of the city had been smashed, leaving the interiors wide open to the elements and everywhere the men looked, Mother Nature was claiming back her ground.

"That's the factory, just up ahead of us," Stan whispered as the six of them sat huddled against the side of a wall.

Ahead of them, an old brick building that looked out of place from the rest of its surroundings was sprawled over a wide area. It was built from red brick with large ornate windows and chimneystacks that towered high into the sky and dominated the land around it. Surrounding the complex was a wall with an old iron gate. The entrance had been violently forced open at some point and sat precariously clinging to its hinges. By whom, they could not tell. It could have been the living, looking for supplies or a place to hide, or it could have been the infected hunting the people that were trying to get away from them.

The place looked deserted. There was no sign of movement beyond the gate or in amongst the buildings of the factory, warehouses, or offices. Beyond the complex, the tall building of the apartment block could be seen. Its modern architecture, mostly glass and steel, was in stark contrast to the nineteenth century brick of the factory. From what the men had seen on the maps and satellite imagery, the apartments shared the same grounds as the factory. The perimeter wall of the industrial buildings had been extended to encompass the new addition with a wall separating the two buildings.

"Marty, Bobby," Stan hissed, "have a look about and give us a call on the radio if it's clear. Bull, give them some cover."

The three men nodded and moved towards the gate. Bull positioned himself close to the entrance's security cabin while the other two moved in to the complex. Stan, Taff, and Danny remained in the street, keeping an eye on the outer perimeter.

The road was filled with burned and overturned vehicles of all shapes and sizes. Bodies lay motionless in the gutters and countless bones and pieces of blood-stained and tattered clothing cluttered the pavements.

Danny noticed the abundance of odd shoes discarded within the street and absentmindedly wondered just how many corpses there were walking about with one bare foot. The thought amused him and caused him to smile fleetingly.

Taff looked at him and raised an inquisitive eyebrow, but Danny shook his head and continued to scan his surroundings.

The buildings facing the factory lay in ruin. Some had been burned to their frames while the remainder bore the marks of the devastation in their masonry. Smashed windows, caved in doors, and bullet holes pockmarking their outer walls. There was no visible sign of the infected but their intermittent moans could still be heard through the adjacent streets and from within the buildings. Apart from the static debris that filled the area, the street was devoid of anything moving.

"All clear. The place looks empty, Stan," Marty's voice informed them over the radio five minutes later.

With a nod from their commander, the remainder of the team moved in through the factory's entrance and met up with the others. From there, they split into three groups. Bull and Danny remained at the entrance, covering the gate with their light machineguns, while the others began a three-hundred and sixty degree sweep of the building's grounds, moving in opposite directions and meeting up on the far side.

They checked the doors, the outbuildings and more importantly, the wall that encompassed the factory complex. Next, they chose their point of entry and prepared to move inside the main building. The two gunners were called up from the gate area to join the rest of their men at the large bay doors leading into the factory floor from the far right hand corner.

Bobby led them in with Bull close on his shoulder. With the extra firepower of the Minimi, it would afford them to put down a massive weight of fire into the confined space of the factory while they withdrew to the open area outside.

Inside they found very much what they expected to see in a building of that sort. Old and rusted machinery, grated walkways, masses of piping, and asbestos-coated partitions that separated the factory floor from the office areas. Corrosion coated nearly every surface, along with dust and dead vegetation. It appeared that the place had not been in use for many decades and weeds and moss had begun to spread over the abandoned equipment and workstations.

Above them, the corrugated roof bore the tell-tale signs of neglect. Large holes gaped up into the morning sky and networks of pipes, some of them hanging from their rickety brackets, crisscrossed the lofty ceiling. The place had probably sat slowly rotting away and steadily becoming forgotten about by the city council. The swathes of graffiti that covered every available space and the empty beer cans and used syringes that carpeted the floor was evidence enough that the place was long out of use.

The six men spread out and advanced along through the main workshop. Their eyes scanned every inch of the ground and peered into every dark recess between machinery and workstations. Small offices and cupboards without windows presented themselves as dark caves needing to be cleared by torchlight and the countless nooks and crannies that could hold a threat had to be checked before the advance could continue.

Everything was done in complete silence and systematically. It took them just over an hour to confirm that the area was safe. They had seen no infected, but evidence of them having been there at some point was in abundance. In one of the offices, Danny had discovered the remains of a number of people. It had been impossible to estimate their number due to the state of their bodies. They were little more than skeletons, completely stripped of their clothing and flesh, dismembered and scattered over the floor.

Next, they moved out and towards the tall apartment block next door. It was separated from the factory by a breezeblock wall with an old rusty gate obstructing the entrance. It was easy for the team to bypass the corroded padlock and enter into the narrow walkway along the side of the building. Again, Bull remained behind to cover the factory and watch their rear. He placed himself at the gateway that separated the old Victorian building from the more modern living space.

"You be careful, fellas," he whispered to them as Stan led the team along the walkway, "and don't talk to any strangers."

"Even if they have a huge bag of sweets?" Taff quipped through his radio as he followed on at the rear of the group.

They made their way along towards the rear of the building. It had originally been the administration offices for the factory, built in the 1970s and had been converted into an apartment complex when the factory had closed down. The car park at the back was still filled with dozens of vehicles and the doors leading in through the main entrance had been barricaded. Like every other defensive position throughout the city, the barriers had not been able to withstand the sustained assaults of the infected. Now, the doors lay smashed and pushed to the side. Overturned furniture that had been hastily piled against the entrance filled the space beyond the threshold and swathes of dried blood covered the walls and floor of the foyer.

Floor by floor, while Danny remained in the entrance hall, Stan, Taff, Marty, and Bobby moved through the building, clearing each apartment as they went. Most of the doors had been forced open or left askew and many were now empty. Trails of blood were everywhere and it appeared that the occupants had either turned or escaped through the chaos. Human remains were in abundance and the powerful stench of rotting bodies was heavy in the air. However, there were no indications that any of the infected were still inside.

An hour later and they reached the final floor. There were six storeys to the building and four apartments on each, except for the top level. There were only two doors there. Much larger and more luxurious than the floors beneath, these had been the penthouse apartments that would have cost their owners twice, maybe three times as much as the rest of the residences in the building.

In the last apartment to be cleared, Bobby was almost taken by surprise. Turning the handle and pushing the door inwards, he was greeted with the gaunt faces and lifeless eyes of two infected that came charging along the hallway towards him. He flung himself to the side of the doorframe and raised his rifle just as the first of the bodies shot out from the gloomy apartment. Bobby's timing and judgement were precise and the stock of his M-4 crashed into the side of the decomposing woman's head as her ghastly face appeared over the threshold. The impact sent her crashing into the doorframe with a loud thud and then into a heap on the floor where she lay sprawled and motionless with thick congealed blood oozing out from the gaping wound in her skull.

As soon as his blow struck the first body, Bobby snatched back his rifle and thrust it into the face of the infected that quickly appeared behind the first. With a loud crack, the weapon struck the dead man square in face. The man reeled back along the hallway as the butt of the rifle crashed into his features, shattering his nose and cheekbones. He let out a startled grunt as the blow landed and he dropped to the floor as his legs continued forward and his body was thrown backwards from the force of the blow. Bobby stepped into the doorway and simultaneously drew his knife from its scabbard. With a single thrust, he pushed the blade through the reanimated corpse's eye and ended its unholy existence.

The rest of the team had remained on the landing, watching Bobby as he expertly dealt with the threat. They knew that he could handle the situation and any attempt to help him would have only resulted in them getting in the way.

Bobby huffed and nodded to the others before disappearing into the dark hallway. Taff followed closely and together, they cleared the spacious rooms, one by one. There were no more infected waiting for them. However, what they did find were the bodies of two children, eaten to the bone, lying strewn across the living room carpet in vast pools of dried blood.

Stan and Taff moved up to the roof to confirm they had eyes-on on their targets and to establish communications with the Operations Room on the Isle of Wight. To the south they were able to see the junctions they intended to use as their muster points for the infected clearly. Visibility was better than they had anticipated and they were able to see far into the distance along the ruined street. There were quite a few reanimates wandering around through the buildings, roads, and intersections but they were not in anything like the expected mass numbers they would be once the sound devices were triggered.

"Should be pretty straight forward," Taff shrugged as they sat at the lip of the wall that ran around the roof's edge. "We have good visibility and there are plenty of routes leading in and out of the area."

Stan grunted as he watched the targets through his binoculars. He raised his view and eyed the buildings directly across from them.

"We've got an audience."

Taff followed Stan's gaze and across the street, over an open patch of ground that had once been a small inner-city park, he saw an office block. It was less than a hundred metres away and almost every window in the upper floors had a sea of pale faces pressed up against it. He snatched the binoculars from Stan and looked for himself. Thousands of vacant eyes stared back at him. He could see their mutilated hands scratching at the glass panes in an attempt to reach across to the men on the apartment block's rooftop. There was no sound but he could hear their hunger filled moans in his mind.

"It's a good thing they're as dumb as a bag of spanners, Stan. We could be in deep shit if they worked out that all they needed to do was walk down the stairs and cross over the road to get us."

"Yeah," Stan agreed, "we'll have to keep our movements to a minimum up here. We'll stay inside the building and keep eyes on the junction during the day from the top floors and only use the roof at night."

"Sounds good to me," Taff replied. He wanted to get off the roof. He did not like the fact that thousands of ravenous corpses were watching him.

The men split into pairs and began working on securing their location. Before they could think about continuing their mission, they needed a base to conduct their operations from. Doors were sealed and holes in the walls were blocked. Escape routes were identified and a sentry system was set in place. On the roof of the building, they placed a number of ropes that run down the wall and into the alleyway leading into the factory complex. From there the men would be able to escape into the road on the eastern side of the perimeter wall and in the opposite direction from the main entry point to the apartments.

Repairing the main gate leading into the factory complex was out of the question. Apart from it being nominated as their primary escape route, trying to lift the heavy iron railings back into place would result in noise and their position being compromised. The gate would remain as it was but a trip-wire attached to an electronic circuit would be placed to cover the gap in the barrier. It would be a passive defence that would alert the team through a flashing light and a small constant bleep in their command post within the upper floors of the apartments. They chose not to place an S-Mine there because a lone wandering infected was not necessarily a threat. Even a few of them, accidentally stumbling into the factory grounds, would be no cause for concern to the men. Triggering a mine at the gate would be a complete compromise and an overreaction and escalation to a situation that could easily be dealt with silently and more effectively.

The entrance to the car park at the rear of the apartments was a simple matter. It would remain open. Due to the distance between the gateway and the building's foyer, where the sentry position was located, it would be easy for the team to see any of the infected entering into the grounds long before they became an immediate threat. Again, providing that the dead did not become aware of their presence and swarm through in large numbers, small groups could be easily dispatched with minimum fuss.

The S-Mines were placed within the buildings where they would cause maximum damage. Inside the factory, which was their fall-back position, the Bouncing-Betties were sited beside the main entrances. One was also placed halfway up the stairs of the apartment block but its wire was left detached. It would be connected only in the event that the men had to retreat to the upper floors. However, the factory mines were rigged and made ready, and they would explode the moment anyone triggered them.

"Okay," Stan said as he completed his checks of their defences, "I'd like to get some eyes on the routes in and out before last light arrives. Bull, you and Bobby are with me. Ready to move in five minutes."

"Bollocks," Bull grunted.

13

For the previous two nights, sleep had not come easily for Christopher. The events that had occurred out in the parking lot a couple of days before remained vividly etched into his mind and stubbornly clinging to the outer edges of his every thought. No matter how hard he tried to blot it all out, the memories would somehow become the main focus of his attention as he relived the events, over and over in his head. He was emotionally exhausted. Since murdering his sister, he had laughed and he had cried, sometimes the two reactions arriving simultaneously and leaving him on the verge of madness as the split in his psyche battled for supremacy of his mental state.

Every time he closed his eyes, he saw the face of Tina and heard her screams and pleas as she dragged her wounded body away from him. He could still feel the pistol in his hand and the juddering recoil along his forearm as the booming shots echoed in his ears. The excited wails of the dead and the gut wrenching shrieks of his sister clawed at his brain long after the events were over.

He sat for hours at a time, reliving that terrible day and questioning himself on his actions. Then, he would slip into a trance, remaining motionless for hours with virtually nothing going on inside his head. Other times, he sat ranting to himself, justifying what he had done and reminding an imaginary audience of the pain and suffering, both physical and mental that his sadistic sister had subjected him to.

Despite his fluctuating emotions, the incident had not dampened his appetite. Within minutes of returning to the office, he had smashed open the storeroom door and began stuffing himself to the point that his head spun and his body shook from the sudden influxes of large amounts of sugar. The diet had clearly come to an end and he indulged himself to the point where he was incapable of standing.

Outside, the moon shone brightly over the car park and the long industrial buildings, casting the landscape in an eerie glow while Christopher lay sleeping fitfully in his sleeping bag. The office space had descended into disarray. Tina was no longer there to ensure that they were organised and the place was kept tidy. Their emergency equipment and packs had been flung across the room and into the corner where they were left and forgotten. The makeshift toilet was close to overflowing and the shower bag remained full to the point of bursting. He no longer bothered to wash his hands or his festering body. He did not care about the colonies of bacteria that took up residence beneath his armpits and amongst his crotch. Christopher would do whatever he pleased now and there was no one to stop him.

The floor was littered with plastic wrappers from sweets and bars of chocolate. Empty boxes, cans, and bottles occupied every surface and would remain there for the foreseeable future. The PlayStation console he had brought up from the warehouse sat useless on the coffee table below the large television set into the wall. He had dragged it from its box and connected all the leads and power supply. He was more than aware that the power was out but for some reason, he had insisted in attempting to start it all up. For a whole hour he had sat staring at the television, willing it to flicker to life. Subconsciously, he questioned what he was doing but he refused to answer.

His large body lay cocooned inside the thick synthetic fibre filled material of the sleeping bag. It twitched and shuddered and his grunts and groans betrayed yet another of Christopher's frequent nightmares. He woke with a start, gasping and crying. Confused and still torn between consciousness and sleep, he called out into the darkness.

"Tina? Are you there, sis?"

The room remained silent except for his heavy breathing. After a moment, he regained his senses and remembered where he was and that he was alone. Reaching his palm up to his face, he wiped at the glistening sweat that soaked his brow.

"Fucking hell," he sighed as he lay back down. "Fucking hell."

In his dream, he had awoken and seen the faint silhouette of his sister sitting in the far corner of the room, staring back at him without making a sound. He had crawled from his bed and moved towards her, grabbing one of the camping lights from the table. As he approached, he could hear soft whimpers coming from her direction and fumbling with his light, he had raised it up so that he could see her more clearly.

What he saw had instantly snatched the breath from him. She was completely unrecognisable as his sister but somehow, he knew that it was Tina. Her face was gone and in its place was a grinning, blood smeared skull. Out from her nose and eye sockets slithered hundreds of maggots and worms, and a cockroach scurried across from one side of her bare cranium to the next. He recoiled in horror, almost tripping over the low table behind him. As he retreated, the body of Tina had risen up from the corner and it began to advance on him, snapping its jaws ceaselessly and laughing manically.

Christopher tripped and landed heavily on his back. Unable to move from fright and shock, he lay motionless while the emaciated corpse of his sister continued to approach. The last thing he had seen in the faint glow of the camping light had been that horrific grinning skull, slowly descending towards his own face.

Now he was awake. His chest was heaving as he fought to catch his breath. He stared up at the foam-tiled ceiling of the manager's office and wondered how long it would be before the visions would finally stop haunting his thoughts and dreams. He wanted the conflicting emotions to cease and leave him alone. He had suffered enough throughout his life and he wanted the pain and torture to be over.

He reached out and felt for the pistol he had left on the floor beside him. He carried it everywhere with him and slept with it close to his pillow. He had seen numerous characters, good and bad, do the same thing in the movies and felt that he too should adopt the same habit. His fingers closed around the cool steel of the barrel and he lifted it towards him, holding it close to his chest for comfort. He was still annoyed with himself for wasting so much ammunition trying to shoot Tina. He now only had one bullet left in the magazine. Again, he silently reminded himself that he would not need it due to the fact that he would never venture beyond the safety of the building's inner walls.

For the next two hours, he lay staring up at the ceiling. He tried hard to drift back off to sleep but all his efforts were futile.

His mind was filled with too many thoughts. Some were memories and others were fantasies. In the end, as the morning light began to filter through the tiny cracks between the thick cloth that covered the windows, Christopher gave up on trying to sleep. He sat up, running his fingers through the thick greasy curls atop his head. He pulled his hand away and rubbed his palms against the sides of his sleeping bag. He considered, very briefly, having a shower but quickly dismissed the thought and instead, opted to have breakfast.

He set up his portable gas cooking stove and proceeded to begin heating a hefty helping of spam and baked beans. He had grown to love and crave that particular meal since arriving at the warehouse. Then, after being starved of that simple pleasure for over a week by Tina's enforced diet, his desire for it had gone into overdrive and he had eaten more than his share of it since breaking into the storeroom.

With his meal ready and his growling belly waiting in anticipation, Christopher snatched up his spoon and made to begin delving into the saucepan. He paused and looked around at his surroundings. The room was gloomy. It was difficult to see into the corners or through the shadows beneath the tables. Suddenly, he felt a shiver ripple through his large body. He was strangely aware of something but he had no idea what it was. He jumped up, clutching the handle of the pan in one hand and made his way across to the windows. He reached up, grabbed the thick material of the curtains, and forcefully tugged them to the side.

He was hit with a barrage of light and he recoiled from its painful brightness against his sleepy eyes. The low sun had just risen above the rooftops of the warehouses at the far end of the parking area and he was bombarded with its full brilliance. He looked away and blinked repeatedly, seeing white spots flashing across his vision. His eyes eventually settled after a few seconds and he was able to turn his attention back to the large panes of glass that overlooked the dead world beyond his sanctuary.

He gasped and stumbled back from the window. He was suddenly overcome with terror, revulsion, loneliness, confusion, and shock. All those emotions hit him in the same instant, overwhelming his already weakened and fragile mind and almost sending him reeling into a black abyss. He let out a whimper and fell to his knees as the vision that greeted him sapped all of his strength and smashed his composure.

Outside, a low mist had rolled into the expansive car park and covered the ground in a metre deep white haze that was impossible to penetrate with the naked eye. The roofs of the abandoned cars poked out from the fog like the hunched backs of mechanical beasts emerging from a swamp, and the light poles that lined the parking bays reached out above the mist like the bare trees of a sparse wood in winter time. It was not the unnerving fog or the inanimate objects sitting within it that had made Christopher recoil with fright.

It was the hundreds of dark featureless figures that stood staring back up at him that snatched his breath away. Visible only from the waste up, they appeared like blackened spectres drifting through the open area, searching for a poor soul to haunt. Now he could hear them. Their low incessant moans drifted up towards him and penetrated the glass barrier, clawing at Christopher's ears as he knelt staring out at them. His mouth hung slack and he did not notice that he had dropped the saucepan from his grasp, spilling its hot steaming contents over the floor and the bare flesh of his legs.

The mass of dead were slowly meandering towards the far side of the car park and the area of the gate where he had last seen Tina, two days ago. More of them were clambering at the main entrance to the building, directly below him. He could see the throng of infected beneath him, pushing and jostling one another as they attempted to claw their way in through the barricaded doors of the reception. The thuds and rattles of their hands striking the impenetrable barrier joined with the wretched voices that he heard filtering into the building. He had not heard them sooner because he had not listened for them. He had felt safe in his hideout, protected by the strong walls and the barricades that he and his sister had built. Now, seeing them out there, his ears had also focussed and he could now hear them clearly, as though they were there, inside the room with him.

The sudden thought made him spin around and his frightened eyes began searching and scrutinising every door and every shadow. He whimpered and his vision blurred with tears. His lips began to quiver and he screwed his eyes shut and began wishing the creatures away, hoping beyond hope that it was all just another one of his frequent and vivid nightmares.

"Oh shit," he whispered as he began climbing back to his feet.

For a few moments, he stood staring out through the window wearing just his soiled t-shirt and a pair of less than brilliant white underpants. His toes smeared the beans and spam into the carpet as he stepped into the mess, oblivious to the hot food that scorched his feet. He leaned close to the window, pressing his greasy cheek against the cold glass as he attempted to see what the infected were doing at the far end of the building.

"Oh shit, oh shit," he repeated, realising that he had somehow brought this upon himself. Shooting his sister had attracted them to him and it was his own fault that hundreds of them were now outside and wanting to get in. He was sure of that.

At the far end, around the area of the side gate, he could see hundreds of them and more and more were joining the crowd by the second. However, he quickly realised that the mass was not growing as would be expected from the increasing numbers. His eyes widened in sudden realisation. The crowd was not growing because they were somehow getting through the gate and into the staff parking area by the loading bays.

"Shit," he exclaimed and turned towards the door.

Still only semi-dressed, he snatched up his pistol and ran into the corridor, heading for the stairs. By now, he was crying again and mumbling incoherently. He could not understand how this had happened. He had closed the gate himself and ensured that the bolts were firmly in place before he headed back into the warehouse.

Had the fence collapsed? Did the dead know how to manipulate locking mechanisms?

He doubted that either was a possibility but he could not think of any other explanation. He *must* have made a mistake somewhere along the line.

Bounding down the thirty-five steps that had caused his so much pain and suffering, Christopher reached the foyer. He stood for a moment, staring at the tables, chairs, and heavy vending machines that blocked the main entrance. The shuddering bangs from the other side made his skin tighten and goose bumps to form all over his body. He was incapable of moving for a short while as the horror of the situation was fully realised. They knew he was there. Somehow, they knew he was hiding inside and they wanted to get in.

His bare feet seemed to become warm suddenly, despite the chill of the linoleum floor of the foyer. The faint sound of trickling water became distinct over the loud hammering of the dozens of dead hands against the doors. Christopher looked down and quickly saw that he had lost control of his bodily functions. A dark wet patch was quickly spreading out across the front of his filth-ridden underpants and streams of urine cascaded along his inner thighs, forming into a golden puddle at his feet.

"Oh God, no," he muttered.

It was not the fact that he had messed himself that caused him to pray to God. It was the hopelessness of his situation. At that moment, he really wished that Tina were there to help him. He began crying louder, calling for his sister to save him from the monsters outside. He wanted her to come bursting in through the door, swinging her crowbar and beating at the heads of the infected and rescuing him from the hideous creatures.

The door leading into the reception area from the small row of offices suddenly flew open and crashed against the wall with a juddering clang. Christopher spun around, believing for a moment that his prayers had been answered and expecting to see his sister come charging to his rescue.

His hopes were quickly dashed as a sea of rotted faces rushed into the foyer. He screamed as the dead poured in, piling through the door and crashing into one another as more of them pushed from behind. At the sound of the high-pitched wail of the large meaty flesh standing in the open space before them, the multitude of walking corpses paused and stared back at Christopher, their pale flat eyes scrutinising him.

The first to recognise the man as their prey let out a gargling moan and the bodies behind quickly joined in with the lamenting chorus. As one, the crowd surged forward and ploughed through the doorway towards Christopher.

He was unable to move, frozen to the spot by the horror of what was happening to him. The army of reanimated corpses advanced on him, groaning and snapping their jaws as they reached out in front of them. Christopher began to step back, almost slipping in the pool of urine beneath his feet. He retreated further and raised his pistol in his shaking hands, aiming it at the lead creature as he began squeezing the trigger.

Nothing happened. The round did not explode from the barrel and the trigger did not click. It merely refused to work. He frantically pulled the trigger again and again but with no result. Tears were running down his face and his vision was quickly blurring as he continued to step backwards towards the stairs.

"Fuck, fuck," he exclaimed in a high-pitched, faltering voice.

He realised that he had not chambered a round. Reaching out with a trembling hand and numbed fingers, he gripped the top-slide and pulled back hard. The bolt scooped up the brass case and threw it into the breach with a metallic crunch and Christopher instantly snatched at the trigger. The round cracked loudly in the confined space and the flash of the muzzle blinded him for a second, as the bullet sprang from the barrel and sailed through the air at lightning speed where it smashed harmlessly into the wall above the doorframe.

With the last of his ammunition spent, Christopher turned and leapt onto the bottom step and began to race upwards towards the offices. He covered the distance quicker than he had ever done during his training sessions with Tina, and within just a few short seconds, he had reached the landing and was in the office again. He slammed the door shut and began dragging the large heavy couch over towards the entrance.

The footfalls of the dead and their incessant moans drifted up from the stairway and along the corridor and seemed to deliberately head for the office he was hiding in, filtering their way through the gap at the bottom of the door. He piled more office furniture on top of the couch, desperately hoping that it would be enough to stop them from getting in. Soon, the corridor outside was filled with the dark figures of the infected. Their hands and faces pressed up against the windows as they beat and gnawed at the glass, staring at him hungrily as he stood crying uncontrollably in the centre of the room.

He looked down at the empty pistol in his hands. The top-slide was locked to the rear, showing him an empty chamber and magazine. He began to cry all the more when he realised that he had wasted his last hope of denying the dead the satisfaction of being able to tear him apart while he was still alive.

"Tina," he yelled up at the ceiling in despair.

The dead beyond the window howled back at him, excited at the sight and sound of a living human being.

On the far side of the car park, a lone figure stood watching the events unfold. She had seen the large plump form at the window staring out at the sight of hundreds of bodies filling the parking area. She imagined the familiar sound of his whining voice as he realised that he had no way out and that the infected were in the building with him. She pictured him struggling to save himself and building pathetic barricades that would be nothing more than a small obstacle to the mass of corpses pushing against them. She heard the shot of the pistol and when no more followed, she surmised that the gun must have been empty. When she saw him moving within the upstairs office again, a faint smile creased her lips at the thought of him throwing away his last opportunity of a painless death.

For a while longer, she stood watching the big windows above the main entrance to the supermarket supply depot. She could see movement in the room but was unable to distinguish exactly who or what it was due to the reflection of the sun. Soon, however, she saw the large body of Christopher crash against the glass. His back was pressed up against the window and his arms were raised out in front of him. Eventually, he sank to the floor and curled himself into a ball as a multitude of other, darker figures piled in around him.

"What goes around, comes around, Chris," she grunted after a while and turned away.

Slowly, limping heavily on her damaged leg, Tina headed for the gateway and the access road leading into the industrial complex.

14

"For Christ's sake, you're not making a flower arrangement, Bobby," Bull whispered impatiently to the man crouching at the curb side beneath him. "Get it secured and let's get the fuck out of here."

"Nearly done," Bobby replied.

Bull remained standing, turning his body in a continuous three-hundred and sixty degree arc as he scanned the street and provided protection for the both of them. He held his Minimi close into his shoulder with his finger resting lightly against the trigger and his eyes peering over the sights as he kept a watch on their surroundings.

It had just gone midnight and Bull was beginning to feel uncomfortable and over exposed. They had been out on the ground for over three hours, slowly snaking their way through the maze of streets and avenues, avoiding the wandering infected and darting from one shadow to the next. They remained on high alert throughout, listening into the night and checking every patch of road through their night vision before exposing themselves from their hiding places. They would move just a few metres, stop and listen, and then begin the whole process of observing and examining their surroundings over again. By now, the constant vigilance, mixed with the suppressive night and the haunting wails of the dead that echoed through the streets had begun to claw at Bull's nerves.

They were far from their operating base in the apartment block, with no support but what they provided for each other. They had hidden in doorways and behind cars, holding their breath while hordes of the dead trampled by just metres away from them as they made their way to their target area. On three occasions they had needed to deal with individual corpses that stumbled too closely, dispatching them with their knives and doing all they could to remain undetected. It was not an easy task to do whilst out in the open and the strain was beginning to show.

Now, Bobby and Bull was situated at the most southern junction that they had earmarked for the final noise box. They were roughly one kilometre away from the factory and on the most extreme point of their operational boundaries. Behind them, headed north in a straight line and leading up to the apartments, two more of the reinforced waste paper baskets containing iPods had been planted at their respective junctions by other members of the team.

Each intersection covered a large expanse of ground. The roads were wide and the pavements were broader still, leaving plenty of open space to be filled by the infected once the operation moved into its next phase. Each noise box had been set at the base of a street light and secured with cable ties and a heavy-duty chain to stop them from being moved once Stan triggered them remotely. With the amount of infected that they expected to converge on the area and begin swarming around the source of the noise, the music boxes needed to remain secure and static. Initially, the team had considered placing them higher up so that they were out of reach but there were too many possibilities of something going wrong and noise being made while setting them up and placing the men in unnecessary danger.

"That's it, done," Bobby said as he raised himself to his feet and unslung his rifle from over his shoulder. "That thing's going nowhere. I don't care how many of those bags of shit pull on it. You good to go?"

"I was good to go the minute we got here," Bull scoffed under his breath. "Let's get moving, Bobby. I've had enough of playing chicken for one night."

The pair of them paused for a moment and checked the sprawling streets around them. Four major roads fed into the area along with a number of smaller avenues, all merging into the centre of the junction from different directions. In the luminescent glow of their NVGs they could see dark shapes, disfigured and lurching, ambling through the shadows and wandering along close to the sides of the buildings. The nearest of the dead were fifty metres away. A small group of them had gathered and clambered around a wrecked truck which lay on its side in the middle of the road. The vehicle had spilled its contents of boxes and steel barrels over a wide area of the street, creating obstacles that the clumsy bodies of the reanimated dead would bump into and tumble over as they blindly shuffled about. The cluster of infected feebly beat their hands against the vehicle's sides, showing no real effort in their attempts to get inside.

Bull turned and began to lead the way. They opted to follow the same path that they had taken on their way out, sticking to the proven route. They walked slowly, keeping their movements unhurried and deliberate to avoid attracting any attention to themselves from the thousands of watching eyes that surrounded them. All around, the streets reverberated with the ghostly moans of the dead and the clangs of objects being overturned or struck as the infected crashed about through the darkness.

Both men could not wait to be back in the relative safety of their base on the top floor apartment, but they refrained from allowing their eagerness to dictate their pace. The last phase of any mission was always the most perilous. Soldiers throughout history had often had a habit of letting their guard down when the end was in sight and it was then, regardless of how proficiently they had performed their task, that they became unstuck.

The two men turned into a street where the night seemed to turn darker still. The shadows of the tall buildings merged into one and blanketed the road that ran between them and rendered everything invisible to their watchful eyes. Even through their NVGs it was almost impossible to penetrate the blackness. The lack of ambient light that could be magnified by their goggles forced them to rely more upon their other senses.

Bull trusted his guts more than any other intuit. Over the years there had been very few occasions when his sixth sense, emanating from the pit of his stomach, had proven him wrong. Now his instincts were screaming at him to find somewhere to hide. He stopped and raised his hand, showing Bobby the flat of his palm while he kept the barrel of his machinegun pointed along the darkened street. A few seconds later, he swept his arm to the side, indicating for them to move into cover.

Bobby did not hesitate. He stepped to the side and took up position beside a low wall that jutted out from one of the buildings on his right. Bull quickly joined him and hunkered down in the shadows behind him.

"What is it?" Bobby whispered over his shoulder but keeping his attention and the barrel of his weapon focussed on the street.

"Not sure," Bull replied. "There's something moving up ahead and coming this way. I didn't see what or how many but they're definitely closing."

Bobby nodded and sunk deeper into the shadows, clutching his rifle tightly and readying himself for a fight. If it were a herd of the infected, they would just have to sit it out and hope that they were not seen. If it were just a few stragglers wandering aimlessly, then the knives of the two men would come into play. They listened intently, waiting for the distinct sounds of scraping feet and low grunts that always announced the arrival of the dead, but there was nothing happening close by. The usual night sounds of the lifeless city could be heard in the adjacent streets and over the buildings as the infected cried out into the darkness but there was nothing in close proximity to the two men crouching behind the small wall.

"You sure you saw something?" Bobby whispered after a minute of silence and beginning to wonder whether Bull was becoming a little too jittery.

"I didn't *see* anything," Bull snorted angrily. "I heard something and just got a feeling that there was something there."

"Oh right, so you were using your Jedi powers and now we're sitting here like a couple of wankers because you felt a disturbance in 'the force'?"

"Fuck off, Bobby. I'm just as keen to get back as…"

The pair of them instantly fell silent as their radios began to hiss in their ears. They could hear a voice but it was distorted and unrecognisable through waves of static. They looked at one another questioningly but neither of them had an answer.

"Unknown call sign, say again," Bobby whispered as he pressed the send button and spoke into the microphone attached to his assault vest.

There was no reply except for the familiar hiss in his ear of an empty carrier wave. Bobby stood up and cautiously looked in both directions, straining to see through the gloom. The street appeared empty, even though his field of vision stretched no further than a few metres. He nodded to Bull and then stepped back out onto the pavement in the hope of getting a clearer signal through his antenna.

"Stan, this is Bobby, radio check."

The radio crackled again but as before, the voice was indistinguishable. Bobby stepped further out into the open and stood beside the slowly decaying hulk of a large silver people carrier. He turned and hunched his shoulders and began speaking quietly into his mouthpiece as he slowly stepped back into the shadow of the broken down vehicle.

Bull remained in position and covering his friend while he attempted to make contact with the rest of the team but as he moved further away, Bull could see less of him. Bobby was soon nothing more than a faint dark shape, barely distinguishable from the blanket of darkness that had begun to swallow him up as he increased the distance between himself and the protection of the wall.

"Stan, this is..." Bobby began trying again.

He felt himself abruptly falling backwards towards the vehicle and was unable to stop. Something was pulling at his harness, catching him off balance and drawing him closer towards the door of the people carrier. His back and shoulders slammed against the frame of the rear window and he felt the cold bony hands of an infected person grasping at the bare skin on the back of his neck from inside the vehicle. He pulled and twisted, trying to break free but he could not get his feet into a position where he could grip against the ground. One of his legs slipped from underneath him and his weight dragged him downwards but the clutching hands refused to relinquish their grip upon him.

Bobby reached for his machete but before he could draw it, another figure shot out from around the other side of the car and pounced upon him. Instinctively, he drove the long blade up through the creature's abdomen but it did not slow his attacker down in the slightest. The sharp steel pierced organs and scraped over bone but the ghastly face in front of him did not seem to notice. Its teeth snapped together loudly as it lunged downwards towards Bobby's face. Bobby snapped his head to the side, the dead man's jaws gnashing on thin air just centimetres away from his cheek. Again, he pushed back on his machete with all his strength, hoping to keep the thing at a distance while he tried to regain his footing and break free from the corpse holding him in place from behind. The hilt of the machete slipped through the weakened flesh of the cadaver with a soft popping sound and Bobby found himself wrist deep in the putrid intestines that began to spill out from the gaping wound. The teeth snapped shut again, just millimetres from his face.

Bull saw a shadow flicker across in front of where he had seen Bobby disappear into the darkness. He heard a dull thud as something crashed against the steel frame of a car and it was quickly followed by the scuffing of feet mixed with the grunts and gasps of a struggle. He jumped from his cover position and drew his long blade, bounding across the pavement and into the road in just a few rapid steps.

Bobby was wedged against the window, being tugged from inside the vehicle while the weight of a reanimated corpse pressed against him from the outside. His hands were pinned in front of him and he was unable to reach for his pistol because it would risk allowing the snapping jaws to gain ground on him.

Bull reached over and grabbing the thing by the collar of its jacket, wrenched the infected away from Bobby. With a mighty heave, Bull tossed the corpse away to the side where it crashed into the wall that he and Bobby had taken cover behind just a few moments before. Its head thumped against the brick barrier with a heavy crunch that snapped its spinal column and split its skull wide open. The body slumped to the ground, dead.

Next, Bull turned his attention to the clawing hands that held Bobby stuck to the window frame of the people carrier. He grabbed his partner by the straps on the front of his harness and pulled him up from the ground and forward towards him. The cold dead hands came with him, refusing to let go of Bobby. The skeletal face of a woman appeared through the opening as she was dragged out from the car's rear passenger seat. As her head and shoulders came free, Bull raised his knife and thrust it down into the top of the woman's head, driving the point of the blade deep into her brain.

They had to pry the fingers free from Bobby's harness as the creature maintained a stubborn death grip upon him. The bones snapped and Bobby was finally free. He stood for a short moment with his hands upon his knees and panting for breath and then moved towards the curb side. Crouching down, he began washing his hands in a puddle to remove the gunk and stench of the rotten corpse's innards.

"Cheers, mate," he grunted up at the big man standing close by.

He was shaken and confused about how he had found himself in such a predicament. He wiped his hands on his trousers and stood back up, turning to face Bull. He could vaguely see the scrutinising expression on his friend's face and swiftly realised that he could virtually read his thoughts.

"No, neither of them managed to get me," Bobby assured him as he rubbed his hands over the back of his neck and his arms, checking for any wounds sustained in the struggle that he had failed to notice.

Bull nodded.

Another sound close by made them turn and raise their weapons. Two figures stepped out from the gloom and cautiously moved towards them.

"Have you two finished dicking about?" Stan's voice asked impatiently in a low hoarse whisper. "We've been trying to get hold of you for the past hour."

Bull and Bobby almost laughed out loud with relief. They had been expecting more infected to come rushing towards them but it was their commander coming to their rescue. Danny stood beside Stan and grinned back at Bobby.

"We could've done with your help a minute ago," Bobby remarked as the four of them huddled into the cover of the wall.

"Yeah, we saw your little scrap but we didn't want to get involved and end up getting our heads bashed in by you both," Danny replied and indicated the sprawled body of the infected man lying close by.

"Your task complete?" Stan asked, looking from one to the other and keen to get away from the area.

"Yeah," Bobby nodded. "All in place and good to go. What about the other two bins, did you get them planted?"

"All good," Stan answered. "Everything went as planned and the baskets are secure. Now let's get back."

At the apartment block, the four men skulked back in through the gate at the main entrance and headed up the stairs. Marty had remained in the foyer, keeping an eye on their rear while Taff had positioned himself on the roof to afford a better over-watch and clearer communications with Stan while he went looking for Bobby and Bull.

"Go on, Bull," Taff sneered. "What kind of drama have you been getting yourself into this time? Stan has been worried sick about you. He was pacing the house, ready to phone the police and report you guys missing."

Stan checked his watch and looked out over the rooftops. The sun would be coming up within the next few hours and with their initial task completed, the operation would be reaching the next phase. He walked across the roof and checked on the factory to their rear. He could just about make out the gate leading in from the street. He eyed the wall that split the factory from the apartments with suspicion, searching for any gaps or weak points that they had not seen earlier. He hoped that once the music began the dead would not begin wandering in from the rear. The first of the noise boxes was just a few hundred metres away and they should be close enough for the infected to zero in on without too many of them straying into the complex by accident.

"We should try to get some sleep," he said glancing at his watch again and looking across to the eastern horizon. "The fun and games will begin soon."

Taff remained on the roof with Danny while the others moved down into the apartment to rest. Once first light arrived, Stan would remote trigger the music and then begin sending situation reports to the operations staff back on the Isle of Wight. The other teams that were scattered throughout the city would initiate phase-two at the same time and before long, there would be a mass exodus of rotting corpses converging on the respective locations and forming themselves into huge swarming targets for the bombers.

"I can see our house from here," Danny pointed out childishly.

Taff turned and looked over to the north. Against the dark horizon, he could just make out the towering building that had once been their home before the spread of the infection. It was roughly three kilometres away and on the opposite side of the River Thames.

"That's a shame," Taff grumbled as he turned his attention back to the south.

"What is?"

"I left a very nice and expensive leather jacket behind in my wardrobe there. It cost me nearly three-hundred quid, mate."

As first light arrived, the men assembled on the rooftop. They had all brewed themselves coffee and brought their cups up with them while they settled in to watch the beginning of the next phase in the operation. There would be very little for them to do other than observe and send situation reports while ensuring that their LTD, Laser Target Designator, remained aiming into the centre of mass. Taff had already set up the guidance system. It was placed on top of an extendable tripod, close to the roof's edge and pointing towards the furthest junction where the first of the airstrikes would hit. He had checked the batteries and ensured that the sight was accurate to where the splash of the laser landed.

Stan squatted close to the lip of the rooftop while the others sat beside him on stools and dining chairs that they had brought up from the apartment, slurping at their drinks with expressions of anticipation. He hit the remote and within seconds, the faint sounds of music began to drift up towards them.

"It's not very loud, is it?" Taff snorted with disappointment as he strained to hear the low and incoherent sounds that only just managed to reach them.

"What did you expect, Taff, a bloody rave?" Bull replied as he turned his head and angled his ear towards the music bins.

Stan fumbled with the control-pad and finally worked out how to increase the volume. Soon, the entire area was blaring with sounds that the city had not heard in a long time while the men squinted, trying to identify the distorted music. Next, he began initiating the other two sound devices that were closer and within seconds, as he maximised the volume on each, the area became alive with music.

"What's on the playlist?" Marty asked.

"I think it's an opera?" Danny replied.

Bull shook his head and held up a silencing finger. The look upon his face was intense and he cocked his ear in the direction of the first junction. He could only hear snippets due to the echoes and distance, and the fact that all three bins were playing together and were out of sync. However, he was sure that he recognised fragments of the music. Finally, he smiled broadly and turned to the others with a glint in his eyes.

"Danny's right," he beamed elatedly and glared at Marty. "It's an opera and it's by Wagner. It's Ride of the Valkyries."

Marty could not hear it clearly but he smiled with pride and delight. He was especially pleased with the fact that the music being played was the regimental march of his and Bull's old parent unit, The Parachute Regiment.

"You Paras," Taff scoffed with a grin and shaking his head. "You're all the fucking same. As soon as you hear that fat chick screeching away, you all get a hard-on."

"Well it's far more stirring than the marching tune that your lot used to play. What was it again? The theme tune to Laurel and Hardy, wasn't it?"

Stan panned his binoculars over the junctions before him. The music had only been playing for a minute or so but already, hundreds of shuffling corpses were appearing out of every doorway and from every street. The sounds of Wagner filled the air and blotted out their moans. The instruments of the orchestra replaced the crashes and bangs of the dead as they bashed about within the buildings. He looked up towards the office block across the street. More faces had appeared at the windows and began pressing themselves against the glass in an attempt to reach the outside and follow their comrades towards the source of the music. He wondered how long it would be before the panes gave way and the bodies began tumbling out into thin air.

"Taff, go and join Bobby in the foyer and keep an eye on our rear. Let me know how we're looking. We'll double up the stags while those things are on the move."

"Roger that, Stan," Taff replied and moved off towards the stairwell leading down from the rooftop.

Inside the building, the music became muffled but it was still audible enough for him to hear and zero in on its direction. He began making his way down the flights of stairs and stopped to check on the S-Mine that they had stationed on the third floor. It was still securely in place and only needed the wire attaching and the safety pin pulling free to arm it. If any of the infected got inside the apartment block the team hoped that the detonation of the mine would buy them enough time to get out of the building and in to the factory complex or the adjacent street via the ropes they had attached to the roof.

In the foyer, he met up with Bobby who was huddled behind an overturned desk set back from the entrance. Up against the doorway, they had rebuilt the barricade as best they could with the furniture and appliances taken from the ground floor apartments. Bobby was watching the car park to the rear of the building and paying particular attention to the wide gate at the far end that lay open.

"How we looking, Bobby?" Taff whispered as he crouched down beside him and peered out through the buckled doorway.

"See for yourself," Bobby replied and nodded to the patch of street that he could see beyond the gates. "I take it that the show has started?"

"Yeah. Wagner is in full swing and Bull and Marty are wanking themselves silly up there."

Taff looked through the sight attached to the top of his M-4 and watched as a crowd of mottled greys and browns drifted along the road beyond the gates. He felt particularly relieved that none of them had ventured into the apartment grounds as yet and that the music seemed to be channelling them all in the right direction.

"Jesus," Taff remarked open mouthed, "there must be thousands of them out there. This place will be teeming with those things in an hour."

"I thought that was the idea, Taff?" Bobby asked sarcastically and reached for the flask of coffee he had sitting next to him.

"No strays as yet?"

"Not so far. They're doing exactly what we want them to do but no doubt, there's bound to be a few that come wandering in."

"We can deal with a few of them," Taff nodded. "I just hope that the batteries don't die on those music bins. We'll be up shit creek if that happens."

"You had to say it, didn't you," Bobby glared at him. "Next you'll mention the rain and then we'll get pissed on too."

Taff grinned back at him.

On the roof, Stan pulled out the antenna to the satellite phone and prepared to send his situation report. It had only been one hour since they initiated the second phase of the operation, and for a kilometre, stretching south and dissected by three major junctions, the road was already packed with the bodies of the undead. By now, the sounds of their cries and wails had merged into a crescendo as they competed against the music that was playing at maximum volume. Still, more and more of them were arriving and converging on the epicentres of the three sound devices. They were packed in between the buildings, shoulder to shoulder, and the sea of rotting flesh surged endlessly as they all jostled, pushed, and tugged at the bodies around them. It was impossible even to begin estimating their numbers.

"Jesus fucking Christ," Danny whispered as he sat staring at the closest of the intersections. A river of rot was flowing in from all angles, adding to the seething mass. "I wonder how the other teams are getting on."

Stan made his call to headquarters. While their commander sent his report, Bull and Marty patrolled around the lip of the roof. They moved in a crouch, ensuring that their bodies were not exposed to the thousands of eyes in the streets below. They stopped at each of the corners of the building and peered down into the avenues running alongside of their position. Nothing of the tarmac or paving stones at ground level could be seen. Everything in the streets had been swallowed up in the torrent of corpses that trundled towards the junctions and the music. The entire city was on the move.

"Lucky for us that those dumb shits are like sheep," Marty commented as they watched the empty car park to their rear and eyed the wall of the perimeter.

No infected had yet veered from the path of the mass and entered in through the open gates. They blindly followed the bodies in front and showed no interest in the wide open space of the parking lot. Bull bleated quietly as he watched the flow of corpses.

Stan closed down the antenna and turned to the others. His face showed no indication of how his situation report had been received.

"Well?" Bull queried up at him as he sat back into his chair. "Don't keep us in suspense. Share the wealth, Stan."

"One of the teams didn't report in," Stan began. "It was one of the Hereford bunch that was moving to their LUP through the sewers and tunnels beneath the city."

"Bad comms or did they run into trouble?" Danny asked.

"Unknown," Stan replied with a shrug.

"Poor bastards," Marty huffed.

"I informed them that phase-two was appearing to be going as hoped. The other teams in position to the east and west are reporting similar results in their lanes. HQ will send up a drone later to have a look for themselves and begin an assessment on enemy numbers that can be destroyed once the airstrikes begin.

"Phase-three, the simultaneous assault on the harbour and airfield, and the start of the bombing runs on London, will still be going ahead and will begin at first light tomorrow. We should see the first of the assault troops being lifted into the south by mid-morning if all goes well at the airfield in Farnborough."

"So we sit tight and wait for the fireworks then? Sounds good to me," Bull grunted.

Still positioned in the foyer, Taff and Bobby cursed as the first of the dead broke away from the exodus and stumbled in through the gates.

15

Peter stood watching in awe as the Chinook helicopters lifted their huge bodies into the air beneath their twin rotors. The four mechanical giants soared into the sky creating a deafening upsurge of noise as their powerful engines went into high gear. He wondered how such bulky machines were able to get off the ground in the first place let alone fly, yet they lifted with grace and ease.

Flanked by a number of smaller aircraft, the troop carrying CH-47s were accompanied by an Apache ground attack helicopter and two Royal Navy Huey Cobras. The three gunships, glistening with a vast and deadly array of heavy machineguns and missiles, would provide close air support as the assault troops disembarked from the Chinooks at the airfield in Farnborough. Once on the ground, the fighting men and women would begin securing the fuel depot and setting up a defensive perimeter while the menacing attack helicopters hovered close overhead.

The scream of the engines began to fade as the aircraft gained height and headed towards the north, leaving a strange calm to settle over the windswept grassy field where more troops patiently waited with their equipment and weapons for their turn to join in with the attack on the mainland.

Peter and his brother, Michael, sat huddled together in silence and watching the goings on around them. There were thousands of soldiers sitting about in nervous anticipation. Many of whom like Peter and his brother, had been recruited into the civilian militia just three weeks before. Some were quiet and others laughed and joked with false bravado but it was clear that *all* were afraid. With only the most basic of training, large numbers of refugees had been armed with rifles and sent to join in on the retaking of the mainland. Some had volunteered, eager to escape from the squalid conditions of the camps and receive the extra rations that had been promised to those who offered their services. Others had been manipulated and forced into joining the newly formed and ill-trained militias.

The regular troops were to be used in the first waves, with the likes of Peter and Michael being sent in only as reinforcements and auxiliaries, helping with rear guard actions, maintaining security cordons, and facilitating with the immense task of resupply. They had been assured that they would not be used at the front unless it was essential and all they were expected to do was to support the men and women fighting in the line and help maintain the security of recaptured areas.

Still, despite the assurances of the army commanders, Peter remained sceptical of their perceived role. He failed to see how they could not eventually find themselves at the spearhead of the assault. The task was far too great for the amount of professional soldiers that the army had available. He had no previous military training but still, even *he* could see that the regular troops would be hard pressed to accomplish their objectives on their own. With the numbers of infected that they were expecting to come up against, it was only a matter of time before the reserve units and militias were thrown into the battle.

Michael, on the other hand, viewed it all as a big adventure. He was delighted at the prospect of riding in the helicopters and treated the whole thing as a game. On several occasions, Peter needed to remind his brother about the danger they were facing. He even had to remove the magazine from Michael's rifle to prevent him from getting carried away and shooting himself or someone else from overexcitement.

Peter was scared. He firmly believed that they should all play a part in the recapture of the mainland, but nevertheless, he dreaded seeing what had become of his country. He reeled in trepidation at the thought of facing the immense numbers of infected that they expected to encounter in and around the city of London. All his life, he had been a sceptic and prone to realistic thinking and now, with the operation underway, his thoughts were flooded with pessimistic views on the outcome of the invasion. Looking around him, he watched the other members of the militia. They were far from the toughened, well-trained, well equipped, and experienced soldiers that had just taken off in the helicopters. They were a rag-tag army of civilian men and women of all shapes and ages, and from all walks of life. None of them had received more than two weeks' worth of training and most of that had been taken up with learning how to handle the weapons safely, never mind how to shoot them with any degree of accuracy.

Peter looked at the grinning face of his brother. The boy was only eighteen years old but his mental ability was much younger. All of his life, Peter had looked out for him. He had sacrificed a career and countless relationships with girls in order to keep an eye on his brother and help him along through a world in which Michael understood very little. When the call to arms had gone up in the refugee camps, Peter had volunteered them both.

For months, they had been living on scraps, surrounded by the sick and the dying, and perpetually at risk of being attacked by other refugees as the strong preyed upon the weak. It was a Darwinian existence within the fences of the camps and the term 'survival of the fittest' had become as commonly used as 'hello' and 'good morning' or, 'I'm hungry'. Peter and Michael were far from being amongst the *fittest* and their survival depended on them getting out of the refugee camp.

Strange looks and questions had been directed at Michael at the recruitment centre and Peter had feared that his brother would be sent back to the camps. With some quick thinking and clever words, Peter had managed to convince the recruiters that Michael would be a valuable asset in the coming weeks and that he would personally look after him. Now, Michael sat holding his unloaded rifle in his hands, smiling broadly, and constantly shuffling his feet impatiently.

"When are the helicopters coming back, Pete?"

Peter shrugged and reached into his pocket for his cigarettes.

"I don't know, Mikey. To be honest, I'm hoping they'll take their time in turning around. This isn't going to be a fun trip, you know."

"Helicopters are fun."

"Not when they're dropping you off into a crowd of dead people that want to eat you, they're not, Mike."

"Oh," Michael said and looked down disappointedly, "I forgot about them. Do you think there'll be lots of them?"

Peter shrugged again and was about to answer when a car horn to their right let out a long single blast. Everyone that was gathered in the field stopped what they were doing and fell silent. They all turned and saw a green painted army Land Rover with a figure standing on top of the roof. The man stared back at them and scanned his eyes over the thousands of bobbing heads that watched him expectantly. It was their Battalion Commander, Colonel Moore.

"Ladies and gentlemen of the militia," the Colonel began as he lifted the megaphone to his mouth. His voice was crisp and clear through the speaker and as always, he reminded Peter of the stereotypical British officer from old war movies.

"As you are all well aware, the counter offensive to reclaim the mainland has begun," the Colonel continued. "As we speak, the forward elements of the airborne assault are moving towards the airfield at Farnborough. There, they will clear and secure the area in order for our aircraft to begin refuelling. Thus, enabling us to bring in more reinforcements from the island and onto the mainland.

"Simultaneously, a joint amphibious and airborne operation is being launched against the harbour at Portsmouth. Once this task is completed, landing craft will then be able to start delivering troops, vehicles, and supplies onto the mainland where they will begin their thrust northwards to link up with the units at Farnborough.

"There, the assault troops will quickly reorganise and then begin moving forward by helicopter towards the southern outskirts of London. Once the break-in is achieved, a ground column will move up from the airfield in support of the break-in while our Chinooks help with immediate reinforcement.

"With the aid of our Special Forces, large numbers of the infected are being herded into mass groups at key points within the city. Aircraft from the navy and air force are about to begin their bombing missions on these concentrations and should effectively reduce the enemy numbers facing our soldiers within the built-up area."

As if on cue, a loud violent roar suddenly filled the sky above them as the first wave of Tornado and Typhoon jets took off from the HMS Illustrious and shot overhead, screeching across the heavens towards the north until they became nothing but black dots in the distance. The deafening howl of their jet engines drowned out any sound made on the ground but Peter saw the faces of the people around him and imagined the gasps of awe as they looked on at the demonstration of power and dominance provided by the pilots.

The atmosphere on the ground was one of extreme excitement and confidence. No one doubted that in the near future they would be returning to their homes and rebuilding their lives and their country as the war against the dead would soon be over. Everyone appeared keen to join in with the fight and many began to cry out impatiently, concerned that the battle would be finished before they had their chance to play a part.

Peter was in no hurry. He hoped that the operation would go according to plan and be successful. He wanted nothing more than to be liberated from the camps and the fear and stress of having to survive from day to day. However, he was free from any of the illusions that seemed to infect all those around him. Their enthusiasm, though infectious to most of the other survivors, gained no ground within Peter's soul. Humanity was on the back foot and severely outnumbered by the army of dead. It was estimated that ninety-five percent of the population either were amongst the ranks of the enemy, or had been consumed by them. The war would not be over any time soon and he was confident that there would be plenty of time and opportunities for the men and women of the militia to get their rifles dirty.

"This will be no easy fight. Our enemy is vast and unflinching in its resolve. The dead feel no fear and are incapable of reason. They have no consideration for the dangers they face and will not hesitate to attack us, regardless of our overwhelming firepower. It will be a hard fight and a fight we must win. Our species depends upon our ability to reclaim our lands and free our cities of the plague infestations.

"That is just the first sortie on their way to London," Colonel Moore shouted through the megaphone with vigour and pointing towards the faint black specks as they headed towards the northern horizon. "More will take off over the next few minutes and wave after wave will decimate the ranks of the monsters swarming our capital. Our soldiers will walk over a carpet of bone and ash as they victoriously take back our beloved homeland."

A cheer went up as the crowd surged with enthusiasm. They clapped their hands together and reassuringly grasped the shoulders and arms of the people standing close by, demonstrating their solidarity.

"Listen to your commanders and have confidence in the men and women who lead you. Protect the people at your side and remember, you are fighting for the human race."

Again, the mass of men and women standing in the field erupted with vivacity and applauded their commander. Colonel Moore gave a nod of acknowledgement to his assembled troops, climbed down into the passenger seat of his vehicle, and headed off, back to the command centre in the town of Newport.

Peter remained unimpressed. Their leader had given them a speech to rile them up and bestowed his confidence in them and their abilities. However, the Colonel would not be joining them on the ground. He would be staying on the island and would command from far behind the front lines with a large body of water acting as a protective moat. His subordinate officers would be leading the fight and it was them to whom the people of the militia would turn to when the battle raged.

"Whatever happens, Mikey," Peter said as he turned to his brother and held him tightly by his arm, "stay close to me. Don't allow yourself to get separated. Do you understand?"

Michael looked back at him in confusion. He could not understand his brother's concern. The thought of sitting in the helicopter was all that was at the forefront of his mind at that moment and he wondered why Peter did not show the same excitement.

An hour later and Peter found himself cursing the Gods as he sat strapping himself into a row of seats along the interior of one of the Chinooks. Somehow, he and his platoon of militia had been selected to be in the first wave of reinforcements to head up towards the airfield. They had been given no information on what was happening or how the counter offensive was fairing so far, only that they, the militia, were moving. Their commander, a young second Lieutenant from the regular army, had ordered them to board the helicopter and all had complied without question.

The aircraft was filled to bursting point with troops and supplies and Peter sat staring at the stacked crates of ammunition in the centre of the fuselage with anxiety. He was no expert but from what he could tell, there must have been a lot of fighting going on around the airfield to require such a large resupply already. He looked about at the nervous expressions on the faces of the other men and women. Their eyes glittered with apprehension and their feet and hands fidgeted continuously.

Michael, however, was beside himself. He was thrilled to be finally getting the ride he had looked forward to so much. He whooped and cheered as he shuffled in his seat, eager to experience the helicopter lift off from the ground. He twisted and turned endlessly, arching his neck so that he could see out through the small round windows behind him and confirming that they were still not yet airborne. He did not want to miss that particular moment. He wanted so much to see the ground receding below them as the aircraft lifted up into the air and gained altitude until the people and buildings below appeared like toys.

Peter rolled his eyes and grinded his teeth irritably. He was not thrilled and he was not particularly enthusiastic. He just wanted them both to survive. He knew full well that his time on the mainland was going to be completely taken up with watching out for the thousands of corpses roaming the land and keeping his brother out of danger, while at the same time, keeping himself safe.

"Michael," he roared into his brother's ear in an attempt to be heard over the noisy engines, "calm the fuck down."

Michael froze and stared at him solemnly. He saw the serious expression in his brother's eyes and knew that he had somehow angered him. He sunk back into his seat and tightened his seatbelt, feeling deflated.

"But I just want to…"

"But nothing, Michael. This is not a game," Peter hollered back at him with the veins of his neck protruding from beneath the skin with the strain of having to shout so loudly in order to be heard.

Michael said nothing but merely blinked back at him as he wiped the flecks of his brother's spittle that splashed against his face.

"You need to calm down and think about what you're doing now. I can't do it for you, Mikey. Do you remember what I said to you?" Peter hesitated for a moment, hoping that his brother would offer up the information without needing to be reminded. "Stay close to me and don't get separated, whatever happens."

Michael nodded his acknowledgement but his eyes continued to drift towards the window, worried that he will miss the take-off.

"People are going to die, Michael," Peter continued, hoping to force his brother into the realisation of the seriousness of their situation. "A *lot* of people will die. I just don't want any of them to be us."

The sound of the engines began to change and the fuselage rocked slightly as the aircraft prepared to rise. Instantly, Michael's attention was no longer in Peter's grasp. His expression changed suddenly and the look of comprehension in his eyes was quickly replaced by the familiar vision of a young man on the verge of soiling himself with exhilaration as he turned to peer out through the window.

Peter turned away to continue staring at the large piles of ammunition and the pale and tense faces of his comrades.

"Shit."

16

"Just do what you can to keep the area clear, Taff," Stan's voice instructed them through their earpieces.

Taff stared in disbelief at Bobby before keying the send button on his radio.

"Like what, Stan?" He asked cynically. "There's about thirty of them already inside and mincing about the car-park. If we can't shoot them, what else can we do?"

Up on the roof, Stan was getting annoyed. Over the last hour while the sun's rays slowly made an appearance over the rooftops a number of bodies had stumbled in through the open gate to their rear. Taff and Bobby, unable to use their rifles for fear of drawing attention to themselves, had been sending regular situation reports to their commander. Even with the silencers attached to their barrels, the discharge of their rifles would still make enough noise that could potentially be noticed by some of the crowd surging by in the street. Instead, they had no option but to sit and watch while the numbers of dead within their perimeter steadily grew.

So far, the meandering corpses had shown no interest to the entrance of the apartment building and remained at a distance, stumbling about in the car park in confusion while the music continued to echo from the walls of the buildings all around them.

The team had just received word from Samantha back at headquarters that the assault on the harbour and airfield had begun. No news on the progress of the advance was available as it was too soon to tell but she also informed them that the first wave of bombers was on route to their location.

"Taff," Stan growled into his microphone, "I don't care what you have to do, just hold your fire and keep out of sight. The airstrikes are inbound and will be here any minute. Once they start, you'll have enough noise cover to deal with them then."

Out to the front of the building was an ocean of rotting bodies. By now, they were in their hundreds of thousands and no patch of ground remained unoccupied. For as far as the eye could see, stretching out to the south, there was a mass of flailing arms and shifting heads. The music still managed to triumph over the moans of the dead but only barely.

"I like big cock in June...how about you?" Bull sang absentmindedly as he watched the surging crowd.

Marty was sitting beside him. He lowered the binoculars and turned to his friend. Watching him closely with a questioning look carved into his face, Marty felt a slight smile tugging at the corners of his mouth.

"What the hell are you singing there, Bull?" He finally asked after listening to the big man singing words he had never before heard to that particular tune.

"It's Frank Sinatra," Bull simply replied without looking at him and nodding in the direction of the first junction. "The song playing down there is one of Ol' Blue Eyes'. I think it's called 'How about you?' or something like that. You never heard it?"

Marty began to laugh, holding a hand up to his mouth so that the sound did not carry and alert anything at ground level to their presence. With the noise of the infected and the music, added to the continuous shifting of the crowd, it was not likely that any of the bodies below were going to notice.

"Yeah, I know the song but I don't remember there being anything about a big cock mentioned in it. I'm pretty sure that it's 'New York'."

Bull turned to him and grinned.

"Yeah, well, I like to mix it up a little."

"Two minutes," Stan said as he folded down the antenna of his satellite phone. "They're approaching from the south. Get the LTD ready and pointing at the southern intersection. They can hit that first and creep their way north towards us."

Danny switched on the Laser Target Designator, aimed it towards their first intended target, and checked the range.

"Target painted, Stan," he confirmed. "One-point-two kilometres."

Far off to the south, through his binoculars, Stan watched as a cluster of small black specks appeared over the horizon. He checked his watch and then returned his attention back to the approaching aircraft. Further to the left and right of the first group were a number of other distant planes, growing larger by the second, as they flew in along their respective flight corridors, guided in by the teams in place on the ground.

Reaching into one of the pouches attached to his assault vest, Stan retrieved the Tactical Beacon, TACBE. Normally used as a personal locator beacon for downed pilots, the TACBE could also be utilized for short-range communications with passing aircraft on the emergency frequency.

Stan pressed the talk-switch.

"Sierra-three, this is Golf-four," he said hailing the particular group of aircraft that had been assigned to his assault lane. "Sierra-three, this is Golf-four. Radio check."

"Golf-four, this is Sierra-three. Strength five," came the crackling reply of the pilot, indicating the strength of the signal he received from Stan.

"Roger, you're good to me. Approach on bearing zero-one-zero degrees, north. Targets in the open and painted with laser. Seen?"

There was a pause in the conversation as the pilot checked his heading and looked for the splash of the infrared laser.

"Roger, target confirmed. Coming in on zero-one-zero, thirty seconds. Get your boys down and into cover. Sierra-three out."

"Okay, head's down, fellas," Stan ordered to everyone around him. "We've got incoming from the south and will be here within the next twenty seconds. Danny, keep the target well painted. We don't want any stray ordinance taking us out."

Stan turned away from the junction and crouched himself down behind the low wall running around the roof of the building. He looked across to Bull and Marty who were doing the same, taking cover before the bombs were dropped. They were well beyond the danger area of the first junction but as Stan had already pointed out, there was always the possibility of some of the ordinance overshooting their target.

"Taff," Stan called through his radio as the growling sounds of jet engines became audible over the city. "Get yourselves low down there. Ten seconds to the first drop."

Down in the foyer, Taff and Bobby readied their weapons, taking off their safety catches and crouching further down into the cover of the barricade. As soon as the first wave of airstrikes was over, they intended to neutralise the infected that had stumbled into their rear area. With the noise of the blasts and the confusion created by the bombers, they would have the cover they needed to begin dealing with the threat.

Danny waited until the last second before taking cover himself as the aircraft engines rose to a tremendous howl. The Laser Target Designator was secured to the lip of the roof and still pointed towards the target. He ducked down and drew his knees up close to his chest, counting off the final few seconds in his head as the roar of the Tornados and Typhoons grew to a crescendo.

At ground level, as the sound of the engines overhead drowned out the music, hundreds of thousands of eyes turned upwards. Every corpse in the area suddenly became still as they turned their faces towards the sky and watched the dark shapes of the bombers soaring in from the south. Their voices had fallen silent and they did not attempt to reach up towards the aircraft or move away to safety. Their hands hung limply by their sides and their attention remained transfixed on the strange shapes above them, hypnotised by the sight. Even when the first black cylindrical shaped object detached itself from the undercarriage of the lead plane and began tumbling towards them, the dead did not move but looked on as the bomb hurtled towards the ground and landed in their midst.

The heavy steel casing crashed into the hard concrete and detonated instantaneously. The blast sent hundreds of torn and dismembered bodies sailing through the air over a wide area. All the windows that were still intact and stubbornly clinging to their frames in the buildings around the intersection and beyond were blown outwards in a silent explosion of glass fragments. The hordes of infected that had been pressing themselves against the glass from inside tumbled out through the empty frames and crashed into the streets below, bursting in clouds of blood and bone on impact with the ground. Structures buckled under the immense pressure wave and abandoned vehicles were flung far and wide at phenomenal speeds, crashing into buildings and scattering the bodies of the walking dead like bowling pins as they tore through the packed street.

A fraction of a second later, every molecule of oxygen in the immediate vicinity was sucked into the centre of the blast where the air immediately ignited into a huge white fireball that surged outwards in a blinding flash, incinerating all in its path. Everything burst into flames and immediately vaporised in the intense heat. Flesh was seared from bone and bodies shattered while steel and concrete melted and fractured.

Stan and the others felt the shockwave of the initial blast as the first of the aircraft, a Tornado, shot overhead. The heat of the firebomb followed close behind, turning the cool crisp morning air into a blazing furnace. The roof shook and the teeth of the men clashed together as the apartment block struggled to withstand the shockwave that ripped through its foundations. Even from a range of over a kilometre, the effects of the blast could be felt and just seconds after the first, there was another massive explosion of heat, and then another as the planes began their individual drops on the first target.

A few seconds later and the four men raised themselves to look out over the lip of the roof. To the south they saw nothing but carnage. Buildings were mangled beyond recognition and blazing wildly as the fires violently spread through their floors and engulfed everything in their path. The centre of the junction was distorted out of shape and awash with the charred and fused remains of thousands of bodies and dozens of vehicles. In that particular intersection, there was very little that remained standing. A small number of infected blindly stumbled towards the raging flames and were quickly consumed. The incendiary bombs had mostly done their job and destroyed everything in the area.

However, within moments, thousands more bodies piled into the intersection from the closest streets. They blindly staggered into the area of the junction, stumbling through the flames and quickly filling the area with blazing bodies.

"Christ," Bull grunted as he looked out towards the south through his binoculars. "That worked better than I expected it to."

"There's more coming," Marty whispered from beside him.

"More aircraft? Yeah, I know."

"No," Marty said and pointed his finger to the streets on the right that were feeding into the nearest junction. "Infected, there are more of them coming."

Bull turned and looked to where Marty was pointing. The exodus of rotting flesh was showing no sign of slowing and more of them were squeezing themselves into the already tightly packed junctions. Despite the losses that they had just sustained in the first airstrike, they continued to advance on the area, showing no signs of retreat.

"Our six o'clock is clear, Stan," Taff informed their leader over the net.

With the thunder of the explosions and the roar of the fireballs, Taff and Bobby had gone to work in clearing the car park at the rear of the building. As plaster dust fell from the ceiling and windows shattered all around them, the two men took careful aim at the heads of over thirty staggering corpses. As the floor juddered beneath them and the walls shook violently, some of their shots missed, whizzing harmlessly through the air and smashing into the brick wall that formed the perimeter. However, with slight corrections to the aim and hold of their weapons, the dead were soon dealt with. They now lay still, their skulls splayed open and the remnants of their brains spewing out over the ground around them.

"Roger that, Taff. First wave complete. Target destroyed. Confirmation from Ops that the other teams are having the same results throughout the city. The second wave will be here in one minute. Stay down."

Out in the street at the rear of the apartment block, the river of dead had turned into a stream. There were still a lot of shuffling corpses headed for the target area but nothing like the numbers that they had witnessed throughout the previous day and night.

"You think this is going to work?" Bobby asked as he changed out his magazines.

"Seems to be working so far, mate," Taff shrugged.

Danny angled the LTD so that it was now pointed at the next intersection. Although the fires were quickly spreading further to the south, the dead at the second target location were mostly unaffected and remained mobile and in vast numbers. Some had been hit with shrapnel and a small percentage had caught fire from the heat wave that irradiated out from the first bombs but overall, they were untouched.

Once again to the south, the team saw the faint dark shapes of aircraft as they raced towards their targets, flying just two-hundred metres above the ground. Stan guided them in on the TACBE again before ordering his men to take cover.

This time, as the bombs detonated at a much shorter range from their over-watch position, the shockwaves were far stronger, the heat more intense, and the rattle of their teeth and bones all the more forceful. The building beneath them shook fiercely and felt as though it was about to come apart at the seams.

Bull was curled into a ball, his hands covering his head with his elbows tucked closely into his chest. He shifted and squirmed, flinching with each thundering impact and gasping as the air pressure around him threatened to suck his lungs out from his chest. He could feel the heat against his bare skin and the sweat that soaked through his clothing.

"Fuck me," he howled over the din of the explosions with popping ears. "I hope those pilots know what they're doing."

As the men sat gasping and trying to recover from the second wave, Stan forced his shaking body up to the lip and peered out over the second target. As with the first, the junction had become a wasteland of scorched earth and charred bodies. The flames from the first two objectives had merged into one large inferno and had begun to spread along the streets and buildings that led into the intersections.

Studying the effects of the strikes, Stan eyed the third and final junction. It was just three-hundred metres away and he began to feel that they were too close for comfort. Danny, Bull, and Marty crawled up and took a look for themselves. They were all beginning to think the same thing and turned to Stan with questioning looks.

"Taff, how we looking in the street behind us?" Stan asked urgently.

"Still plenty of them out there, Stan. Not as many as there were, but enough to ruin our day. You thinking of bugging out or something?" Taff replied from the foyer.

Stan did not answer but turned and reached for the satellite phone. He fumbled with the buttons and cursed himself under his breath as he struggled to make contact with the command centre on the Isle of Wight.

"Danny," he said as he raised the phone to his ear and heard the dial tone, "get the LTD ready and pointed at the first junction. Make sure it's secure because we won't be here to correct its aim if it slips."

Without needing to be told, Bull and Marty began checking their own weapons and ammunition, grabbing only what they needed to fight and dumping their heavy packs to one side. They pulled out their water bottles and began taking large gulps then passing them onto Stan and Danny who were both busy with other matters.

"Taff, Bobby, prepare to move in one minute," Marty called into his mouthpiece while Stan sent his situation report to HQ and informed them that they were withdrawing from their over-watch position.

Ready to move, the team headed for the door of the stairwell. Stan followed at the rear as the others began filing through and descending the first flight. There had been no time to guide in the next wave of airstrikes but with the ground ablaze, it would be impossible for the pilots to miss their targets. They had their approach bearings and the LTD had been left aiming its laser into the centre of the closest junction.

Stan took a glance back over his shoulder before passing through the door. Far off in the distance he saw a new set of dark objects making their way up from the south. They were bulkier than the first two waves and moving at a much slower pace. They were the first of the assault troops moving up in the Chinooks. The break-in had begun. Stan knew that at that same moment, a column of vehicles would be thrusting northwards from the airfield to open a corridor of resupply and reinforcement for the forward elements. They did not have enough helicopters to transport them all so a ground element needed to be established also. Soon the southern outskirts of the city would be a war zone as the advance pushed forward through the streets, clearing the buildings and destroying the infected that remained in the area.

Something else caught Stan's ever-vigilant eyes. Above the black silhouettes of the CH-47s another cluster of specks appeared. It was the third wave of bombers. They were approaching fast and ahead of schedule. Stan's eyes grew wide as he realised that they were out of time. The Tornados and Typhoons would be overhead within a matter of seconds and they were only just beginning their descent into the staircase.

"Move," he yelled down to the rest of his team as they reached the bottom of the first set of stairs. "Incoming, incoming. Move, move."

Without pausing, Danny, Bull, and Marty began bounding downwards, clearing each short flight of steps in just a few strides. Stan was racing along behind them, screaming at them to run faster before the bombs began falling. By now, the sound of the jet engines had grown to an ear-splitting screech as they streaked over the apartment block and shook the building. The thunderous roar reverberated within the confines of the stairway and the men instinctively ducked their heads as they continued downwards. Stan knew that the bombs had been released and were already falling through the air towards their targets. It was only a matter of seconds before they detonated.

A dazzling white light filled the staircase, momentarily blinding the men of the team and forcing them to shield their eyes as they stumbled and crashed into the walls and bannister. Then the building seemed to lift from its foundations and crash back to the ground, throwing the men to the floor and pressing them into the hard concrete. The blast wave, like a hurricane travelling at the speed of light, ripped through the apartments, blowing the windows in on themselves, tearing doors from their frames, and warping the walls as the structure struggled against the violence of the explosion.

The air disappeared from around Stan and his men, threatening to suck out their innards in the vacuum and causing their eardrums to burst and their eyes to bulge as the fuel-bomb ignited and spewed out devastation in a wide arc. The heat wave scorched its way through the building, incinerating everything around it and almost boiling the blood within the veins of the living men.

A second later, another detonation, not as large but much closer than the first, rocked the building from further down the staircase. Debris flew in all directions, crashing into the walls, bursting into flames and smashing against the bodies of the soldiers who lay pinned to the floor, gasping for air and screaming with pain and shock.

Within just a second or two, but seeming like a lifetime, the immediate effects of the bombs subsided. Although the air was clogged with debris, dust, and smoke the four men could once again breathe. The apartments around them were burning wildly and the smoke was quickly filling the stairwell to the point where it began to choke Stan and the others. The men dragged themselves to their feet, holding onto one another for support and calling out into the swirling black clouds enveloping them.

Stan was screaming down to them from somewhere above. His words were unintelligible and distant in their rattled minds. He continued down towards them, holding the sleeve of his shirt over his mouth and nose to stop him from succumbing to the smoke. He felt a body in front of him and recognised it as the huge bulk of Bull.

"Marty, Danny," he called urgently as he pushed Bull forward into the blackness. "Answer up for fuck sake. Marty, Danny…"

"Stan, we're here," the answer came with the distinct Glaswegian accent of Marty from below on the next flight of stairs. *"We're okay… I think."*

Stan and Bull crashed into the others and quickly realised that their escape had been cut off. The next two flights of stairs had disappeared from beneath them. A result caused by the S-Mine detonating when the blast wave hit the building and ripped the trip-wire away from the firing pin.

Without hesitation, Stan turned and began to climb the stairs, heading towards the roof again. More bombs would be falling soon but this time, they would be high explosive. Now that the fuel-bombs had created the initial damage and set the dead on fire, spreading the flames amongst their ranks and igniting the buildings in the immediate area, the HE detonations would finish them off, blowing them to pieces and damaging them to the point that they were no longer mobile. It was also hoped that the high explosives would help contain the fires by blasting them apart and at the very least, making them more manageable once the mopping-up operations commenced.

"Up to the roof," Stan called over his shoulder. "Get up to the roof, quick. We'll go down by the ropes."

From far below them, the voices of Bobby and Taff could be heard calling up to them through the wreckage of the stairway. Miraculously, both of them had somehow survived the devastation and they were in a good enough condition to have control of their senses. Mixed in with their calls were the distinct dull snaps of their silenced weapons as they fired at something unseen to Stan and the others.

Stan clicked his radio and called into his microphone. It was dead, damaged in the explosions. He paused just long enough to lean out over the mangled bannister and shout down into the chasm of what remained of the staircase.

"Taff, bug-out, we'll meet you at the ERV."

Bobby raised himself to his feet and loosed off another volley into the wall of gaunt faces that were spilling in through the gates of the parking area. He fired with rapid single shots, peering over the sights and relying on the accuracy of his instinctive shooting skills. Even at a range of fifty metres, many of his rounds were slamming into their intended targets. He squeezed the trigger again and saw the head of the nearest body snap backwards and a dark mist plumed up behind it as the 5.56mm bullet ploughed its way out from the other side of its skull. Its legs collapsed from underneath it and Bobby turned his attention to the next corpse in line.

Above, he could hear the voice of Stan but he was unable to understand their commander's words while his ears still rang, the flames around them crackled, and his M-4 snapped unremittingly as more of the dead converged towards them. He felt a hard slap on his shoulder and allowed his attention to be fleetingly snatched away by Taff.

"We're bugging out, Bobby," the Welshman screamed into his ear. "If the airstrikes or pus-bags don't get us, this building definitely will when it falls on our heads."

Bobby nodded and snatched up the small med-pack he had tucked into the corner of the barricade. He quickly slung it over his shoulder and continued to fire at the approaching infected.

"What about the others?" He asked as he secured his kit and fired another group of five shots, dropping two of the infected.

"They're heading back to the roof," Taff called back over his shoulder as he began scrambling over the pile of ruined furniture stacked against the doors. "The stairs have been wiped out so they're brushing up on their abseiling skills. We're heading for the ERV."

On the other side of the barricade, Taff stood his ground and began despatching the grotesque figures that lurched towards them while Bobby climbed out from the foyer. From the rear of the group, a flurry of movement caught Taff's eye. He turned, pointing his rifle towards the potential new threat. A runner, moving fast, had shot through the gate and was racing towards them from between the parked cars to the left of the parking area. Taff fired, the first shot missing the creature by just a few millimetres and hitting the corpse of a woman behind it. The round punched through her breast bone, causing her body to twitch but otherwise showing no sign of damage. He fired again, and again, missing with each shot. With just a few metres to spare, his fifth round finally hit its mark. The speeding copper plated missile blasted its way through the man's lower jaw and virtually severed his head from his brittle spinal column. The corpse dropped to its knees, its head lolling to the side for a moment before it crashed face first into the tarmac.

Bobby was now over the obstacle and joined Taff in the melee. He fired rapidly and downed a number of bodies before the bolt locked to the rear within the body of his rifle, revealing an empty chamber and magazine. He had already turned and was moving to the right towards the narrow walkway that led along the side of the apartments and connected them to the factory complex through the old rusty gate. It was pointless to stand still and change out his ammunition, presenting himself as an easy target. A magazine change should always be done on the move, either while advancing or withdrawing.

"Magazine," he urgently called out to Taff.

He fell back and headed for the corner where the wall met the alleyway. His right index finger pressed against the protruding release catch just in front of the trigger guard. The empty magazine dropped and clattered against the ground while simultaneously, Bobby's left hand had already closed over the replacement that he dragged out from a pouch on the left side of his assault vest. With a single, well-practiced motion, Bobby clicked the fresh magazine into place, thumbed the bolt release catch, sending a round into the chamber, and brought his weapon around to bear as he turned and covered Taff's withdrawal.

"Taff, move," he shouted out as he began to fire again.

Still using his instinctive shooting skills, Bobby kept both eyes open, maintaining visual contact with Taff as he turned and headed towards him. Bobby adjusted his aim as the short stocky Welshman bounded for him in a semi-crouch. Careful not to shoot his partner as he sent rounds heading towards the wailing bodies, Bobby swayed to the side as he fired, his rounds snapping by, very close to Taff's head as he hurtled for the alley.

In the narrow passageway, Taff and Bobby bounded along beside the wall and headed for the gateway leading into the factory. A loud crunch above them made them look up just in time to see a large bulky shape hurtling through the air and away from the roof's edge. Three more bodies quickly followed the first figure. It was Stan and the others. They had made it to the roof and were flinging themselves into thin air, using the ropes to control their fall, but slowing them only marginally.

The first to land was Danny. With just a metre to go, he expertly tightened his grip to the point where the tips of his boots lightly touched the ground before his heels made contact and he came to a graceful landing with bending knees that absorbed the impact. The rest were nowhere near as elegant in their descents. Bull, the least of all.

While Stan and Marty landed heavily on unsteady legs but managed to remain upright and balanced, Bull smashed into the concrete pathway. A small crater formed in the centre of a spider's web effect in the broken cement, the cracks branching out from the site of the impact. He landed with a heavy splat and bounced into the wall of the factory perimeter with a loud huff.

"Fuck…," he gasped.

Without waiting to see if Bull was conscious or free from injury, Taff began heaving him to his feet just as the first of the infected rounded the corner of the apartment building. Bobby raised his rifle and began firing while the others retreated towards the gate, hobbling and dragging one another through the narrow entrance.

Bobby slammed the gate shut but discovered that there was nothing to secure it with. The alleyway was now packed with the infected making their way along towards where they had seen the men disappear through the gap in the wall.

"Leave it, Bobby," Danny was shouting over to him from the door leading into the main factory floor. "Leave it and move."

Bobby turned and from the peripherals of his vision, he saw movement to his left within the courtyard of the factory complex. A wall of dead faces were staring back at him and staggering in his direction. They had entered through the main gates, having caught sight of the men as they began climbing down from the roof and naturally turned in that direction, spewing in through the twisted iron barriers of the gatehouse. By now he could hear their moans and excited cries as they caught sight of his animated movements and radiant flesh.

"Watch the wire," Danny called frantically, pointing down towards the threshold of the factory doorway as Bobby leapt towards him. "The wire. Watch the fucking wire, Bob."

Bobby looked in time to allow himself an extra-long stride and cleared the trip-wire connected to the S-Mine that was situated at the side of the doorway on the outside of the building. The hair-thin cable stretched across the bottom of the frame and ran up alongside the door and would trigger the mine if the entrance were breached. As Bobby landed inside the factory, Danny connected the end of the thin line to the door handle.

Bobby and Danny fled through the factory, ducking between the machinery and hurdling over pipes and fallen ducts in the wake of the others. As they made their way through the maze of rusted steel obstacles, their ears detected a deep rumbling from outside and beyond the factory walls. The noise grew in volume and ferocity and soon became a screaming snarl as the fighter jets returned for another bombing run.

"Incoming," Stan howled from somewhere up ahead within the warren of machinery. "It's HE coming in. Get down."

Danny and Bobby threw themselves to the ground and scampered across the dust covered surface of the factory floor, crawling towards a huge rusted iron piece of equipment towering above them that would hopefully provide them with some cover from falling debris. By now, the noise of jet wash raged within the building, sounding as though a storm was blowing in amongst the abandoned industrial equipment.

"Down, get down," Stan's voice continued to echo around them.

Bobby and Danny curled themselves into balls and clenched their teeth, waiting for the inevitable impacts of the high explosives.

The Tornados and Typhoons were now overhead.

17

For hours, the battle had continued to rage for control of the airfield. The first troops to land had very nearly been overrun as they desperately held onto the ground that they had retaken. The CH-47s, packed with troops and flanked by gunships screeched in low and fast, barely slowing as they swooped in with their wheels bouncing against the runway. While the soldiers poured out from the rear ramps, thousands of corpses wandering through the local roads, fields, and built-up areas turned and headed for the noises of racing engines, thumping rotor blades, and chattering gunfire.

As the troop carrying helicopters, barely on the ground for more than a few seconds, returned to the island to pick up reinforcements, the vastly outnumbered soldiers left behind formed a perimeter around the landing zone. They fought off wave after wave of undead as they ferociously charged at the terrified men and women throwing up a hail of bullets from rifles and machineguns into their path. Before long, massed crowds of ravenous bodies were assaulting the besieged airbase from all directions.

The air droned with the incessant sound of battle as hordes of the dead were cut down. Tracer rounds zipped out in all directions like laser beams, tearing through flesh and bone. The airfield was quickly becoming sodden with the congealed blood and putrefied brains of the infected and a vast swathe of bodies was beginning to pile up around the beleaguered defenders as they valiantly stood their ground. They had no choice but to stand and fight. There was nowhere for them to retreat to and there was no possibility of surrender. This was a war of attrition against an enemy who asked for and gave no quarter.

In a number of places, the reanimated corpses had broken through but the soldiers who had been kept in reserve for that exact reason quickly plugged the holes in the line. The few vehicles that had been carried across from the Isle of Wight raced from one crisis to the next, carrying the Quick Reaction Force. The QRF, made up of the hardest veterans, relentlessly counter-attacked along the entire line to support the crumbling defences and throw back the attackers.

The support helicopters above them did what they could, concentrating their fire on large clusters of the infected moving towards the airfield but they could not afford to waste valuable ammunition on individuals and smaller groups. That task was left to the troops below with controlled firepower and dogged determination in the face of death as they stood together, fighting for the people beside them.

Casualties were sustained. Some were hurt from the explosions that erupted around the perimeter as the Apaches and Cobras blasted the dead. Others were bitten and torn as groups of the infected managed to crash through their defences and wreak panic upon the terrified men and women.

The aid stations were slowly becoming ineffective as the wounded began to pile up around the handful of medics that were expected and equipped to deal with much smaller numbers. Some of the bite victims took their own lives but many needed to be helped. Most of them screamed in protest and begged to be spared as the Military Police stepped in to deal with them before allowing them the chance to die and return.

Only when reinforcements and resupply began to arrive did the tide begin to turn in the favour of the living. The hopes of the men and women on the ground soared when they looked to the south and saw the large dark silhouettes of the Chinooks as they approached, returning from the island. After being alone for almost two hours, their confidence grew and their fighting spirit lifted as the reinforcements began pouring onto the airfield and were launched straight into the attack. With the extra manpower and ammunition, and the landing zone secured, the assault troops went onto the offensive. They advanced out from the perimeter and began pushing the enemy back, leaving a trail of devastated bodies in their wake as they formed a new defensive line.

More vehicles arrived and attack helicopters from the island relieved the Apaches and Cobras already on station, allowing them to return for refuelling and rearmament. The offensive on the Farnborough airfield was beginning to take shape. The more soldiers arrived, the further the defences were able to push outwards until eventually a ring was formed around a great swathe of the runway and buildings, including the all-important fuel depot.

With the airfield in their hands, the troops were able to begin refuelling their support aircraft on site, rather than having to send the helicopters back to the island. Huge amounts of soldiers and material began to disembark onto the runways as the Chinooks stubbornly continued their shuttle runs to and from the island.

Peter and Michael had been amongst the first of the militia to arrive. They stepped off the aircraft and into a raging hell. Smoke swirled around them, pouring out from the buildings lining the runway that had caught fire from the burning tracer rounds and the rockets fired from the gunships. The sound of clattering gunfire echoed all around and the tortured screams of the wounded could even be heard over the howl of the helicopters.

Their commander led them towards an area just to the rear of the forward defences. The terrified militia sat clustered together, unable to form a clear thought in their racing minds as they watched the defenders running about just metres away from them, screaming to one another and endlessly firing their weapons.

The loud crack of a grenade exploding just twenty metres away caused Peter to flinch and yelp involuntarily. He turned and saw a small dense murky cloud of debris and smoke where, only a moment before, there had been two soldiers desperately fighting against a number of the dead. He clutched his rifle tightly and huddled close to his brother.

Michael was just as shocked and terrified. His gaping eyes darted in all directions as he watched hundreds of twisted figures falling beneath a storm of gunfire all around them. The helicopter ride had been fun and exciting but he would have gladly refused the adventure if he had known what to expect once they landed.

Eventually, the battle had been all but won. The avalanche of corpses slowed and petered out to a trickle as the bodies began to stack up around the perimeter. Shots still rang out from all around the defensive line but they were intermittent now instead of the raging hailstorm of thundering guns. The attack helicopters continued to circle the area surrounding the airfield, keeping a vigil for the people below and loosing off the occasional rocket or burst of cannon fire into clusters of approaching infected.

The airfield was quickly being reorganised and the civilian militia, who now numbered in their thousands, were tasked with replacing the fighting men and women on the line and holding the perimeter. The regular soldiers were withdrawn into the centre to resupply their weapons and ammunition in preparation for the next phase, the assault on London.

Peter and Michael had not been sent to the front. They had gladly accepted the task of helping to unload the helicopters as they came in to drop equipment, vehicles, personnel, and pick up the wounded. For well over an hour, the two brothers toiled and sweated in the early morning chill as the airfield buzzed with activity around them. Concentrating on what he was doing, Peter was almost able to forget where he was, and about the fact that millions of the infected surrounded them.

"Are we winning, Peter?" Michael asked as he dropped a heavy crate of machinegun ammunition onto a huge stack.

"I don't know," Peter replied, pausing and arching his aching back. He looked around at the preparations being carried out all across the airfield. "I think we are."

"Good, because when this is all over, I want us to live in a big house with a swimming pool. I want two puppies and a helicopter of my own." Michael looked up at one of the menacing Apaches as it flew over the airfield towards the east. He raised his hand and waved before turning back to his brother. "Do you think they'll teach me how to fly one of those when it's all over?"

"Yeah, Mike, I'm sure they will," Peter replied dryly as he went back to hefting the ammunition onto the stack.

Unfortunately, their respite from the horror of the battle was not long lived. As the long column of trucks, loaded with ammunition and soldiers moved out towards the north where they would push through into the southern outskirts of London and link up with the air-assault troops, Peter's platoon, along with many others, were ordered to follow their commanders. They picked up their weapons and equipment and moved towards a row of waiting helicopters. Their engines were already running at full revolutions and the Loadmaster was frantically waving them forward towards the ramp.

Peter looked around, knowing full well where they were headed. His hands trembled and a cold sweat began to trickle down from his neck and along his spine. The four regular soldiers that had been attached to each militia platoon were standing to the rear of the group, herding them forward and ensuring that none of them attempted to flee. Since landing at the airfield, Peter had witnessed a number of summary executions being carried out on deserting men and women by officers and soldiers alike. He glanced down at Michael standing beside him and appearing completely oblivious to what was going on. He was back to looking excited and eager to climb aboard the Chinook. Peter wondered just how far they would get before they were cut down by gunfire if he decided they should run. He eyed the faces of the regular troops. They were tough and vigilant, expectant of such actions from the militia.

Not very far, he reasoned.

"Are we going in the helicopter again, Pete?"

"Yeah, looks that way, Mikey," Peter replied, feeling forsaken.

"I've decided," Michael said, turning to his brother with a broad and innocent smile. "Chinooks are now my favourite helicopters."

"Good for you, Mike," Peter said hollowly. "Good for you."

The militia moved forward and stepped up onto the tailgate of the CH-47. The Loadmaster impatiently pushed them along, slapping his hand against the shoulder of each man and woman who passed him and screaming over the noise of the engines for them to move along and find a seat.

Crammed into the fuselage like cattle, the press-ganged soldiers crouched and sat wherever they could. No one had told them where they were going but most of them had worked it out for themselves. The assurances of them not being thrown into the front line unless it was really necessary seemed to have been forgotten. There were still a large number of regular and better trained and equipped soldiers at the airfield and it was becoming clear to Peter that they were being used as infected fodder.

Surely, it can't be going that badly at the front already? Peter wondered as he looked around the aircraft at the frightened civilians who were about to be thrown into the thick of battle against an enemy that, in his mind, could not be beaten.

Once again, he felt the now familiar lift of the aircraft as the rotors tilted forward and the wheels left the ground. Through the small round windows along either side of the fuselage, Peter watched the other CH-47s as they all climbed in unison, quickly rising into the air above the airfield and heading to the north.

"Michael," Peter yelled down to his foolishly grinning brother, "remember what I told you before the last helicopter ride?"

A look of deep thought swept over Michael's face for a moment before he turned back up to Peter with no indication of having found the answer. Peter leaned down, holding onto one of the cargo-nets hanging from the bulkhead behind the cockpit as the helicopter shook and lurched, threatening to throw him into the wall.

"Stay close to me. Don't leave my sight, Mikey. Move only when I move and stop only when I stop. Don't do *anything* unless I tell you to. Okay?"

Michael nodded enthusiastically and held up his thumb. He held it there for a while, keeping his eyes locked on Peter before turning his attention back to the window and staring out at the landscape below them.

It was not long before Peter noticed that the aircraft was slowing down and had developed a slight tilt as the nose lifted and the tail dropped. He looked around at the expectant faces surrounding him. Eyes shone brightly with fear as they turned to one another with silent questions and looked to the regular troops amongst them for answers.

The veterans were climbing to their feet, checking their equipment, and readying their weapons. They turned and began shouting orders, barely audible within the fuselage, to the militia who just sat staring back at them, too frightened to move or completely unaware as to what was expected from them.

Peter leaned over and looked over Michael's shoulder and out through the window. The ground below was no longer the sprawling green fields that they had been travelling above for the previous fifteen minutes. It was now a jumble of buildings, houses, and clogged roadways with broken down traffic. The landscape was no longer whipping by as the engines of the Chinook forced them along at speeds which defied the cumbersome size and shape of the aircraft. They were now moving at a much slower pace and the distance between the CH-47 and the ground was decreasing rapidly. They were coming in to land.

Peter reached down and slapped his brother on the shoulder.

"Stay close," he reiterated as he shouted into Michael's ear. "Do you understand me? Stay close, Mike."

"Yeah, Peter, I understand. I will stay close and only move when you tell me to," Michael screamed back up at him with a proud look on his face for having remembered the instructions his brother had given him earlier.

By now, everyone on board either had climbed to their feet voluntarily or had been dragged up by the people beside them. The smell of exhaust and aviation fuel was quickly becoming diluted by the stench of vomit, urine, and the distinct smell of human excrement. Peter's nose wrinkled as the pungent odours drifted into his nostrils. With the interior being so tightly packed, it was impossible to tell who were to blame for the variety of stinks filling the aircraft. Accusing looks were swapped between many of the militia and soldiers but no one openly owned up to the responsibility. Peter suspected that most on board had played at least a small part in adding to the new and offensive atmosphere.

Peter was doing his best to remember the small amount of training that they had received. The rifle in his hands had still not become the extension of his body that the instructors had promised it would one day be. His equipment, packed with ammunition, was heavy and uncomfortable. The straps dug into his shoulders and caused his back to ache. He was far from being prepared for battle. He was a civilian and his brother was even less prepared. Peter would need to look out for Michael while trying to remember how to work his own weapon and keep himself safe.

"Thirty seconds," the Loadmaster screamed from the far end as he stood close to the tailgate with his hand hovering over the control panel, ready to lower the ramp.

The veteran soldiers, standing close to the tailgate, turned and repeated what the Loadmaster had shouted, passing the message along to the people behind them. Peter felt his mouth suddenly become dry and a cold hollowness form inside his abdomen.

Aircrew that had been sitting squeezed into the gap between the cockpit and the passenger compartment jumped down and pushed their way through the civilian militia that were standing in their way. Climbing over people and equipment with no regard for where they placed their feet, they reached for the machineguns that were attached to the side doors with their barrels pointed outwards. As soon as they were there, the aircrew pulled back on the cocking levers, chambering rounds from the long shining belts of 7.62mm ammunition leading into the feed-trays from the steel containers attached to the sides of their guns. They began to swivel from side to side, searching for targets on the ground.

Peter watched them with curiosity. They reminded him of the door-gunners he had seen in numerous Vietnam War movies, hanging from the Huey helicopters. Over the din of the engines, he saw the aircrew on the starboard side begin to judder and a flurry of brass casings began to fly through the air from the right of his machinegun. Then the muffled rattling of the gun as it fired rapidly reached his ears. It seemed an eternity before the gunner took his finger away from the trigger and began looking for more targets and Peter wondered just how many of the dead were down there, waiting for them.

"Five seconds," the Loadmaster by the tailgate roared and hit the button to begin lowering the ramp.

Everyone took in deep breaths, trying to control their fear in the face of having to step out into the hell that had once been the city of London. They had no idea what to expect when they landed. All they knew was that the forward elements of the air assault had made their break-in and were in heavy contact with the enemy. Every eye was now focussed on the ramp as it slowly lowered and more of the blue sky, swirling clouds of black acrid smoke, and eventually, rooftops came into view.

The faces of the civilian troops were pale and coated with sweat. Their knees shook and their stomachs twisted. The stench of fear and human waste suddenly became all the more overpowering inside the fuselage as the men and women prepared themselves to step out into battle.

With a heavy bump, the wheels touched down on the tarmac of a wide road, flanked by tall buildings and filled with the scorched remains of people and vehicles. Fires blazed all around within the structures and the nerve clawing sounds of battle could be clearly heard, even from within the helicopter.

The Loadmaster turned and began shouting into the depths of the helicopter as he waved everyone forward.

"Go, go, go..."

18

Time seemed to slow down to little more than a snail's pace. The roar of the Tornado and Typhoon engines became a thunderous rumble in their ears, mixing with the sounds of their pounding hearts and the echoing voice of Stan as he continued to scream out to them to get down and into cover.

With his head cradled between his own elbows and his forearms locked tightly together to protect his face, Danny peered through the narrow gap between his wrists as he waited for the high explosive bombs to land. Seconds had turned into hours and it began to feel like he had been braced and expectant of the impacts for an eternity.

The walls of the factory suddenly caved inwards with a deafening roar. The old Victorian bricks and the stained glass windows shattered into a million pieces of flying shrapnel as the blast wave flung them through the air at lightning speeds. The floor seemed to rise beneath Danny and then tumble back to its foundations, dragging his shocked body with it and slamming him into the hard surface as everything around him was turned upside down and pulled and twisted out of shape. The heavy iron machinery above them swayed and strained against the brackets and bolts holding it in place. It juddered and clanged as chunks of masonry slammed against it, tearing valves and pipes away to join in with the flying debris punching holes through the remaining walls around them.

Danny felt his ears burst and his ribcage being squeezed. It felt as though his body was about to implode and then explode a moment later. Bobby was screaming something unintelligible beside him as the building collapsed all around them under the force of more detonations. Pipes and ducts showered down from the ceiling and crashed to the floor, bouncing from machinery and crushing the workstations throughout the factory. His vision blurred and he felt a heavy weight slam down on his lower legs. Something had landed on him and pinned him to the floor. With panic quickly rising inside him as he realised that he was trapped,

Danny began screaming and trying to pull his legs free of the solid iron grate that had fallen from the roof and now ensnared him.

After the first set of detonations were over and the debris ceased falling, Bobby began pushing at Danny's back, knowing that it would not be long before the next bombardment began, or until the infected made it into the building.

"We need to move, Danny," he was screaming frantically as he heard more fighters approaching their position in the distance. "Danny, move."

Danny was howling with pain and Bobby realised that his friend was unable to comply with his demands to crawl out from their cover. He glanced along the length of Danny's body and saw the rusted piece of walkway that had dropped onto his legs. Even at just a glance Bobby could see that the skin had been broken and bones had probably fractured. He climbed over Danny and searched around him as he scurried out onto the remains of the factory floor. All around them were piles of twisted metal, smashed brick, and shattered glass. Up above, Bobby saw that the roof had disappeared entirely and all that remained were a few of the twisted and buckled iron girders that had once held the tiles and sheets of corrugated iron securely in place.

He crawled around to the side of the machinery that they had taken cover beneath. The metal plate that had landed on Danny sat flush with the side of a large cylindrical tank and would need to be lifted in order to free him. Just one look at the object confirmed to Bobby that he would not be able to move it on his own. It must have weighed at least two or three-hundred kilograms.

To his left, he saw the gaping hole where the entrance into the main factory building had once been. The S-Mine had done its job well and now it was nothing but a jagged hollow in the wall with the mauled bodies of dozens of infected mixed in with the rubble.

A figure appeared out of the dust that swirled around the gap, tripping over fallen bricks and body parts as it began climbing into the building. Its eyes fell upon the man standing just a few metres away and it let out a yearning moan as it doubled its efforts to negotiate the tricky ground underfoot. Bobby raised his M-4 and shot it squarely between the eyes. Its head arced backwards and it tumbled out into the factory yard. Another body soon appeared and there were more of them arriving as Bobby began taking well-aimed shots at their heads while Danny continued to struggle and scream beneath him.

A noise from behind made Bobby turn just as the huge bulk of Bull appeared out of the billowing dust and smoke. He vaulted over a large fallen iron pipe without it affecting his pace in the slightest and landed with perfect balance just a metre away from Danny's head. With a look of rage and hatred stamped upon his face, Bull raised his Minimi machinegun and let off a burst into the crumbling doorway, shattering the heads of a number of the infected and splintering the bricks that were precariously clinging to one another around the hole.

Bobby looked back at him as the bodies began to fall under his heavy weight of fire. Bull's face was smeared with blood and his wide terrifying eyes seemed to glow white from within the swathe of crimson liquid that covered his face. He had a long bloody gouge stretching from the corner of his mouth towards the curve of his jaw that exposed some of his teeth and the muscles around his jawbone. Bobby also noticed that an entire ear was missing from the left side of Bull's head. The wounds were pouring with blood but they did not seem to have any disabling effect upon the big man.

Bull eased off the trigger and stepped across to the side of the machinery where Danny was trapped. He nudged Bobby aside and quickly evaluated the situation. Marty had by now arrived on the scene and took up position beside Bobby and continued to fire at anything that appeared from around the doorway.

"This is going to hurt a little, Danny," Bull roared down at the trapped man and took a wide tight grip on either end of the iron plate.

With every ounce of his strength and growling through gritted teeth, Bull heaved the section of walkway upwards and away from Danny's legs. He felt it move but already it was beginning to slip from his grasp. His shoulders, back, and biceps were screaming at him with the strain and his legs were beginning to shake as he fought to keep the heavy iron from crashing back down onto Danny.

"Grab him," Bull cried as his face turned an even brighter shade of red than it already was from the blood. The veins protruded angrily from the skin of his neck as he jerked his head back and howled. "Bobby... grab Danny... I can't hold it."

Bobby jumped to Danny and Bull's aid while Marty continued to cover them. He gripped the wounded man by his forearms and wrenched him out from beneath the machinery and onto the factory floor. Danny screamed in pain as his battered legs were dragged across the rubble, opening the wounds further and bashing his damaged bones. Behind him, a heavy metallic thud indicated that Bull had released his grip on the fallen walkway. With no time to waste, Bull reached down and hurled Danny up from the ground, slung him over his shoulder, and then turned and began to plough his way back through the ruined building. Marty and Bobby brought up the rear, firing continuously as the infected began to climb in through the shattered doorway.

A torrent of gunfire burst over their heads, forcing them to duck as glowing red tracer rounds zipped by just centimetres above them. Stan and Taff had climbed onto a walkway that remained intact and covered their withdrawal.

"They're coming in," Stan called down to them, referring to the approaching aircraft rather than the undead that were clambering through the doorway. He raised his MP-5 and fired off another group of rapid shots at the crowd that were quickly filling the building behind the fleeing men. "Move your arses. They'll be here any second."

The six of them crashed through a side door and out into the open. They were in a small open-air corridor that linked the main building onto one of the outbuildings. They needed to get out from the factory complex before the next wave began dropping their ordinance and causing the remains of the walls to tumble in on them.

Stan doubted that they could withstand another direct hit like the previous one. They were all hurt to some degree. Splinters of steel and glass had penetrated everyone's flesh and flying lumps of heavy masonry and machinery had caused further injuries within the group. Virtually no one remained completely unscathed. Danny was badly hurt. His legs were bleeding and possibly broken but they could not yet afford to stop and check him over. Taff was covered in blood but he assured Stan that it could not be his, as he could feel no injuries. Bull had lost an ear and sustained a wound to his lower jaw and Bobby was hobbling. Only Marty seemed unhurt or at least, unaffected by any wounds he had suffered.

Stan continued along the short narrow alleyway and soon found himself looking out onto the courtyard. Fifty metres away, he could see the twisted iron rails of the factory's main entrance and beyond it, the street they had entered from a few days before. There were infected milling around on the outside and headed for the gate but he concluded that their numbers were manageable. They had very little choice but to make a dash for the gate because the alternative could already be heard coming in fast overhead.

"Move," Stan called over his shoulder as the first of the aircraft raced over the rooftops of the city. "Move now. Head for the street."

Bull jumped out into the open and charged for the gate. Over his shoulder, Danny's wrecked body bounced with each stride and he grimaced with agony as he fought to keep hold of his light machinegun and his consciousness.

Carrying his Minimi in his free hand, Bull wielded the weapon like a bat, swiping at anything that stood in his path and firing wildly at anything beyond the range of his forceful swings. He shouted and cursed as he pounded across the open, throwing caution and stealth to the wind and relying on his aggression and power.

Marty shot passed him and began leading the way and firing on the move, clearing a path for the others as they hurled themselves towards the street. Behind them the bombs began to obliterate the junction again, pulverising the buildings and the dead into a pile of rock and organic mush. Their heavy thumps shook the ground cracked the air. Chunks of debris rained down over the courtyard but the men had no intention of taking cover. They needed to get out of the danger area before they were all killed by their own people.

The shockwaves of the explosions ripped the apartment complex apart. Its walls burst outwards and its roof began to cave in on itself. It collapsed in a rumbling cloud of dust and falling girders as the team reached the gate. The factory took another hit and a fountain of iron and brick flew high into the air. More debris shot outwards from the centre as the remains of the building imploded.

"Jesus," Bobby shouted over his shoulder as plumes of smoke, dust, and human wreckage rocketed into the air from the factory complex. "Those pilots are flinging their ordinance about like a mad woman's shit."

By now the six men were tearing along the street, barging through the lurching bodies and swatting away the clumsily reaching hands as they fled from the scene. The perimeter wall of the complex absorbed a lot of the devastation that headed their way and provided them with a degree of protection. However, the material thrown into the sky from the explosions still had to obey the laws of gravity.

Man-sized blocks of concrete and metal crashed into the streets behind the factory. Some pieces were close enough to cause the men of the team to adjust their stride and direction while other pieces of debris dropped far to the side or in their wake. The infected in that area were not spared either. A dense group of advancing corpses that were standing in Bull's path were bowled over by the rear end of a Volkswagen Beetle that had been ripped apart and hurled out from the parking area at the rear of the apartments. Bull looked up and silently thanked the pilot responsible as the gaggle of infected were swept aside.

They turned right and into an empty street. Their footsteps seemed to grow louder, bouncing from the tall buildings on either side of them as the sound of the raging battle for the city faded into the distance, cushioned by the walls of the buildings. The ground still shook with the impacts of the relentless airstrikes, and the streets echoed with their *whumphs* and *thwacks*, but they were now out of the immediate danger area. The hordes of infected that had converged on the intersections were being decimated and mixed in with the booming thuds of the airstrikes, the sound of small arms and heavy machinegun fire could now be heard far off in the distance.

Apart from a few corpses that were badly damaged or too decomposed to move at a speed that was more than a crawl, the street appeared deserted. The team slowed their pace to a steady walk, having broken contact with the dead and extracted themselves out of the line of fire from their own aircraft. It was now time for them to find a place to rally and take stock of their condition.

Further along, Stan stepped off the street and moved to the left. He paused for a moment, checking along the road in each direction and then scrutinising the black chasm of a large doorway that led into one of the buildings. He looked up and read the sign that was embossed into the discoloured granite stone of the doorway's plinth. Before the outbreak, it had been a bank.

Most of the windows, made from thick reinforced glass, remained intact. Some of the panes bore the signs of the turmoil that had broken out during the early stages of the plague. Bullet holes had caused craters, surrounded by networks of fractures stretching out across the glass but the building's integrity seemed to remain more or less complete. The door had been left open but did not appear to be damaged. It was as good a place as any for the men of the team to go static and reorganise themselves.

Stan nodded to Marty and they both moved forward together. The others took up cover positions along the wall and watched the street. Bull squatted, keeping Danny slung over his shoulder like a rolled up rug.

"Put me down, Bull," Danny grunted. "I can manage."

"Can you fuck manage, Danny. Just shut up and keep still. I'll put you down once Stan finds somewhere for us to get you sorted out."

A few minutes later, as Taff and Bobby finished dealing with the few infected that crawled and staggered towards them, Stan and Marty returned and gave them the all clear.

Inside the bank, they moved through the large foyer and towards a security door that hung open beside the teller counters. Bobby secured the main entrance and followed on behind, kicking his way through piles of bank notes that littered the marbled floor.

"Fucking hell," he whispered loudly. "We're rich. Look at all this. There must be at least a few million lying about in here."

Through the security door, they entered into a passageway with offices branching off to either side. The rooms beyond the narrow panes of glass set into the doors were dark. No faces lurched out from the gloom as the men peered in through each window as they passed. At the far end, they found a staff area with chairs and tables and a kitchenette. Stan and Marty immediately went to work, pushing a number of the dining tables together and kicking the other furniture to one side.

"Right, Bull, get Danny onto the table so I can have a look at him," Bobby ordered and began opening up his medical pack.

While Bobby began his examination of Danny's legs, the rest of the men checked their weapons and ammunition status. Marty swapped his M-4 for Danny's Minimi light machinegun and stripped him of his belted rounds. At least a half of their ammunition had been spent during the withdrawal from the apartments and factory and the gunners were restocked from the reserves that the rest of the team had been carrying for them. As the men began to see to themselves and their weapons, Bobby tended to Danny.

The building continued to rattle and vibrate around them. Dust and plaster cascaded down in fine mists and the glass in the windows and doors clattered lightly with each low concussion. Everyone instinctively looked up to the ceiling as another wave of distant explosions sent the walls into convulsions.

"How'd you think it's going out there?" Taff asked to no one in particular as he finished off repositioning the magazines within his assault vest.

Nobody bothered to answer him. Beyond the walls, it sounded as though the city was being steadily flattened. The battle was still in its early stages and a huge amount of weaponry and ordinance was being brought to bear. One thing that they were all very aware of was that there would be no second chances. Manpower and ammunition stocks would be severely depleted once the battle was over. All resources would need to be reconsolidated before they even began considering the next push. Every bullet, every aircraft, every drop of fuel, and every available man and woman was being thrown into the counter offensive. If the assault failed then their hold on the mainland would be lost and never recovered.

Everyone remained silent for a moment, still staring up at the ceiling and listening to the sounds of aircraft and the fearsome battle that was being raged outside in the streets of the capital city of Great Britain.

"They *have* to win," Taff said quietly as he turned away and continued plucking out the slivers of steel and glass that had lodged themselves into his flesh.

Danny's fibula on his right leg was broken clean in two and his ankle was badly crushed. Bobby suspected that the tibia may also have some fractures but he could not be sure. His left leg was severely lacerated but as far as he could tell, Bobby saw no breaks. With the help of the others holding Danny down, Bobby began work on resetting the broken bones. Danny writhed and thrashed as he bit down on the collar of his shirt, trying desperately to hold in the scream that was fighting to get out from between his clenched teeth.

Bobby bound his damaged legs with anything he could use. First he lined the bones up and then retrieved a thick roll of box tape from one of the drawers of the kitchenette. He tightly wrapped it around each leg so that Danny's boots became fused with his body and it was virtually impossible for his ankles to move and cause further damage. Next, Bobby took a couple of financial magazines that had been brushed from the table. He folded them around both of Danny's lower legs and then proceeded to bound them with multiple layers of tape until there was nothing left on the roll. The end result was that both of Danny's legs were set with rudimentary casts and would hopefully be enough to support his wounded limbs. At least that way, Danny could walk unaided if he needed to. His treatment was completed when Bobby gave him an injection of painkillers.

"It's not exactly morphine, mate, but it should be enough to take the edge off the pain. We wouldn't want you stumbling about while you're smacked off your tits, would we?" Bobby said with a smile.

"Cheers, Bob," Danny grunted while looking down at the strange casts that their team medic had secured to his lower legs.

Next, Bobby turned his attentions to the mighty Bull. The huge man was sitting in the corner, using piles of bank notes pressed against the hole where his missing ear used to be. He looked up at their medic and grinned, stretching the wound running along his cheek and exposing a number of shining white teeth.

"Those twenty-pound notes are doing nothing in the way of stopping the bleeding, you dick head," Bobby pointed out, shaking his head as he squatted down beside Bull to begin examining the wounds. He winced and grimaced as he pulled back a cluster of notes displaying the blood smeared face of Queen Elizabeth II.

"Hey, it's the most expensive first-field-dressing I've ever seen, so I thought I would treat myself," Bull shrugged.

Bobby went to work. After a few minutes of hissing and groaning as the wounds were cleaned and then hurriedly sewn together, Bull ceased his torrent of abuse and physical threats against the man who was trying to help him.

"Fuck me," Marty grunted as he looked down at Bull's disfigured face. "You look like something that just crawled out of Frankenstein's lab, mate."

"I'm still better looking than you'll ever be, you ugly shit."

"Trust me, Bull, that audition for the first post-apocalyptic boy-band you wanted to go to... I think you should reconsider your options, mate," Taff added.

Once their injuries were dressed and the men felt ready, they prepared to move.

"What's the plan?" Taff asked, turning to Stan.

Stan shrugged. They had two real options as far as he could tell. They could either try to reach the front lines of the offensive and link up with the assault units there, or move to the river's edge in the hope of getting picked up by Captain Werner and his boat. Making it through to the troops fighting in the south of the city would be difficult, if not impossible. The infected were attacking the lines in vast numbers and there was also the added threat of getting shot by their own soldiers or bombed by their own aircraft.

The river was their best option. They would need to make their way back towards the north, through the city. However, they could not be sure that the submarine would still be there. Werner was only expected to stay in the river for twenty-four hours after the drop-offs were completed and then move to a safe distance within the estuary to avoid being hit by any stray ordinance.

"Can you walk?" Stan asked as he turned back to Danny.

Tentatively, Danny lowered himself down from the table and tested the ability of his encased legs to take his weight. He grimaced as he allowed more pressure to be added, slowly building up to the point where his lower limbs were supporting him entirely. He grunted and huffed with each movement. Finally, he was standing unsupported and he took a slow step forward. His face was ashen and the pain he was suffering could clearly be seen in his glittering eyes but he was determined to walk unaided. He hobbled forward a few paces, sucking in air through clenched teeth with each agony filled step. He stopped and looked up at Stan.

"Do you think you can make it?"

Danny nodded.

"I can manage, Stan," he groaned as he checked the M-4 that Marty had given him in place of his much heavier and bulky Minimi. "Just don't be trying to break any records on the pace you set. I'll look like a right clown trying to run with Bobby's homemade callipers on."

19

The veterans were the first to jump down on to the London streets. The militia followed closely behind them but with much less vigour and enthusiasm. As Peter and Michael hopped from the rear of the Chinook, they were both grabbed by other soldiers and pushed forward to where the rest of their platoon nervously stood in a tight cluster and waiting for further orders. The moment that the helicopter was empty, its wheels started to lift again and the Loadmaster began closing the ramp. He watched the civilians as they stared back at him with frightened eyes and gave them an encouraging wave, followed by a thumb's up. The ramp closed and the Chinook lifted high into the air and headed back towards the airfield.

"Stay here," the militia Platoon Commander shouted to them, "and whatever you do, don't fucking wander off."

All around them, they could see troops running through the streets in all directions, firing their weapons and screaming to one another as they cleared the buildings with machineguns and flame throwers. Overhead the sky snarled with the sound of fighter aircraft as they continued to pummel the forward positions with rockets and bombs. Loud detonations boomed out through the streets, shaking the ground below the feet of the terrified militia. Buildings were collapsing under the onslaught of high explosives while bodies were flung through the air for great distances.

As Peter ducked with each thundering detonation, he pulled his brother in close. He had never seen or felt anything like it. It was hard to tell what was happening or how the break-in was progressing. In his eyes, it was complete chaos.

Close by, a cluster of soldiers stood talking loudly. Radios hissed and orders were barked. Peter recognised their commander and soon realised that he was receiving instructions from the senior officer for that patch of ground. He could not tell what was being said but the conversation seemed to be going only one way. The area commander was instructing the young regular officer on what he wanted him and his platoon of militia to do.

A moment later and they received their own orders. From what Peter could surmise, they were going to move forward and cover an area of ground that was out towards the left flank of the assault. He was unable to hear the rest of the orders being barked at them because another sortie of fast moving aircraft rocketed directly above their heads. Even if he could hear what the officer was saying, Peter doubted that he would understand much of it because tactics and military jargon had not been covered during their brief period of training and preparation back on the Isle of Wight.

The Tornados and Typhoons, appearing like black monsters from out of the clouds, swooped in low over the buildings and released their rockets. Peter looked up and watched as the missiles burst forward and soared away over the rooftops to the north and disappeared, leaving a faint streak of white smoke in their wake. A second later, he felt and heard their impacts as they exploded. He cringed and pulled Michael down with him, expecting a shower of debris to begin raining down upon them. They were suddenly yanked to their feet and the angered, soot smeared features of one of the veterans that had already been in battle for a number of hours began screaming into their faces and ordering them to follow him. The Platoon Commander tagged along on his heels and the militia followed, flanked by the four regular troops who kept an eye on them as they headed for the front line.

They passed through a number of streets, stepping over the mangled and charred bodies of the dead and making their way through the detritus that covered every part of the roads. The ground was littered with chunks of masonry, twisted metal, and deformed limbs. Exhausted soldiers, having been pulled back from the line to rearm and rest for a few precious moments sat staring out into space, their uniforms tattered and covered with dust and the ever present smears of blood. Their faces looked gaunt and their eyes hollow from fatigue and revulsion at what they had experienced in such a short space of time. Most of them were silent and impassive to the fresh men and women who marched passed them. Others wished the troops of the militia luck, acknowledging that they were all in that particular mess together, regardless of where they had come from.

As the skies continued to roar with the sound of jet engines and the heavy *whumphs* of huge detonations, the men and women of the militia were led into a street and told to take up defensive positions. Against a backdrop of clattering machineguns that echoed from every direction, the anxious and inexperienced platoon formed themselves into a line and took cover behind the vehicles that remained sitting at the roadside. The main battle now seemed further away, the sound buffered by the buildings that surrounded them on either side. The street, virtually untouched by the ravages of the offensive seemed almost like an oasis of calm within a desert of chaos and death.

Close behind them, Peter could now hear the conversation between the filth encrusted veteran and the officer in charge of their platoon. The soldier spoke in a low voice, careful not to allow the ringing in his ears to dictate his volume of speech.

"The front is becoming bogged down, sir. Every time they try to move forward they get flanked by pus-bags. We don't have enough men to cover every street so we need to protect their left flank and if possible, fill the gap between ours and the next unit along to the west. There are still thousands of infected moving in towards the landing zones and that street is causing us all kinds of dramas," the soldier grumbled and nodded along the road and indicated the junction up ahead where another street crossed its path. "Twice now we've tried to push forward but ended up getting attacked by those fuckers coming along on our blind side."

"Roger that, Corporal," the young second Lieutenant replied, nodding his head and then looking along the street with probing eyes. "What do you need from me and my men?"

The Lieutenant was doing his best to sound in control of things and unfazed by what was happening around him, but it was clear that he was scared too. The veteran just stared at him for a moment with a blank expression on his face. Then his features twisted into a snarl and his eyes became ferocious.

"What the fuck do you think I need?" He growled hoarsely. "I need you and your band of fucking boy scouts to hold this line."

The officer looked shocked for a moment and was about to reply, no doubt intending on waving his rank around and pointing out the fact that a lowly corporal had no right to speak to him in that way, especially since he held a Queen's Commission. However, the unflinching brutal look in the battle hardened soldier's face was all the encouragement that the Lieutenant needed to decide it was best to allow that one little slip of discipline and respect for the chain of command to slide.

"Listen to me, *Rupert*," the veteran continued impatiently and referring to the Lieutenant with the nickname given to all British officers. "All you have to do, is stop those things from getting through here. I'm here with you and I'll call in the airstrikes. B Company is going to start moving around through the streets to our left in an attempt to join up with the first-battalion and it is our job to cover the gap in the meantime. Have you got that? Keep your men under control and leave the thinking and tactics to me."

The soldier turned away and left the officer sitting and staring up at him with his mouth hanging open and a glazed expression covering his face. Behind them, the militia's regular soldiers had gathered and watched the veteran expectantly, waiting for his recommendations. They moved off to the side and began talking quietly amongst themselves, clearly discussing what needed to be done once the dead began attacking.

Peter looked across at the officer and felt a pang of sorrow for the young man. He looked deflated and close to tears. He was clearly a fresh faced second Lieutenant with little or no experience. He was doing his best to lead his platoon into battle and put on a brave face but the veteran had just snatched the frayed rug from beneath his feet and his delusions of grandeur with it. On the other hand, Peter also understood that there was no room from peacocking or pulling rank within the battle torn city. It was the men and women who had quickly needed to learn how to survive that held the knowledge and experience that was vital to the outcome of the offensive. Peter decided there and then that the veteran was the man he would turn to and follow when the fighting started.

They did not have to wait for long. Within a few minutes, as the battle raged a few streets away, the first of the infected showed up at the far end of the road. The men and women hiding behind the cars and pressing themselves into doorways, watched as a number of ghostly figures stumbled through the wispy smoke that seemed to drift along between every building within the city. Some of them continued across the junction and towards the next street while others, turned and headed towards the hidden defenders and followed the sounds of the living as they struggled to wrestle London from the grasp of the dead.

The veteran watched them with his fearsome eyes, instructing the militia troops to hold their fire until he said otherwise. The infected stumbled along the street, and headed straight for the ambush that was lying in wait.

Peter remained huddled behind the wheel-arch of a broken down vehicle that sat at an obscure angle in the centre of the road. Michael was beside him, watching his brother's every move and expression with fearful eyes and waiting for further instructions. He would do nothing unless Peter told him to. He trusted his brother completely and he had looked out for both of them from the very start of the outbreak. He had no reason not to trust his judgement now, even whilst in the city and surrounded by millions of the infected.

More bodies appeared from around the corner and followed on behind the first cluster. There were more of them arriving with each second and Peter began to wonder whether there were deliberate tactics being employed on behalf of the dead. It was almost as if they knew that the left flank was the weak point and that they should attack from there. He shook the thought from his mind, subconsciously knowing full well that the reanimated corpses were incapable of any higher thought or reasoning. It was just blind luck that they wandered that path and besides, to think anything else would be horrifying.

The road between the buildings was quickly becoming packed with a large crowd of wailing bodies. A wall of them advanced along the street and before long, it was impossible to guess their numbers or judge how deeply their ranks stretched.

"Fuck it," the veteran grunted as he crouched beside the second Lieutenant. He ducked down and reached for the handset of his radio. "Zero, this is Charlie-One-Zero-Bravo. I need an airstrike on the left flank, over."

"Roger that, One-Zero-Bravo. What is your location and the Target Reference?" The voice of the radio operator asked.

"There is no Target Reference," the veteran replied angrily and impatiently. "We're on the left of the main assault, between A and B Companies. Just tell those clowns to look for the red smoke and take out everything north of it."

Without waiting for confirmation, the veteran reached into one of his pouches and retrieved a smoke grenade. He pulled the pin and stood up, cocking his arm behind him and hurling the grenade as far as he could. It landed just in front of the first rank of infected. It popped, hissed, and then began to emit and faint red mist. Within seconds, thick crimson plumes were billowing out from the canister and filling the street with blood coloured smoke.

"Fire," he screamed to the militia around him.

Every weapon in the street suddenly opened up on the throng that lurched towards them and dozens of bodies were instantly torn apart under the weight of fire. They tumbled to the ground in droves and were trampled by the feet that relentlessly surged forwards from behind them. Within a very short space of time, the tarmac and pavements were carpeted with the twisted bodies of the fallen but more took their place and pushed on towards the living men and women throwing up a wall of fire from further down the street.

Guns jammed and magazines were expended. The weight of fire began to wither as the poorly trained militia clumsily changed out their ammunition or attempted to clear their stoppages. Their drills were slow and their handling of the weapons was far from being second nature to them. What would have taken a professionally trained soldier only a few seconds to do, took the civilians much longer to accomplish. They wielded their weapons in a painfully slow manner, unsure of what they were doing and hesitating at every turn. They fumbled ineptly with their rifles and ammunition, panicking as the wall of death slowly approached. Some dropped their weapons on the ground and covered their ears, screaming to themselves while cowering into cover. Others turned and fled as the dead advanced to within fifty metres of where they hid.

The regular troops that were standing their ground behind the militia, firing into the sea of dead faces, did what they could to prevent the rout. They alternated their fire from the reanimated bodies and the terrified civilians that were tearing down the street away from the front line. The seasoned soldiers screamed for them to stop, threatening to open fire if they did not stand their ground. Some of the men and women were brought under control and flung back into the line but others were cut down under a hail of bullets from the rifles of their own men as they fled in blind panic.

Peter was sending round after round into the lumbering bodies in front of their position. Tracers whizzed along the street, smashing into flesh and concrete, shattering the remnants of glass still clinging to the window frames of the buildings.

Michael was beside him, firing wildly and doing very little in the way of aiming his rifle. Suddenly, his weapon fell silent and he looked down in panic, unsure of what was wrong. Peter noticed his brother's confusion and without a word, reached down and whipped away the empty magazine.

"A fresh one," he hollered to Michael and pointed down at the SA-80 rifle sitting ineffectively in his hands. "A fresh magazine. Put a fresh magazine on, Mike."

Finally, Michael realised what was expected of him and within a few seconds he was back to spraying the street with un-aimed and inaccurate shots.

A loud whoosh overhead made Peter duck and turn just in time to see the rocket shoot over the street and slam into the centre of the crowd. A bright flash dazzled everyone for a fraction of a second as the shockwave launched them back and onto the ground. A plume of black smoke erupted from deep within the writhing mass of corpses, flinging debris and bodies through the air then falling back to the earth in twisted lumps. Another rocket rushed in and exploded further along the street and against the building closest to the junction. Its bricks and steel frames burst outwards as the missile blew apart with immense force from within. Its deafening boom and blast wave flattened anything still standing over a wide area as shrapnel zipped through the air and tore apart anything that it came into contact with.

From behind the front line, a sound similar to that of ripping canvas but amplified by a thousand, grated on the ears of the living men and women below as the rotary cannons of the Cobra began pouring an immense stream of fire into the infected. The dead tumbled and fell in heaps. The heavy 20mm rounds, firing at a rate of six-thousand per minute, smashed the bodies of the cadavers to pieces as piles of empty brass cases piled up below the hovering angel of death with beating rotors and snarling guns.

Some of the militia cheered and clapped their hands, waving up to the pilot triumphantly and relieved that the enemy advance had been halted before they were overwhelmed. Others just stood and stared in awe at the devastation inflicted upon the street and the infected by the weaponry of the Cobra.

The attack helicopter remained hovering just above the rooftops for a while longer, blasting away with its heavy guns and firing more rockets deeper into the withering enemy. Eventually, its guns ran dry and it needed to leave for rearmament.

A stillness settled over the destroyed street as plumes of smoke rose from every quarter and smouldering debris littered ground. Amongst the wreckage crawled and slithered the mangled remains of the infected that had not sustained injuries to their heads. Some were crawling on shattered limbs and others were nothing but a set of arms with a head, determinedly clawing their way towards the militia.

As the sounds of the Cobra faded, Peter became distinctly aware of more explosions and gunfire coming from close by in the streets to their left. The thunder of battle was creeping closer and soon, the pain filled cries of human beings joined the clatter of rifle and machinegun fire. Out in front of them, a number of corpses lumbered along, still advancing, but they were no longer an immediate threat after the gunship had dealt their attack a crippling blow. Now, the danger seemed to be in the other streets around them.

Suddenly a cry went up from the junction to their rear. Everyone turned in time to see a number of soldiers racing away from the road that joined onto theirs from the left. Some were wounded and being dragged by their comrades while a few was firing blindly into something that Peter and his platoon could not yet see. Others, having flung their weapons away, stormed along the road and continued towards the landing zones. A few seconds later and the first of the infected appeared from around the corner.

One of the retreating soldiers, moving slowly and realising that he would not be able to outrun the crowd, dropped the wounded woman he had been helping to withdraw. He drew his pistol and fired the entire magazine into the mass of bodies until it was empty. Without a second thought, he turned and fled, leaving the injured woman on the ground and screaming for help. No one moved to her aid, but the dead were more than willing to fall upon her. The gut wrenching screams did not last long as dozens of clawing hands tore into her flesh and began ripping her apart.

"Move," the veteran ordered with a roar as he turned to the militia and began charging up the street in the opposite direction from the infected. "It's B Company, they're overrun."

With panic gripping them, the civilian troops turned and followed after the veteran. The regular troops, along with the young officer also followed having seen more of the dead pouring in from the side street and cutting off their escape back towards the landing zones.

Peter grabbed Michael by the collar and wrenched him to his feet. Without allowing him the time to gain his balance, he dragged him along in his wake. Michael stumbled and crashed into a number of vehicles, screaming at his brother to slow down. His pleas fell upon deaf ears as Peter refused to let go and chased after the fleeing militia and the veteran.

They were headed towards the intersection that had been ruined by the Cobra gunship. The buildings on either side, blasted open by the rockets, smouldered and crumbled as they passed. Vehicles lay in their path, twisted and wrecked after being blown apart from the missiles, and everywhere the living people placed their feet, they either stepped on body parts, or splashed through thick rotted blood.

A number of infected reached out for them but they were either cut down by bullets or they were swept to the side. There were more staggering figures up ahead but compared to the size of the crowd spilling into the street behind them, going forward was their best option.

The veteran was sending a desperate situation report as he ran, hoping to call in another gunship to help them. Nothing was available. The left flank of the assault was crumbling fast, being rolled up by vast numbers of undead that had survived the devastation of the airstrikes that morning. The veteran tossed the handset to the side and continued to lead the terrified militia deeper into enemy territory. He had hoped to be able to swing around to the right and meet up with the forward elements of the assault but every street they passed was crammed with the walking dead.

Not everybody followed. As they travelled deeper into the city, some of the civilians began to break away in an attempt to find somewhere to hide. Little by little, the numbers of men and women remaining in the platoon dwindled. Even the second Lieutenant had vanished, along with two of the regular soldiers assigned to the group. The platoon that had once numbered nearly thirty soldiers had shrunken to just eight men and women.

At a corner in one of the streets that seemed relatively quiet, the veteran paused and allowed the people still following him a moment to catch their breath. They were terrified and exhausted.

"Get your weapons sorted out and make sure you have a fresh magazine on. Check your ammo and drop any unnecessary kit," the veteran instructed them.

It was quickly realised that the remnants of the platoon were beginning to run low on ammunition. With the help of the regular soldiers, the magazines were evenly distributed amongst the survivors, giving them all an equal chance at defending themselves. All of them took the opportunity to drink some water but it was not long before the veteran was inundated with questions on where they were, where they were going, and how they were going to get back to safety.

"How the fuck should I know?" The veteran growled at them through clenched teeth. He was clearly just as frightened but it was him that they all turned to for leadership. "We're completely cut off from our own lines and by the sounds of it, the left flank is overrun. I'm just trying to get us away from those fucking things."

Once they were ready, the veteran ordered them up onto their feet again and continued onwards. It seemed that the majority of the infected from within the city centre had converged upon the southern outskirts. The streets, compared to the battle that raged behind them, seemed quiet. There were still a number of wandering corpses that needed to be dealt with but they were nowhere near like the mass numbers that were attacking the front lines.

A few hundred metres further on and the veteran led them into another road leading off to their right. He suddenly stopped and raised his rifle, about to let loose with a volley of shots but took his finger away from the trigger at the last instant.

Before them, just twenty metres away, were six figures standing in the centre of the street and staring back at the militia platoon as they all came bounding around the corner and then coming to an abrupt halt. The six men were covered in dust and blood and their features looked twisted and battered with pale grey complexions. Their eyes burned with savagery and their body language was far from welcoming. But they were clearly alive and they were also heavily armed.

For a few seconds the two groups said nothing and remained where they stood. Finally, the veteran lowered his rifle and stepped forward, careful not to make any sudden or aggressive moves in their direction.

"The left flank has collapsed," he reported to the men in front of him. "We're trying to find a way around."

"The whole fucking assault is collapsing," replied a man standing slightly in front of the others and appearing to be their commander.

Another of the men began to speak. He was much larger than the first and with a red face from all the dried blood that coated his skin.

"The counter offensive is failing and we're trying to find a way out of this rat-trap," he began as he eyed the remnants of the militia platoon. "You'd be as well following us if you knew what was best for you."

The veteran nodded his appreciation and gladly accepted the offer of the fearsome looking soldiers. He turned back to the rag-tag civilians who had somehow become his charge and looked at each one of them in the eye. He began to wonder whether any of them, including him, were likely to survive.

"Stay close to me," he whispered back to the militia survivors as the six men turned and began to move along the street and away from them. "Do everything that these guys tell you and for fuck sake, don't get in their way."

With wide eyes and fear coursing through their veins, the motley bunch of partially trained men and women tagged along behind the strange soldiers that led them along the street. The newcomers were clearly professionals. They moved as a unit and seemed to know what needed to be done without being prompted. While two remained on the flanks and cleared the doorways and windows of the buildings on either side, another two pushed forward, checking corners and the numerous vehicles that littered the streets. One of them appeared to be badly injured and limped along in the centre with his lower limbs wrapped in thick rolls of brown tape and aided by one of his comrades.

On a number of occasions, lone wandering corpses were dealt with in silence with blades pulled from their belts and thrust into their brains. No words or orders were needed.

Peter, up until that point, had been considering leaving the group and finding a hiding place for him and Michael. However, just one look at the six soldiers offering to take them along was enough to convince him that staying with the group was the safest option and their best chance at survival. At least for the time being. His main concern was looking out for himself and his brother.

"We'll be okay, Mikey," he whispered as they walked. "We'll get through this."

20

A blue/grey haze had formed just a few metres above their heads and clung to the atmosphere of the Operations Room. Samantha, having only recently taken up the habit of smoking again, was already going through two packs per day. The time span between cigarettes was down to a matter of just a couple of minutes at times. Her nails had gone, having been chewed to the point where the beds had begun to bleed, and the last of her hairclips had been twisted and snapped out of shape over two days ago. Now her hair was pulled back and tied into a tight ponytail with a rubber band securing it in place.

As usual, she was hovering over the shoulders of the command staff, pumping them for information and situation reports on the various parts of the operation. The cigarette clutched tightly between her lips glowed brightly in the dimly lit room and many of the people around her were quietly choking on the fumes. No one dared to complain. Gerry had questioned her, very briefly, on why she thought it was acceptable to be smoking within the building but he had soon retreated and dropped the matter. Samantha's blazing eyes and taught expression was enough for him to concede.

The counter offensive, though it had started off well, had become bogged down and then began to turn into a defeat. The airfield at Farnborough was still securely in the hands of their troops and the perimeter was holding and being reinforced. The harbour at Portsmouth, however, was a different story. After the initial bombardments, the dead had been reduced to ash and the troops began quickly pouring ashore with the support of helicopters and airstrikes. To begin with, the beachhead had been secured in a very short space of time and it was not long before the troops and vehicles were ready to begin their thrust northwards to link up with the elements at Farnborough and then begin leapfrogging towards London.

Unfortunately, the convoys had become stuck, moving at a crawl along the roads leading northwards from the harbour due to the heavy amount of static vehicles clogging the roadways. It was not long before mass crowds of infected began arriving in the area and attacking the slowly moving vehicles as they wormed their way through the crammed lanes and communications with entire columns were lost.

As the dead attacked, the militia tasked with holding the vital junctions within key villages and towns were gradually being forced to abandon their positions, and many of the regular troops were diverted away before they got to the front at Farnborough and sent to support the civilian soldiers in the south. Enemy numbers in those areas had been greatly underestimated and as soon as the helicopters, planes, and troops began moving in, every corpse in the south seemed to converge upon the harbour and outlying urban areas.

More and more resources were being syphoned away from the main assault on London to help reinforce the collapsing front around Portsmouth. Without the harbours, the continued resupply of manpower, vehicles, and equipment that was needed to be massed for further operations could not be brought to the mainland in sufficient numbers. By aircraft, running shuttle missions, it would have taken too long and momentum would be lost.

Casualties were heavy and a large number of men and women were listed as missing. It was not long before the commanders on the ground began a tactical withdrawal, hoping to gain some breathing space and the chance to reconsolidate their assets and manpower before pushing on with a fresh assault.

As the line began to retreat, the dead feel upon them, overrunning their positions and pushing deeper into the secured areas. The withdrawal soon turned into a rout and no matter how many regular reserve soldiers were thrown in or how intense the airstrikes, the living began to flee towards the south in panic as the infected refused to yield against the heavy defences.

In London, the Special Forces teams had done well. Only one of them had failed to reach their operational area and all communications with that particular group had been lost. Once on the ground, the small units had set up their noise devices and had begun gathering huge numbers of the dead into their areas. The airstrikes had gone according to plan and had wiped out an incalculable amount of enemy forces but again, their numbers were underestimated and the dead continued to swell the streets.

With the attack in the south around the harbours going badly and needing extra support, the assault on London was becoming bogged down within just an hour of the first troops landing on the ground. The airstrikes were still flying and gunships continued to provide close air-support but the front was steadily crumbling under the continued pressure of vast numbers of reanimated corpses.

It was not long before reports began flooding in of a collapse on the left flank. After a number of 'blue on blue' incidents, friendly fire, due to the lines being so fluid, the dead had broken through and began pushing eastwards. With the men and women reeling against the incoming fire from their own air-support, the dead had rushed through the gaps created by the confusion and obliteration caused by the Tornados and Typhoons.

Within minutes, the dead advance was threatening the centre where the main thrust was being conducted. The landing zones were quickly being swamped by retreating men and women and soon being followed by hordes of the infected. Helicopters transporting vital troops and equipment were unable to land while the soldiers on the ground were under threat of being completely surrounded and cut off.

The offensive had already lost one Chinook when the brave pilot, seeing how desperate the situation was, flew in with a company of reinforcements and attempted to land his aircraft at a critical point where the front needed them most. As soon as the wheels of the CH-47 touched down, with the rear ramp already lowered to allow a fast unload, thousands of corpses rushed towards the machine and overwhelmed it before the pilot was able to take off again. They charged up the tailgate and through the fuselage, tearing through the men and women on board. Before the pilot was able to raise his aircraft again, the dead were in the cockpit. Shortly afterwards, the helicopter exploded into a ball of fire.

The battle for the mainland was failing. Samantha, staring up at the large screens attached to the walls of the command centre, showing the dispositions of their forces, could do nothing but look on in horror. It was only a matter of time before the defences at the harbour collapsed completely and the troops that were trapped within London were overrun. All their reserves of manpower and aircraft had been committed out of desperation to shore up the various fronts. However, it was not enough.

Regular reports of ammunition stocks flooded in through one radio, informing them of the rapidly depleting state of their ordinance. While other radios buzzed with updates on movements and the status of ground forces. The casualty reports from the medical arm were just as alarming as any of the others.

Samantha looked from one screen to the next, comparing the information she could see to the reports she held in her hands. The figures were adding up to a catastrophe. She turned and looked towards Gerry. He was sitting staring up at the huge operations screen that displayed the map overlays of the harbour, airfield, and London. He looked shocked and his mouth was agape as he watched in disbelief.

The green dots and rings on the screens, superimposed onto the live satellite imagery, denoted the men and women on the ground and where their lines were at that moment. The swathes of red indicated the dispositions of the dead and it was apparent that the map screens would soon be nothing but a shroud of scarlet.

There was very little that any of the command staff could do. The offensive was descending into chaos and communications were breaking down between the different elements. The air arm continued their bombing missions but it was becoming increasingly difficult for them to distinguish between enemy and friendly forces. As whole units were swallowed up and fell silent the communications staff continued to do all in their power to gain accurate reports but as the command structure fell apart, so did the control.

The troops in London were trapped in an ever shrinking pocket as the dead pushed in from all sides. Their escape routes, via land and air, had been cut off. Resupply and reinforcement would not be able to reach them until the men and women on the ground were able to stabilise the front. Even the relief columns that had departed from the airfield had been stopped short of the city by immense hordes of the dead. Reports from the various commanders on the ground claimed that it would be impossible to break through to London.

Despite Samantha's attempts to reboot the attack by diverting their air-support with orders to begin concentrating their attacks on the south in an attempt to open a corridor for the relief column, the soldiers in London remained trapped inside a noose of rotting flesh. No matter how much ordinance was dropped on the roads and buildings between the reinforcements pushing north from Farnborough and the ensnared men and women in the city of London, the dead refused to relinquish their hold upon their hard won prize.

The door to the Operations Room opened and the tall gangly figure of General Thompson entered. He looked worn out. His naturally gaunt face was paler than usual and his eyes were rimmed red. His hands were shaking and his body appeared frail and weak. He had been receiving the same real-time information that the rest of the command staff had been. He had watched as the attack started well, feeling confident in their ability to reclaim the mainland. Then, he had looked on with growing concern that eventually turned to complete consternation as his forces were stopped, pushed back, and then overwhelmed as the offensive reverted into a calamity that he knew they would not be able to recover from.

Everything had been planned down to the minutest detail. They had prepared for all eventualities, as far as he was concerned, and nothing had been left to chance or overlooked. However, regardless of their preparations, planning, and assets the truth was laid bare for all to see upon the electronic tapestries around the command centre.

"The bastards," General Thompson whispered hoarsely, shaking his head while staring angrily at the screens. "The rotten bastards."

"General?" Samantha said with clear concern as she watched the face of the 'Prince of Darkness' and saw the faint tear that trickled down over his cheek.

Thompson did not reply.

Samantha and Gerry swapped questioning glances. The whole Operations Room was silent as the men and women turned to look at the General with anticipation as frantic cries and reports flooded in over the radio waves along with the sound of gunfire. The units in London were fighting desperately and pleading for someone to help them. Some of the command staff was crying silently as they listened to the torrent of despairing and terrified voices, unable to do anything to help them.

Thompson stood bracing himself against one of the desks, using his hand pressing down against its hard flat surface to support his body, as though he would collapse without its help. He seemed to be unaware of the people around him, as though he was in a world of his own. His eyes, burning with sorrow and anger, remained locked upon the shrinking rings of green that were overlaid onto the map of London.

"Bastards…"

Finally, he turned towards Gerry and Samantha. They could see the regret and sadness in his eyes. Gone was the tall striking figure that exuded confidence to the people around him and instilled fear into anyone who crossed him. Now he appeared like a broken man. A man who had lost everything and was quickly losing his life force along with it.

"Bring them back, Sam," he uttered quietly and looking completely deflated. He turned to begin walking back towards the door. "Bring them all back."

As the door closed behind him the people in the Operations Room wasted no time in calling all their forces back, ordering them to retreat. Each unit and asset of the operation had its own radio operator assigned to it within the command centre and now, messages began streaming out over the net, informing them that the offensive had failed and that they were to begin extracting, immediately.

"Where are they?" Samantha barked at a young corporal sitting to the far right of the room and staring at a computer screen.

Gerry stood up from his desk and began overseeing the progress of the retreat, leaving Samantha to deal with the status of the Special Forces teams.

"I'm not sure," the communications technician replied, shaking his head and nervously tapping a pencil against a cluster of small red dots on the screen. "At their last ping, they were two kilometres north of the front line in London, Captain, but their signals have stopped transmitting. The other teams are headed for their extraction points, if they can get to them, but I have no idea where Stan and his men are or where they're headed."

"Do we have comms?"

The corporal shook his head.

"Their last sit-rep said that they were pulling out from their over-watch position due to the proximity of the airstrikes. I've heard nothing from them since but they were steadily moving in the opposite direction, away from the ground assault."

Samantha stood back and watched the screen for a moment. The beacons were not moving and it had been over an hour since they last updated. The bio readouts indicated that all six members of Stan's group were still alive and well. She studied the red blips and traced the route that they had been moving along. They were headed away from the lines on a general bearing of northeast through the city. She was trying to place herself into their shoes and attempting to anticipate Stan's intentions.

"There's a reason that they're there. They don't do *anything* without knowing what their next move is and it's up to us to know what that move will be."

There was something that she was not seeing. She took a step closer and leaned in over the shoulder of the corporal and studied the map overlay displayed on his computer screen. The six red dots were clustered within a prominent junction on the south side of the river and roughly two kilometres inland from the southern bank. She reached across and zoomed in on the map. Again, she racked her brain and studied the ground where Stan and his men had last been seen. They were too far away from the front line to expect a helicopter extraction and besides, she suspected that they were no longer in that area and the signal was just a ghost of their last transponder update.

"Where the fuck are you, Stan? Where are you leading us?" She grumbled, rhetorically.

She shook her head and thrummed her fingers against the desk for a while as she studied the map. Then she saw it.

"Get hold of Werner," she said urgently and patting her hand down hard on the corporal's shoulder. "And get me a map of the London tube stations."

Gerry looked across to her from amidst the frantic activity of the command staff around him and their anxious voices as they attempted to control the withdrawal.

"They're heading for the river," Samantha said with a nod of confidence as she reached into her pocket and began lighting yet another cigarette. "Those crazy bastards…, they've gone underground."

21

While the battle continued to rage in the streets above, the team and the remains of the militia platoon moved deeper underground. Visibility was down to almost nothing and they relied on their dancing flashlight beams and night vision goggles to expose any danger lurking in the darkness. The booms of the high explosives continued to vibrate through the foundations of the city, shaking the walls of the tunnels beneath and dislodging clumps of masonry as London struggled to withstand the ferocious bombardments.

Stan and his men, wearing their NVGs, led the way down through the dark subway station. Danny was being helped along by Taff while the others fanned out ahead and swept their weapons from side to side, clearing their path as they went while the militia, under the command of the veteran, brought up the rear. The dark basement of London resounded with the fear filled heavy breathing of the survivors.

The ground was covered with the skeletal remains of hundreds of unfortunate victims of the plague. Those travelling through the underground rail networks had been easy prey for the infected when they overran the city. They were trapped and soon became easily disorientated as they fled through the tunnels in panic, searching for the exits. Many never made it out as terror spread and people fought for their own survival. The youngest and oldest were the most vulnerable and as the commuters scrambled for safety, the frail were abandoned or pushed to the side. The infected quickly found the weak and fell upon them. Now their bones carpeted the cold floors and were being trodden on by the living as they too attempted to escape from the city.

Further in, as Stan led them in what he believed to be the general direction of the river, they found themselves in water that had risen up to their knees. Since the power had failed, the pumps had ceased to work and now the River Thames was gradually flooding into the maze of tunnels that criss-crossed beneath the city. The subways reeked of sewage and human decomposition, mixed with the pungent smells of oil and mildew. Already, the survivors were beginning to feel as though they were suffocating and craved the far from clean air that was above ground.

"What the fuck are we doing down here?" Danny whispered rhetorically through pain gritted teeth as he held on to Taff's shoulder and limped through the filthy water.

The painkillers that Bobby had supplied him with were beginning to wear off. Each and every step now shot excruciating pain up through his broken bones and along the length of his body and the network of his nervous system. The agony sent him in to minor convulsions that made his body twitch each time he placed his weight upon his damaged legs. Every stride forced a surge of hurt that rocketed up to his brain with an almost electrifying zap.

"Trying to find a way out, mate," Taff replied as he kept his eyes on Stan and the men in front of them. Their shapes glowed bright green against a backdrop of black through his NVGs. "How you doing, Dan?"

"I won't be doing any breakdancing for a while."

Behind them the sound of sloshing water rippled through the tunnels as the five civilian troops, led by the veteran and two regular soldiers covering the rear, waded their way through the subterranean river of noxious water. Their lights flickered continuously as they nervously checked in every direction and peered into every corner.

The walls of the subways were still adorned with framed posters advertising theatre shows and fast-food restaurants amongst sign-posts giving directions to the various platforms and parts of the stations. Globs of dried blood covered the white tiled walls in vast smears while putrefied and bloated corpses drifted along like flotsam on the gentle currents that flowed through the tube networks. Turnstiles and rail guard boxes sat broken and empty and machines that had once dispensed snacks and train tickets loomed out of the darkness like the rusting hulks of robots that had long since ceased to function.

On the surface, Stan and his followers had been left with no choice but to venture into the depths of the city's subways. It was impossible to guess where they had come from but the streets around the river were crammed with the corpses of the living dead. They were all headed for the sounds of the battle in the south and there was no way that Stan and his men could have circumnavigated around them. Finding a hiding place was out of the question. Due to their sheer numbers, it could be a long time before the area was clear enough for them to continue their journey.

Some of his men were wounded and needed medical attention and the civilians were at the point where their nerves were so tautly stretched, it would not take much pressured to cause them to snap. Hiding whilst surrounded by thousands of infected would result in a number of mental breakdowns, Stan reasoned.

They needed to reach the Thames and prayed that Captain Werner and his crew were still somewhere within the river. Stan had surmised that the staff of the Operations Room would be monitoring their movements and hoped that Samantha would be able to guess correctly where they were heading. The satellite phone had proven useless in making contact with their command staff and Stan suspected that it had been damaged during the bombing of the factory. The TACBE was also proving to be just as ineffective. Despite repeated attempts, the pilots were either not hearing him due to range or equipment failure, or they were just too busy trying to stabilise the faltering front lines. As a consequence, Stan needed to rely upon the intelligence and anticipation of the men and women that were controlling the operation from the Isle of Wight. If that failed and Werner and the U-boat was nowhere to be found once they reached the river, they would have to attempt to find their own craft to carry them away from the deadly shores of the mainland.

A bloody rowing boat would do, Stan whispered internally.

Bull and Marty, carrying the Minimis and wielding the greater firepower, had taken point. Up ahead they paused at an intersection. They stepped to the side, took up positions on either side of the curved tunnel, and poked their heads out into the open, clearing the passageways leading off to the left and right.

Stan directed them to move into the passage that led them on a general bearing eastwards. He was navigating by dead reckoning and following the faded and waterlogged London underground tourist map he had found discarded and floating amongst the wreckage. It was hard to be one-hundred percent sure of exactly where they were and many of the signs were faded with rot and mould or had been burned in the fires that had spread through many of the stations during the outbreak. He was relying on his own built-in compass and estimations of distance from his pacing.

Further along, they stepped out from the narrow confines of the tunnel and onto one of the station platforms. An abandoned train, its windows smashed and its doors forced open, sat silently resting on its flooded rails. Blood was smeared over many of its interior surfaces and around its doors, and piles of discarded baggage and clothing lay strewn over the seats. The water had reached high enough to flood the floor of the carriages and a steady brook flowed through the train, carrying debris and body parts out over the platforms.

Bull raised his hand and signalled for everyone to remain still and quiet. The sound of trickling water could be heard echoing through the tunnels as the Thames pushed through the ground and rivulets sprang from the cracks between the tiles. Amongst the drips and streams, heavier splashes could be heard coming from within the train. They were getting louder and all lights were turned and pointed towards the direction of the open set of sliding doors in the nearest carriage. As Bull and Marty pushed to the left and right to cover either end of the platform with their machineguns, Bobby crept forward with Stan backing him.

Their rifle and sub-machinegun barrels entered into the carriage ahead of them, aiming into the corners as the two men cleared the entranceway into the compartment and then searched further along the rows of seats.

"Stan," Bobby whispered and indicated something in front of him.

Through the green hue of their night vision goggles, the shape that was slowly making its way along the floor towards them was hard to make out. It awkwardly dragged itself through the murky water and towards the bright light beams it could see shining through the broken carriage windows. They did not need to identify it to know what it was. The corpse had been cut or torn in half and its internal organs floated along behind it in a long trail like a string of grotesque and partially inflated balloons.

It had been trapped down there in the train probably since the beginning, too badly damaged to be able to follow the others up to the surface as they rampaged through the streets and buildings, and feasted upon the population. Its body was bloated and waterlogged from months of floating about in the flooded train but now it was determinedly crawling towards the living men standing illuminated in the doorway by the shaky lights behind them.

Stan stepped forward, pulling his long heavy blade from his belt. With a forceful chopping motion, he slammed it down against the back of the creatures head. Its face splashed down loudly in the water and the crunch of its skull was audible through the train as Stan's machete extinguished the creature's existence.

They continued deeper into the city's underground. They came across more of the infected, clambering blindly at the walls, rails, and blocked doorways in the pitch-blackness. At the sight of the militia's lights, they always turned and began wading through the greasy black water, groaning and gnashing their teeth excitedly. The men in front dealt with them without needing to fire their weapons. Rifle butts, machetes, and knives were used to despatch the pathetic creatures that lurked within the dark.

According to Stan's pacing, they had covered a distance of roughly one-point-five kilometres through the dank subterranean atmosphere, stopping at various stations along the way, checking their position, and taking a tentative peek at what was happening on the surface. Each time the reports came back of mass crowds of infected still filling the streets.

"Where are they all coming from? I thought the airstrikes were supposed to have wiped them out by now?" Taff asked, shaking his head in wonder.

"There must be some bridges still intact enough to allow them to cross the river from the north. Unless they've learned how to swim?" The veteran replied. It was the only explanation that he could think of.

By Stan's judgement, they were now only a few hundred metres from the river's edge. He looked at the faded map in his hands and suddenly realised where they were when he saw the name of the next station along. The significance of their approximate location was only just occurring to him because he had been too concentrated on heading for the river. They were not all that far from a site that they all knew well and with their general direction of travel, they were likely to pass close to a place from their past that had once helped to play a part in their current circumstances.

They would need to find a point where they could surface soon or they would end up on the northern bank, an even more heavily crowded side of London. With all the noise in the south, it was only fair to assume that every corpse in the metropolis had headed for the riverside, packing the streets along that side of the Thames.

They began to head eastwards as much as the tunnel systems would allow them to. Around them, the walls resounded with drips of water, the splash of feet, and the frightened heavy breathing of the militia. The distant ghostly wails of the dead that remained lost and trapped in the underground joined in on the haunting opera that clawed at the mental state of the survivors that were desperately searching for a way out.

At a prominent fork in the tracks, the group turned off to the right and entered into a passageway that seemed to be separate from the rest of the subway tunnels. There were no rail tracks underfoot and it soon became apparent that they were steadily climbing along a gradual slope. Within one-hundred metres, the ground below them became dry as they continued along the strange corridor. As they pushed onwards, the shaft began to narrow. Gone were the tiles of the tube station walls and glitzy posters and advertisements. Now it was just bare concrete with thick steel supports jutting out at evenly spaced intervals.

Eventually, they began to see glowing maintenance signs informing them that the way ahead was blocked and access beyond that point was strictly prohibited. Security signs also warned of cameras, guards, and prosecution for anyone caught trespassing. Further along they came to a large gate that lay open and showed the tell-tale signs of having been blasted with shaped explosive charges. To the right of the gate, there were an electronic key panel and a pad for biometric scanning.

Stan ordered a halt and stared up at the frame of the gateway. It was strong and constructed with thick steel bars that were embedded deep into the walls of the tunnel. He was confident that the entrance way and the chasm beyond had nothing to do with London's underground rail networks. The walls appeared to be relatively new and the gate, along with its security systems, was far too technologically advanced for it to have been in place for more than a few years. He stood and peered into the darkness beyond the entrance then checked his map. The tunnel was not marked on the tube station diagram, confirming to him that they were indeed at the location he had suspected they were headed towards earlier.

Danny, seizing the opportunity, hobbled over to the wall and slid downwards with his back pressed against the concrete and taking the weight off his painful legs. Bobby crouched beside him and offered him another concoction of painkillers to take the edge off the agony he was suffering. Danny waved them away. His eyes were closed tight and his teeth were clenched together behind his curled lips.

"No," he gasped, "I can manage. I just need to rest, mate."

Bobby nodded and offered him something to drink. He took the time to check on how the makeshift casts were holding out and saw that they were sodden with water and beginning to fall apart. They had lost their rigidity and were now nothing more than piles of mushy pulp that were wrapped around Danny's battered legs.

"Hey, you," Bobby hissed across at the two regular soldiers that were attached to the militia platoon. "Find a couple of able bodies amongst your group that can help."

Two of them were called forward and made responsible for the continued mobility of the wounded soldier. Bobby instructed them to stay with him at all times and that they were not to worry about fighting or anything else other than ensuring that Danny was kept moving and away from harm.

"What about those things?" Michael asked nervously.

"You two just worry about my friend here," Bobby cut in before Peter was able to reply. "We'll do the rest and as long as you're close to Danny, you'll be safer than being amongst that gang-fuck over there."

Bobby shone his light and nodded his head towards the two women and one man that remained in the tunnel behind them.

They nervously shone their torches in all directions, spinning their bodies and aiming their weapons at every sound, no matter how slight.

Peter followed Bobby's eyes and saw that he was referring to the remnants of his platoon. He did not feel any particular loyalty to the militia soldiers that he had been part of but at the same time, he did not appreciate them being referred to in a derogatory way. They had been through a lot and suffered just as much as any of the regular soldiers. However, the look in Bobby's eyes convinced him that he should keep his opinions and protests to himself. Instead, he assured the man that they would stay with his friend and keep him moving.

Bull snatched a light from one of the other soldiers and shone it into the black void beyond the shiny steel bars. The beam brushed over the smooth surfaces of the walls and what looked to be a junction further along and illuminating a number of bundles that he interpreted as corpses scattered over the floor. Directly in front of them, roughly thirty metres or so, it appeared that there was another set of security doors, made from thick solid sheets of steel or iron. They too lay wide open.

"What do you think this place was, Stan?" He asked, leaning in over the threshold of the gateway but reluctant to step through.

"We should *all* know," Stan replied and received a number of quizzical looks in return. They had no idea of what the place was.

"Through there," Stan continued and nodded to the second set of blast proof doors at the far end, "is our old headquarters."

The rest of his men turned and shot him a look. After a moment they realised that Stan was right. They had not recognised the place without the bright lights that were fitted into the ceiling and constantly blazing overhead. They were also used to seeing it from a different angle, from along one of the corridors branching off to the left and right of the main entrance. They had never approached the bunker through the underground rail tunnels. Guards were normally posted on either side of the doorway, controlling access in and out while a continuous flurry of men and women were always moving in different directions along the passageways. Now the place was silent, dark, and unrecognisable as the former hiding place of their command centre.

They moved through the gate and towards the bunker doors. Nothing but blackness greeted them from the other side of the complex's entrance. Even the beams of light aimed through the doorway seemed to be swallowed up in the thick blanket of darkness. The place had become an unmarked grave for the people who had failed to make it out when the command centre was overrun.

Stan looked over the door and its locking mechanisms. Bloodied claw marks with human nails that had been broken off and became embedded in the thick congealed blood covered the outer surfaces. Thousands of hands had pounded against the barrier in their attempts to break in but the entry point would never have given way against a million bodies pressing against it.

The bunker had once been part of Winston Churchill's underground labyrinth during the Second World War and later, a nuclear fallout shelter designed to withstand a direct hit on the city above and keep the remains of the government safe below ground. It was virtually impervious to a direct assault, even with explosives.

The heavy deadbolt locks that were made from titanium appeared to be untouched and undamaged. Stan stepped back and grunted in realisation that someone had opened the doors from the inside or possibly by remote, having broken through all the firewalls and sophisticated programming of the computerised security systems.

"What do you reckon, Stan?" Taff asked as he scanned his light over the ground around them. The beam glinted against something that reflected brightly in the otherwise inky darkness and he moved towards it. "Shit."

Stan turned and saw Taff crouching down beside the remains of a body. There were a number of corpses lying around them but this one in particular was clearly different. It was armed and appeared to be fresh. As he moved closer, Stan recognised the man's face. Most of the side of his head had been blown away but he could clearly see that it had once been the commander of the SAS team who had gone missing during the insertion. It was the same man who had slipped from the side of Werner's U-boat and had almost been lost in the Thames. His weapon lay beside him, spattered with blood and grey matter while more of his skull's contents decorated the wall directly behind the remains of his body. His limbs and internal organs had been ripped away and all that remained of him was his head, shoulders, and the upper part of his ribcage that was still protected and held together beneath his assault vest.

Taff reached down and picked something up that was lying beside the remains. It was a folder of some sort and filled with a thick bundle of laminated pages. He looked at the front of the beige coloured file and then turned it over, looking for a label of some sort. It was blank and gave no indication to what it was for.

"What do you think?" He asked as he passed it across to Stan who then began flicking through the pages that were filled with graphs, numbers, and diagrams. Stan knew exactly what the file was and what it was for.

"Launch codes," he said, shaking his head as he stared down at the folder.

Taff looked at him with a raised eyebrow and then back at the weighty file of documents in Stan's hand.

"They're launch codes for ICBMs," Stan clarified. "These poor bastards were obviously sent in to retrieve them from this death-trap."

"Nukes? Why would they be in here looking for the codes to launch nuclear missiles? We have enough trouble as it is."

Stan shrugged and turned to look back up at the open blast doors leading into the bunker complex.

"Maybe whoever opened this place up couldn't find them, or never made it out?" He reasoned aloud. "Thompson may have sent these guys in to retrieve them before someone else did. We were all brought up to speed on that lunatic in the north, Gibson, wanting to use heavy nukes on all the cities. Maybe the Prince of Darkness was afraid he would find them down here and wanted to keep the codes from falling into the wrong hands?"

"So where's the rest of the team?" Taff asked as he glanced back down at the pale ruined face of the SAS commander.

"All over the fucking place," Marty's voice replied from behind them.

Stan and Taff turned around and looked at the bodies that were sprawled throughout their immediate area. Marty was right, the SAS team were still there. They had been ripped apart by the infected and their body parts lay scattered and mixed with the corpses of their attackers. Clusters of bullet holes that had not been noticed sooner began to appear in the walls all around them and piles of empty brass cases carpeting the floor glinted in the beams of light. By the looks of things the SAS men had been caught unawares from all sides and trapped there, fighting it out with the undead until they steadily run out of ammunition and then took their own lives.

"Jesus, there must've been hundreds of those things in here," the veteran gasped as he shone his light over the piles of corpses stretching in either direction along the two tunnels. "Poor bastards never had a chance."

A noise in the passageway leading back into the tube tunnels made everyone spin around. There was something approaching them from within the darkness and the sounds of heavy scraping feet could be heard creeping towards them along the vaulted ceiling.

A loud bang to their right made everyone reel as one of the militia fired off a round. Its muzzle flash was like a bolt of lightning, flickering from the walls and blinding anyone that was facing in the general direction of the firer. The weapon's report in the cramped space boomed and pressed violently against the eardrums of everyone, causing a flurry of gasps and curses as they instinctively raised their hands to the sides of their heads.

Stan was about to cry out, ordering everyone to hold fire, but a number of other rifles opened up almost immediately after the first. The airspace in front of the bunker's entrance erupted with deafening cracks as the militia began firing blindly into the darkness behind them. The veteran was screaming for them to cease-fire as he launched himself against the man who had been the first to pull his trigger. He slammed into him with his shoulder, flattening the civilian against the wall and ripping the magazine away from the rifle in his shaking hands. The man stared back at the veteran in terror for a moment as his weapon ceased firing.

The ear-splitting blasts of the weapons continued uncontrolled, illuminating the tunnel with flashes of brilliant white as glowing red tracer rounds spun away into the dark passages and ricocheted from the walls. Men and women alike were suddenly knocked from their feet as Stan and his men set about trying to bring the militia back under control and having no choice but to hit them with forceful open-handed slaps across the sides of their heads. Some of them dropped to the ground and others tumbled across the narrow space, colliding with the people beside them and either dropping their weapons or releasing their death grips on their triggers.

Behind them, as the militias fire began to whither, another series of loud snaps emitted. They were not the same booming reports of the SA-80 rifles that the civilian soldiers were carrying, but the muffled sounds of a suppressed M-4.

Stan whirled and saw a figure standing close to the bunker doors and a rapid series of flashes blasting outwards from the rifle in its hands, firing a long burst into the dark opening. It was Bobby, shooting at something that was unseen to the others. There was another form at his feet. Its legs kicked frantically as it writhed and thrashed against the cluster of withered hands pulling it back into the doorway. Bobby reached down and grabbed one of the man's legs and began attempting to pull the figure back towards himself while still firing his rifle into the gap between the bunker doors.

The man on the floor was Marty. He screamed with pain as he felt a set of incisors clamp around the soft tissue of his hand and begin crunching down on the bones of his fingers. The sharp searing pain of his flesh being torn was quickly mingled with the agony of digits being crushed and gnawed as he continued to fight to free himself from the multitude of hands that refused to let go. More of the infected began to pile in around him.

Bobby's rifle continued to blast away at their attackers but it was not enough to stop them. His M-4 suddenly fell silent as the magazine became empty and he let it fall to his side, hanging from the sling attached to his harness. He drew his pistol and began to pump rounds into the heads of the infected. Some of them fell back beyond the doorway and others landed on top of himself and

Marty. He could feel his body being pulled into the darkness beyond the threshold as he fought to tear himself free while keeping a tight grip on his friend's leg. He could smell the rotting stench of the dozens of reanimated corpses that clamoured around him, pulling at his clothing and clawing his kicking legs as he tried to climb back to his feet while fending the infected away from Marty.

Another bright flash of pain flared in front of Marty's eyes as the skin around his neck was torn and a large gaping wound began gushing with a torrent of blood. More teeth began sinking into his soft flesh as he was pulled away from Bobby and set upon by a mob of ravenous monsters. They tore and bit at him, digging their fingers into his soft tissue and biting at any part of him they could reach. His hand was suddenly pulled backwards and a large hole was ripped out from his wrist. Arterial blood instantly began to spray from the wound in long jets, coating the grotesque faces of the dead and driving them into a frenzy as they tasted the warm metallic life fluid of their victim. Marty howled again, his blood curdling screams echoing through the tunnels of the underground labyrinth.

Bull vaulted across the militia soldiers lying prostrate on the ground where they had been bowled over by the heavy whacks of the men behind them. He landed at Bobby's side and instantly reached down for his friend who was half way in through the door, kicking and screaming as the dead piled in around him. Bull grasped Marty's thrashing legs, and yanked him back into the tunnel and away from the bunker as Bobby scrambled backwards away from the entrance.

Without pausing, Bull swung his Minimi around and loosed off a long burst into the bodies that surged out from beyond the doorway, gnashing their teeth and growling angrily at the man who had taken their prey away from them. They fell into a heap beneath the hailstorm of fire that was thrown against them but there were more of them charging towards the entrance from the black depths of the bunker.

The rifles of the militia began to fire again. There was more movement in the passage behind them as wandering corpses lost in the tube tunnels began to converge on the sound of gunfire and the screams of the living.

Stan ran back over to Bull's side and joined him in firing into the mass of bodies that were advancing on them from the corridor beyond the bunker doors. There must have been hundreds of them, climbing up from the lower floors and crawling over one another as they fought to reach the living above them.

The militia were beginning to fall back, fumbling with their rifles as they attempted to change out their magazines. As the fire faded from behind, faint shadows of disfigured bodies grew along the walls of the tunnel in the flickering light, accompanied by the long moans and gurgling howls of the advancing dead.

"Move right," Stan screamed over his shoulder to the others as corpses began spilling out from their old headquarters. "Get into the tunnel on the right. We're bugging out."

Some of the militia, facing in the opposite direction from Stan, retreated into the wrong access channel. By the time that they realised their mistake, it was too late and their route back had already been cut off by a number of corpses that began charging into the tunnel after them. More screams echoed around the chamber as Stan and his men began to retreat.

One of the regular troops had been knocked over by the fleeing men and women and as he climbed back to his feet, he was set upon by a horde of the infected that spotted him in the dancing light that continued to flit around over the chamber. The blaring crackle of gunfire continued as both groups fled in different directions. The agony filled howls of men and women as they were slaughtered at the hands of the infected echoed along the tunnels for great distances, attracting the attention of the thousands of dead that were wandering through the subways.

Bull raced along the passageway with Marty slung over his shoulder while Taff helped Danny to hobble along through the long winding corridor. Behind them, Bobby, Stan, and the veteran covered the retreat, taking it in turns in throwing up a wall of zipping tracers into the avalanche of walking dead that were following close on their heels. Reaching a set of stairs and instantly recognising where he was in the narrow beam of light he held in his hand, Bull began climbing the steps. As he reached the second flight, the stairway below them was rocked by a bone crunching detonation. The ground shook and the grenade's shrapnel *thwacked* and pinged against the walls as it flew out in all directions.

"Up, up," Stan was shouting from below. "Keep going. Faster."

By now, Bull should have been exhausted. He was carrying the entire weight of Marty, including both their equipment and climbing dozens of flights of stairs but he felt nothing in the way of fatigue or physical pain. His closest friend was hurt badly, slumped over his shoulder and bleeding severely from multiple wounds. At that moment, Bull could think of nothing but getting Marty to safety.

"You're okay, Marty," he said over and over again. "I've got you, mate. You're going to be okay. Just hold on, Marty, for fuck sake."

At the top of the stairs they burst out into the storeroom of a small independent book shop. The team had used that particular entrance into the bunker complex on many occasions. Bobby pushed ahead of them and took the lead through the main part of the store, striding over piles of scattered books and magazines and slamming the butt of his rifle into the side of the head of a single corpse that stood staring back at them, bewildered at their sudden appearance. The dead woman's skull caved inwards as her body was sent flying across the floor and slamming into the wall.

Out in the street, Bobby began firing his rifle at the corpses that turned and lurched towards them. Bull crashed through the door and into the open, not bothering to stop and paying no attention to the misshapen figures that moved towards him. He turned and raced off to the left. Behind him, Taff and Danny emerged, closely followed by the two militia soldiers who had been tasked with helping their wounded comrade.

"Here," Taff growled as he passed Danny across to them, "take him and run. Follow Bull and stay with him. Don't let him out of your sight."

Raising his rifle, Taff began to help Bobby clear a path as the wounded were evacuated from the area. Windows shattered from stray rounds and bodies dropped all around them but more appeared from around the various corners and from within the numerous doorways.

"Take a right," Stan howled as he crashed into the street and followed after Bull and the others. The two militia were just ahead of him and complied with his orders as they reached the junction at the head of the street.

"Right, go right," Peter called after Bull, passing the message on and watching as the big man made a change in his direction without a single glance backwards and disappeared around the corner.

Bobby and Taff dropped back to protect the rear and followed in Stan's wake. The veteran was still with them but he was limping badly, having caught some of the shrapnel in his leg from the grenade he had tossed into the tunnel in an attempt to stem the tide of infected snapping jaws that were chasing after them. His teeth were gritted and his face was creased with pain but he was determined to keep up, wielding his rifle in one hand while the other was pressed firmly against his bleeding thigh.

Bobby came alongside him and placed his arm under his shoulder for support and helping him to keep moving. Taff remained close and continued to cover them, firing in all directions as the infected sprang from every door, window, and alleyway. They reached the corner and saw Stan and the two militia soldiers with Danny just ahead of them. Below their feet, a trail of bright red blood spattered the pavement and far in front they glimpsed the back of Bull and the bouncing figure of Marty hanging from his shoulder. Nothing was standing in the way of the man and the few bodies that managed to get close enough were knocked to the side by his powerful blows.

"Stay with me, Marty," Bull gasped as he slammed his fist into the face of another corpse. The body of the dead man was lifted high off its feet from the impact and hurled almost to the other side of the road. "I've got you, Marty. Everything's going to be okay."

A hundred metres further on and Bull came to an abrupt halt. Marty, severely weakened and barely able to form his words, had demanded that his friend put him down and after a brief argument, Bull reluctantly complied. As the rest of the men caught up, Bull began checking Marty's wounds, trying valiantly to stem the flow of blood as the others formed a protective ring around them and began picking off the few corpses that were appearing in the immediate area.

"Leave it," Marty groaned while shaking his head.

Bull ignored him and continued to apply direct pressure while Bobby ripped open a field dressing. Marty's wrist needed immediate attention and he had already lost an incredible amount of blood through the torn artery. He also had a large bite wound in the soft tissue between his shoulder and neck and his clothing was stained dark with glistening wet blood. His face was pale and coated in a fine layer of sweat and his lips were tinged pale blue through loss of blood. He was fading fast and as Bobby pressed the dressing down onto Marty's bleeding forearm, Bull reached for his tourniquet in a last ditch attempt to stop the loss of Marty's precious life fluid.

"For fuck sake, Bull, leave it," Marty growled again weakly.

The huge man paused and looked back at Marty's sunken eyes and withered cheeks. Bull's own eyes were glazed with a film of tears and his vision blurred as he gazed down at his dying friend.

"There's nothing you can do, mate."

"We can stop the bleeding," Bull reasoned in a breaking voice and began gripping the wound in his friend's arm even tighter. "You'll be okay, Marty. We'll get you sorted soon. We're nearly at the river."

Marty shook his head. He was barely able to open his eyes and already he had lost the vision in his peripherals. His legs were numb and he could feel a great coldness creeping its way up along his body.

"You know you can't," he said with a faltering voice and a slight smile. "You know you can't help me, you dick head."

Bull was oblivious to the cracks of rifle fire around him and the anxious shouts of the defenders as they called out targets to one another and recommended that they should move. He could feel an invisible hand beginning to squeeze at his throat. It was strong enough almost to stop him from breathing and an immense pressure seemed to be welling up from inside his chest and pushing against his sternum.

"It's okay, mate," Marty croaked as a large pool of dark red blood began spreading across the paving stones beneath him. "It's alright."

Bull released his grasp on Marty's arm and gently placed his hand around the side of his friends head, cupping the crook of his neck. He pulled him close and buried his face into Marty's matted hair. The tears were beginning to flood and his body jerked slightly as he fought to hold back the sobs. He kissed Marty's head and lay him back down. With his other hand he reached for the pistol on his hip, nodding slightly to himself as he painfully accepted that he was about to lose his best friend.

Marty stared back up at him and gave a slight shake of his head.

"Don't," he said hoarsely. "Save your rounds, mate. You'll need them."

Bull watched as his friend weakly lifted his arm and moved his hand towards his own mouth and parted his lips. He knew what Marty was about to do and he shook his head and raised his own hand to interfere. Marty feebly knocked his hand away, staring back into his eyes with the last of his determination.

"It's okay, Bull. It's okay."

Bull nodded and looked on as Marty removed the cap from one of his rear molars. With a final withering smile, Marty bit down hard. His body twitched suddenly and arched backwards for a moment, as though a jolt of electricity had passed through him. His head shot back and his right eye bulged out from its socket then instantly turned black from the massive haemorrhaging of his brain. The side of his face turned a deep purple as the capillaries and veins around the area of the tiny explosive burst and within seconds, blood began to seep out from his nose and ears.

Bull paused for a moment, staring down at Marty's lifeless face and stroking his hand across his pallid left cheek. He nodded with heart-breaking acceptance as he leaned forward and tucked his arms beneath Marty's knees and around his shoulders.

He paused for a moment and took in a deep breath.

"He's coming with us," he growled as he raised himself to his feet, holding Marty's limp body in his arms and turning to walk away without paying any attention to the men and infected around him. "We're not leaving him here, so he's coming with us."

Stan and Bobby stepped back, leaving the firing to the others as they watched Bull carrying the sagging dead body of yet another of their team. Stan showed no outward emotion but it was plain to see on Bobby's face. His features were awash with a collage of rage, sorrow, and confusion. It had all happened so fast at the bunker and he felt guilty that he had not been able to help Marty. His hatred for the infected and grief at not being able to save his friend were surging through his body as he dropped the blood soaked field dressing to the ground and took control of his rifle.

Bull broke into a run, continuing towards the river with tears streaming down his face. The others followed as the crowd at the end of the street swelled from the hundreds of infected that tumbled out from the buildings all around them. The streets to the left and right were swarming with them and the team were in danger of being cut off.

By now, they could see the gates leading into one of the dockyards. They had no idea whether or not there would be anything of use to them at the water's edge but it was a risk they had to take. They had nowhere else to go. Their only other alternative was to barricade themselves into one of the many buildings but it would only be a matter of time before the dead managed to break in.

In the distance, the heavy thuds of explosions continued to rock the city as the remains of Stan's men, along with the veteran and two militia soldiers, Peter and Michael, raced for the opening in the fence line that led into the dockside. They slammed the gate as they passed through and Bobby and the veteran did what they could to secure it. The bolt locks they slid into place would not hold for long and already the iron rails rattled loudly as hundreds of corpses threw themselves against the flimsy barrier. Bobby and the veteran withdrew, taking nervous glances over their shoulders as the gate began to bow and buckle beneath the mass of bodies pressing against it.

Stan turned a corner and stopped dead in his tracks, raising his MP-5 simultaneously and firing a volley of shots into a cluster of mangled figures that turned to face them. Two of them dropped, their skulls shattering beneath the hail of Stan's rounds.

"Fuck you," Bull hollered with rage and took off at a sprint, barging his way through the corpses that stood in his path. "Fuck you."

Many of them were felled by the big man and trampled beneath his feet as he lumbered forward towards the river, determined to carry the body of his friend to safety and away from the dead city. The rest of the men followed, firing wildly then swinging their rifles like batons when their magazines run dry.

Bobby pulled his pistol and shot a round through the face of a woman as she pounced towards him. Her head snapped backwards but her body continued forward and slammed into him, knocking him to the side and forcing him to vault over a barrel lying on its side that he was about to crash into. Behind him, a scream rang out as one of the militia was tackled to the ground. The man was too far away for him to help and there were too many infected between him and the civilian soldier. He fired a couple of badly aimed shots in the general direction of the militiaman and continued after Stan and the others.

Taff and Danny were working in tandem, acting as the two halves to one body. While Taff supported the wounded man, he used his right arm to fend off the dead that were on his side. Danny took care of the left and together, they forged forwards after Stan and Bull.

"What do we do when we get to the fucking water?" Danny grunted as he continued to hobble through the dockyard.

"Fuck knows," Taff shouted back at him as the barrel of his M-4 smashed against the head of a body that was little more than a jumble of clicking bones covered with leathery skin. "We'll burn that bridge when we've crossed it."

Stan and the veteran watched as Bull turned to his left and disappeared from sight along the narrow jetty leading to the water's edge. A moment later and they too made it to the corner and bolted along the wooden planks without slowing their pace. At the far end, Stan had hoped to see the big grey monster that would be their ride out of there. Instead, they saw nothing. There was no sign of Captain Werner or his boat. He looked in both directions along the river, desperately scanning the water for the U-boat.

With nowhere left to run, they stopped on the rickety dockside and turned to face their enemy as the remains of their group arrived. They formed a defensive line along the end of the jetty and prepared their weapons, slamming in fresh magazines and checking on what they had left. They were all beginning to run low on ammunition.

"I'm down to four mags, Stan," Bobby called out as he raised his weapon into the aim. "When I get to my last, I'm going for a swim."

Stan swivelled and looked into the murky water of the Thames. He nodded back to Bobby in agreement. They would probably drown, being sucked under by the currents, but it was worth a try. He ripped away his assault vest and dropped any equipment he did not need. The rest of the men followed suit and stuffed their pistols and magazines into their pockets, dumping any unnecessary weight.

Bull gently placed Marty on the ground at his feet and stood ready to protect his friend's body to the very end. He checked the state of his weapon and ensured that he had a full belt of two-hundred 5.56mm rounds clipped into the feed-tray. Marty's Minimi had been lost in the bunker attack and Bull's gun was down to his last belt but he was determined to make every round count. He checked his pistol and vowed that he would save the last shot for himself.

"Where's the others?" The veteran called out when he saw that the two brothers from the militia were missing.

"They're gone," Bobby replied with a shake of his head.

It did not matter, they were all about to die anyway. They could jump in the river or take their own lives but either way, they had gone as far as they could go.

As the first of the infected reached the far end of the pier and turned towards the six men standing at the water's edge, Stan and the others readied themselves to hold their ground, using the bottleneck of the quayside to their advantage.

Bull opened up with controlled bursts of three to four round groups that smashed into the lead infected. The impacts sent scraps of clothing, bone, and flesh flying through the air and shattered bodies tumbling in all directions. The rest of the men joined in, making each shot count.

The dockside erupted into a clamour of ear-splitting snaps and cracks as the guns fired relentlessly into the advancing mass. A large pile of bodies was quickly forming over the wooden planks of the pier but there were hundreds more behind them, taking their place as they surged against the wall of devastating fire.

"Magazine," someone cried out from the right.

"Stoppage," another hollered.

"Behind us," Danny suddenly shouted from the left as he slammed the last of his magazines into his M-4.

Stan pivoted, expecting to see a threat approaching them from behind.

Just two-hundred metres away, he saw the glowing white bow-wave of the Type-XXI as it cut through the water at speed. Now, he could hear the thrum of its diesels as they hammered away at full revolutions. It was headed right for them and showing no sign of slowing. A figure in the conning tower was waving his hands frantically and shouting something that Stan could not make out. The boat was approaching fast and within seconds, as the survivors on the quayside continued to pour all their fire into the advancing crowd, the gap was down to less than one-hundred metres.

Looking down at the water's edge, Danny suddenly realised what the figure on the bridge was trying to tell them. His eyes bulged with the realisation and he turned to the others and began to push some of them forwards and to the side.

"Move out of the fucking way," he yelled.

Everyone turned and saw the bow of the boat, now almost on top of them. They jumped to the left and right, narrowly avoiding being ploughed under by the point of the submarine's forward deck as it crashed into the jetty with a shattering crunch. The impact sent up a huge wave of Thames water and smashed through planks of wood and thick support beams like they were matchwood, flinging them into the air as the boat came to a shuddering stop amongst the wreckage of the flimsy pier.

Already the engines were racing again as the Chief Engineer slammed the diesels into reverse gear, wasting no time in pulling the vessel away from the dock wall.

"Stan," Werner screamed down from the conning tower with urgency as his sailors began firing into the mass of dead from their positions on the aft deck. "Get your men on board. And be quick about it, will you?"

22

Far to the south, the horizon blazed, casting up an orange glow into the sky above London. The low concussions of explosives and the faint crackle of heavy machinegun fire could be heard even from a distance of over forty kilometres. They could see the faint silhouettes of helicopters buzzing about over the streets and the streak of fast moving aircraft as they raced across the skies above the doomed city.

"I knew it wouldn't work," Al said as he placed down the handset of their radio. He turned and looked back over the landscape and then up at the sky. "We should think about finding somewhere to go static for the night, Tommy. It'll be dark soon."

Tommy was sitting beside him, taking small nibbling bites from a digestive biscuit as he stared down at his feet in deep thought. Lean and gangly, he always appeared to be on the verge of tripping over his own legs that seemed to have a mind of their own. His limbs were out of proportion to the rest of his body and at times, he looked almost alien. However, despite his appearances, with his crooked nose and snarling features, he was an extremely professional and experienced soldier.

"What are they saying on the radio, has it all gone to rat-shit then?" He asked as he turned his attention back to Al.

"Looks that way," the big man nodded, solemnly. "From what I'm hearing, they're calling for all their units to withdraw. The troops in London seem to be cut off and everyone else is bugging out, back to the Isle of Wight."

Al and Tommy had been friends for many years. Their unit, having been decimated during the outbreak, had been instructed to occupy a Forward Operating Base, FOB, situated within the Midlands. Since the mainland was evacuated, they had sat patiently waiting for orders and information on when the great counter strike would begin and what their role would be as part of it. Three days earlier and they had finally received the call that they had all been waiting for and were placed on standby.

Rather than sitting around and being drip-fed information from the staff of MJOC, the people in the FOB had decided to carry out their own information gathering operation. Prior to the start of the invasion the two men had volunteered to venture out from behind the walls of their base and move south in the hope of gaining some first-hand intelligence on what was happening once the attack began. They had watched and listened with optimism during the opening phases but their positivity slowly changed to disappointment as the tide steadily turned and the battle was lost.

"Jesus, those poor bastards don't have a chance. By nightfall, anyone remaining in the city will be left there and I doubt there'll be anyone left by the time daylight arrives."

The radio transmissions were a jumble of cries for help with panic filled and screaming voices, pleading for support and rescue. Neither Al nor Tommy needed actually to see what was happening on the ground. They could fill in the blanks for themselves.

"We'd better let the people back at the FOB know about what's going on. I'm pretty sure they won't have been informed yet of what's happened," Tommy said as he slung the remains of the biscuit down the hill.

"Let's sleep on it, mate. I don't have the stomach to begin a lengthy conversation over the radio just yet. Let's just find somewhere to sleep for the night, then we'll begin heading back in the morning. In the meantime, I'll have a think about how to break the news."

Al was huge. He was well over two metres tall and almost just as wide. He had reached full height by the time he was fifteen years old but his body had continued to grow outwards. Along with hard training and an active lifestyle, he had slowly grown from a scrawny teenager and into a burly and powerful man. Despite his size, he was very capable of running for long distances with ease. Although he was far from being a natural sprinter, he was still able to keep pace with most of the people around him and outdistance the vast majority.

Al and Tommy had first met when they attended a promotions course while serving in different companies but in the same battalion. From there, they bonded a close friendship that had lasted for over ten years and would continue until the day they died.

"We'll head for that farmhouse we saw a few miles back," Al suggested as he climbed to his feet and slung the radio over his shoulder.

"Sounds good to me."

They were both about to move off when Tommy saw something moving at the foot of the hill, close to the edge of the treeline and on the opposite side of the road. It could have been one of the infected with its lunging gait and dishevelled appearance but Tommy noticed that it appeared to be more alert than any of the dead they were used to seeing. He clicked his fingers to draw Al's attention and then pointed to the body as it stumbled out into the road and began to climb the hill clumsily.

Immediately they both knew that it was a living person. The figure struggled to negotiate the slippery grass and the undulating ground but refused to give up. Whoever it was, they were hurt and exhausted but determined to keep moving. The figure's face turned upwards towards Al and Tommy and they saw that it was a woman. She saw them too and for a fleeting moment, their eyes remained locked. Behind her, the woods reverberated with the sounds of heavy footfalls, snapping branches and the poignant wail of the dead.

Tommy began to walk down the slope. Al, after a moment's hesitation, joined him and they both headed towards the limping woman. When they were within ten metres of her they stopped and eyed her with suspicion. She stared back at them, her face showing a catalogue of pain and fatigue. The two men slowly advanced towards her, their weapons pointed at her and ready to fire if she showed any sign of aggression.

Al noticed the blood seeping through her trousers around her lower leg. She was dressed strangely, wearing a boiler suit with heavy work boots and a thick jacket that was three of four sizes too big for her. She swayed on her feet and looked as though she was about to collapse. Her face was pale and withdrawn, glistening with sweat as though she was suffering from a burning fever.

Al watched her and took a slight step forward, peering into her sunken eyes as he continued his visual inspection. His finger remained lightly pressed against his trigger and the barrel pointed at her chest.

Tommy glanced across at him nervously as the crashes and thuds drifted across the road from beyond the trees, growing louder as the dead continued their pursuit.

"You been bitten?" Al demanded, abruptly, and nodded to the blood sodden wound on the woman's lower leg.

She blew out a sigh of exhaustion as she continued with her struggle to remain on her feet. Her eyes were becoming heavy and her head seemed to be swimming around in a circle that was increasing with speed. Her vision was beginning to dance and blur and her ears were filled with an electrifying buzzing noise.

"My...my," she stammered as her energy reserves were spent and her stance faltered for a moment. Her wounded leg almost collapsed but she corrected it just in time to prevent her from falling. "My brother... my brother did it. He... shot me... He..."

She stumbled forward and fell to the ground. Tommy jumped to her side and placed his hands over her back to prevent her from rolling down the hill. He turned her over and stared down into her face. Her eyes were rolled into the back of her head and he suspected for a short moment that she had died. He checked her pulse and breathing and then nodded up to Al, confirming that she was still alive.

"I think we should take her with us, mate."

"She's not a stray dog, Tommy. You'll have to see if she wants to come with us before we decide whether or not to keep her."

Tommy glanced back over his shoulder and saw the first of the infected as it crashed out from the wood line and stumbled into the road. It stopped and searched around its immediate area, looking for the living woman that had been trying to escape them. It seemed confused and continuously pivoted in a tight circle, looking in either direction along the road. Its head began to rise as it followed the lay of the hill in front of it. Its eyes locked on the two men that were half way up the slope and it let out a long moan as it lifted its arms and began to stagger towards the foot of the embankment.

"We'll ask her that later," Tommy replied as he began scooping her up from the grass. "Come on, Al, give me a hand here."

Together, they helped the woman to climb the hill. Her head rolled and her shoulders sagged as they dragged her along. She was barely conscious and incapable of moving under her own steam.

"Where…where are you taking me?" She mumbled weakly during one of her fleeting moments of clarity. "Where are we going?"

"Somewhere safe," the big man on her left replied as they reached the peak of the hill.

"Tina," she huffed. "My name's Tina."

"Please to meet you, Tina," Al said cheerfully. "I'm Mickey and this is Donald. Goofy is waiting for us back at the Neverland Ranch. Now shut up and save your energy."

END

CHECK OUT OTHER GREAT ZOMBIE NOVELS

Z BURBIA
by Jake Bible

Whispering Pines is a classic, quiet, private American subdivision on the edge of Asheville, NC, set in the pristine Blue Ridge Mountains. Which is good since the zombie apocalypse has come to Western North Carolina and really put suburban living to the test!

Surrounded by a sea of the undead, the residents of Whispering Pines have adapted their bucolic life of block parties to scavenging parties, common area groundskeeping to immediate area warfare, neighborhood beautification to neighborhood fortification.

But, even in the best of times, suburban living has its ups and downs what with nosy neighbors, a strict Home Owners' Association, and a property management company that believes the words "strict interpretation" are holy words when applied to the HOA covenants. Now with the zombie apocalypse upon them even those innocuous, daily irritations quickly become dramatic struggles for personal identity, family security, and straight up survival.

ZOMBIE RULES
by David Achord

Zach Gunderson's life sucked and then the zombie apocalypse began.

Rick, an aging Vietnam veteran, alcoholic, and prepper, convinces Zach that the apocalypse is on the horizon. The two of them take refuge at a remote farm. As the zombie plague rages, they face a terrifying fight for survival.

They soon learn however that the walking dead are not the only monsters.

SEVEREDPRESS

CHECK OUT OTHER GREAT ZOMBIE NOVELS

900 MILES
by S. Johnathan Davis

John is a killer, but that wasn't his day job before the Apocalypse.

In a harrowing 900 mile race against time to get to his wife just as the dead begin to rise, John, a business man trapped in New York, soon learns that the zombies are the least of his worries, as he sees first-hand the horror of what man is capable of with no rules, no consequences and death at every turn.

Teaming up with an ex-army pilot named Kyle, they escape New York only to stumble across a man who says that he has the key to a rumored underground stronghold called Avalon..... Will they find safety? Will they make it to Johns wife before it's too late?

Get ready to follow John and Kyle in this fast paced thriller that mixes zombie horror with gladiator style arena action!

WHITE FLAG OF THE DEAD
by Joseph Talluto

Millions died when the Enillo Virus swept the earth. Millions more were lost when the victims of the plague refused to stay dead, instead rising to slaughter and feed on those left alive. For survivors like John Talon and his son Jake, they are faced with a choice: Do they submit to the dead, raising the white flag of surrender? Or do they find the will to fight, to try and hang on to the last shreds or humanity?

CHECK OUT OTHER GREAT ZOMBIE NOVELS

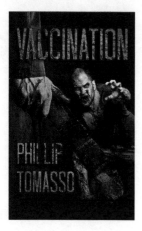

VACCINATION
by Phillip Tomasso

What if the H7N9 vaccination wasn't just a preventative measure against swine flu?

It seemed like the flu came out of nowhere and yet, in no time at all the government manufactured a vaccination. Were lab workers diligent, or could the virus itself have been man-made? Chase McKinney works as a dispatcher at 9-1-1. Taking emergency calls, it becomes immediately obvious that the entire city is infected with the walking dead. His first goal is to reach and save his two children.

Could the walls built by the U.S.A. to keep out illegal aliens, and the fact the Mexican government could not afford to vaccinate their citizens against the flu, make the southern border the only plausible destination for safety?

ZOMBIE, INC
by Chris Dougherty

"WELCOME! To Zombie, Inc. The United Five State Republic's leading manufacturer of zombie defense systems! In business since 2027, Zombie, Inc. puts YOU first. YOUR safety is our MAIN GOAL! Our many home defense options - from Ze Fence® to Ze Popper® to Ze Shed® - fit every need and every budget. Use Scan Code "TELL ME MORE!" for your FREE, in-home*, no obligation consultation! *Schedule your appointment with the confidence that you will NEVER HAVE TO LEAVE YOUR HOME! It isn't safe out there and we know it better than most! Our sales staff is FULLY TRAINED to handle any and all adversarial encounters with the living and the undead". Twenty-five years after the deadly plague, the United Five State Republic's most successful company, Zombie, Inc, is in trouble. Will a simple case of dwindling supply and lessening demand be the end of them or will Zombie, Inc. find a way, however unpalatable, to survive?

Made in the USA
Middletown, DE
14 July 2016